ROOSEVELT'S BOYS

ROOSEVELT'S BOYS

JOHN C. HORST

THORNDIKE PRESS
A part of Gale, a Cengage Company

Farmington Hills, Mich • San Francisco • New York • Waterville, Maine
Meriden, Conn • Mason, Ohio • Chicago

Copyright © 2017 by John Horst.
Thorndike Press, a part of Gale, a Cengage Company.

ALL RIGHTS RESERVED
This novel is a work of fiction. Names, characters, places and incidents
are either the product of the author's imagination, or, if real, used
fictitiously.
The publisher bears no responsibility for the quality of information
provided through author or third-party Web sites and does not have
any control over, nor assume any responsibility for, information
contained in these sites. Providing these sites should not be construed
as an endorsement or approval by the publisher of these organizations
or of the positions they may take on various issues.
Thorndike Press® Large Print Western.
The text of this Large Print edition is unabridged.
Other aspects of the book may vary from the original edition.
Set in 16 pt. Plantin.

LIBRARY OF CONGRESS CIP DATA ON FILE.
CATALOGUING IN PUBLICATION FOR THIS BOOK
IS AVAILABLE FROM THE LIBRARY OF CONGRESS

ISBN-13: 978-1-4328-5483-6 (hardcover)

Published in 2018 by arrangement with John Horst

Printed in the United States of America
1 2 3 4 5 6 7 22 21 20 19 18

For Hazel
and
to the memory of OHP

From fearful trip the victor ship comes in
with object won.

—Walt Whitman

ACKNOWLEDGMENTS

Special thanks are given to Belkis Torres for help with the Spanish phrases in this book, and to Amelia and Eliza Burnett for the German.

CHAPTER 1

Jonathan Whelihan snatched glances as the Indian followed, stubborn, willful, vexing, through the high Arizona desert, through the unforgiving land, past petroglyphs and ruins of the peoples who'd passed in and out of existence. Past the burrows of rabbits and snakes and scorpions and tarantulas, through the land that offered few second chances for those who did not have their wits about them. Land that either destroyed or strengthened the resolve of men.

He knew well that this would continue, mile after mile, until the last one hundred yards. Knew that he should never look over his shoulder while racing, as it broke the rhythm of his stride, broke his concentration and ability to give full attention and effort to the task, but he did anyway. He did it every time, and, every time, the Hopi would overtake him.

The wagon was not far behind and, as if it

were under steam power, effortlessly passed them, Rocky Killebrew laughing like an imbecile as he cracked the whip over the gelding's rump. The horse and driver, in short order, were well ahead of the running men.

Whelihan was certain to lose, angry that he'd not demanded a longer head start. He called out to his brother. "Not in the riverbed! Not in the riverbed, Rocky! Damn it to hell, not in the riverbed!"

But it was too late, and the words fell on deaf ears anyway, as Killebrew was not the type to take orders from anyone, let alone his adopted brother. The horse was soon in to its chest, the driver tumbling, covered, sinking to its knees in Arizona quicksand.

"Damn it!" Whelihan took it all in, slowed, lost concentration, lost the momentum as horse and driver flailed, covered in wet sand.

They were all right. He pushed himself, the end near, the Indian unwilling to race on to the finish line. Another hundred yards and the prize would be his.

He jogged back to his companions, breathlessly grinning, watching Louis Zeyouma work the horse free of the mire.

"I won. I won, boys, I won. First time I beat you, Louis. First time in my life I beat you. I won, I won!"

The Hopi comforted the animal, pretending to take no heed of the declaration. In a proper contest, he could beat his lifelong adversary with little effort. He always had. "The welfare of the horse is more important than winning a foot race, Jonathan."

Jonathan waved him off as he considered the ancient phaeton, buried to the wheel hubs and Rocky rubbing his forehead, grinning as if he'd been told a funny joke.

"Told you to stay out of it, Rocky. Damned riverbed's like soup this time of year; you goddamned well know that."

In a little while, horse and buggy and driver were clear, and the men worked together, erasing any vestiges of mud, any evidence of an infraction against the patriarch of the Whelihan ranch.

"Your father loves this old carriage, Jonathan." The Hopi shook his head, looking disappointed that the others were less worried over it than he. They damned well should have been.

They found shade at the edge of an arroyo covered with patches of Mormon tea and buckwheat and rabbitbrush, Killebrew attempting, unsuccessfully, to pass a bottle amongst them, pleased that the athletes never imbibed, his offering never more than a courtesy.

Jonathan grinned as he gulped water from his canteen. "Guess we're all in."

The Indian shrugged indifferently while he worked, cleaning the clumped mud from the running moccasins, a present from his sisters the previous Christmas.

Rocky Killebrew blew smoke at the sky with a vengeance, for he was a small man and wore his smallness on his sleeve, daring the world to question or deride it. He did about everything with a vengeance, as it bothered him to be small. Even his carriage — the way he walked, stood, talked, generally behaved — told the world, told anyone who'd take notice, that he was a small man and that he hated it.

"When did you say we go, Jonathan?"

"Next week."

The Indian looked up from his moccasins. "And, again, remind us why?"

Jonathan's lips quirked into a self-conscious sort of smile, in a way that it was clear the answer was not plain to him. "To fight! To fight the Spaniards, of course!"

Rocky grinned, face contorted by the effects of the spirits. "To hell with the *Maine*, remember Spain!"

"The other way around, Rocky."

"Right." He pulled on the bottle with

enthusiasm. "To hell with *somebody*, anyway."

Zeyouma tied his moccasins. "Come on. Dinner'll be ready soon. Your sister deserves that we should not be tardy." He dusted his trousers' seat clean. He wanted to return to the ranch as, when Rocky commenced imbibing, there was little one could do to stop him. Killebrew was not exceedingly articulate sober, and downright impossible inebriated.

"What's the hurry?" the lad grinned, holding up the bottle for inspection. "We have plenty o' hooch, shade, tobacco, and" — he looked off at the sun working its way across the sky — "more than enough time before supper."

Sean Whelihan tilted his head in the direction of his dinner plate as his daughter said grace. He hesitated long enough at its conclusion before digging in, to remind them that he was in charge of everything. *Everything,* from the running of his ranch to bedtime and the start of the day and even the consumption of victuals.

The senior Whelihan belonged to that race of men who forever found themselves at the wrong end of the stick. The race of men who did not fit in. His ancestors were Irish and, more damning than that, southern Irish and, even worse still, Catholic Irish. They were poor, his father and grandfather and great-grandfather before him. And they were proud, unwilling to bend or assimilate.

They'd fled to America, escaped the British as much as the Great Hunger, as Sean's father had, once again, taken up with the wrong side — the losers, the nonconformists, the rebels. This was the lot of the Whelihans for as long as anyone could remember. It was why the current patriarch had never lost the telltale brogue. His father, due to an error in direction or judgment, or bad luck, had ended up, not in New York or Boston where there were too many Irish to count, where they could have blended, been swallowed up, accepted simply by default, but in the southern part of the land of opportunity, in a place where few of his kind were known to exist. And, because of this, he'd resigned himself and his family to a kind of self-ascribed sequestration, in the backwater of the backwater, where he hoped no one would care to bother them.

From the beginning, it had been clear that few, if any, in his new community wanted or needed his kind, as there was little use in the land of Dixie for poor Irish dirt farmers or blacksmiths or gunsmiths or farriers.

That was what slaves were for, and these were all enterprises at which Patrick Whelihan excelled with vengeful resolution.

All that was fine with the senior Whelihan, who did not want or need help or charity from the community, and most certainly not from the government. Every Whelihan from the beginning of time reveled in the concept of living independently, and they'd either thrive or die trying.

He'd found his acre of land and lived on it, walling himself and his family off from the rest of the world. At least they could work a little in peace, without the meddling and injustice of what he was convinced was a government as venal and untrustworthy as the empire of Victoria Regina, as he was certain that there could exist no other kind.

His success or failure would be measured strictly by the hard work, the labor he and his family applied. And it had worked until that damned war, the war that would permanently rob him of one son and damage the other for life.

The current patriarch had essentially done the same. He'd found his acre of land, uprooting all and moving west to Arizona to evade the tyranny of, not the British, but his own tormentors, the American Republic.

His hard work and deliberation, and the

hard work and deliberation of his family, were applied to the acquisition, the nurturing, and breaking of not the sod of the earth but the horses that roamed free in the Arizona desert.

Every endeavor in which Sean Whelihan engaged was carried out deliberately, and this evening would be no different. On this night, he'd play the role of deliberate inquisitor, Jonathan was certain of that, as he'd seen it played out many times since the year of his mother's demise. The lad waited and, by the end of the first course, was not disappointed.

"How is it that the rig was in quicksand?"

Jonathan responded, almost instinctively. "Oh, well, it wasn't, eh, exactly, Father."

"Liar!" He stopped himself. He did not like to lose his temper at the table. It put him off the victuals and gave him indigestion that would burn away in his gut until early morning. He turned his gaze to Ellen, seated opposite him. His dead wife's place.

He counted ten under his breath, considering the bread he'd cut with the precision of a surgeon. He spoke quietly. "Do not take me for a fool, boy."

"My fault, sir." Killebrew knew when to take responsibility for his actions. The old man was constantly annoyed with him, but better for him to be the subject of the Irishman's ire than for it to fall to Jonathan, especially when the shenanigans were of his own doing.

"How so?"

"I run her into the bad stuff, sir. We were having a race. I was on the phaeton, Louis and Jonathan, of course, afoot. I tried to take a shortcut. Mired her like you read about, sir."

"The horse?"

The Hopi spoke up. "He's fine, sir. No injury. He walked home with no problem."

"And I take it you won again, Louis." Sean Whelihan glanced at his daughter. "You *always* win."

"Not today, Father." Jonathan grinned. "I took the prize today."

"Which was?"

He cast his gaze downward. "The braggin' rights, sir, that's all."

"In a pig's eye!" The old man glared accusingly at his daughter, the mistress of the spread, and then at the Hopi. The Indian seemed always underfoot, distracting the lads and his daughter from their work. Visiting! Eating the old man's food. Did he not have a home on the reservation?

Turning his head side to side, he sneered, knew they were all conspiring against him.

19

"What gave you the idea that you could beat a horse in a foot race?"

"Oh." Jonathan smiled, nodding to his adopted brother. "Rocky had to give us a head start, and he was driving Jug Head."

The old man blew air between his pursed lips. "Jug Head? That bag of bones? No wonder. That's no race at all." He looked up from the gristle on his plate. "I ask ye *again, what* was the prize?" He cleared his throat, as was his custom when irritated. "Never mind. I know well enough. Off to war. Off to another ridiculous adventure, conjured up by our venal government to line wealthy men's pockets." He glared at Rocky. "Another pair of Whelihans, off as lambs to slaughter."

His own father's words came to mind, as if it happened only yesterday. "Go on and fight, you bloody fools! Go on and serve the British crown. That's right! The British crown! Mark my words: these southerners, these so-called confederates, will be revealed for what they are, the pawns of the English bastards. Mark my words!"

And when that did not move Sean Whelihan or his brother, the old man raged on. "Fight so that some bloated bastard can keep his niggers! One nigger's worth more than both of you put together. That's it, you fools, march off to war, to defend the interests of the slavers and the bloody British bastards!"

Sean Whelihan smiled, as if to signal a sort of epiphany. "Oh, no, that's right." He pointed an arthritic finger at Rocky. "You answer to that damned Ulster name. Killebrew! *Killebrew* and *Whelihan,* they'll make fine engravings on your headstones." He grinned. "But then again, you'll not have headstones. Headstones are far too dear. Wooden crosses that'll be rotting away in some godforsaken field in the middle of nowhere in a year's time will be good enough for the likes of you. Stone monuments are for men of means. Bloated bastards of importance. Another fitting end for the best our country has to offer. Another fine chapter written in the book of Whelihan."

Ellen stood, motioning for the lads to clear out. She'd deal with the old man in her own way. "Father, there are a few hours of daylight. The boys need to finish cutting out the horses that we are selling to the army."

She moved past them, stealthy as a mountain lioness picking her way through an arroyo. She placed a wedge of cake before the old man, patting him gently, as one would a surly old canine. She kissed his temple.

"Your favorite, Father. The mercantile had coconuts."

"Bless you, child." He glared at the rest. "At least there's one in this family still loyal. One in this family with a modicum of sense and propriety."

Ellen Whelihan was twenty-seven and looked nearer to forty. Her hair had silvered prematurely. She had her father's jaw, the shape of a lantern, which gave her face a gaunt, sad look, even when she was in a pleasant mood. Her intelligence and kindness were what made her beautiful, but only to those who knew her well, as she was a private woman and wholly devoted to her clan.

She watched her brother brood, staring out from the porch, looking south. Handing him a cup of coffee, she gave him a reassuring hug.

"All right?"

Jonathan stared at nothing. "I . . . sometimes" — he faced his sister, bearing the expression of a drowning man — "I feel like I'll burst, Ellen. I'm like I could jump out of my skin. I feel that if I don't do *something, anything,* other than this, something with some kind of adventure, some sort of purpose, by God, I'll bust wide open!"

"So you're all volunteering."

He searched her eyes. Provoking his father was worrisome, but the one he dreaded disappointing more than anyone was Ellen, more a mother to him than a sister. "Will you forgive me if I do, Ellen? Will you forgive me if I run off, leaving you to deal with *him*?" He pointed with his head toward the house. "Take Rocky and Louis and run off on our adventure? Leave you with all the worry and work and misery?"

She pulled him close, resting his head on her bony shoulder. "I'll worry about you, worry about each one of you, but no, Jonathan. To deny you this — I might as well take you out and shoot you." She nodded. "Have your adventure. Find some peace, and don't worry about Father. I'll handle him."

"Why's he have to be that way, Ellen? Why's he have to be so darned angry and belittling all the time? I try and try to please him. Nothing I do is ever enough."

"Because he loves you too much."

"Darned funny way of showing it."

"And he's scared, Jonathan."

Her brother guffawed. "Ha, that's funny! Father scared? Father's never been scared of anything in his life." He thought of the tintype on the mantel, the picture of his father and uncle, posing with their pistols and Bowie knives, back when they were young and full of life. Back in the second war for independence. Back when men were men.

"Brother, I would not wager against that." She smiled at her sibling's ignorance. He was such a man, such a copy of his father, and didn't even know it. "You leave him to me."

She looked him over, as if deciding whether or not he was fit for duty. "Next week, I'll ride with you to Prescott. I'll see you and the boys off, *if* they decide to take you."

He smiled at her gibe and immediately looked hurt, the thought of it terrifying. "Do you suppose they . . . they won't?"

"Won't what?"

"Take me?"

"No, little brother. If they wouldn't take you, then, well, I don't know what they'd want in a soldier. You promise you'll be careful. Promise you'll come home safe."

He caught her heading to bed. He'd been drinking, and Ellen knew the despondency was at its worst when Father was in his cups. He rarely did anything to excess, and the drink had no hold on him. She could tell by the tone of voice that he'd worked himself into a funk. He sat on the porch in the dark with a dog's head in his lap, the glow of the cigarette the only indication of his presence. She stood in the moonlight and waited.

"So, it is such, isn't it, Ellen?"

"They're volunteering, Father. Yes, they're leaving."

"Even Louis?"

"Yes, Father, even Louis."

"Goddamn them. Goddamn every one of them."

She stood before him as would a vassal before her king. She knew more about her father by listening in on his nightmares than by any words he'd ever outright spoken.

"No swearing, Father."

"Goddamn them. Goddamn the politicians and bastards. They took me brother and now they'll take me boy."

"Boys," Ellen muttered under her breath. Rocky was always overlooked, ignored.

"Tell me, Father. Talk to me. Tell me what happened in the war."

"Gettysburg. Gettysburg is what happened in the goddamned war. That perfumed son of a bitch and that old stupid man sent us on a fool's errand, sent us across that field, and me brother, me brother worth a hundred of the sons of bitches, we marched and marched, and then it was he and I and he . . . he stepped right in front of me. Knocked me to the ground. Stepped right into the path —" He could not finish.

He stared into his lap, running his fingers over the dog's ears as he tried to work the words out. He took a trembling breath, attempting to quell the panic running through his mind. "Oh, God, Ellen, oh, God, me boy, me Jonathan does not know what he's in for. Doesn't have a notion what it's all about."

She stepped into the darkness of the veranda, rubbing his back as she'd done when she had no words to comfort him. As she'd done when the darkness had overtaken him. She could think of nothing. Fact was, he was likely correct. She wondered if Jonathan or Louis or Rocky would see Christmas.

Most times he infuriated her. Most times she wanted to grab him by the shoulders and shake him until he stopped his nonsense. This time, she wanted to cradle him in her arms and knew as well, he'd never have it. Like a spirited puppy held against its will, he'd squirm and kick and protest until he was left to his own destructive devices. She retreated back into the silver-lit yard, nearly as bright as sunlight in the morning.

Sean Whelihan spoke to the glowing tip of his cigarette. "I know this place is not exciting. I know a wandering soul, an inquisitive mind, needs more, and I would make it right, Ellen. Allow him some time, a little money for some adventuring. I don't mind that. I'd like to see him off East maybe to college. He has a sharp mind. Not as good as yours, but a sharp one enough, bright as some of those easterners who come swaggering here, throwing their money around.

"And we've money, thanks, in part, to that blood money from the goddamned army for the herd. We've the means, and I was planning . . . soon as the money got a little better, soon as we beat this terrible slump, but — well, I don't know. I don't know, Ellen. Not this! Not this way, my God, not this way. Not the way of the bloody army."

He searched her eyes as she stood before him, as if he were looking for an answer, for a way to articulate it. "I know I'm not easy to live around, Ellen. Know I vex you and the boy, know I make hurtful comments, and I'm . . . well, I don't like to do that, but, oh, God, I'll lose him as I've lost your mother. Your mother and me brother."

He brightened momentarily. "Maybe you

could tell him, tell him he can have his adventure. Travel East to college. That might change his mind."

"He's nearly twenty, Father. He's a grown man. His mind's settled on going to war." She turned her head from side to side. "College won't entice him."

"Ha! A *man*!"

"He *is*, and he knows his mind; he knows what he wants, and we must let him follow his own path, Father. Leave it to providence, and pray to God for his safe return."

Sean Whelihan stood, pushing the dog from his lap, retreating, escaping, as one freeing shackles from his limbs. "*You* pray to Him, Daughter. I've prayed enough, and, to tell the truth, I might as well pray to that dog, all it's ever done me."

She'd helped him to bed. Finally making it to her spot, consulting her watch as she stretched her tired back. *Her* time. A few precious moments before she could hold her eyes open no longer, a few moments where she could lose herself in Dickens or Brontë or Austen.

She lit the lamp, placing it closer to the rocker as she thumbed the pages. A coyote's call pulled her gaze to the ranch yard, all silver basked in moonlight. She loved the place so.

Louis Zeyouma called from the shadows. "Ellen?"

She could smell him often before she could see him, smell that he'd been on a run, the metallic tinge of sweat, Louis's odor. There was none other like it, and she'd known it for as long as she could remember. She stood to offer him a drink, as Ellen was first and foremost a servant and hostess to anyone visiting her ranch.

He waved her off, nodding for her to retake her seat.

"What has you running so late?" She knew he ran late when he had a lot on his mind.

He turned his attention to the moon. "Pleasant evening."

"Night."

"I guess it *is* late." He considered the time. His visits were typically initiated well before sundown.

"Jonathan and Rocky are off somewhere." They started every conversation the same way. A sort of dance, a ruse, carried out for the benefit of no one. They could both pretend all their interludes were happenstance.

"Care to walk?"

She glanced longingly at her copy of *Tales of the Punjab*. Ellen was a traveler through

29

her books, her only outlet, a mental reprieve from the mundane.

"It *is* late, Louis." She stood automatically, as if her legs had a mind of their own. She could not deny a guest anything.

He pulled the shawl from the back of the rocker, covering her shoulders, brushing them with the palms of his hands. He waited as she blew out the lamp.

They walked to the corral and then along the road west toward Flagstaff, Ellen speaking into the night as they strolled. "I suppose this is the best it'll ever be."

She smiled but was not happy. Louis continued the ritual.

"I guess so."

They walked together when the day's work was done, when Ellen had no further obligations and everyone had retired for the evening. The two of them, alone, together. Friends.

"Thank you for going with them, Louis." She turned from her usual gaze at the road before them. "I know you care not a whit for any of this."

"I don't know. Perhaps I've become a patriot."

She grinned. "As Father would say, *in a pig's eye!*"

They stopped at the boulder they'd used

since the time they started the ritual, about the time Louis had become a man.

Their rock. The rock that offered the most splendid vantage point to the valley below. It was here he'd present her with the solitary cigarette, the pre-twisted fancy ones she liked from back East, the ones Louis special ordered. Ellen's one vice. Ellen's one departure from propriety and decorum and denial of creature comfort.

He lit it for her and watched, another part of the ritual, their ritual. She leaned back, blowing smoke at the stars. His heart melted when she assumed that pose, as Louis always considered Ellen to be beautiful.

"Regardless of your reasons, I'm glad you will be with them." She turned, a little desperately. "Watch over Rocky, Louis. Please, watch over Rocky."

"I'll watch over them both."

"I know you will. But it's Rocky who worries me so. Jonathan — well, you know. Jonathan has always lived the charmed life. Jonathan . . . to him, everything comes so easily. But Rocky —" She turned her head, felt the emotion building; she swallowed to keep it from choking her. She faced him. "And, Louis, please, take care of yourself. I don't know what I'd do without you."

For the first time in their lives, he pulled

31

her into his arms, threatening to crush the glowing ember of her cigarette as he embraced her.

He kissed her, and she did not resist. She held him a little desperately, speaking into his ear. "Well, this is rather unexpected."

Louis watched her as she pulled away, regarding the cigarette. She dropped it between them, crushing it into oblivion.

"You do not mind?"

"No." She took a deep breath, felt the flutter in her chest, knew he could feel her trembling.

"Yet you retreat."

"I'm sorry."

"Why? If you do not mind, why are you sorry? Why do you retreat?"

"I . . . I don't know. But I'm glad it happened."

"I am glad, too, Ellen." He ran his fingers across her forehead, over her eyes, tracking the contours of her face as would a blind man remembering something lovely and dear to him. "I have wanted to do that since I was sixteen." He kissed her again. "I've wanted to do that for too long."

"This war business is certainly triggering some unusual emotions." She smiled, remembering so many lines and scenes from so many novels. "I suppose we're all caught up in the emotion of it."

"I am not caught up in anything."

"Then why did you kiss me?"

"Because I love you, and it is time I did something about it, Ellen." He kissed her again, each kiss more electrifying than the last.

She pressed fingers to eyelids, holding back the tears. Turning from him, she once again fixed her gaze to the silver-lit land before them. "Oh, Louis, it's no use. It's no use." She smiled. "I have had the same feelings for you, and I guess you know that." She patted his hands as they enveloped her waist from behind, grasping her about the womb. It was more comforting than anything she'd known. More comforting even than her mother's touch, a touch she'd not known for what seemed an eternity. "But it's no use."

"Why not?"

"Because," she pressed her body against him, knew he wanted her as desperately as she him. "Father. Father would never allow it, and I can't . . . I can't, Louis. I cannot do this to you."

"To me? Do what?"

"Cause trouble. Hold you when there's nothing for you. It's preposterous. I know the church has plans for you. You are committed to service as a missionary. Return to your people; marry a pretty maiden, Louis, marry a young, pretty girl. She'd be better suited to your future, your purpose, your —" She turned and looked down upon him. Louis was no prize, but to Ellen, he was a handsome man. "Find a pretty young Hopi, not a gangly old maid like me."

Louis kissed her again. "You are not gangly *or* old."

"I'm nearly ten years your senior."

"No, you're not! There are only seven years between us."

She ignored the challenge. "Please, Louis, do not delude yourself and do not patronize me. I'm worse than plain. I'm *hideous.* And beyond the age for marrying."

He hugged her again, whispering into her ear. "Not to me, Ellen. Never to me. To me you are beautiful. You are in my thoughts and dreams and with me constantly. Please, Ellen, when I return, promise you will remember what I have said here tonight. Promise me that you'll reconsider."

She wanted to turn and say something profound and clever, something from one of her novels. She caught herself. "No, Louis. I will not. I will not do anything but continue on with my life running this ranch. This is my destiny. This is my future, to . . .

to stay here and care for this place, take care of my father. I'll not do anything to cause you heartache or pain. I love you too much, and, well, our paths will separate when you return. There's nothing for it. There is no alternative." She held up a hand, a barrier, as symbolic as physical. "There's an end to it. We will be friends but not lovers, Louis. So there's an end to it."

She looked at him, running her fingers through his dark hair, kissing him one last time. "It's late, Louis. Let's go back. It's time I'm to bed. It's time we said good night. Tomorrow promises to be a busy day."

CHAPTER 2

Jonathan Whelihan had had his own cabin since he was seventeen. He had wanted to leave the ranch house and move in with the boys, the hired men, but his father would have none of it. Thus the compromise, and the little outbuilding sat, equidistant between two worlds. The place in which he forever seemed to languish.

He was not a hired hand or even a foreman. He was the son of the rancher, and it was his duty to behave as such. Mixing in a familiar manner with the help was not conducive to the maintenance of proper decorum, Sean Whelihan was certain of that, and that was Jonathan Whelihan's plight pretty much for as long as he could remember. He did not fit in with the family, and he did not fit in with the wranglers on his ranch, and the situation with Rocky did not help. Rocky was supposedly his brother, yet the old man treated him differently, even taking it so far as to banish him to the bunkhouse once his drinking had begun to consume him.

Yet, his adopted brother ate dinner with the family every evening. Another one of Sean Whelihan's strange incongruities. It was all rather tiring to keep straight, and, because of it, Jonathan lived in a state of constant flux. It was likely what contributed the most to his restlessness.

But he was embarking on an adventure, and the cabin felt small. Small and inconsequential and suffocating as he worked well into the evening packing what he thought would be useful in battle.

Ellen had mended and washed his underwear. She'd laid out ten pair and socks enough for a whole troop. He'd manage with four sets, tucking the rest in the drawer of his chifforobe.

He'd wear his best suit, the one he'd had tailored for him in Phoenix the year before, as it added a level of maturity and, at least according to Francesca, sophistication. He frankly did not know what they'd be looking for in recruits, but he'd always looked younger than he was and a little gaunt from the running, though he was not by any means weak. He'd even been in a fight with a wrangler they'd hired a while back whom

Rocky had smarted off to and caused a bit of a kerfuffle.

He didn't really know how to fight. Never had to all the years growing up. Even when he'd ventured into town, there was never any call to fight. Everyone liked Jonathan Whelihan. He was handsome and respectful and charming. But he did fight that day, awkwardly, and, in the end, the job had been done and the ruffian put in his place and fired from the ranch.

Later, they learned that he was a rather bad hombre who had killed a man and was wanted for that murder and some burglaries, for which Jonathan was a bit proud, as facing down a fellow was a tough enough undertaking, but facing down a bad fellow was all that much more an accomplishment.

He wondered if Rocky would behave as his adopted brother had been misbehaving pretty much from the time he was weaned from the wet nurse's tit. Rocky was a foundling, taken in by the late Mrs. Whelihan, cared for and loved as if he'd been the fruit of her own womb.

It was soon discovered, to the chagrin of Sean Whelihan, that the boy had a temper worse than the old man's and a nearly insatiable appetite for spirits, causing him to be downright stupid when he'd indulged too much, which was often.

Truth was, Rocky Killebrew was not at all stupid — likely the smartest of the family — only profoundly pig-headed, often unwilling to learn anything that might ease his way through life and perhaps inspire it to a happier one.

It seemed he reveled in misery, worked it as a craft, treated it as a vocation, a calling, and, to someone as inherently happy-go-lucky as Jonathan, it was an altogether vexing way to conduct one's life.

The late Mrs. Whelihan sure loved them both, and it was she, really, who was the only one to ever truly calm him. Control the fits of rage. She understood Rocky.

It was soon after she'd passed that he started in on the drinking. Sean Whelihan declared that he plain had bad blood, bred wrong, like a degenerate colt, and the best that could have happened to him was to have never been born at all.

But Rocky had been born and, at least physically, had flourished and would likely have ended up, like his brother, a rather splendid fellow had his adopted mother not passed so early out of his existence.

Jonathan was determined to watch him on this adventure, yet, he knew, it would be the Hopi who would excel in that undertaking.

Louis had a calming influence on the both of them. The Indian would help him control the wild Rocky. It would be Louis who'd bring them all home safe.

He was packed and checked the clock on the wall. Nearly ten, and she was not yet there. He took a walk where he knew he'd intercept her, on the road that linked the two ranches. He enjoyed the walk, especially when the sky was clear, when there was a chill to the air. It helped calm his mind. The moon was full, turning all to silver streaked with dark shades of grey. He could see a long distance.

He considered that the same moon shone, that moment, on the battlefield, somewhere in Cuba, somewhere many miles away, some place where he'd ultimately be tested, and this caused a shiver, like a plunge into an icy river, to run through him.

Off to the west, the boys could be heard in the yard out front of the bunkhouse, sitting around an impressive campfire. One called out, offering him a good night.

Another couple cheered, impressed with some feat of Rocky's, presently taking full advantage of his comrades' hospitality in giving him a proper farewell party. He'd be in for a right raging hangover in the morning.

She rode up fast, sidesaddle, the joy nearly overwhelming him as it meant she'd be wearing that dress, the especially beautiful one, and no petticoat under. He loved that dress above all in her impressive wardrobe.

She stopped next to him for a moment, nodding a little devilishly, pulling at the collar, revealing the gifts bestowed upon her by the Almighty. She urged her mount on. He'd have to jog to catch up, but instead he lingered to give her time to settle. The anticipation was thrilling, not unlike Christmas morning when his mother was living.

It had been foretold, from the time they were children, that Francesca Rogers would be Mrs. Jonathan Whelihan, and this was never disputed nor was it challenged, by anyone, not even Sean Whelihan, a man who did not condone the mixing of races. With Francesca, he knew when he'd been bested.

Jonathan himself did not mind the arrangement, as, from the time he decided girls were pretty and special and desirable, he'd been smitten. She'd been a beautiful child and had grown into the kind of woman any red-blooded man would be proud to have as a lover, a companion, a wife. He never entertained any other future.

She possessed more than a hint of Latin

41

blood, since her family had lived first in California and then Arizona for more than thirty years, descended, at least on her mother's side, from the Californios. Other components contributing to her lineage included a bit of Scandinavian, Dutch, and a great-grandmother who was allegedly a full-blood Tarahumara.

Tall and slight, with an olive-colored complexion, green eyes, and hair raven black, no man or boy lucky enough to see her could refrain from overtly admiring her. Yet everyone knew, she was Jonathan's woman, as certainly as if it had been preordained by the Almighty.

A few months shy of twenty and an only child, she was the mistress of her ranch, her dear father departing this earth two days after her seventeenth birthday and her mother a year and a half later.

Francesca had no difficulty rising to the challenge. She could outride, outshoot, and out negotiate anyone she'd thus far encountered. By the more surly merchants and traders of the region she was known, more or less affectionately, as *that little bitch,* a moniker she bore with pride.

He was a little disappointed when he peered into his room. She'd ridden too quickly, undressing before he could assist.

She reclined, like Bathsheba, in his narrow bed, under his crisp white sheets, awaiting his arrival. His disappointment was immediately ameliorated, as Francesca, with nothing more than a smile, could distract the most focused of men.

Soon beside her, he pressed his body to hers, feeling the warmth of her sex. He was pleased to find her so aroused.

"You smell wonderful."

"You smell like leather."

"New travel bag." He motioned with his head. "Ellen ordered one for each of us as a present."

"Love me?"

"With all my heart, Francesca."

She moved deftly, positioning herself astraddle as was her wont. She could control things better, move better for both of them, and it offered the best vantage point to see his expression of wonder, reverence, worship as she worked her magic.

He tried to focus. "How do you get your hair so pretty?"

"*Only* my hair, Jonathan?" She smiled, following his eyes, his gaze, as it moved over her long neck, pretty, ample breasts, and flat belly. They'd had such carnal knowledge for the past year, and still he regarded every act with the same reverence as if it were their first time.

"No." He smiled. "And your pretty face, and neck, and bosoms, and, and . . . oh, God, Francesca, I love you."

Afterward, they lay, bound together in post-coital bliss. He petted her sex, and she did not stop him, instead pressing her body against his hand.

"Tell me again why you want to leave, Jonathan."

"I, I . . ."

"You don't know."

"I . . . no, I *do* know, Francesca. I *do* know. I want to fight for my country." He turned, the jingoistic zeal trumping carnal desire. "I don't want those Spanish bastards to keep doing what they've been doing."

"You mean for the past four hundred years?"

He looked injured. Francesca likely knew more about the current state of affairs than he. "What's that supposed to mean?"

"For four hundred years, the Spaniards have controlled Cuba, Jonathan, yet all of a sudden, it's a travesty."

He rose and fetched a glass of water. He fed some to his love, then took a long drink. He returned his attention to her and wanted her again. He wanted her always, and the thought of not having her inspired him to regret the entire enterprise.

She smiled devilishly as his ears reddened. "I did not know the Spaniards were such a terrible race."

"Oh, what of the *Maine*? What of that young woman pictured in the paper" — he could not expunge from his memory the image, simultaneously provocative and revolting, as the poor creature could have been Francesca's twin — "the one those devils stripped naked and ogled on that ship?"

"That's a lot of nonsense. Uncle read the real story to me. That never happened. Uncle says all of this is the orchestrated silliness of a bunch of politicians and journalists. Roosevelt's War, that's what they're calling it, you know. Uncle says —"

"I don't care what your uncle or the newspapers say!" He stopped himself before it deteriorated into a quarrel. Of all times, he did not want to quarrel this night, their last together for God only knew how long.

He paced about the room, adjusting objects while searching for the correct words to articulate. "I *have* to go, Francesca. I don't know why, don't know what's right or wrong anymore, but . . . but I *have* to go, that's all."

She smiled as a mother would her

tantrum-throwing child. "I know, Jonathan. I know."

"Why won't you marry me, Francesca?"

"I will, when you've finished with this silly adventure."

"Why not now?"

"I've already told you. I don't want to be a twenty-year-old widow, Jonathan."

His eyes widened, as if the thought of not returning had just occurred to him. "What if . . . you know, what if you end up in the family way?" He turned his gaze to her flat belly, wondering for a moment how she'd look pregnant. In all likelihood, ravishing.

"Then I'll marry you when you return."

"And if I don't come back?" He felt like a grown-up man saying that.

"Well, then I'll go to San Francisco and have the babe there. I'll take a trip and bring it back as a foundling or a cousin. It's not the first time such a thing has happened, either around here *or* in my family."

"You're a wicked, wicked thing."

"Thank you. Now, shut up and turn out that light, Jonathan. I want you again. In the dark this time; I like it that way."

CHAPTER 3

Clara Maass would be twenty-two in June and already had been the head nurse of the Newark German Hospital for nearly a year. It would be an extraordinary feat for a woman many years her senior, especially as her slight frame would almost ensure that she'd not be taken seriously, let alone accepted as a candidate for the daunting job of staff nurse in a hospital.

It was the state of her hands, red and worn by hours of toil as a mother's helper and matron at the neighborhood orphanage, that had captured the attention of Anna Streeber, the superintendent of nurses, the woman who would forever change Clara's life.

Clara had barely turned seventeen when she'd submitted her application; the minimum age for entry into the training program was twenty-one.

But first appearances were often deceiving, and deceiving she was with her delicate features, blue eyes, and hair that mimicked spun gold in sunlight. A frail schoolgirl she was not, and one needed only a brief encounter for that misconception to be dispelled. No one who met the pretty German-American could argue that.

She loved her work as a nurse, and at least the drudgery part of it, the part that involved only the skills of a housemaid with the strength of an army mule, came easy to her; she'd been doing such work since the age of ten for wages, earlier if she counted helping her mother.

The intellectual part was nearly as easy, for Clara possessed a keen mind and hunger to learn. Almost immediately she was fully competent in the practice of the nursing arts, assisting and guiding physicians and fellow nurses alike in the principles of Nightingale's *Notes on Nursing* in addition to the most up-to-date theories on medicine brought over from the German practitioners of the healing arts.

As soon as she'd heard that proper nurses were needed for the impending war, she wrote a letter of inquiry. She re-read the reply with enthusiasm. From the office of Dr. Anita Newcomb McGee, she was to report to the Seventh Army, presently located in Jacksonville, Florida.

It was for her, not unlike the motivation for Jonathan Whelihan, an adventure, and the generous salary would offer significant assistance in the care of her parents and many siblings.

As she undressed for bed, she thought of the terse surgeon whom she'd won over. He was downright distraught at the idea of losing her, and, as she combed out the golden locks and regarded her image in the mirror, she wondered if it had not been only for the loss of her skills as a nurse.

She was beautiful and knew it and knew that everyone else knew it. She once heard someone say that being beautiful was a sin but was convinced that was not true. The Virgin Mary was beautiful. Beauty was no sin, but vanity was, and Nurse Maass guarded against it with the veracity of a soldier in the Black Watch.

The oval glasses helped tone it down, but there was no denying that Clara was a stunning young woman. She could not change that, nor did she necessarily want to. To Clara, her beauty was a kind of weapon used to advocate for her patients. If she could not persuade through intelligence or competence, she'd not hesitate to allow her allure to manipulate the men who often held the power to heal or destroy, to make them behave and act properly, more often than not without their conscious understanding of it.

She crawled between the sheets, preparing for some well-deserved and needed rest, as it had been a long sixteen hours, and she'd be up again in another five to do it all over again.

Her body began to relax in slumber when the knock on her door came with enough zeal to force her to answer, knowing at once who it was. At least she'd not been called for another emergency.

"Clara!"

"Constance."

"Oh, Clara." The distraught woman pushed her way in. "I still cannot believe it. Off to war. To war, Clara, my goodness, to war!"

"Yes, to war, Constance." She stared longingly at her bed.

"I brought us a little brandy."

"I don't drink spirits, Constance, you know that."

"Oh, nonsense. It'll help you sleep."

"I don't need help to sleep." She was asleep as soon as her head hit the pillow. Due to a pure mind, her mother said. A person who could sleep like Clara was pure of mind and heart.

Constance plopped down, pouring generously for the both of them. "Clara, Dr. Kopf was so upset, I heard he went to his club and got drunk this evening."

"Dr. Kopf goes to his club and gets drunk every evening."

"I heard he" — she looked left and right, as if there might be eavesdroppers — "I heard he's sweet on you, Clara."

"Constance!" She suppressed a laugh. "He's as old as Methuselah, and married, and besides, his breath stinks, as well as his feet."

Constance cocked her head like a curious pointer. "How do ya know his feet stink?"

"I was in his office last week reviewing cases, and he had his shoes off under the desk." She waved her hand in front of her nose. "He needs a thorough scrubbing."

"Well, I heard from one of the orderlies, who heard from a cook whose wife works at the club, that he was drunk as a lord. Made comments, Clara; said he'd leave his wife for you if only she didn't have all the money."

"Well, that means nothing to me, Constance. I'm to help the soldiers, and I care not one bit for what Dr. Kopf thinks or doesn't think." She tried to look terse. "And

I'll thank you not to talk about it again. It's scandalous and a sin. Shame on him if has such thoughts." She stood, ushering her rotund companion toward the door. "Now, we both have work to do" — she looked at the clock on the mantel — "in less than four hours, so I suggest you go to sleep."

"Oh, Clara." Constance grabbed her in a bear hug. "I'll miss you."

Further south in Baltimore, M. Mary Bonaventure, Sister of Mercy, had recently celebrated her fifty-first birthday. Of those, thirty-one had been spent tending the sick poor in Baltimore. She'd never been involved with war, was too young for both the Crimea and the American Civil War, but nursing was nursing, and she'd spent enough years fighting in the hospital ward, battling disease and infection, dysentery and typhoid fever and broken bones and difficult childbirths.

In another week she'd be on a train south, along with five of her colleagues, to Camp Thomas, Chickamauga Park, Georgia. They were Sisters de Sales Prendergast, Loyola Fenwick, Celestine Doyle, Mercedes Weld, and Nolasco McColm.

She was the eldest; the youngest, Celestine Doyle, was thirty-one.

She was not only the oldest but known by everyone as the *kind* nun. Not that she was a push-over. She was not, but she had learned to forgive certain behaviors of both her patients and parishioners.

During the terrible heat of the Baltimore summers, she'd allow the young new mothers to bare their legs, which was singularly forbidden, to the cooling effects of the fans running in each corner of the ward. But, as no men were permitted other than physicians, Mary Bonaventure could see no harm. "Only the Lord and the nuns will see," she'd quietly chastise her more Victorian-minded sisters as they covered the legs of the sweat-soaked mothers.

She, on the other hand, would never be caught without the full symbol of her order, a habit of black material, mercifully of cotton in the summer, covering from chin to feet. A long train, not unlike a wedding dress, was looped when at work on the wards, and the habit was tied with a leather girdle and rosary. A veil of black completed the ensemble, long and flowing to cover her hair as tribute to her devotion, despite the oppressive Baltimore heat. The physicians who served with her were convinced she was not human.

■ ■ ■ ■

Minerva Trumbull was not a nurse, though at twenty-seven she had done the work of nursing for more than eleven years in the Sibley Memorial Hospital that was more her home than anyplace else. At least she spent more time there than at home, working twelve to sixteen hours, six days per week.

It was the nursing matron who told her about the contract nurses needed for the war effort. Of course, as Minerva was no nurse, she'd not taken any of it seriously.

But the fear of yellow fever and malaria was overwhelming, and the need for immune nurses outstripped the supply. As her matron reasoned, Minerva knew more about nursing care than any of the young women fresh out of formal training. She convinced her to submit her application.

It was Minerva's goal to become a *real nurse,* as she called it. A real nurse with a real cap from a genuine school of nursing, and she knew it would one day happen. Now that her grandmother had passed, she'd be free to travel north to the hospitals where Negroes, at least those with adequate references, could withstand the rigors of the admission process.

The only thing lacking was funds, and the salary the government was willing to pay would fill that void amply. If she could hold a contract for a year, she'd have more than enough to study and live so far from home.

The matron checked on her as she finished her last day on the ward. A woman of sixty and a devout Christian, Wilhelmina Connelly was the daughter of an abolitionist who, after the war, devoted her life to serving the poor.

She wound up in North Carolina as the superintendent of nurses, responsible for not only hiring Minerva but encouraging the notion that she could fulfill her lifelong dream.

"All sorted, Minerva?"

"Yes, Nurse Connelly."

"I have something for you." She handed her a package, standing by proudly as the young woman opened it.

"A . . . a nurse's uniform?"

"Yes, this is the uniform of my school, Minerva." She held it under the young woman's chin. "I had it altered to fit you." She reached over, pinning on the cap with care. "This is mine."

"I . . . I can't. I can't."

"Yes, you can, and you will." Standing

back to survey her ministrations, she said, "You look very nice." She smiled. "I'm not saying to lie, Minerva, but, well, you wear this. Wear it proudly, dear. You're more of a nurse than a lot of the school-trained girls I've encountered." She nodded. "I've written of your qualifications, and they know what to expect. You're a proper contract nurse, and you leave it at that. If you don't know something you're told to do, you let them know. Like you do here, you do what you know, and you tell us when you don't know." She patted Minerva gently. "Doubt much if you'll be expected to do anything you've not already done here for years, dear. You have confidence in yourself. Confidence in your knowledge. I know, in no time, they'll love you as much as you're loved here.

"And, when you return, we'll send you north, up to one of the schools that'll have you. Maybe my alma mater, Phipps. I told you, they matriculated Mary Mahoney; why not you?"

Minerva had to look away. "I want to thank you, Nurse Connelly. Thank you for everything. I'll do you proud, do your uniform proud. I promise, ma'am."

"I know you will, dear." She handed her another parcel. "Go on with you, and remember everything you've learned. And, Minerva, remember, you might be immune, but it doesn't mean you cannot die. You take care of yourself, dear. Take care and come back to us."

CHAPTER 4

Rocky Killebrew rode the last leg of the journey to Prescott, vomiting the better part of the day, thankful he was not required to work, as he was in no position to do anything but stay mounted, and that with considerable difficulty. He held back, far behind the carriage. In this way he avoided the wrath of the old man.

Louis drove, and next to him sat, proud and in charge, Ellen Whelihan, who periodically checked the lovers behind them.

It was both a sendoff and a business transaction, as the elder Whelihan had been contracted to deliver a herd of range horses to Alexander Brodie and his volunteers. There were over a hundred and the promise of cash payment upon delivery. Sean Whelihan kept the pace a brisk one. The sooner this was over the better, as, in a way, it felt as if he'd contracted a deal with the devil. He could not shake the ominous foreboding and subsequent pain that often ran through his gut, into his soul.

They arrived at Fort Whipple, more a carnival than a military recruiting depot. Men wandered here and there, some swaggered, and others stood about waiting. Men of many stripes — cow punchers, prospectors, Indians and Indian fighters, teamsters, lawmen, lawless men, young, old, and in between. Some were easterners, educated and well-dressed city men, desperate to join the fray. Some gambled; a few fiddled about the quartermaster's checking the equipment and uniforms.

Sean Whelihan sneered, pointing a crooked, arthritic finger, as if he'd identified the source of all evil. "There's the bastard politician and his henchman."

Buckey O'Neill, captain of the First Arizona Volunteer Cavalry, stood and smoked with his former ranger scout and deputy, Tom Horn.

Jonathan grinned at his father's rant. The elder Whelihan was the quintessential iconoclast. He hated all manner of politicians and celebrities. The junior Whelihan could not resist provoking him a little.

"What's wrong with Buckey?"

"Ha! Buckey! You know well enough. And that bastard Horn. He — well, at least his murderous ways'll come in handy soon enough in battle, *if* he doesn't turn coward and run." He spat on the ground between his feet. "Which would not surprise me. Everyone with half a brain knows he's the one responsible for the Pleasant Valley war; everyone knows he has blood on his hands in that, and the blood of children no less, certain as the turning of the earth."

Jonathan looked off in the distance to a group of men gathered under a marquee tent. "And there's another one, Father! Standing by the tent pole."

Sean Whelihan sneered. "You're right, boy. Chock full of the bastards. The ass, Brodie." He turned his head in disgust. "I don't envy you, boy. Like wading among a pit of vipers, by God."

Whelihan pulled his son aside, walking him to a grove of trees, away from the family and crowds.

"I want to talk to you, boy."

Jonathan waited uneasily. He'd never seen his old man act in such a peculiar way. "Yes, Father?"

Sean Whelihan ran his fingers under the lapels of his boy's suit jacket, pulling the young man into position so that he'd face him. "You mind yourself, lad. No heroics. You do your duty, and do as you are told, and nothing more." He wagged a finger in Jonathan's face. "You volunteer for *nothing,* lad. Nothing! You understand me? Nothing!"

"Father, I —"

"Shut up and listen. My God, you're so much like your mother. Could talk a dog down off a meat wagon." He looked off at his family, at his daughter and Rocky and his son's girl and Louis Zeyouma standing indifferently off to the side. "You take care of Louis. The Hopis are not fighters, son. They are no cowards, but they are no fighters, and you take care of that boy." He opened a satchel and removed his old CSA belt. "I wore this in three battles." He held it up, showing his son the buckle. "You see that dimple? That's from a Yankee minié ball. It saved me life, boy." He nodded. "Put it on."

"It's likely not regulation for this outfit, Father."

"Regulation be damned. You tell that politician O'Neill that it'll bring you and the brigade luck." He had another thought. "And be careful of Rocky, lad."

"Yes, Father."

"He . . . he's a good boy, but he's not one of us, Jonathan. By God, we tried, your mother and me. We tried, but he's — well, he's of bad blood. Bad northern blood, and you be careful with him lad. He'll . . . I swear, I've worried so much o'r the years. I swear he'll be our undoing."

"I'll watch him, Father. I'll watch over them both. I promise you."

"All right, now." He pulled the lad's lapels again, running the backs of his fingers over his son's bony chest. He nodded at the garrison belt as Jonathan fastened it. "There. It fits. It suits you."

The old man fidgeted, and Jonathan waited. He had something more to say, and the young man knew he had to give him the time to articulate it.

"My brother Jonathan —"

"Poor Uncle Jon."

"Yes, lad. He . . . died for me, Jonathan. You cannot fathom such a thing." He blinked. "But, I fear you might learn soon enough." He patted his son's shoulder. "You come back safe. I've lost too much, lad. Don't know if I can endure any more."

"I promise, Father. I promise." He pulled his father into his arms. It was the first time he'd ever hugged him. "I promise, Father. I'll be home soon."

"Which clan?" Colonel Theodore Roosevelt peered through dusty pince-nez at Louis

Zeyouma, the third in line next to Rocky as men clambered, pressing in to see the maestro himself. Roosevelt had slipped in, unannounced, to review the first Rough Riders to join up. The Arizona boys, he called them. He appeared pleased at what he'd seen thus far.

Jonathan Whelihan, for reasons he could not fathom, answered in the Indian's stead. "Rope, sir!"

Zeyouma nodded, adding, *"Tchuf mongwi."*

"Ah, an esteemed member of the Antelope Society. Do you run?"

Rocky Killebrew guffawed, eliciting a glare from the colonel, seated like a judge behind his camp desk, the fly of the marquee tent flapping ominously in the breeze. Killebrew straightened his back as all attention was directed toward him.

"These boys can outrun an antelope, Mr. Roosevelt."

"And you are?"

Rocky stood at attention. "Rocky Killebrew, sir, of the Circle W, sir. We brought them horses you all were so impressed with." He nodded. "This is my, ah, stepbrother Jonathan Whelihan. His pa owns the ranch. Louis, there, he runs down to Winslow all the way from Oraibi to watch the trains pass. Louis and Jonathan, they're runnin' sons of bitches, sir."

"And you are profane, young man." Roosevelt looked the three over while drumming a blotter with his pencil, speaking almost to himself. "We can use a runner" — he turned to Louis — "but not a Hopi, I regret to say."

Jonathan spoke without thinking. "Why not?"

Captain O'Neill interjected, "That's *why not, sir,* and the answer is it's because the colonel said so, son. You boys might want to remember this is the US Army, where you address colonels as 'sir' and don't demand a rationale for their decisions."

Roosevelt waved him off. "It's all right, Captain." He turned to the young men. "Very simply stated." He looked at Rocky. "Tell me, young man, what does the term Hopi mean?"

Rocky replied, "It's — well, sir, it's the name of Louis's tribe. Hopi. Means Hopi, like Apache means Apache or Navajo means Navajo."

Roosevelt straightened in his seat. "It's a shortened name for *Hopituh Shi-nu-mu*" — he turned to Louis — "which means," he nodded, "tell us, young man."

"The peaceful people."

Roosevelt nodded. "The peaceful little

ones." He looked each man in the eye. "And, that, gentlemen, is why he may not ride with us." He sat forward in his chair. "There are two tribes that I will not have" — he nodded — "and the Hopi are one of them, as they are a peaceful folk, and I'd no sooner ask one to fight than I would a Quaker to take up the sword."

Buckey O'Neill turned. "And the other, Colonel?"

"The Apaches."

Rocky once again spoke out of turn. "Why not the Apaches? They're some mean bastards. Some fightin' sons of bitches."

"Young man, you will have to control that filthy tongue." Roosevelt turned to O'Neill. "Captain, fine every man a quarter for each time they swear when speaking to an officer, or, for that matter, in a military capacity. I'll not lead a rabble." He looked back at the others. "Apaches are too difficult to control in battle. It is like the old Celts; they become unmanageable." His face changed, and the colonel looked a bit like a lecturer. "Why, do you know, gentlemen, that the Celts were known for their fits of mania in battle? *Riastradh,* it was called, and so wild they'd become that they'd start killing their own. That, too, is the way of the Apache, and, well, I cannot have it, not in a modern,

European-style war."

He stood, pulling his Brooks Brothers tunic in place. "You two may come along. Any men involved in the breeding of such fine beasts will certainly prove useful to the cavalry." He extended his hand. "But you, young fellow, return to your people, and help them survive. We are on the eve of a new century, a new, modern world." He nodded. "And I see you've been educated in the ways of the white man. Return to Oraibi, young man, and teach your people how to endure."

He turned. "Captain O'Neill, let's inspect those mules."

"This way, Colonel."

"You say they're from that breeder Walsh, down near Tombstone?"

"Arvel Walsh, yes, sir. Best mules this side of the Mississippi."

"He's a captain of Arizona Rangers, isn't that correct?"

"He is, sir."

And before they could respond or salute or protest, Colonel Roosevelt was off, like an excited schoolboy on holiday, to his next adventure.

It was like a hammer blow to everyone except for Louis, and the women, of course, as they were heartened to see the Indian relieved of the obligation. Louis was no warrior. He never had so much as an unkind word for anyone.

By early evening everything was settled. The Whelihan clan rested under the shade of a Palo Verde as the boys sauntered up in their new kit.

Ellen stood them together and snapped pictures with her Kodak. "You two look very handsome."

Jonathan looked himself over. "Not certain how these heavy shirts'll feel in the tropical sun. Feel fine when there's a bite in the air, but it's a nice outfit sure enough, Ellen."

He wandered away from them with Francesca, beyond the edge of the camp and the men whose necks craned to catch a glimpse of his love as she moved past them.

They sat together in silence for a while as Jonathan thought of the correct words to say. Her nonchalance was not a little vexing.

"So, this is it."

"It is, Jonathan." She smiled. "Are you happy?"

"Oh, yeah, sure, I'm happy."

"You don't seem very happy." She smiled coyly. "You seem a bit put out."

"Oh." He could not deny that the homesickness was already setting in. He felt silly in the new stiff flannel shirt and duck trousers. Felt an imposter, as if he didn't belong.

Her lack of concern provoked him. "Well, you sure seem to be taking it well enough."

She shrugged, not changing her impish grin. "What do you want me to say, Jonathan? 'Don't go? Please come back home?' What do you want me to do? Fall to the ground? Grovel at your feet?"

"No!" He wiped the dust from his new boots. "I . . . I don't know, Francesca. Don't know, only thought —"

"I'd be crying and gnashing my teeth?" She smiled. "Jonathan, I love you. I want to have your children."

His eyes went to her womb. "Children?"

"Yes, of course, children."

He remembered the conversation in the cabin. "You're sure not yet?"

"I don't know. Perhaps."

"What do you mean, you don't know? What do you mean, *perhaps*? Don't women know these sorts of things?"

"Do you know immediately when one of your broodmare's and stud's union has taken, Jonathan, as soon as you put them together?"

"Don't talk like that!"

"Like what?"

"Like we're horses, like we're common animals. Jesus, Francesca, you are scandalous sometimes."

"We *are* like horses, and dogs and cats, and swine and my cattle, and even the scorpions and snakes that writhe about on the ground. We *are* common animals, Jonathan, plain and simple. We're animals, and I don't know if I'm growing your babe inside me or not." She smiled. "I ought to be, with all the carrying on we do."

He went pale, running his hand through his hair in what could only be described as a kind of panic. "What if, Francesca, what if —"

"Then I'll deal with it if it happens. I already told you not to worry about that. Jonathan, I want to spend the rest of my days with you, but I will not have you moping about for the next fifty years, wondering what it would have been like to run off to war with these Rough Riders and have your adventure." She stood, pulling him to his feet, giving him the most provocative kiss of his life.

Holding a palm to his cheek, she said, "Remember that kiss, Jonathan. Remember it and remember there is a lifetime of such kisses" — she smiled — "and much more, waiting for you when you come home." She nodded. "And you remember to come home, Jonathan. Remember to come home." She pulled a locket from around her neck, transferring it to her lover's. "Open it, Jonathan."

"Your hair, and" — he felt his face flush — "your picture in a . . . a *chemise?*"

"It's the sheer one that you like so much, Jonathan. The one that shows off my bosom the way you find so maddening."

He looked hurt, sounding a bit like a child vying for his mother's affections. *"Who took it?"*

"That perfumed dandy in Flagstaff."

"He saw you in almost *nothing?*"

"Relax, darling. He's not the kind of man who finds such interesting." He looked it over again and wanted her. Wanted to strip naked of the confining, itchy uniform; wanted to find the nearest hotel and pull her into his arms, into bed, and love her as he'd never done before.

She closed his fist around the locket. "Remember me, Jonathan. Remember me."

Colonel Roosevelt stood before the men, the definition of incongruity, sporting the Brooks Brothers uniform and slouch hat, a gleaming saber affixed to his side. An intellectual in a uniform too well-tailored for proper battle. He no longer sported the pince-nez; these had been replaced by oversized steel-rimmed glasses of a sturdier construction.

Buckey O'Neill saw to it that the men stood at attention, a foreign concept to most of them.

"At ease, men." Roosevelt walked up and down the line. "Men, you are now proud members, actually the first members, of the First United States Volunteer Cavalry.

"Hold yourselves proud, as you've been chosen to represent all that is best about America, about your home land of Arizona.

"Remember this, men. The eyes of the world are upon you. The eyes of the world are upon the US volunteers, and I know in my heart that you will not disappoint them.

"We are embarking on a crusade, men. A crusade, not unlike the crusades of old, to end the tyranny of the people of Cuba, who shall soon know the freedom we Americans genuinely cherish and enjoy.

"Over the next several weeks, you will hone the skills you've brought from hard years of toil and adventure. You will learn to be military men, learn to shoot the enemy as military men, ride, and bear yourselves and interact with your fellow troopers in such a way that would do the most seasoned West Pointer proud. And all of this without losing that unique pioneer identity."

"Here, here!" A lanky fellow spoke up.

Roosevelt nodded. "That's right, here, here!" He pointed. "Though I will warn you, trooper, what's your name?"

"Davies, sir."

"Trooper Davies, we are not a rabble. And future speaking out of turn will result in a fine. Be warned, young man."

"Yes, sir."

"Speaking of rabble . . . You men will soon find out, if you do not already know, I hold myself to a very high standard. I am a teetotaler." He qualified that. "Well, except of course in the warmer months, I might partake of a mint julep at bedtime, to help me sleep. But I imbibe in no vices, except, well, in the form of politics. I do not take drink or tobacco, do not swear or gamble. I am a happily married man.

"That said, I do not begrudge a man certain proclivities, and, as imbibing of alcoholic beverages and tobacco are not yet illegal in these United States, I will not ban their use in our outfit, at least not within reason, and when a man's work day is done, nor will gambling be forbidden so long as the man engaging in such activity is neither a cheat nor without the funds to support such a habit.

"I will, however, not tolerate the practice of usury. Additionally, fighting amongst yourselves will not be tolerated. Any disagreements will be settled in the boxing ring, Marquess of Queensbury rules applying.

"Lying with women shall be forbidden."

He waited for the sniggering to abate. "Except, of course, among married persons, between, of course, husband and wife. But be clear, gentlemen: I will not tolerate a trooper in a house of ill repute."

A backwoodsman near the front whispered to his companion. "What's a house a' ill repute?"

"A bawdy house."

"A what?"

"A brothel."

"A what?"

"A whorehouse."

"You don't say!"

Roosevelt continued. "These offenses will be dealt with by the most draconian measures, from fines to imprisonment to expulsion from the corps.

"As for capital offenses" — he looked each man by turn in the eye — "meaning infractions incurring punishment by death penalty, such as desertion, cowardice, murder, rape and, for that matter, any cruel or unjust treatment of women, children, or the infirm, will be carried out with extreme prejudice. Is that clear?"

"Yes, sir!"

"Capital! Now that the air is most abundantly cleared, men, anyone unwilling or unable to rise to this challenge, any man considering himself incapable of behaving like a proper warrior and gentleman, simply report to me, and I'll relieve you without further obligation."

He waited, and none replied. "Capital! Now, men, I'm leaving you in the competent hands of Major Brodie and Captain O'Neill, as I'm off to San Antonio, where I'll be waiting with the rest of the troop. At that time, we'll commence training. Until then, Godspeed, and remember, the eyes of the world are on the men of Arizona! Do us proud!"

He nodded to Captain O'Neill. "Dismiss the troop, Captain."

After the swearing-in ceremony, Jonathan felt proud, felt it was real now that he'd pledged to act like a soldier and do his duty. He absentmindedly fidgeted with the locket Francesca had given him. Thought about the baby possibly growing in her belly. Had it happened? He took a deep breath, pushing away the feeling of foreboding and panic. He *had* to come home alive and well.

He watched Rocky returning from a chuck wagon, plate heaped high, as a scrawny man with grey stubble plopped down beside the young Whelihan, much to Rocky's chagrin. Jonathan attempted to lighten the mood, motioning for his brother to find another seat.

"You ought to have sides welded to that plate. My God, Rocky, did you leave any for the rest of the men?"

"Oh, plenty." He surveyed the beans. "I wonder if them Mexican ladies are comin' along. If'n they do, we'll be needing fatter uniforms." He nodded. "Old timer, you're in my place."

"It's Pep Young, laddie" — he looked at the stump he was using for a stool — "and I didn't see no engraved nameplates."

"Well, my name's Rocky, old-timer, and I'll thank you for finding another spot. Not in the habit of repeatin' myself, and ain't much in the habit of pushing around scrawny old men." He offered a cocky smirk. "So, again, I'm askin' you nice, move outta my seat."

The Indian was on him from nowhere, touching Rocky on the shoulder, eliciting enough of a startle that Killebrew dropped the plate at his feet.

He glared at the Indian. "What the hell'd you do that for?"

"I am sorry, but you must sit somewhere else. It is not for you to bother Pep."

"What are you, his nursemaid?" He pushed the Indian, who responded with a quick right hook, dropping Rocky like a man through a trap door.

Jonathan went into action. "I'm mighty sorry, men." He held up a hand in a way of apology. "Rocky hasn't been around you kind of fellows much." He grabbed his brother under the arms, dragging him from the circle of dining troopers.

The Indian joined him, helping Jonathan to prop his brother against a tree. The stranger patted Rocky's face, and he soon awakened.

"I'm sorry for that, young fellow, but that's Pep Young, and you don't know him, but I will tell you one thing. My right hook would appear a no more significant injury than a fly alighting on your nose, compared to the drubbing you'd receive from him."

Jonathan grinned. It was Rocky's luck to tangle with such an hombre. "You don't say?" He remembered his manners. "I'm sorry, mister, name's Jonathan Whelihan."

He nodded. "That's Rocky Killebrew you clobbered."

"Your brother."

"In a manner of speaking."

"William Pollock."

Rocky rubbed his cheek. "Why ain't you got an Indian name?"

"I do, but you can call me Pawnee Pollock. Everyone else does. My Indian name you would not understand, nor would you be able to properly say it."

Rocky stood. "Well, you can go to hell, *Paw-nee* Pollock, and I'll thank you to stop helping me." He pulled himself from Jonathan's grasp. "Both of you can go right to hell."

The headache was nearly unbearable, and not even the heavy pull on the cheap rye he'd secreted in his pack helped mitigate it. He sneezed and opened a torrent of blood that ran over his lips and down his chin. "Goddamn it!"

He was working himself up, and when that happened it was headache time, one that could lay him up for days, and this was no time for such.

He looked off in the distance and saw the men laughing. Jonathan was there, as always, accepted right away as one of the gang. The goddamned golden boy. Sometimes he hated him for that.

He wondered why he was there. He didn't even know where Cuba was. Didn't know anything about Spain until he'd heard all the nonsense from Jonathan. He felt that he might vomit.

A friendly voice pulled him from his self-pity.

"Try this. It will help with the swelling."

He looked up at a dapper man with a uniform as well tailored as the one worn by Colonel Roosevelt. An easterner by the accent, not young, actually nearer to forty, and he looked a bit odd in the plain uniform blouse. An educated man at that. He certainly should have, at the least, been a lieutenant.

Rocky turned to face him, taking the gift of ice wrapped in a blue silk polka-dot scarf.

"I'm thanking you."

"Not at all." He nodded to the spot on the ground next to Killebrew. "May I sit down?"

Rocky looked into his lap. "Suit yourself."

The easterner handed him a neatly rolled cigarette. Rocky refused it, holding up a hand.

"No, thank you."

"Name's Kane, Woodbury Kane. You are,

I believe I heard someone say, Mr. Kille-brew?"

Rocky laughed at the thought of anyone addressing him as mister. "Yeah, Rocky. You can call me Rocky."

"Woodbury." He extended his hand. Rocky waved him off, holding up his own for inspection. "Sorry, mine's bloody. God-damned bloody nose."

"Sit up, Rocky, tilt your head forward and pinch your nose. That's right." He smiled. "Does the ice help?"

Rocky offered a sideways glance. No one other than Jonathan had ever been this nice to him. The man was a dude, no doubt, impeccably groomed with waxed mous-tache, chiseled features, and skin browned by the sun. He'd heard of men who fancied men. Wondered if he was in the company of such. The thought of it turned his stomach. He could not hide his suspicion. "Why are you treating me so decent, mister?"

Kane smiled. "Because you are my brother." He held the sleeve of his coat forward as if to offer proof. "We are broth-ers, members of a band of brothers, and it is fitting and proper to care for one's own." He pulled the bottle from Rocky's coat pocket, opened it, then took a drink. "Ah, that bites a bit, doesn't it?"

Rocky found him intriguing. He wondered how such a gentleman would fare in battle. At least his headache was bearable. His nose no longer bled.

"What you mean *band of brothers*? Never heard such talk."

"It's Shakespeare:

But we in it shall be remembered —
We few, we happy few, we band of
  brothers;
For he to-day that sheds his blood with me
Shall be my brother; be he ne'er so vile,
This day shall gentle his condition;
And gentlemen in England now-a-bed
Shall think themselves accurs'd they were
  not here,
And hold their manhoods cheap whiles any
  speaks
That fought with us upon Saint Crispin's
  day."

Kane took another sip of the rye, slapping Rocky on the knee. "Let us adjourn to the local watering hole, young trooper Killebrew. Your drink is simply one too vile on which to retire."

Rocky looked left and right. "Is it allowed?"

"Most certainly."

"What are you, some kinda officer?"

Kane straightened his back. "Certainly not! I'm a trooper, same as you, young Killebrew."

Rocky smiled. He liked the sound of *young Killebrew,* especially when stated with the clipped, sophisticated accent. "So how you so sure it's allowed?"

Kane pointed with his head in the direction of the marquee tent. "Captain O'Neill sanctioned it. We, who are not on guard duty, have the evening off. Free to wander."

He sprang to his feet with the energy of an athlete. "Come, young Killebrew. I know just the thing to fix your dark mood. Follow me, lad."

They stopped at Kane's tent. He nodded to an empty bedroll. "My bunky's Bill McGinty. Do you know him, young Killebrew?"

"I don't."

"He's a wrangler like you. Capital fellow."

Kane retrieved a shoe brush and ran it deftly across his boot tops. He handed it to Rocky, nodding. "Always look your best, young Killebrew."

He looked Rocky over with a clinical eye. The bleeding had stopped, but his face was liberally smeared with dried blood. Kane handed him a wet washcloth. "Hand me

81

your jacket, young Killebrew. I'll remove that blood from the lapel."

In short order both men looked fine enough to grace the cover of *Harper's*. "There. We are ready to take the town!"

On his first night as a trooper, Jonathan pulled the duty of the first guard. He didn't mind. He was too excited to sleep and really didn't want to hear Rocky's inevitable whining about the drubbing he'd received from the Indian.

Maybe this place would make a man of him. Jonathan could only hope, as Rocky had stopped maturing around the age of fourteen, when his adopted brother had discovered the wonders of spirits. He'd be twenty on his next birthday. It was all becoming tiresome.

For his own part, Jonathan never doubted that he was already a man. He had a woman he'd soon marry, had a lead position on the ranch, and, despite his father's constant meddling, still did good service for it. Hell, he and Ellen really ran the place. Now, he'd prove himself as a soldier and a warrior. Not even the chill of the night air could diminish his spirits.

He smelled the captain's smoke long before he saw him and thought he'd make an impression, calling out a challenge as the officer picked his way through the dark.

"Good evening, Trooper."

"Evening, Captain, sir."

"It's 'captain' or it's 'sir,' son; you don't need to say both."

"Yes, sir, Captain."

They both grinned. O'Neill started a fresh cigarette off the smoldering butt he'd all but finished. He offered one to Jonathan.

"No, thanks, sir. Bad for my wind."

"Oh, that's right, you're Sean Whelihan's son, aren't you? The runner."

"I am, sir."

"He doesn't much like me, your father."

"Oh, no, sir, it's not that. It's — well, my father, he's not much for politicians." He shrugged. "The war and all." Jonathan's grin turned sheepish. "My father might well be the only southerner, the only former confederate, to curse the memory of Robert E. Lee." Jonathan nodded. "It's nothing personal. His brother died at Gettysburg. He never forgave any of them. Never trusted the government — *any* government — after that."

"Understood, Trooper. There's no denying I'm a politician" — he stared at the glowing tip of his cigarette — "a savvier politician than any was General Lee. I guess all great generals must be politicians."

"Well, sir, don't know about all that. I've heard you done a lot." Jonathan worked to slide the Bowie into its sheath, as he'd been fiddling with it.

"Let me have a look, Trooper."

O'Neill held it to the moonlight. "A wicked damned thing."

"Not too keen on taking a man with it, to be honest with you, Captain. Never was much for using a blade on *anything,* except, of course, for butchering dead critters."

"In the Sepoy Rebellion of fifty-seven" — O'Neill spoke to the blade, distantly, almost absentmindedly, as if he were reading a long forgotten text — "the mutineers, on their knees before the British, they'd plead for the bullet and not the blade." He nodded, handing the hellish piece back to Jonathan. "If you keep your Colt and your Krag handy and in order, young Trooper, you won't need to use that thing" — he turned to walk away — "unless it's to open cans of beans or to chop firewood, I dare say."

Rocky was having a much more pleasant evening than his brother, as he and Kane had ended up at the Hotel Burke, the most opulent place in Prescott. His new friend seemed well at ease, more properly fit amongst the sophisticated décor of the elegant stag bar. Rocky admired an expansive canvas of a nude reclined, hanging above them.

"What is your pleasure, young Killebrew?"

"Don't know, never been in such a fancy place. You pick for me, Mr. Kane."

"It's Woodbury, young Killebrew. Remember, it's Woodbury, or Woody to all my friends." He smiled at the barkeep. "Two Manhattans, if you please."

"My pleasure." The barman was a friendly old fellow, a veteran of the GAR. He nodded at the troopers. "Wish I could go with you boys."

Woodbury raised his glass in toast, acknowledging the man's lapel button. "I dare say you've done adequate service to your country, sir. We'll take a Spaniard or two in your honor."

Rocky downed his quickly as Woodbury looked on, waiting for the barman to leave them. He spoke to his reflection in the mirror. "Young Killebrew, the Manhattan is a drink meant to be consumed slowly." He took a sip as if to offer an example. "It's meant to be savored."

Rocky flushed. "Sorry."

"I am, like Colonel Roosevelt, not a fan of drunkenness."

It was the first time Rocky did not feel offended by lecturing against his proclivity toward the stuff. He understood Kane's meaning, looked at his polished boots and then back at his reflection. He did not recognize the dapper fellow standing beside the dude from the East. "It won't happen again, Woodbury. I'm sorry."

"Oh" — he waved him off — "no need for apologies. Only, it's so much more pleasant when in the company of a man with all his faculties." He grinned. "Wouldn't you agree with that?"

"Yes, Woodbury. I'd agree with that."

The man caused his heart to flutter. He was a gentleman, a wealthy and educated man, a member of one of the old families of America, and a kinder, more sincere fellow, Rocky had never met. No one had ever been so decent to him. Well, at least except for Jonathan, but Jonathan was more a brother. He *had* to treat Rocky right; they were all but kin.

But Woodbury . . . Rocky'd already figured, only knowing him this little time, he was more a god than a man. A mentor bordering on father figure. Rocky could not believe his luck. He felt his head clear. His headache was nothing more than a vague memory. He was even sober. He felt damned well.

Woodbury pulled him from his reverie. "Young Killebrew. You've not had dinner!"

"Oh, I'm all right."

"Nonsense!" He called to the barman. "Sir, may we have a table in the dining room? My brother here has had nothing to eat all night."

"You boys are brothers then?" The barman looked each over. "You sure don't look alike."

"We are brothers in arms, my good man, as I'm certain you remember from your days in the civil war." He turned his attention to the dining room. "Seat us next to those two lovelies." He elbowed Rocky. "We could stand some feminine company."

Rocky lost his smile. The women were no doubt of means, more akin to Kane's social circle, miles from that of a saddle bum. "I . . . I don't think that's a good idea, Woodbury. Make a damned fool a' myself."

"Nonsense." He pulled the lad by the arm. "Smile, and look handsome in that suit. Leave the rest to me, young Killebrew. I'll do enough talking for the both of us. That, my friend, I can guarantee."

CHAPTER 5

Sean Whelihan watched his men work in
the corral as evening and the setting sun
brought to a close another day.

He stared dubiously into the cup of tea
Ellen pushed into his hand.

"No coffee?"

"Not this late, Father. You know how it
aggravates your insomnia."

She put an arm around his bony shoulder.
He'd never reciprocate, but the easing of
the tension in the sinew and muscle was
enough to let his daughter know, she was
unconditionally loved.

His eyes wandered to the oversized barn
and bunkhouses and pasture land. Not bad
for a man who had little more than the
clothes on his back when he'd arrived in
Arizona nearly twenty-five years past. He
used to quip that his spread would have
been twice its size, had his brother lived.
Had the incompetent fools not led him into

oblivion.

"Penny for your thoughts, Father."

He smiled as he turned to regard her. He brushed an errant lock of silver from her forehead. "Good old Ellen. You will never leave me."

She turned to face the last hand, pulling a saddle from a range pony. She nodded a good night. "No, Father, I won't."

"The men are taking up the slack, now that the boys are run off. Guess there'll be not too much of a hole left by them after all."

"I don't think there'll be any, Father. Jonathan's trained the foreman well enough that he can assume Jonathan's duties as well as his own until he returns." She watched Agata hang wash rags for drying. "And selling so many horses — well, until the herd is built up again, they'll have an easy enough time of it, and, frankly, everything runs more smoothly when Rocky's not in the mix, God bless him."

Sean Whelihan harrumphed. "You can say that again. Your mother, God rest her soul, she was too kind, Ellen." He shook his head, trying to look more provoked than he was at the thought of Rocky and his foolishness, as he did love the hapless young man. "Don't know what got into her head when

89

she decided to adopt that boy."

"Well, Father, you must agree on one thing about Rocky. He keeps it lively around here."

He became angry. Turning, he snapped at her. "What the hell were they thinking, running off to some silly war and leaving us with all this work and worry."

She patted him on the arm. "Now, now, Father. You're certain to give yourself indigestion. What's done is done, and, besides, with fewer mouths to feed, it's, in many ways, easier." She lied. She missed the lads terribly.

She pulled him by the arm. "Come, it's off to bed with you. It's been a long day, and a longer one's awaiting us tomorrow."

"You're a loyal daughter, Ellen, and when this is over, and those two dunces are back, I want you to take a trip to California. San Francisco, maybe."

Her lips thinned. "We'll see, Father, we'll see."

Sean Whelihan dreamt the same dream he'd had a thousand times. The nightmare was especially vivid when things weighed heavily on him.

It always started the same. The extraordinary heat, the sun devils rising off those

90

Pennsylvania fields, distorting the hellish line of blue uniforms three-quarters of a mile away. It was supposed to be cooler up north, but it certainly was not on this day.

His brother, as always, happy and smiling. He never was bothered by battle or, for that matter, much of anything.

The sweat would run like torrents off his forehead, into his eyes, the kepi a worthless thing in the sun. He wished he'd kept his straw hat, but his brother said they'd have to look like proper soldiers, and an old beat-up straw hat was not part of a proper uniform. He'd blink and wipe, blink and wipe, yet he could never clear his vision enough to face the dreadful task before them.

They wouldn't let them sit, and they waited and waited, standing in that heat, no shade, sapping the energy, waiting for the bombardment to soften the Yankee line, but that did nothing but obscure the view, the air hanging heavy with black-powder smoke, stinging sweaty skin, hands and face and neck as it hung, like a wet funeral shroud, engulfing them, bathing them in the acrid stuff.

Some boys off to the right were having green apple battles, pelting each other as if attending nothing more serious than a

Sunday social. He could not understand their ambivalence.

The perfumed ass, hair curled in ringlets like a freshly outed debutante, sat a-horse above them, giving the order to advance. He could hear it in Pickett's voice, could hear it as clearly as if, instead of telling them to move forward, he was saying, *"On to your graves, lads; march straight on to oblivion."*

Pickett knew, Longstreet knew, they all knew it was too much to ask of the most dedicated warriors to ever tread the planet, and these boys were that. They were fighters, fearless and expert at killing, at behaving bravely, but the charge, this charge — well, anyone with a modicum of sense knew it would have been more a kindness to tell them to turn their Enfields on themselves. Do as Kipling had said: *"Just roll to your rifle and blow out your brains and go to your God like a soldier."* At least they'd not have to march that field in the crippling midday sun.

He checked his cartridge box. The flap seemed welded shut or, at the least, lined with sheet lead. He wondered if he'd be able to reload and fire quickly enough. Would he fumble with his caps as, in the heat of battle, they felt so tiny, and he as if his digits had magically turned to thumbs.

Would it be enough? He squinted into the

distance, seemingly miles away, at the blue bellies secreted behind the stone walls. Would there be any point in it?

His brother, as he'd done a thousand times in as many dreams, turned and smiled. He nodded as if to assure him it would all be fine.

Halfway there, whole platoons fell around them. "Dress that line! Look sharp, boys, dress that line!"

Minié balls buzzed like carpenter bees, and he was now twelve years old, tearing down a rotten chicken house with his brother. Jonathan swatted them like shuttle-cocks, using an old piece of board and laughing. In one blink he was Jonathan the brother, in another, his only son. It was all confusing, and he regretted the times he'd chastised his boy for some silly, inconsequential infraction. He was a thoroughly good boy, and he'd never told him that, and now he knew in his soul that his boy would not come back from Cuba, and he'd never have the chance to tell him how proud he was and how desperately he loved him.

A round struck him in the belly, knocking him down. Jonathan, the brother, pulled him to his feet, checking his younger sibling for a wound, laughing at the newly created dimple between the *C* and the *S*. "You are one lucky devil, little brother! One lucky devil fer sure!"

"Dress that line, soldiers, dress that line!"

He looked off to the lieutenant and wanted to shut his mouth with a ball through his brain.

The young officer glared back. He was not one of Sean's, as all of his men had been killed or, at least, lay dying behind him. The Yankee sharpshooters had a steady aim that day. "I *said* dress that line, soldier. Don't be looking at me; you fix your eyes on those mudsills ahead. Show those blue bellies we are no rabble. We are the Army of Northern Virginia, by God, and we'll show 'em!"

Then Louis Zeyouma ran past them wearing naught but his running moccasins. He held the colors high and nodded at Sean Whelihan. He blinked the sweat away and saw that he and his brother were surrounded by the herd he'd sold to Roosevelt's Rough Riders. His beautiful cow ponies, his stock. A shell-burst dropped every one, and horses and men lay all around him, screaming and bleeding and dying. He broke ranks to comfort one, a dapple grey that he remembered had the loving disposition of a puppy, and he cradled its lolling head in his arms, watching the life drain from its horror-stricken eyes. Again, the surly lieutenant commanded him back. Back in line, back with his brother, following Louis Zeyouma to his death.

At three hundred yards he came upon Rocky Killebrew, sitting on a fence post all alone, waiting for them, pulling greedily on a bottle of rye, and, when Sean Whelihan stopped to address him, the young man turned into a tremendous black vulture and spewed vomit all over his sweaty shirtfront. The bird turned to the Yankee line, pointing with a straggly wing for Sean to move ahead. Move on. Move on, to your end.

He blinked again and felt his legs heavy, as if wading, thigh-deep, in Arizona quicksand. He turned to his brother, who grinned and said something that Sean could not understand. The explosions too loud, eardrums too tortured. He could hear nothing but a kind of low humming, like the din of electrified power lines.

His brother pointed forward to cannon, miraculously appearing at point-blank range, and, before Sean could duck or attack or recoil, his brother broke ranks, pummeling him, knocking him down into a low spot on the field, placing himself between Sean and the load of canister spewing shot and hot death at the remaining line of grey uniforms.

All was confusion and smoke and pain, and Sean Whelihan was sitting upright, legs crossed like an Indian with the remains of his brother dripping from his hair and chin. He looked down, and his boy's head, face up, sat smiling in death in his lap, and that is when Sean Whelihan had his fit of apoplexy.

CHAPTER 6

Minerva Trumbull sat, ramrod straight, as if she were balancing the nurse's cap pinned to her hair. The rhythm of the train, taunting, click-clack, "You're a fraud," click-clack, "You're a fraud," beat a steady cadence in her ears.

She'd learned from the time she could remember that lying was a sin and for the lowest of the low. She'd never lied in her life, and now she felt she was the most reprehensible liar ever to tread the earth. It gave her a terrible worrying feeling in the pit of her stomach. Not even the basket prepared by her former co-workers could entice her to eat.

Next stop was Baltimore, and she re-read the instructions for about the tenth time. She'd meet the nun there, then to New York to a transport sailing south, either to Florida or Georgia, her own self-doubt compounded by the confounding instructions.

Why would she, a North Carolinian, travel north in order to go south? It defied logic, and Minerva wondered at the wasted effort and expense. She lived only a short distance from Florida or Georgia, a short train ride to any of the hospitals that had been springing up to accommodate the sick soldiers.

The train lurched, and she felt the cap tip. She touched it, checking the pin holding it in place. The cap pressed down on her, feeling as if it weighed a ton, as if Superintendent Connelly had placed an anvil there instead.

Her boss's words were, at least, a comfort: "Be yourself, be truthful, do your duty, Minerva, you know how. God bless you, you know how."

You know how, you know how. It was true; Minerva knew how. If only they had not considered her a nurse. *Anything* but a nurse. An orderly, a housekeeper, a . . . what? A *something,* an *anything,* other than a nurse! Oh, Lord Jesus, what had she gotten herself into?

Seemingly by magic the imposing figure dressed in black was upon her. Like the grim reaper, she hovered, extending a hand. What was this? Had they come to take her? To where? To a police station, to a military court where'd they'd deem her a fraud, clap her in irons, and throw her in jail with all the other liars? The criminals?

"You must be Nurse Trumbull." The smiling nun broke her daydream.

"How . . . how did you know that?"

Sister Bonaventure plopped onto the seat facing her new companion. "You are the only nurse I see in" — she checked the slip of paper — "car three-twelve."

"Yes." She nodded, then blurted, "Not a nurse, Sister. I'm not a nurse."

"Oh." She peered at the pretty young woman. "You look as if you are." She consulted the paper again. "Says here I'd be traveling with an immune nurse, a Nurse Trumbull."

"I'm not a nurse, Sister. It was all explained to the board. They're desperate for immunes, and — well, I've worked for the hospital a long time. The superintendent of nurses at my hospital explained it, and — well, they accepted me. But . . ." she felt the rush of panic envelop her. The nun's garb, her mere presence, power, confidence! She could never hope to meet the standards of the legendary Sisters of Mercy. It was overwhelming.

Bonaventure looked her over and did not like what she observed. "Do you not feel well, child?"

Minerva mopped her brow. "It's so close in here." She peered out as the station's platform slowly passed them by.

Bonaventure opened the window. "Summer has come early to Baltimore." She knew well that the heat was not the source of the infirmity. "Nurse Trumbull."

"Oh, I *do* wish you'd not call me 'nurse'! Please, I'm Minerva. Minnie to my friends."

The nun grinned. "That may prove problematic, child." She thought quickly. She needed to know what the young woman knew, as they'd likely be working together.

"How long have you been caring for the sick?"

"Oh, just shy of eleven years."

"That's a long time."

Minerva liked her. Did not know nuns, only a few Catholics in her time, but had heard of nurse nuns, these Sisters of Mercy. They were legend, famous for their intellect and competence. Why did it have to be a nun? And why this one?

The sister was an intimidating and imposing woman, yet, there was some certain kindness. She had kind eyes.

Minerva fixed her gaze to her lap. "I guess so."

"What kind of patients have you cared for, Minerva?"

100

"Oh, all kinds. Helped birth babies, took care of folks who had suffered apoplectic fits, new mothers, folks who'd been in farm and factory accidents."

"Any typhoid cases, influenza, smallpox, cholera?"

"Typhoid fever, yes, ma'am, and cholera, lots of cholera." Her eyes brightened. They were easy-enough maladies to nurse, at least with the skills she had cultivated. "And, yes, ma'am, smallpox and influenza. But no yellow fever, never seen a yellow fever and only a few malaria cases; most folks stay home and wait for it to pass. That's what they say I'm to do, ma'am, take care of such as I'm immune from malaria and the yellow jack."

"Well, I believe you are up to the task, Nurse Trumbull. The army has seen fit to designate you nurse, and I see someone has given you her cap."

Minerva once again reached for it, ensuring it was secure. "My superintendent, yes, ma'am."

"I've never known a nurse who'd give away her cap if it wasn't to someone worthy. I see no reason to question the veracity of the army's decision, nor the decision of your superintendent."

Minerva smiled, touching the cap again.

"Did I say something amusing, Nurse

Trumbull?"

"The wisdom of the army, Sister." She shrugged. "Why would they send two southerners on a train north to take a ship south?"

Bonaventure grinned. "You have an excellent point, Nurse Trumbull —"

"Please, call me Minnie."

"All right, Minnie." She was convinced now that they would be friends and have a compatible working relationship. "The other sisters of my order left a few weeks ago. I stayed behind for a particularly bad surgical case. They traveled south by rail and are currently in Florida."

"Which town?"

"Oh, I've lost track. They've moved them three times in two weeks. The army does seem to lack organization."

"How long have you been a nurse?"

"Oh, longer than you've been alive, my child, longer than you've been alive."

"It has always been my dream to be a nurse. Superintendent Connelly encouraged me to try for a contract. With the money I receive, I plan to go north and study."

"No family, no husband, to hold you back?"

"Oh, no, ma'am. I had no one but Grandmother, but she's passed. No one keeping me." She stared out the window. "Nothing keeping me but money."

Sister Bonaventure patted her knee. "Well, then, we'll have to make certain you come back with bags of it to fulfill that dream, Nurse Trumbull."

Clara Maass was pleased that she'd taken her mother's advice and worn her nurse's cap and uniform. She was no longer just another young woman, traveling from New York to Florida. She was a nurse, and everyone nodded respectfully and addressed her as "nurse," and they knew she was off to war, to do the work of the military nurse as had so many of her sisters before her.

She looked down the dock at the USAT *Thomas* loading with men and provisions. She breathed deeply, filling her lungs with the pungent odor of the East River and burning coal and creosote-coated pilings, rope and grease and fresh oak packing crates. And to Clara Maass, it all smelled of adventure.

As she cleaned her spectacles with a fresh handkerchief, a kind old gent with white whiskers, sporting a nautical cap, offered her a seat in a shed out of the sun, as it was bright and warm for this time of year. He fixed her a cup of tea. He patted her on the shoulder, giving a grandfatherly smile. "I love nurses."

In a little while she was joined by the nun, imposing in her severe black garb, the stiff under-veil adding a half foot to her impressive height. In tow was a diminutive woman. Clara smiled as they approached.

"You are Nurse Maass from New Jersey?"

"I am, Sister." She stood and proffered her hand.

"This is Nurse Minerva Trumbull, of North Carolina," she said smiling, "and I am Sister Mary Bonaventure from Baltimore."

"Pleased to meet you, ladies."

Minerva spoke up. "I'm not a nurse." She looked self-consciously at the nun, then fixed her eyes on the dusty floor of the outbuilding.

Sister Bonaventure interjected. "Nurse Maass, Nurse Trumbull is one of us but for a certificate. She is an immune and has done service in her hospital for many years. On our trip up, I read the letter of recommendation from Minnie's superintendent of nurses. As far as I'm concerned, she's a nurse, and we'll say nothing more on it."

Clara nodded. She could work with such women. She liked them immediately. "I whole-heartedly agree." She smiled, addressing Minerva. "You know how to mix a batch of carbolic acid solution, no doubt, and that's likely the lion's share of the work we'll be doing. That and scrubbing."

"I've not worked in surgery. Not given injections, ladies, not mixed medications or done any labor of the real nurse."

Sister Bonaventure replied, "You know how to keep clean beds, dressings, how to spot a fever; you know the important aspects of nursing, child." She nodded to Clara. "From what I've read and from the letters I've received from my colleagues already working away, it's fever and dysentery, as in the Crimea and the last war, we'll be facing more than traumatic wounds. Already, hospitals are filling up, and they've not yet fired a shot."

Clara spoke up. "So, there's an end to it. You are Nurse Trumbull —"

"I'd rather you call me Minnie."

"No, no." Bonaventure held up a hand. "Not that I stand much on formality, but Nurse Maass is correct. We must maintain a sense of distance and decorum, ladies. A little formality is always in order under such circumstances. Men in times of stress need structure and discipline, especially when it involves mixing with the fairer sex." She smiled. "Especially beautiful ones.

"In private, we might call each other by

our Christian names" — she bowed toward Minerva — "or our pet names, but in an official capacity, you will be addressed as Nurse Trumbull and Nurse Maass, and I as Sister Bonaventure."

She turned to observe the progress of the loading, checking a watch she kept pinned to her wimple. "I was told a Major Johnston would be escorting us once our lodging has been arranged." She looked about. "Let's see." She smiled at the old sailor. Taking command, she said, "My good man, how about some more tea and perhaps a few biscuits for some army nurses?"

If there had ever been any qualms about the slight Clara Maass's ability to handle the rigors of an army nurse's life, these misgivings were soon allayed as she took on her first officer.

She reached her tallest height of five-four, peering through the lenses of her impeccably polished spectacles into Major Johnston's reddening face.

"All due respect, *Major,* but Nurse Trumbull is a contract regulation US Army nurse, same as I. The same as the Sister, here. It is not remotely acceptable for her to sleep in the steerage."

"I am sorry, madam, it is specifically *not*

the steerage, but —"

"If you please, Major, the term is 'nurse,' not 'madam,' and there are no buts about it. Nurse Trumbull will sleep in our quarters" — she cast her gaze at the opulent stateroom assigned to them — "as you will have another bed placed in here. There's ample room for ten nurses" — she nodded to Sister Bonaventure — "and at least another four nuns."

She watched him leave and looked calmly upon her companions, doing her best to control the quivering in her voice. She was not nervous or scared; *she* had her German up.

Minerva blew air between pursed lips. "Clara, you are bold to speak in such a tone to a high-made officer."

"Officer or surgeon, I have never met a man yet who did not back down when I was in the right. And I am in the right, and you'll see, we'll have a bed in here for you in no time." She turned to leave the room. "I believe I'll do a little exploring before dinner time."

Sister Bonaventure followed Clara with her eyes. She smiled at Minerva. "My word! And I thought it was the *Irish* temper one had to watch."

Clara admired the Statue of Liberty as it disappeared from view, turning her attention bow-ward, to the open ocean. A steady, pleasant breeze blew across her back. She trembled with excitement. She was born for adventure, and this one, she knew in her heart, was only the first. There'd be many more to come.

She wondered what her mother and siblings were doing at that moment, the twinge of homesickness palpable even though she'd lived at the hospital for nearly four years and the orphanage before that as a resident caretaker. But neither was ever more than a long walk to return home, which she did at least every other Sunday.

Father would be home in a little while. He'd be tired and do nothing more than eat and go to bed, as fourteen hours in a hat factory took a toll on any human being, and her father was an old man, much older than his years.

A scrawny fellow approached, younger than she and only a hair taller. He clutched an old rifle, a relic from the last war, as if he were warned not to misplace it.

Stomping to attention before her, he

saluted awkwardly, much in the way of a child playing at soldiering.

"Evening, ma'am!"

"Good evening to you." She looked him over for insignia and found none. "How shall I address you?"

"Private, ma'am, Private Hogan of the Fourth New York Volunteer Infantry." He said it as if he were reading from a roster.

"Well, Private Hogan of the Fourth New York Volunteer Infantry, how may I help you?"

"In charge of guarding you, ma'am. You and the other nurses." He clutched his rifle more tightly, as if worried someone might take it from him. "Where you go, I go, ma'am. Major Johnston's orders."

"Guarding *me*?" She looked left and right. "Guarding me from what?"

He looked confused, as if he did not know the answer to her query, yet certain he should. "*Danger,* ma'am, danger, and . . . and such."

"Well, then, Private Hogan, I suppose we shall be spending a lot of time together." She nodded, suppressing an urge to laugh, as she'd caused him to blush.

From an early age she had the gift, the ability, to render men of all ages smitten and speechless. It was in part, of course, due to her beauty, but something more profound than that. She possessed an other-worldly femininity, almost goddess-like, that turned most men to putty.

She extended her hand. "Please, call me Nurse Maass, and I'll call you Private Hogan." She tipped her head toward the cabin. "The others are Sister Bonaventure and Nurse Trumbull." She waited for him to absorb the information. "Private Hogan, I will warn you, Nurse Trumbull is a Negro" — she turned her head from side to side — "and I'll have no trouble on account of that. Is that abundantly clear?"

"Oh, no, ma'am. I mean, yes, ma'am, I mean yes, *Nurse.* I got nothing against any darkies. The ones I've known, they're some fighting sons of guns." He looked embarrassed. "I mean the men, ma'am . . . Nurse, I mean, you know, the soldiers. I ain't never known no nurses." His voice trailed off, almost as if he were talking to himself. "Not that nurses would fight, I guess." He shrugged, offering a hapless smile.

"Well, that's fine, then, Private Hogan. Please follow me. I'll introduce you to my companions."

Private Hogan took up his post, a comfy seat next to the cabin door and a lounge replete with wool blanket and down pillow.

He chewed gum and read dime novels to pass the time.

Sister Bonaventure peered at him through a porthole. "At least he doesn't take tobacco. A filthy habit. I could not imagine the idea of it, the smoke, wafting in here."

Clara smiled. "He seems harmless enough." She watched the ladies finish unpacking. "I had never given needing a guard much thought."

"Not all soldiers are saints, Clara." The sister regarded her companions. Minerva was nodding. She was more worldly, world-weary, and wise in the ways of the wicked than was the young beauty from New Jersey.

Clara hung up her one fancy dress as her companions admired it. She shrugged self-consciously. "Not that I expect I'll be wearing it, but, I thought, it doesn't weigh much, doesn't take up any room; I reasoned there was no harm in packing it."

And, as if on cue, an authoritative knock on the door followed by the snapping-to of Private Hogan presented them with a visitor in the form of an Olympian god of a soldier by the name of Captain Mortimer Hollander.

He bowed. "My compliments."

"Good evening, Captain." Sister Bonaventure positioned herself between the visitor and her self-ascribed charges. "How may I help you?"

"Major Johnston requests the presence of Nurse Maass at the ship captain's table this evening."

Clara peered around the nun's massive girth. "Why?"

"I beg your pardon?"

"I said, why? Why me? Why not the three of us, Captain?"

"Well, I, ah, we — that is, I mean the major, madam, he did not expect a nun would find such a thing, well . . . interesting."

"As eating? A nun eats, Captain, and so does my companion Nurse Trumbull."

"Well, madam . . ." Mortimer Hollander blanched. He was not used to interrogation, or being put in such an embarrassing situation. "I —" He nodded to Minerva. "It's, well, not —"

"Thank you all the same, Captain, but we'll dine together in our quarters." She looked about the stateroom. "As you can see, it has more than the comforts of home." She touched him by the elbow, leading him out. "Tell Major Johnston that —"

Minerva interrupted. "That Nurse Maass will be ready to be escorted from her stateroom at, should we say, a quarter till eight o'clock?"

Captain Hollander smiled. "Oh, capital!" He nodded a kind of salute, appearing almost Prussian in his military bearing. "Until then, madam." He nodded yet again. "Ladies." He offered a special look of gratitude to Minerva. "Thank you."

Sister Bonaventure turned to the wardrobe. She pulled out the dress, holding it under her chin as she regarded her reflection in the mirror. "If there were three of these sewn together, I could fit into it." She turned to Clara.

"Well, child, it looks as if you'll have a use for this after all, and on your first night."

"Why'd you do that, Minnie?"

"Oh, come now, Clara. He's a beauty, and you will have a wonderful time. I will not allow you to sit around with us and lose such an opportunity. We'll find plenty to do. Maybe we'll teach the private to play whist while he's guarding us."

Minerva was correct. Captain Mortimer Hollander was a handsome man, tall, nearly a foot more so than Clara, with an athletic build, face and hands bronzed by many days spent with his men on the parade field. He was a New York lawyer when not a volunteer soldier.

He extended his arm stiffly, escorting her to the captain's dining room.

"Is there something wrong with my glasses, Captain?"

"Oh, no. Why do you ask?"

"You keep staring at them."

"I was wondering what you looked like without them."

"A bit like a mole."

"I doubt that."

"You are rather familiar."

"I don't mean to be."

She liked him, despite his obvious attention to his own appearance, and a certain haughtiness. It was evident to Clara, there was something genuine underlying the façade, something genuine in his attention to her.

"The ship's master is an old friend of the family. He and his wife invited me to dinner, and when I, from the first I laid eyes on you —" He knew at once he was wading into potentially inappropriate waters. He tried to recover. "I mean — well, I thought it might be a bit of a treat for you to dine with us, ah, I mean, them."

"I thought that all this was the major's idea?"

"I — well, that was a bit of subterfuge."

"You mean a lie."

"I prefer subterfuge. In my profession, that's what we call it."

"Which is something other than soldier?"

"Oh, yes, I'm a volunteer in a military capacity. My full-time profession is that of lawyer."

"I see. So lawyers lie and call it subterfuge, and that makes it acceptable."

Clara's coldness alarmed him. She pulled her hand from his forearm. "You may take me back to my cabin this instant, Captain."

"Now, now, please." His expression of shame seemed genuine.

"I am not that kind of girl, Captain, and certainly I do not accompany men under false pretenses. Your actions might be those of a lawyer, but they are not of an officer and gentleman!"

Her reprimand and insult elicited the opposite response. Instead of appearing contrite or even offended, he beamed, enjoying her nerve and sense of independence.

"What's so funny, Captain?"

"You know your mind, Miss Maass."

"I do, and it is Nurse Maass, as it is Captain Hollander. And I'll thank you to return me to my quarters."

"Please, I'm sorry." He thought desperately for a way to move her toward the threshold of the sea captain's salon door.

They were close, but Clara was buying none of it.

"*This instant,* Captain. This very instant!"

But before he could be defeated, the ship's master and commander burst upon them, his wife in tow.

"Mortimer!"

"Captain Bradley." He nodded. "Mrs. Bradley, may I present Miss Clara Maass. She is a contract nurse."

"Oh, she's a little angel." The captain's wife pulled Clara by the arm. "You don't look old enough to be a nurse, sweetheart. Come. You'll sit next to me."

They were delightful, kind and attentive. The captain's wife prattled on through the evening. She was smitten, captivated by both Clara's choice of vocation and deportment. Inevitably, the talk turned to women's suffrage, as Captain Bradley's wife was convinced the fairer sex deserved all the rights and opportunities afforded any man.

The seaman sighed, listening patiently to his wife's diatribe on the matter, an argument that, by now, he could recite in his sleep.

"My old gal would have ladies sailing ships, Nurse Maass."

"And why not? There are women nurses, women physicians. Certainly if there are women such as Dr. McGee, who found such treasures as this darling nurse here, or Clara Barton, running the Red Cross single-handedly, then there is no doubt in my mind a woman can steer a boat, for heaven's sake."

"It's a ship, dear-heart, not a boat. A ship."

"A ship or a boat, I'm telling you, Horace, a woman given the proper training and opportunity can do as well as any man." She leaned forward. "What do you think on the subject, Mortimer?"

"I'm a part-time soldier and full-time lawyer, Aunt Rose. I leave the politics to the politicians."

"Wise boy." Captain Bradley winked. "I suppose the cat is out of the bag. Mortimer is my nephew, Nurse Maass. A little known family secret." He worked on a cigar until he realized it was not agreeing with his guest. He stubbed it out. "You two look good together."

"Horace!" Rose smiled. "He likes to pink up the cheeks of young beauties, Miss Maass. Ignore him."

"I will not be silenced." He turned to his nephew. "Miss Maass, Mortimer is a self-made man! My dear brother-in-law, God rest his soul" — he reached out, giving his wife's hand a squeeze — "died when Mortimer was a lad. He's taken care of his mother and siblings. Been the man of the house for the past fifteen years."

"With your help, Uncle" — Hollander smiled at his aunt — "and yours, of course, Aunt Rose."

"Nonsense! Nurse Maass, you will never know a more dedicated family man as our Mortimer. I'm proud of him." He raised a glass in toast. "And I'll say it again, you two look darned good together."

She found herself walking with Mortimer Hollander anywhere but in the direction of her stateroom.

"Then I'm forgiven?"

"Oh, I suppose." She stopped, gazing off the starboard bow. The Cape May light blinked in the distance. "Is that New Jersey, Captain?"

He squinted. "I believe so."

"Have you really been the man of the house for so long?"

His arm brushed her shoulder as he worked on lighting a cigarette. He offered her one.

"No, thank you, I don't."

"Of course you don't."

"What is that supposed to mean?"

"You like to spar, don't you, Nurse

Maass?"

She did not know why she was so defensive, so combative with him. She shouldn't be. He was actually very attentive. Perhaps it was simply her lack of practice. Clara, like the young captain, had been so busy being the caretaker, the head of the family, that she'd not had opportunity for pleasant conversation with members of the opposite sex.

"I apologize, Captain. My work often forces me into a defensive posture when it comes to powerful men. Sometimes I feel all I do is fight and advocate for my patients." She smiled. "Forgive me."

He patted her hand and as quickly withdrew, not wanting to provoke her.

"I've been told it is not healthy. Medical people claim cigarettes and alcohol are poison to the body. That's all I meant. I assumed you'd not indulge in such an unhealthy activity, being in the profession."

"That's true." She liked that he called her work a profession. Few had so much respect for nurses.

He returned the cigarette to the case. "And besides, the sea air is more agreeable without the stench of burning tobacco."

He folded his arms over the rail, leaning with a foot on the bottom rung, almost as if posing for a photograph. "It sounds more heroic when my uncle describes my upbringing."

"You are full of incongruities, Captain."

"I'd rather you call me Mortimer."

"Not yet."

"When?"

"Later, when we've known each other for more than an evening."

"What do you mean by incongruities?"

"When we first met, I thought you one of those society elites, those wealthy club men who play at soldiering. Now I see you are not unlike me."

"You?"

"Yes. I've been supporting my family, my siblings, for a long time. It's one of the reasons I've become a nurse, and now a contract nurse for the army. For the extra money."

"Your father, too, has passed on?"

"Oh, no!" She resisted the urge to be defensive. "My father's a hard-working man, but there are nine of us children, and, well, the money he toils so hard for does not stretch enough for all, at least to my standard."

"Your standard?"

He smiled and wanted to kiss her. The lenses of her glasses reflected silver from the moonlight, making it difficult for him to concentrate.

"Yes. I want life to be better for my siblings than it has been for me and my parents. Want it to be better for —"

"The next generation."

"Yes, Captain, that's exactly right. It seems to me that it is what we should do with our lives, I mean, other than to serve God, of course. We should ensure the lives of our family, of those we love, are better than they were for their antecedents."

"Miss Maass, you are refreshingly ambitious."

"Refreshingly?"

He sighed, peering down at the wake pushing away from the bow. "Yes, refreshingly." Turning to face her, he gently removed her glasses. She let him.

He pinched her chin between thumb and forefinger, tilting her head first left, then right. "Aha. As I thought, you have a magnificent profile, when not obscured by these." He removed a crisp handkerchief and breathed on each lens, giving them a thorough polish. He returned them, gently, reverently, as if he were presenting her with a gift, fragile as a robin's egg.

She would not argue or protest. She took them but did not put them on.

Smiling, she looked off at the lights of New Jersey passing steadily to the north as she gently admonished him.

"You are too forward, I think, Captain."

"I'm sorry." He said it in a way that reassured her that he was not. He meant every forward and provocative word, as they'd come, not from one possessing a clever, silver tongue, but from a man with a full heart.

"Apology accepted." She hoped he would not feel her trembling. She reached for his arm. "It is late and time I'm to bed. I'm certain you have plenty of soldiering to do before retiring."

"May I see you again, Miss Maass?"

"If you wish."

They eventually arrived at the entrance to the stateroom, Captain Hollander taking the longest, most circuitous route, to Private Chester Hogan stretched out on a deck chair, ensconced, like a chrysalis, in a heavy wool blanket. Throwing it off, he snapped to when the couple arrived.

"All in order, Private?"

"Oh, yes, sir. Fine and dandy, sir." He nodded toward the door. "Ladies snug in their beds" — he stuttered at the potential impropriety of such knowledge — "at . . . at least I guess, sir. I'm thinking they're in bed anyways."

The captain bowed again, in his old-world, old-time chivalrous manner. He took her hand, kissing a knuckle, holding it for a little too long. "You have wonderfully soft hands, Miss Maass."

She tried to hide her smile. "Oh, I've had a few days' reprieve, they're usually as raw and red and chapped as a —"

"Nurse's?"

They laughed together.

"Yes, as a nurse's. Precisely."

"I will call in on you, let's say, at seven for breakfast?"

He did not await a response, instead turning to young Hogan, who stood, yawning and a little dreamy. "Carry on, Private."

"Yes, sir." He saluted as he watched Clara sidle into her stateroom, then at the Captain, carrying himself away on a rather giddy swagger, and, at that moment, Private Hogan wondered what he'd have to do to become an officer.

She waited to drift off as Sister Bonaventure snored peacefully in her ear. Minerva was silent, resting comfortably in the roll-out at her feet. She regretted that her new friend had to take such a poor excuse for a bed.

She'd switch with her in the morning, or, if Minnie would not have it, at least take turns. It was only fair.

She sniffed the back of her hand and could discern just the hint of his tobacco. He *was* a glorious man. A beautiful man, and Clara wondered if he was the one.

She wanted to marry, had always wanted to marry and marry well. She was tired of her family living in poverty. Certainly an attorney would provide more amply than a hatter.

She loved her father, but she would never marry a man like him. Father was, for all intents and purposes, a failure as a provider for his family. He was not — what? Hardworking? He was. He was, simply, not what the captain called her — refreshingly ambitious.

Was he the one? He was not wealthy, but he seemed a moral man, in his own right an ambitious man. That would do for her. She never imagined marrying someone wealthy, an old-money man. Knew the wealthy of that type married their own. Those types would never consider a working woman. Nor would she marry a physician. Physicians marrying nurses was not done. No, she never had any inclination toward physicians.

Did he have faith? He did not give any indication of such when she mentioned her service to God as they strolled about the stern. In fact, he seemed rather silent on the subject.

Was he one of those modern men who believed only in science? She'd known a physician or two like that. Men who were not only agnostic, but disdainful of faith. What did they call religion? Yes, opiate of the people.

She'd need to know that. She'd need to know where he stood. Would she reject him if he had no faith? What if it was not *her* faith? What would she do if he were a Catholic? She'd never thought on that before. Or a Jew? Mortimer Hollander — what kind of name was that? German, like Maass? Dutch? Who knew? If he wasn't Lutheran, what would she do? There frankly weren't all that many Lutherans in New York. Church of England or some other Protestant faith more likely than anything, or, of course, with all the Italians and Irish, Catholic. How would they raise their children? It was all rather overwhelming.

What of her calling? What of her career as nurse? She loved what she did. Would she become a wife and give it all up? She'd known a few nurses who had husbands and families. They managed. Perhaps her mother could mind the children while she pursued her vocation. Her obsession. Her calling. Her career.

She felt ridiculous. She'd known of the existence of this Olympian ideal for fewer than eight hours, yet already she was mapping out their lives together. Her mother would laugh at that. Her mother would smile and push the errant golden lock that always seemed to escape the hair pin. She'd kiss her forehead and say, "There she goes again, my thoroughly German Clara, forcing order to her universe, planning, mapping, demanding sense of the unknowable."

She turned on her side, away from the snoring, and fell into a deep, albeit restless sleep.

CHAPTER 7

They'd been riding for more than three hours on the roof of the last passenger car. Following them were half a dozen open livestock wagons. It offered a clear vantage point from which the lads could keep an eye on the horses and mules, and the fact that Captain O'Neill had assigned them the task was not lost on either of them.

Jonathan grinned as he watched his adopted brother worry over the herd.

The young man stared back accusingly. "What?"

"Oh, nothing. Wondered what you did that last night in Prescott. You're like a new man."

It was a left-handed compliment certain enough but not unwarranted. He actually felt a changed man. Woodbury Kane had that sort of effect on people, especially lads like Rocky, lads who constantly needed reminding that they were of value, who had a difficult time believing it.

"Oh, Woodbury and I, we went to the hotel for dinner and drinks, spent a right pleasant time in the company of two ladies."

"Ladies?" Jonathan thought on it. Rocky was hopelessly intimidated by women.

"Yep, ladies. That Woodbury fellow, you know, he's not a young pup like us — near forty and one of the richest men in this country. Maybe in the whole damned world."

"I did not know that."

"Yep, he says there's a bunch of them comin', men like him, men that are friends with Colonel Roosevelt. All rich as hell and like ol' Woodbury."

"Well, Rocky, I never took you for a society type."

He turned angry. He generally could handle Jonathan's teasing, but now, any derision, especially of his relationship with his new friend and mentor, acted as a sort of hair-trigger on him. "Don't make jokes on it, Jonathan."

"No, sorry, Brother, meant no offense." He turned to look Rocky in the eye. He didn't want to damage the magic worked by the wealthy clubman. "Honest, Rocky, I'm sorry."

They rode in silence for a while, enjoying

the countryside. They'd ride late into the evening and stop on the other side of the New Mexico/Texas border to feed and water the animals.

It had warmed up, and they stripped off their coats, rolling up their sleeves. Rocky caught Jonathan admiring himself in his uniform.

"Thing I don't understand, Jonathan, what's all this rank and such?"

"What do you mean?"

"There's corporals and sergeants and lieutenants and captains and majors and colonels. Hell, a fellow told me there's two types of colonels, a lieutenant colonel and a regular colonel, and there's a whole different bunch of generals. And Woodbury said there's some officers you salute and some you don't. I don't know, Jonathan. I don't much understand a bit of it."

"Well, Rocky, I'm not the one to tell you yet, as I've not been through it all myself, not had the chance to study on it, but one thing's for certain. We are privates, and there's no one lower than us, so I'd say it's safe to bank on every one of them being in a position to order us around. Best thing we can do is keep our mouths shut and ears open and do whatever they say, so long as it's not illegal or a sin. That's the best way to stay clear of trouble in the army, I think."

"Kind of like playacting, all this, ain't it?"

"What do you mean?"

"This whole thing — meetin' men like Woodbury, wearing these fancy suits, all of it. People look at me and smile and act like I'm some kinda hero. No one's ever smiled at me when I walked by. They're all smiling and nodding and thanking me. It all don't seem real. Takes a bit of getting used to."

"Rocky, you are a philosopher."

"Jonathan, I don't even know what that is."

"One thing's for certain, though, Brother."

"What's that?"

"When those Spanish bullets start flying, it won't be playacting."

They were informed that they'd have four weeks of training and then battle, an ambitious goal for the most well-trained army, and these men were far from that.

Jonathan was more game than ever and resolved to keep fit, despite the fact that they'd be mounted when facing the Spaniards. Right after sunrise, he sprinted past the colonel's tent as Roosevelt conferred with his boss and mentor. The excited New Yorker called out.

"You there!"

Jonathan stopped, returning to the colonels. He saluted. "Yes, sir!"

"Oh, you're the fellow from Arizona. The one who sold us the splendid horses."

"Yes, sir."

"I remember you were with a Hopi. My goodness, man, I remember you said you could run." He turned to Colonel Wood. "He's as swift as a Thomson's gazelle."

He turned again to Jonathan. "Do you know the creature, Trooper . . . what's your name?"

"Whelihan, sir. I'm with Company K, sir, the Arizona contingent, under command of Captain O'Neill and, of course, Major Brodie, sir."

"Right, right. Young trooper, the Thomson's gazelle." He turned to Colonel Wood. "I met him once at my club in New York. Thomson, you know, he's a splendid fellow. Naturalist. Spent time in Africa, hunted with Woodbury Kane."

He began writing furiously. "Trooper Thomson, pass this to Captain O'Neill. You are no longer with K Company. You'll serve as my runner."

Colonel Wood smiled at Roosevelt's zeal. "Cavalry doesn't generally have runners, Theodore. Being mounted renders a runner all but obsolete."

"Well, a man of Thomson's talent . . . No, I can see the potential, Colonel Wood, if you will indulge me. I think Trooper Thomson will be an immeasurable asset to our staff."

"Ah, sir?"

"Yes, what is it, Trooper Thomson?"

"My name's not Thomson, sir, it's Whelihan."

"Of course it is, my good fellow, of course it is, but I have a lot on my mind these days, and you look like a Thomson. And now that you are my official runner, the name association will free my mind for other things. Thomson it is." He waved a finger. "Do not worry, if you are killed, we'll ensure it's all recorded in proper order." He had yet another thought. "You have a brother, don't you?"

"Yes, sir. Rocky Killebrew."

"Yes, yes, the one with the foul tongue. I saw him handling mules not long ago. He's a capital fellow with mules. Fetch him here, Trooper Thomson. I want a word with him."

He turned his attention to Colonel Wood again. "Did you know that the Thomson's gazelle, or more properly known as *Eudorcas thomsonii*, or tommie by the locals, is one of the fastest creatures on earth? Even though it resembles its larger cousin both in

132

shape and color, I dare say —"

Wood interrupted him. "Do you suppose we should dismiss the trooper, Theodore?"

Roosevelt looked surprised, as if the idea should have been apparent to him. "Oh, of course, of course. Dismissed, Trooper Thomson. Fetch me your brother, toot sweet!"

San Antonio was like a holiday for Jonathan. As the colonel's runner, he had the best of all possible worlds, as he was constantly in the company of the officer staff. Essentially invisible, he was not expected to pull guard or dig privies or trenches, or perform any of the other unpleasant duties of the private soldier. The golden boy had once again been handed plum pickings.

It was at this time he'd fully learned about Colonel Roosevelt and Colonel Wood, Major Brodie, and Captains Capron and O'Neill. His confidence in his leaders grew every day.

He also became good friends with the colonel's manservant, Marshall, a Negro who was at least ten years older than Jonathan's father, yet as fit and spry as the young runner himself.

The man seemed never to sleep. He was up and dressed when Jonathan arrived for duty in the morning and was still up and dressed late into the night.

Jonathan even had reason to be in the colonel's presence once, going on two in the morning, and still Marshall was there, present and alert, ready to do the colonel's bidding, regardless of the task or hour.

It was in San Antonio that he fully realized how much he loved it. He loved the discipline and comradery, the constant hustle for food and equipment, the lack of organization of the regular army, and the way his shrewd leaders figured a way around the multitude of problems.

He loved the tough men he was meeting and the wealthy and educated ones as well. He loved every moment, every nuance, as every day offered a new extraordinary adventure.

It was here he fully learned the true nature of men, tough men, honest and passionate men. Men who could kill an animal, even the human kind, without hesitation, were the same men who lived with their emotions on their sleeves. Men who could be brought to tears by a terse reprimand from Colonel Wood, as was the case with two troopers forced to share something so rudimentary as a dinner plate, the childlike squabbling used to teach a lesson in both humility and comradery. This is what made the Rough Riders, and Jonathan could not be happier with his choice to ride with them, with the colonel's choice to accept him.

Jonathan had not seen his adopted brother for more than three days, and, as Colonel Roosevelt was off to dinner with some politicians and reporters, he had the evening to himself. He decided to track Rocky down, check on how he was faring.

He was, as usual, with the mules. Jonathan approached cautiously. When his brother sat in that certain way, hunched up like a cripple, he was most certainly in one of his dark moods.

What he did not expect was to see his brother with another bloody nose, and this time broken, lying rather awkwardly to the left of its normal position, as the injury was, no doubt, the result of a rather deftly landed punch.

Rocky glared at him. He was drunk and had, by the state of his puffy red eyes, been crying.

"Where'd you find the hooch, Rocky?"

"A couple of Australians. Veterans of what they call the New South Wales Mounted Rifles, whatever the hell that is." He took a long drink from an unlabeled bottle, hesitating, appearing for a moment as if his body might reject the terrible stuff. He swallowed it down. "Tastes like old piss, but it works. Say it's rendered down from shoe polish."

Jonathan sat next to him, alone on a pleasant slope shaded by a wide old anacua until a pair of black mules, so alike they could have been twins — perhaps were — sauntered up to them. Rocky petted each in turn as they, like a pair of loyal canines, gave him a loving lick on the hand.

"How'd you get a broken nose?"

"Bastard Texan. One of those boys from a unit come up from around here. Bastard son-of-a-bitch!" Rocky wiped the freshly sprung tears from his eyes. He never hid them from Jonathan.

"Why?"

"They were calling those New York fellows — you know, Woodbury and them — they were calling them the *'la-de-da boys,'* and I told them to shut their yap, and then one of 'em clobbered me."

He leaned forward, elbows on knees, palms cradling his forehead. His voice cracked. "That ain't the worst of it, though."

Jonathan wetted his scarf from his canteen and, wringing it out lightly, laid it across the nape of his brother's red and sweaty neck.

"What do you mean, that's not the worst of it?"

"I was feeling pretty low, and I ain't visited Woodbury in a while. I went to his tent and some ass sergeant, some ass from the real army, he pushed me around, told me that I had no business messing around an officer. Old Woodbury got made a lieutenant. That sergeant said I had been fighting, and he'd have me fined or worse for it."

"So, you know how the army is, Rocky. They're not about to change up rules for the likes of you or me."

"Yeah, well, I seen him, Woodbury, or guess it's *Lieutenant Kane* now. He was talking and laughing and having his grub with a bunch of officers, and he glanced over at me, but he didn't stop that sergeant. He didn't wave me in or nothin'. Didn't even ask about my bloody nose. Didn't do a damned thing, Jonathan. Treated me like some hired help. Like some field nigger you'd pass by picking cotton. Treated me like a nobody. After that night in Prescott . . ." He sniffed hard, his voice quaking. "Just a nothin'."

The mule pushed at Rocky's hands with its velvet muzzle. The beast clearly loved him. Rocky, no matter how low his mood, would never hurt a mule or *any* animal.

Jonathan nodded. "You have a way with mules, Brother."

"Your father said I love mules better than humans or horses."

"*Our* father, Rocky."

"*Your* father."

Jonathan changed the subject. There was no reasoning with him when he was so far into a funk. "These are some of Arvel Walsh's, aren't they?"

Rocky looked up into the soft, brown eyes of each. "Yeah. You can always tell a Walsh mule. They got heart *and* soul, that's certain."

He turned to Jonathan. "You know why I like mules better than any other creature?"

"No."

"Because they're different. They don't fit in with any animal in nature. They're freaks. Like me. *And* they don't judge me. Don't care what a man's like. They treat you the same, no matter who you are or where you come from."

Jonathan pulled Rocky's tobacco bag from his shirt pocket and twisted him one. Though he never took tobacco, he could twist a cigarette better than one rolled in a factory. "You're wrong as you can be about that, Brother."

Rocky turned to him, his anger deflating as Jonathan licked the paper shut. He stuffed the cigarette between his brother's lips and continued.

"Why do you suppose so many people hate mules, Rocky?"

"Because most people are ignorant and most times stupid dumb asses, and they don't know shit from shoe polish about mules."

"True."

Rocky looked up at the nearest mare. He wanted to cry when he thought she might be hurt in battle. It was all right for a man to get himself shot or blown up; that didn't bother him. But the animals, they hadn't chosen such a fate. They were victims. Victims of man's hubris and stupidity. He worried over them constantly.

"Most folks don't know that a mule's a hundred times smarter than a stupid horse. Don't know you got to respect that about 'em."

"Right, Rocky, and you do. You know that, and they know that about you."

"What do ya mean?"

"A mule knows a trustworthy man once that man proves himself. Hell, dumb old horses, they'll follow anyone feeds and tells 'em what to do, but a mule, a mule chooses his man. Decides if the man can be followed. You're such a man, Rocky, so that's why I say you're all wrong about mules." He took a long drink from his canteen, handing it over to Rocky. He deftly removed the bottle of rotgut from its place between Rocky's feet. "Mules are the most critical judges of men in the animal world, Rocky, and they judge you, and they see a man they can trust, a man who will look out for them. My God, Rocky, a mule's about ten times smarter than you are, I'd reckon."

"Why do you say that?"

"Because they see something in you that you don't see in yourself."

Rocky harrumphed. "Well, I will say this. A mule'll never walk out on you like . . . like . . . oh, never mind."

"No, tell me, Rocky. Like what?"

"Like our mother."

"What the hell you talkin' about? Our mother died of a cancer, you dope! I swear to God, you cause me to wonder if the mules aren't full of shit sometimes. They know you're a good man, know you better than you know yourself, and you end up saying the stupidest things."

Rocky felt his nose. "Don't feel so good."

"Well, you are. Mother always said that,

and Father, though he might be cranky and mean as hell most of the time, he thinks that about you. I know it. He'd even say it if he wasn't so damned stubborn and proud."

"Well, they'd be liars if they did."

"Don't dare say that about our mother, Rocky! *Never* call our mother a liar! As long as you live, never say anything like that about our mother again!"

"Yeah, well, I'm sorry, I shouldn't have said that, but it woulda been better she had never clapped eyes on me. Better to never had her at all than to know her and then have her walk out."

"Walked out on you! Walked out on you! Jesus Christ, she had a cancer and died! She never walked out on you, Rocky, never walked out on anybody! Ellen even said, the doctor told her, Mother lived longer than anyone with such a cancer ever should have. She lived long as she could so's she could be with us.

"You are a pig-headed dope. Damn you for your goddamned North Ireland stubbornness. Like Father! How could you possibly say such nonsense, you dumb ass!"

Rocky searched for the bottle, turning accusingly to Jonathan. "Hand it over."

Jonathan reluctantly complied.

Rocky took another long drink, hiccupping twice, working to keep it down to no avail. He vomited. "Jesus Christ!"

"All right, Rocky. All right. Come now, you're gettin' yourself worked up. You need to calm down. You need to stop drinkin' that shit. Just stop it."

"I'm sorry, Jonathan." The tears ran. He wiped them with the wet scarf and continued. "She passed on before I could go in and see her. Never got to say good-bye."

Jonathan felt the twinge of guilt. Rocky was always overlooked, always shut out. "I remember."

"Oh, God, I miss her, Jonathan." He pushed the mule away as it sniffed the spot, investigating the pool of vomit.

"Well, I know you do, Brother. And I did see her! I was able to have a talk with her, and she said that I was to take care of you like you were my real brother. She said you were one of the joys of her life."

"She said that?"

"Yep."

"I'll be."

"Mother loved you as much as she loved me. Just know that, Brother. Know it, and please don't ever think that not knowing her would have been better than knowing her for a short time. She was the best thing to ever happen in our lives, even if it was cut short."

"You're right, Jonathan. Oh, God, it hurts so bad. I miss her so much. It hurts to remember her."

"I know, Brother. I know." He changed the subject, as dwelling on her was often too overwhelming. "Rocky, don't be so hard on that Woodbury fellow. My God, if you'd have come to my tent all beat up and bloody, I might pretend to not know you, either."

"No, you wouldn't."

"All right. No, I wouldn't. But still, Rocky, don't be too hard on him. And don't feel like you have to fight every man who says somethin' ignorant or stupid. Jesus, you want to fight the whole world sometimes. Wait a while. I think you'll have plenty opportunity to fight, time comes. Time we land in Cuba, you'll have 'em lining up to fight with you."

"Jonathan?"

"Yes, Rocky?"

"I'm worried for the mules."

"I know you are, Brother."

Jonathan rose, grabbing the bottle of spirits at Rocky's feet. He threw it down hard, shattering the vessel, the contents immediately absorbed in the hard Texas ground. Rocky did not admonish him.

"Well, Brother, best be getting back. The colonel's set me on a strict exercise regimen. That's what he calls it. A regimen. Running ten miles every morning." He smirked. "Didn't mention to him that Louis and I used to regularly do fifteen."

"How is he?"

"Oh, Colonel Roosevelt?" Jonathan nodded. "I like him. He's a talking son of a gun. Never seen a man knows so much about so much. He talks of things I have no idea what he means." Jonathan smiled. "He changed my name to Thomson."

Rocky cocked his head. "Why?"

"He says I remind him of a deer from Africa, called a Thomson's gazelle, on account I can run so fast and for so long." He turned his head, his face bearing an expression of reverence. "He's a talker, all right. That man, like Father says, talks fancier than a Philadelphia lawyer."

"Do you think he'll be all right . . . I mean, in battle, Jonathan?" Rocky cast his gaze to the mules.

"I think so. I know he's not a real military man. One fellow called us amateurs. Some ass reporter. I thought Colonel Roosevelt was going to clobber him. But he's sure taking it serious enough, and the other colonel,

Colonel Wood, he's a sharp soldier sure enough. No amateur. And smart. All these men are smart. Wood is a doctor on top of being a soldier. He fought Geronimo, you know. Rounded up the last of the Apaches. And Colonel Roosevelt, he hangs on Wood's every word." Jonathan nodded. "I think we're in good hands, Rocky."

A chipper voice interrupted them as Woodbury Kane picked his way around the expansive anacua. He smiled at the brothers. "Young Killebrew?"

Jonathan pulled his brother to his feet. He snapped to attention, saluting smartly, all the while nodding at Rocky to follow suit.

"Yes, sir?"

"I *thought* that was you at my tent earlier." He grimaced. "Young Killebrew, you've been pummeled again."

"Yes, sir."

Jonathan nodded. "If I'm dismissed, sir, I'll take my leave. Got to get back to the colonel."

Kane smiled. "You are young Killebrew's brother, aren't you?"

"Yes, sir."

Kane extended his hand for Jonathan to shake. "Pleased to meet you." He nodded. "Certainly you're dismissed. If you please,

145

offer my compliments to Colonel Roosevelt."

"Yes, sir."

Jonathan wandered off, enjoying the sound of his brother treated so well by the *la-de-da* boy. It was a comfort to him.

"Young Killebrew, come with me. I've a surprise to show you."

Rocky grinned. His brother was a genius. He wiped his face clean.

"Young Killebrew, it's called a Colt's machine gun." Kane admired it.

Rocky was impressed, which was significant, as little ever impressed young Killebrew.

It *was* beautiful. Gleaming steel and brass. It was fed by a belt, the shining missiles, lined side by side in a canvas webbing, ready to deliver instant death or, worse, mutilation.

It was a hellish contraption, and Rocky wondered at what it would be like on the receiving end. Felt a little sorry for the Spaniards who'd find themselves in its path of destruction.

Kane nodded to a handsome clubman. "Young Killebrew, this is Sergeant Tiffany. We call him *not that Tiffany,* on account that everyone inquires if he's a member of the glass makers, which he is not. Not remotely related. His family and my sisters donated these machine guns to the regiment."

Sergeant William *not that Tiffany* nodded, extending his hand. "Trooper Killebrew, pleased to make your acquaintance."

He was another of the *Fifth Avenue boys,* as they were called, mostly by the news-papers. Part of the circle traveled in by Colonel Roosevelt, and a man obviously of the same kind demeanor and fine breeding as Kane.

"My idea, William, or shall I say, *Sergeant* Tiffany, in keeping with the highest stan-dards of the military" — he tilted his head toward Rocky — "is to have young Kille-brew transferred to our machine gun unit. He's a master of mules, and, as these machines are so God-awful heavy, I believe such a fellow will prove indispensable."

Rocky smiled. How could he have read Kane so wrong? "I'll do my duty, sir."

"Of course you will." He patted Rocky on the shoulder. "Never doubted it for a mo-ment, my fine man." He turned to Tiffany. "How many mules do you suppose we'll need, William?"

"Oh, three. One for each gun and tripod, and one for ammunition."

"Can you handle three mules, young Kille-brew?"

"With pleasure, sir. Know exactly which ones, too."

"Capital!" Kane smiled. "Gentlemen, this will be the first use of such guns in military history."

Kane turned to another man, riding up on a spirited thoroughbred. A fine animal from Kentucky.

"Hamilton!"

"Woodbury, I mean, *sir!*" He saluted, then dismounted, bearing a wide grin. "Apologies for the lack of bearing, Lieutenant."

Kane ignored him. They were all slowly becoming accustomed to military order.

"Young Killebrew, this is our friend Hamilton Fish, the second-best polo player in North America. Ham, may I present Trooper Killebrew, half-man, half-mule. He speaks their language. He'll be our mule handler. An integral and indispensable part of our team."

Rocky nodded respectfully. Fish shook him warmly by the hand. "Woodbury's right. I'm second." Pointing his head toward Kane, he said, "He's first, the best horse-man and player in the land, but he's aging, Trooper Killebrew. One day, I'll surpass him."

Kane addressed him with an air of excitement. "Young Killebrew, I almost forgot!" He retrieved an envelope from his breast pocket. "A letter for you arrived only this morning." Holding it to his nose, he breathed in deeply. "Smells lovely! Eau de Verveine, if I am not mistaken."

Rocky looked it over as if it were a foreign object, some item he'd never in his life laid eyes upon.

Kane pulled him from his reverie. "From those two lovelies we dined with back at the hotel in Prescott." He nodded. "Go on, young Killebrew, read it. It's addressed solely to you." He winked. "I received one as well. They called us their brave heroes, their men in uniform."

Rocky smelled it and could at that moment remember every detail of each beauty: the lines of their lovely faces, the well-formed noses, the pink cheeks and porcelain skin, the curves of their bodies, the beautiful shimmering hair, the delicate, slippered feet. One of them he swore — no, was convinced — wore silk slippers.

He put it in a pocket, securing it with the button. He'd read it later, in private, where he could savor every word and nuance.

Rocky stood off, watching the men work

the machine gun. Each with the acumen of a scientist, and the dexterity of a mechanic. These clubmen were no worthless dandies. In mind, spirit, and body, they were thoroughly accomplished gentlemen.

He'd learn all! Immediately, his mind turned to the mules. They'd need special racks; they'd need to become accustomed to the gunfire, as the machines caused a terrible racket.

He, as well, would learn all, how to assemble and disassemble them. How to clean and maintain them. He'd not let his crew down.

At that moment he was convinced: he'd walk through hellfire; he'd stop a bullet; he'd do *anything* for Woodbury.

CHAPTER 8

They bathed him as Sean Whelihan lie in bed, stupefied, eyes fixed to the ceiling, jaw agape, in a state of catatonia.

They rolled him left and then right, changing the soiled sheets. Agata placed a washcloth in the hand that was bound up like a claw. She nodded to Ellen and Francesca as she left the room. Ellen called after her.

"I'll sit with him awhile, Agata. Get some sleep."

They rocked in matching chairs for a long time, waiting for the old man to close his eyes, fall back to sleep, perhaps into oblivion. Francesca broke the silence.

"How long did the doctor say?"

Ellen smiled. She'd never be angry at Francesca's candor or pragmatism, as, like Ellen, the young woman had grown up in a land that did not allow the luxury of inordinate grieving.

"Not long. Dr. Gillespie said maybe

another few days at the most. He said Father cannot eat or drink. He'll likely starve to death."

Francesca stood, peering into the old man's eyes. She could not force herself to care too much. To her mind, Sean Whelihan was an ass and a bastard, the way he treated his children. Especially the way he treated Rocky. She'd sooner use her Colt to put him out of his misery than shed any tears.

She held out a hand to Ellen. "Come on. It's to bed with us. He's sleeping. Nothing will come of us sitting here, staring at him."

Ellen complied and in a little while was lying in bed, Francesca joining her as she'd done every time she'd stayed over, at least until she'd started sleeping with Jonathan. Francesca pressed herself against Ellen's strong back, petting the spinster as she would a kitten.

"Are you all right, Ellen?"

"I don't know, Francesca."

"Tell me."

"You'll think me wicked."

"No I won't."

"I can't say it."

"Then I'll say it for you, and you can tell me if I'm wrong."

Ellen turned to face her. Buried her head in Francesca's breast and cried, speaking as clearly as her sobbing would allow. "All right, say it."

"You're a little relieved that your father will soon be dead." She felt Ellen's body tense at the profane declaration. "You feel as if you've been freed from prison." She waited to be told she'd taken it too far. "Now you can pursue a life of your own, a life of fulfillment and happiness. Now you can pursue your love with Louis."

Ellen sat up, wiping the tears from her cheeks. "What did you say?"

"Which part?"

"The part about Louis."

"Now you can pursue your love with Louis."

"Where on earth did you arrive at such a preposterous notion?"

Francesca smiled. "Oh, Ellen, *please*, don't insult my intelligence. I — we've known, my God, for years, that you and Louis adore each other."

"Who else?"

"Jonathan, Agata, *your* father, even rock-headed Rocky, for goodness sake, and probably most of the hands, at least the ones not completely stupid when it comes to the affairs of the heart. Everyone knows, Ellen, everyone but you and Louis." She brushed the hair from Ellen's forehead. "Everyone knows it's your father who's kept that from blossoming. Your father who won't have a dirty Injun in his family, but soon he'll be dead, Ellen, soon he'll be gone and —"

"Don't talk like that!"

"Why not? It's true. It's true, and saying it is neither right nor wrong. It's stating the obvious. It is stating what is true."

"Oh, Francesca. I'm so old, and . . . and ugly."

"Not to me. Your inner beauty is more profound than what's on the outside, at least to me, to people who count, to Louis." She smiled. "And let's face it, Ellen, Louis isn't about to win any beauty prizes himself, and I've always thought the Hopis a rather handsome race, but, my God, Louis is not a pretty man."

"You are wicked, Francesca." She spoke in mock derision.

"I *am not.* I'm truthful."

Ellen spoke at her hands. "I've never found him unattractive." She wanted to tell her of the interlude, the passionate kiss that night they had all announced they were marching off to war. She couldn't.

Francesca pulled herself from bed, found one of Ellen's combs, and began running it through the grey-streaked hair. "You have pretty hair, Ellen."

"No, I don't; it's hideous. I'm hideous. Look at me, Francesca. I'm built like a man. I've the jaw of a jack o' lantern. I'm gawky. There's nothing ladylike about me."

"You are not gawky, and I believe we could do something with your hair, something different, Ellen, to better frame your face. You wear it pulled up so tight. You look like a Quaker."

"I won't color it. That's for low-living women and prostitutes. I won't color it, Francesca, so don't even suggest it."

"You won't have to." She pulled Ellen up to a seated position at the side of the bed. "Let's have a look."

In a little while, she had Ellen's hair arranged in a rather flattering style. She returned the comb to the dressing table and retrieved a hand mirror. "Would you look at that?"

It was remarkable, but, then again, Francesca was an expert in the science of beauty. Not that she needed any help. She was a natural.

Ellen looked a little pleased. She remembered Francesca's comment.

"What do you mean about Louis?"

"Don't play coy, Ellen. You must know he's in love with you. And you with him."

"This is not the time to talk of such.

Father is dying in the next room and I —"

"Dead. Ellen, he's dead, not dying. That's a shell of a man. Soon the spirit will have flown, the process complete, but the reality is that your father is dead, and you must grieve, but you must also go on living." She stood. "I'll leave you to get some rest, get some sleep. Tomorrow is a new day. Tomorrow, you begin living."

Ellen pulled her back to bed. "No, Francesca, please don't leave. Stay with me tonight."

"All right, but only if you cheer up a little." She held up a hand. "Only a little. I know you've had a terrible shock, but a little cheer would do you well."

She held her for a long while, but neither could sleep. Ellen eventually broke the silence. "Francesca, what's it like, you know, to be with a man?"

"Why do you think I know?"

"Ha! Now it's my turn to admonish you! Everyone knows you've had carnal knowledge with my brother. Don't pretend you haven't. Don't insult *my* intelligence."

Francesca rolled onto her back, staring at the ceiling, considering how to articulate it. "You know when you're riding kind of fast on a saddle with a narrow seat rise, and you have that little feeling that runs right through you?"

Ellen flushed. "Francesca, you're scandalous!"

"You asked. Anyway, that's how it feels, only a lot more so."

"It doesn't hurt?"

"Not a bit, if you know how to control your man." Francesca was becoming distracted. Thinking such thoughts caused her to miss Jonathan. "It is quite pleasurable."

"I suppose we should call the boys back, Francesca. I imagine the army would allow them to come home to a dying father."

"I think we shouldn't."

"Why not?"

"Because Jonathan would be mortified to miss the war, and by the time you cable, and they track them down, and come back here, all they'll come home to is a freshly planted grave. They'll see that soon enough. It's not called for, Ellen. Let them finish what they started. Let them come home when they're through adventuring. They'll both be better for it." She turned on her side, pressing her back to Ellen's. "Try to sleep, Ellen. Dream of making love with that Hopi runner. Tomorrow we ride to town and have a proper hair dressing and, perhaps, a new wardrobe. I'm tired of you looking like a sodbuster."

"You are scandalous, Francesca."

"Thank you."

CHAPTER 9

Clara Maass could not decide which she felt more profoundly, sadness or excitement. They'd be in Key West in the morning and then off to her duties as an army nurse. It was her last night with her captain, perhaps for the rest of their lives.

She'd let him hold her hand and thought that this night, their last, if he said the right words, behaved properly, she might let him kiss her, and on the mouth, not the cheek.

She was giddy at the prospect, as she had thought, when she first saw him, that day he lied — committed subterfuge as he referred to it, convinced her to dine with him, that she might be in love, and now, after four days, she was convinced of it.

He greeted her with that usual look of love, adoration, and respect, but this evening things were different.

With a sense of urgency, he took her by

the hand, pulling her along a little too quickly.

She pulled her skirt up to avoid tripping. "What's the hurry?"

"I have something to show you."

They hurried to the portside bow as a group of soldiers formed along the rail. He pulled her close, pressing his chest to her back. He pointed east. "Sight down my arm, Clara, and don't take your eyes from the spot."

A whale breeched, clearing the water by several feet. Clara gasped, squeezing his hand.

"Oh, it's thrilling. What kind is it, Mortimer?"

"One of the seamen said it was a humpback. They travel these waters this time of year." He pulled her closer, shifting her attention further north. "There! There's another, and another!"

"And another! Oh, Mortimer, thank you. It's thrilling to see such magnificent beasts." She pressed his hand to her shoulder, the grasp, the warmth of it coursing through her, like electricity.

They stayed that way many moments, long after the whales and others moved on. She dared not shift or even speak for fear that the moment and their embrace would end.

With reluctance, Clara broke the spell. She turned to face him, so close their lips nearly touched.

"I guess the show's over."

She peered into his blue eyes. "I guess so, Mortimer." Her eyes tracked downward, to his embrace. "I suppose we should —"

"Marry me, Clara."

"I beg your pardon?"

He looked left and right, not certain of the impropriety of dropping to one knee while in uniform. The emotion and the moment trumping decorum, he knelt, pulling her hands together in a loving grasp. "Marry me, Clara. I love you. I can't bear the thought of living one moment longer without you."

"My word!" She'd not cried since childhood, not been allowed the luxury of such an emotion, as it was for the young or the frail, and Clara gave up being both at age nine. She cried now.

"It's . . . it's all so fast, Mortimer, I don't know what to say."

"Yes would be nice."

She pulled him to his feet, the German too imbedded in her psyche to allow emotion to guide such a life-changing decision. "I love you, too, Mortimer —"

"But?"

"But . . ." she turned away, holding onto the rail. She pulled him by the arms, in close, so that he, like a comforting blanket, enveloped her. "Hold me, Mortimer; hold me for a little while."

Her mind raced, and his breath, warm and provocative, bathed the nape of her neck. He kissed her at the hairline, raising a regiment of goosebumps across her back.

"That tickles."

"I'm glad."

"Mortimer?"

"Yes, love?"

A thousand thoughts invaded her mind. What of all the questions? Where would they live? What was his faith? Did he want children and how many? What of her career as nurse?

"You've overwhelmed me."

"Tell me, love, what's causing you to hesitate?"

"I don't know." She turned. "I've taken this adventure, this assignment to serve my country, to help the sick, to serve God." She pressed the front of his uniform with her palms, more to simply feel it, admire it, feel his body beneath it. She felt him trembling, and the thought of him trembling came as a comfort to her. *She* caused him to tremble. "I never expected to fall in love.

Never expected to find you. I . . . I'm not ready for this."

"But you *do* love me?"

She did not need to think for a moment about how to answer. "With all my heart, Mortimer."

"Well, then the rest is insignificant detail."

"How so?" She felt the little twinge of anger. Controlling her emotions, she recovered, as she didn't want to be angry with him. Yet the many unknowns were not *insignificant detail* to someone with her calculating mind.

"Where would we live, Mortimer? I don't know if you have faith, and if you do, what it is. I don't know whether you want children, your wants and needs and desires. I don't know what —"

He stopped her with a kiss that caused her head to swim. "*You* are my wants, my needs, my desires, Clara. I love you, and I am yours. I turn my heart, my mind, my life, my soul, my flesh and bones over to you. How does that sound?"

"Too wonderful to be true." She kissed him. Her knees buckled, and he felt it.

"It's not, my Clara. Please let me into your life, let me be with you, be for you, be whatever you want."

He pulled a small box from his pocket,

presenting a rose-cut diamond ring with an impressive stone at its center.

He grinned, knew telepathically what was in her mind. "My aunt's, Clara. Uncle and Aunt had no children. This is a family heirloom. My aunt said it came from Austria. It's nearly a hundred years old. I hope you like it." He slipped it onto her finger. "It's loose; you're so tiny." He pulled it to his lips and kissed the knuckle of her hand.

"Uncle wanted to marry us aboard ship, but I want to do it properly. I want to ask your father's permission. I want you to be married in a church with all the ceremony such an event deserves. I want everyone to see my beautiful Clara in the appropriate setting."

"Oh, that would be splendid. At my hospital, they have a chapel, Mortimer."

"The hospital where you are the superintendent of nurses?" He relished the thought of his tiny Clara in such a powerful position.

"Yes, where I'm superintendent of nurses." It sounded nice to hear him say it.

She held the ring to the moonlight, then turned to him with a pragmatically German comment. "I can't wear it when I'm working, Mortimer. I'll ruin it with the rough work I do."

"I know, love. Later, we'll find a simple wedding band. You can wear that while working and this when you're off duty."

"That would be grand."

"You are so, so beautiful, Clara."

"Beauty fades, Mortimer. I won't look this way always."

"What did Luther say: 'The mere union of the flesh is not sufficient. There must be congeniality of tastes and character.' " He smiled, kissing her again. "You most certainly have my tastes, and you have character, at least the kind I find attractive."

"You know the words of Martin Luther?" Her heart leapt. "Are . . . are you a Lutheran?"

He spoke quickly, as if the words could destroy his happiness, according to how she'd respond. "I was raised Episcopal, Clara" — he looked at the deck between his feet — "but I don't currently . . . well, practice any formal religion."

"You are no atheist!"

"Oh, heavens, no! None of that, Clara. I'm a Christian. I believe in God."

"I see. But you know the words of Martin Luther."

"I know the words of many historical personages. I can recite the Gettysburg Address if you wish. Or the first three acts of

Shakespeare's *Macbeth.*"

"Don't be impertinent."

"My point is, Clara, that I am putty in your hands. If you want our children to be Lutheran, then Lutheran they shall be. If you want them to speak German or wear lederhosen, or eat pickled cabbage with every meal, or learn to recite the alphabet backward, then that is what shall be."

"How many?"

"How many what?"

"Children?"

"As many as you wish."

"Ten?"

"Certainly."

"Or only one."

"Fine by me."

"Or none?"

"As long as there's some trying."

Her face reddened. "Oh, Mortimer, you are wicked."

She smiled playfully. This was rather a fun game.

"Where shall we live?"

"New Jersey, New York, Altoona, Kalamazoo, anywhere you like!"

"May Mother and Father and my many siblings live with us?" She smiled. "And Mortimer, I do mean *many.*"

"How many?"

"Nine."

"Oh, that's not so many." He kissed her. "As you wish."

He led her to a chaise in a dark corner, out of the wind and light. She was teasing him, and that was a good sign. They plopped down together and kissed as they'd never kissed in their lives.

"May I continue to be a nurse?"

"Only if that is what you want."

"You are very accommodating."

"I have to be. Uncle said that if I didn't convince you to marry me, he'd force me to walk the plank. And the coast of Key West is famous for its man-eating sharks."

"Then I suppose I must say I'll marry you, Mortimer. We simply can't have that." She kissed him again, a little aggressively. "So, the answer is yes, Mortimer, I'll marry you. I'll marry you with all my heart."

She walked in at midnight. As expected, the ladies were asleep. She turned on three lights and they rose up on elbows to see Clara sitting forlornly at the foot of her bed, holding a bandaged hand as if it pained her beyond bearing.

Minerva was first into action. "Clara, what on earth?"

"Oh, silly me. I burned it, on one of the stacks."

Sister Bonaventure, putting on her under veil, found her reading spectacles and adjusted one of the floor lamps. "Let's have a look."

She unwound the gauze, again and again. "Whoever wrapped this must have studied with the Egyptians."

The nun's eyes widened. "It doesn't *look* burned."

Minerva screamed. "A ring! A ring! Oh, Clara, you're to be married!"

Sister Bonaventure smiled. "Oh, my dear, he's a lucky man."

CHAPTER 10

Bill McGinty sat a-horse, watching Rocky work the mules. It was Woodbury Kane's idea to put them together, as between Rocky, Jonathan, and Bill, they were the best wranglers in the outfit.

Rocky nodded to him, stopping long enough to mount one of the saddle mules. He wanted to be on the same level with his new partner, and Bill McGinty had, thus far in his colorful and illustrious life, arrived at the conclusion that no man should be subjected to traveling afoot if it could be avoided. In fact, he had a rather sophisticated theory on why cowboy boots were not comfortable to walk in, and that the mere wearing of them precluded a man from traveling about in any way other than a-horse. Bill's mantra was: "If God meant for man to walk, he'd never have invented the saddle."

Rocky liked him. McGinty was one of his

favorite troopers.

"Bill."

"Rock." It was McGinty's name for his fellow range boss.

"She sets nice."

Rocky acknowledged his mount. Walsh had sent a few mules bred and trained for riding, though few men would consider using them. Too stubborn, too hard-headed to appreciate the mule. McGinty was not counted among those critics of mules as other than pack animals.

But Bill *was* an old-time bronc buster. He thought you had to master horses and mules, thought one had to plant fear in them to force obedience, and Rocky could not have been more opposite.

Actually, it was his father's view and that of Arvel Walsh, the mule breeder who operated a little north of Tombstone. These men had taught Rocky to be tough yet compassionate with the beasts, and that's why they'd worked for him so splendidly.

He remembered the day, five years past, at the Walsh ranch. He'd quirted a mule pretty hard because it committed some infraction Rocky thought deserved such rude treatment.

Arvel Walsh grabbed that quirt and tapped Rocky across the back with it. It smarted like hell. He still remembered the breeder's words. "A mule or a horse can feel a fly land on its rump, young man. And it can certainly feel the sting of a quirt. You remember that."

Walsh and his father also told him that, as in marriage, when one treats a woman, one's wife, with cruelty and threats, he'll likely have a compliant wife, but if he treats the same with love and respect, he's certain to have a loving one. That's what Rocky Killebrew knew of mules and horses.

But old Bill, he'd sooner quirt or beat or tie down or terrify a spirited horse than treat it with some kindness. He obtained results and looked damned tough doing it, but Rocky knew he'd accomplish a lot more if he'd employ a different strategy. And he never would hold any of it against Bill. Bill was doing what he'd been taught, what many others had done, because they knew no other way. But Sean Whelihan knew and so did Arvel Walsh and so did Rocky Killebrew. They knew a different way.

He thought about his own feelings and actions along these lines. Before this adventure, before Woodbury and the sergeant who had kept him from his Fifth Avenue friend and Colonel Roosevelt, he would have probably had words with Bill McGinty, and likely another bloody nose for his trouble. Bill McGinty was that sort of man. Rocky tried a new tack.

"I give your experiment a try, Rock, on that devil roan they brought in from New Mexico the other day."

"Yeah, Bill? The biter?" Rocky twisted his new partner a cigarette, handed it to him, and then twisted one for himself. They smoked together.

"I'll say, Rock," he nodded, almost pleased at both the enlightenment, and his own ability to take direction from a man several years his junior. "At the end a' the day, he turned out to be a damned fine horse, and I didn't need my usual headache powder." He rolled his arm at the shoulder as a way to demonstrate he'd not been fatigued by the breaking session. "Never even got bit!"

Rocky did not gloat. He smiled, staring at the glowing tip of his cigarette. "Mighty glad to hear that, Bill. Mighty glad."

"Reminded me a little of Sergeant Fish. You know, he took a devil we thought about givin' up on, Rock. He's an animal lover like you. He worked with that horse day and night, and like you, with kindness, not a quirt, and you know, Rock, that horse follows him around like a loyal hound."

This put Rocky's relationship with his

adopted father in a different light as well. Sean Whelihan was a cranky son of a bitch most times, and Rocky often pondered that. He'd be gentle with a horse or mule or even cattle or dogs, but with his own kin, and with Rocky, he could be a tyrant.

Ellen had challenged him about it once. "Why must you be that way, Father?" she asked. "You are good with the stock, and plain cruel with us more often than not."

He remembered the old man's reply, which was to erupt from the dinner table and storm from the room. Over his shoulder he sneered. "Because animals are too dumb and innocent to know any better. Humans have a thinking brain. They know right from wrong. That's why."

CHAPTER 11

Clara had fully prepared for a sad farewell when the ship deposited them onto Key West. But in typical army style, her parting would happily be delayed for another several nights.

Due to some inefficiency, they were assigned to a hospital literally flooded with nurses. Contract nurses and nuns and immunes were everywhere.

Sister Bonaventure felt especially at home, as the hospital was located on the grounds of the Sisters of Mary Immaculate. There was little for them to do but wait idly while someone in authority found another assignment.

Mortimer Hollander was as lucky. His men were delayed until they could board a transport to Tampa. He had little to do and occupied every available hour exploring the key with his betrothed.

First stop was to the shops along Duval

Street, where Clara was to be fitted out in the best money could buy. Mortimer insisted she have at least two new dresses, and he'd hear none of her protests.

She was learning that he was a kind man but certainly not one to be pushed about. She imagined the furniture they could buy with the amount spent on the dresses.

"Mortimer, I believe there are more Cubans here than whites."

"It's the cigars, and we're only ninety miles from the island."

She hugged his arm. "I like it."

Minerva was finding her own adventure pleasing as well. Life was different now that her grandmother had passed, and, for the first time, she'd not known constant toil.

The change of scenery was exciting. She had discovered a wonderful companion in Sister Bonaventure but soon found herself alone, as the nun had been pulled into the world of her comrades at the convent.

She was not alone for long, however, as a housekeeper and leader in the local church struck up a conversation about North Carolina. The woman had relations in the area, though Minerva did not know them.

Her celebrity as a nurse was more pronounced when she found herself among the community of housekeepers employed at the convent. They were respectful to Minerva, and again she had to push away that twinge of guilt, that notion that she was somehow a fraud. She could not bear to tell them she was not a real nurse.

Yet she did not feel entirely guilty, and that could be attributed to both Clara and Sister Bonaventure, as throughout the voyage south they quizzed her and conversed about nursing. Clara had loaned Minerva books on pharmacology and care of the surgical patient, allowing her to discover that she knew a good deal more than she originally assumed. It did not take long for her to ignore, as Clara put it, the *insignificant detail* of not having an official certificate. And anyway, that would be remedied soon enough, as soon as this adventure was over, as soon as she had the money from the government.

And what was more significant in all this was the attention paid to her by the several bachelors of the community, as Minerva was a handsome woman. She'd kept her figure, and she had a pretty face. It was flattering to be so well-regarded. She'd all but given up on the idea of having a man of her own, a family. She'd contracted mumps late and assumed that she'd never bear children.

That put an end to that idea. Her grandmother had kept her so busy, all through her late teens and long into her twenties, that the time she'd have the most likely success at finding a husband had passed.

It felt like revisiting an old friend. These men, the ones interested, were older, which was not entirely unwelcome. At least they were mature. Most were widowers and perhaps less inclined to want a family. It was a pleasant distraction to have the attention and interest of the opposite sex.

The food was a welcome change as well. Caribbean, Asian, and Spanish influences. The abundant seafood, both different and not so different from the fare of her home. She found that she was especially fond of the way the conch was prepared by the locals.

At the conclusion of a particularly pleasant evening, she found herself in the company of a dour man, a mulatto, evidently Cuban by his dress, walking beside her as she returned to her room at the hospital.

He rather menacingly nodded for her companion to leave them alone, and the housekeeper did not like it, but he was important in the resistance, and she did not want to defy him.

Her escort checked Minerva for approval

before taking her leave. Minnie nodded, and the two were soon alone.

"I am Juan José Julián Pérez." He nodded, speaking with authority, but he did not extend a hand.

She did not care for his arrogance, or his lack of manners. She decided to be a little brave, a little like Clara. She took a deep breath, turning away from him and speaking in the direction of the street before her. "And this is supposed to be important to me?"

"Ah, I have forgotten." He looked at the tip of his cigar as he blew smoke at the sky, moving up quickly so as to walk abreast of her. "I am dealing with an American. Even the women are overly confident."

She stopped. Turned and faced him. He was a handsome man, a mix of Spanish and African blood; he wore his wavy hair a little too long and sported a small, well-trimmed mustache. The bright white of his linen suit accentuated skin a shade or two darker than his Caucasian ancestors, but far lighter than Minerva's.

"What do you want?" She was giddy at the remark. She felt as if Clara were speaking.

"I heard that you were one of the nurses destined for my Cuba."

"Perhaps."

He blew another lungful of smoke, which evidently did not agree with her. He dismissively tossed his cigar into the gutter.

Minerva was curious. "What is this to you, may I ask?"

He handed her a thick envelope. "It is imperative that this reaches someone in a small hamlet outside of Siboney. I will have you carry it for me. Mention my name to any local, and they will ensure its delivery."

She looked at it as if she were beholding a bomb. "You will have me carry it for you!" She turned, calling over her shoulder as she tossed it back. "Good night."

"One moment," he commanded, as Minerva continued on. She quickened her pace, and this seemed to infuriate him.

"I *said,* one moment!"

She wheeled, staring him in the eye. Straightening her spine, she remembered Clara's behavior and body language when she'd witnessed the German's method for dealing with unpleasant or dismissive men. She wagged a finger in his face.

"No, you wait a moment!" She could not resist admiring him. He *was* handsome. Strong and confident and powerful. Perhaps dangerous. Most likely dangerous.

She could tell that he was a man who did

not generally take no for an answer. Well, he'd take no now! She'd heard about these Cubans, especially the rebels, the insurgents. They did not like the Americans, but they hated the devils from Spain even more.

"I am not a courier *or* a spy, and I'm certainly not taking anything from *you* to Cuba."

He looked away, rather hurt, and his expression melted her anger. Before she could speak again he held up a hand.

"I am sorry."

"I doubt it." She turned again, toward the hospital and to bed, when he reached out, touching her arm. She wheeled again. "How dare you lay your hand on me!"

"No, no, I am sorry, miss, I am sorry. I do not know your name. Please, may I buy you a cup of coffee, as an offer of an apology? A peace offering?" He removed his panama, rubbing his sweating forehead. "I have forgotten my manners, Miss . . . ?"

"Trumbull. *Nurse* Trumbull."

"Of course." He bowed. "Please, Nurse Trumbull." He patted his chest, to the place where he'd placed the letter. "Let us forget about my request —"

"You mean your demand."

"Yes, yes, it *was* a demand, a rude and impertinent demand." He pointed with the hat in his hand to a lively café down the street. "One cup of coffee? I can assure you, it is safe, and quite public."

"I'll have tea." She suppressed an urge to smile. Another lesson from Clara: do not surrender completely. She was pleased with only partially accepting his offer. "I'll have tea this late. Coffee after supper gives me insomnia."

He bowed again. "As you wish. Please, this way, madam."

He reminded her of someone she could not immediately place while he conversed about many subjects with passion and authority. Not her father; he died before Minerva had been old enough to know his name. Not anyone in her family or community. They were the working poor, the sharecroppers and the laborers. This one was like no one she'd ever known, at least on friendly terms. He was captivating. Not white, not Negro. He was unusual. That was the only word she could conjure in her mind. Unusual, almost feminine with that generous growth of wavy white-man's hair and high cheekbones, a well-formed, narrow, white man's nose, and teeth white and straight as a board fence.

She had an epiphany, laughing aloud. He

appeared confused at the outburst.

"Did I say something amusing?" He looked askance, not used to saying anything that elicited laughter. As a rabble rouser, he was in the habit of saying the opposite. The consummate troublemaker. A man of action. A man whose purpose in life was to topple governments.

"No, you remind me of someone, and now I have his image fixed in my mind."

"Who?"

"Oh, no one of importance. No one you'd like to hear about."

His voice softened. "I'd like to hear, nonetheless."

Minerva shrugged and immediately could see that flash of anger. "You are not used to not getting your way, are you, Mr. Pérez?"

She detected a hint of a smile. He looked into his coffee cup, then arrogantly held it high for the barman to refill. "I suppose not."

"Buford Wilcoxon."

"Who is that?"

"The man I thought of when you were relating the evils of the Spaniards, and everything else."

"And who is he?"

Minerva smiled. Clara, her dear Clara, had given her this voice. It caused her to feel good to do something more than sit back and let another control the conversation. She took a sip of tea and cleared her throat.

"Buford Wilcoxon was the most powerful man in our county. He owned about everything. Before the war, he had over three hundred of us, and, after the war, he still treated us the same. Called me nigger-girl when I was nursing him."

"Were you born a slave?"

"I beg your pardon! How old do you think I am?"

Her companion blushed, which amused her. It meant she had a little control. It meant he had a conscience. It meant he felt anxiety about provoking her. "No, no forgive me. It is — well, slavery only recently ended in my Cuba, not like your America. I've lost the sense of timing."

"I did not know that. When?"

"1886, but, in many ways, it is still as it was in the old days."

Minerva smiled. Still as it was in the old days. She thought of Wilcoxon. Some things are universal, no doubt. Some things never change.

"You, honestly, Miss . . . I mean, Nurse Trumbull, do not look a day over twenty, eh, twenty-two."

He pointed at the barman for more tea. He looked at the clock on the wall. It was nearly eleven. He commanded her. "Tell me how I remind you of a slaver?"

"Oh, not that part." She smiled again. "The part — well, I don't know how to say it. He was the most impatient, grouchy man I have ever known." She spooned sugar into her fresh cup. She nodded to him as she held it to her lips, blowing the words across the rim to cool it. "Thank you. This is nice tea." She continued. "None of the other girls could handle him, but I could. Superintendent said I was like Belle."

"Belle?"

"In the story. You know, the old fairytale from France. Superintendent called it *La Belle and the*, the . . ."

"More Anglo nonsense." He waved her off. *"La Belle et la Bête."*

"Does *everything* make you angry, Mr. Pérez?"

"Almost." He liked that she teased him. "Especially when it comes to the subjugation of our race. Especially when all our stories are derived from white men, white culture. I'm tired of it."

"*Our* race?" She smiled and held up her hand. "You are only half like me. Maybe even less."

He took her hand. Gripped her like a vise, though gently. Forcefully and gently and with power. She dared not pull away, instead, allowing him to examine it. "For a working woman, you have attractive hands." He released her when he felt resistance.

"Tell me more of the slaver."

"He came to my hospital to die, but he didn't die right away. He had a cancer in his stomach. I don't know what you know of such diseases, but dying from such a cancer is about as horrible as dying gets." She looked into his eyes, remembering the details. "You know, Mr. Pérez, some of the girls, and I don't mean only us Negroes, but some, were a little glad he was in so much pain." She turned her head slowly. "Good Christian girls, glad to see a man in pain." She placed her cup in its saucer. "I could not understand that. But in the end, when there was no more to do for him, I was given a bottle of laudanum. Doctors said I could give him all he wanted, all he needed, and, well, I stayed with him, day and night. He paid the hospital extra, for me to stay all the time by his side." She looked into the cup. "First time I ever slept in the same room with a man." She looked at him again and was comforted to see his expression.

"The last thing that man said before he departed was, 'I am truly sorry, Nurse Trumbull.'"

She stood, remembering Clara, her mentor. "It is late, Mr. Pérez, time I should be returning to the convent."

He sprang to his feet. "Of course, of course. I'll escort you." He snapped his fingers for the bill. Throwing dollars at the table, he followed her.

She looked up into the clear night sky. "It is surely a glorious night, and so late. I am never up past nine."

He took advantage, pulling her into his arms, kissing her.

She pulled away. "How *dare* you!" She slapped him across the cheek and, with every fiber of her being, resisted the urge to kiss him back. It was the most thrilling experience of her life.

He rubbed his jaw, smiling. "I will not apologize."

She turned toward the hospital, speaking over her shoulder. "I'm not surprised at that." She stopped, holding up a hand like a traffic cop. "Keep your distance, Mr. Pérez."

"Oh, I must walk behind you?"

She slowed. "Of course not, but you are too familiar."

"I am sorry."

"I bet you are."

"Do you believe I am so casual with all women?"

"Ladies?"

"Yes, of course, ladies. I am sorry. I . . . we . . . Nurse Trumbull, you must forgive me. In my culture, women are not so, how do I say?"

"Independent?"

"Yes, yes, independent. That is the word exactly."

They walked in silence for a while. "It was never such a way in my family. My mother, she would not have it. My mother taught me to be respectful of women, but, well, Nurse Trumbull —"

"I'm not a nurse." She looked up at the archway over the gate, the entry to the hospital convent, the imposing words, welded to the wrought-iron grating, like a statement, to be memorialized for all time. They felt heavy as she stood under the ominous sign. *Hospital.* She felt a fraud.

"I beg your pardon?"

"I'm not a proper nurse. I'm one of the immunes. The rules were changed for us. Allowed us as nurses on account we're immune to yellow fever and malaria."

He pulled her into his arms again, kissing

her in a way that caused her to feel scandalous.

He held her. Breathing the scent of her hair, he whispered into her ear, so close it tickled. "Nurse Trumbull, please believe me. Trust me when I tell you this. There is no such thing as a natural immunity to the yellow jack."

CHAPTER 12

Francesca awoke late to an empty bed, put on her robe and slippers, and wandered to the dining room, where Louis Zeyouma sat cattycorner to Ellen seated at the head of the dinner table. Her spot, her mother's spot. They looked as if they bore the weight of the world upon their shoulders.

Francesca spoke through a yawn into the back of her hand. She stretched, and Louis averted his eyes, as Francesca often caused proper young men to avert their eyes. She adjusted the housecoat to hide the sheer negligee it partially concealed. "So, he's dead."

Ellen looked up with desperate, watery eyes. "He's taking oatmeal, in his rocker." She pointed with her head, in the direction of her father's bedroom. "He's taking oatmeal, Francesca. Nearly an entire bowl *and* coffee."

Louis stood, appearing as if he'd been told

his family had been slaughtered by a band of marauding Apaches. He pushed the chair back into place. "I'll go, Ellen." He reached to touch her shoulder, thought better of it, recoiling as if the act would kill him. He nodded to Francesca. "Have a good morning, Francesca."

"No!" She pointed. "Sit! Both of you just sit there. Sit there, and don't move until I've told you otherwise. Understand?"

They complied.

She charged into the sick room, offering Agata a good morning. She smiled at Sean Whelihan as the old man worked on a mouthful of warm cereal. She patted the housekeeper on the arm. "I'll take over, dear. Go on, you've your chores to do."

Waiting for the door to close, she turned to Sean Whelihan, who looked her over with wild, wondering eyes. Still appearing bewildered at his predicament.

"You are one tough son of a bitch, old man."

His eyes widened, and she shoved a spoonful into his mouth before he had time to react. "I told Ellen you'd surely be dead by now." She looked the room over. "Thought certain you'd be with your dear wife, though perhaps not. Hortense was a sweet lady. You might not be heading where she is at all, if

190

you understand my meaning." She shoved another mouthful in. He took it, sputtered and coughed, spitting a gob, which ran down his chin.

"Oh, sorry, too much? They say, you give a man in your condition too much, goes right into the lungs. Ends up dying from pneumonia."

She found a wash rag and roughly rubbed his face. "There, all clean." She looked about the room again. "I'll give you this, you kept the room as dear Hortense decorated it. I know you loved her. No denying that. You sure loved her."

He cried and tried to mouth words. He could not articulate.

"What's that? Sorry? Did you say you're sorry? I didn't know you understood the meaning of the word. Didn't know you had it in you.

"No? You're not sorry? Or are you?" She took the teapot filled with coffee, fed him some through the spout. "Some of Agata's horrible coffee. You've always hated her coffee, I know. Now, you'll drink it or it will run down your clothes. You'll do exactly what we say, old man, now and until your miserable carcass gives up the ghost. You'll do whatever we say, and there's not a single thing you'll be able to do about it."

She stood, walked about the room; she found a pillow on the divan, carrying it to where he was seated. She spoke as she fluffed it, fiddling with the tassels hanging on each corner.

"You hate me, don't you, old man?"

He gestured in the negative. The man who'd killed tough men with his bare hands, scared of a girl of twenty. The irony amused her.

He had never let on that he hated her. *That little bitch.* That's what the men in the saloons and stockyards called her, and for good reason. He hated that his boy was involved with this half-breed, more Indian than white. He was powerless to prevent the relationship, and Francesca was too much of a woman not to feel arrogant about it.

"Oh, be honest, yes, you do. Only tolerate me as I'm not too dark; little Mex, little Tarahumara, more or less white, and, besides, you'd never really do anything to vex your darling Jonathan. You tolerate me, and that's a good thing, old man, because I'm carrying his baby." She stood, holding the pillow over her womb to mimic a pregnant belly. "I'm carrying his little child, his little dark Mexicano, his dark Indio baby. They say with dark blood, you know, with people like me, sometimes one will be born black as pitch. Something to do with bad blood, you know. And, boy do I have it!"

She sat again. "You know, you're much like a newborn yourself, old man." She pushed him back into the chair, clutched his face, pinching it in her grip. "Why, I could place this pillow over your head, kill you dead, kill you dead, and no one would ever be the wiser."

She looked back at the door. "Let's try." She placed the pillow over his face, holding it there a moment. She pulled it down and smiled. "You see, old man, see how easy it would be? You can't fight me. You're too weak. Too weak to fight a woman half your weight. Half your size." She smirked. "To let you in on a family secret, we're not Tarahumara at all. Oh no, those are the peaceful Indians; they're like our darling peaceful Hopi. The Hopi of Mexico. The peaceful runners. No, I'm not Tarahumara at all." She stood straight, pressing her thumb into her chest. "I'm Yaqui!"

His eyes widened.

"Oh, you know the name Yaqui, old man? That's good. The Apaches' nonsense appears as child's play compared to the Yaqui when it comes to savagery. We know how to kill. How to ensure the lives of our enemies are a living hell, right before we snuff them out."

She found a handkerchief, dabbing his cheeks dry. "Now that we understand each other, old man, and now that it seems that you will not be dying any time soon, at least as long as no one murders you, we are going to strike a deal, a nice — What did the whites call it, when they dealt with the Indians, stole their land, their way of life? Oh, yes, a treaty. You and I, we're to have a treaty, or, should I say, a pact. And here is what it will entail.

"First, you will give your blessing to Ellen and Louis Zeyouma." She nodded. "That's right, a full-blood Indian and your daughter. They love each other, and you are the only thing keeping that union from happening, so now, you will give your blessing, and that will be that, and when Louis impregnates your daughter, and *if* you live long enough to see the birth of your little half-breed child, you will give your blessing in that as well.

"Second, when Jonathan returns, you will welcome him and not deride him or chastise him for any of his actions. He's a good lad, and you know it, and I know you love him, and you're to start acting like it.

"Third, you are to stop riding Rocky. He's

a good boy, too, and deserves better. I know he's wild and still very much acts like a child, but that's partly your fault. When dear Hortense died you should have been more attentive to him. You should have been more attentive to them all. They deserve a father who is not bitter and miserable. You're to start counting your blessings and start conducting yourself as the proper man of this house."

She sat and watched him and pulled the pillow to her breast. She looked into his watery eyes and smiled, reaching out to again brush his cheek dry.

"Can you do that, Sean Whelihan? Can you take up your place as the proper man of this house?"

He tried to speak, tried to form words that would not come. He nodded in the affirmative, trying to swallow the drool working its way out of his mouth. Francesca dabbed his chin.

"You *are* a good man, Sean Whelihan. You are a fine, fine man and a caring man, but you will not torture your children with your temper any longer. You will not deny them happiness or love because of your own old-fashioned ideas on mixed races. You will stop wallowing in this ridiculous self-pity."

She patted him on the knee. "It's time that

195

this was a happy home again." She nodded to the portrait of Hortense. "It's time to bring the home back to the glory days when it was run by your angel of a wife. It's time, Sean Whelihan, and it's what I require."

He worked his right hand, found hers, and squeezed it weakly. She stood. "Good, and here is my promise to you, dear future father-in-law." She kissed his forehead. "I will ensure your days are spent in as much comfort as possible. I promise you'll want for nothing. Jonathan and I will marry and merge our ranches. You'll be one of the wealthiest men in Arizona. You'll be the head of a fine household, and you'll love all your grandbabies."

She wagged a finger in his face. "But remember, Sean Whelihan. I *break* horses, I do not coddle them. Ellen's coddled you for too long, and what's it gotten her? I'll tell you what. Days of sorrow and longing." She turned her head side to side. "That's unacceptable. Remember that, Sean Whelihan. I *break* horses. It's my way."

She washed his face and combed his hair. She buttoned his pajama shirt to the neck as she watched him deflate. The ordeal, the threats, the emotion — too much for him. Francesca helped him into bed.

"Now, I've Ellen and Louis waiting at the

dinner table. I'm going to go tell them the good news. All right?"

He nodded.

"Splendid! I knew I could rely on you." She touched his cheek. "When you are feeling stronger, you can tell them yourself." She kissed him. "Rest, Sean Whelihan. When you awaken, I'll be waiting for you."

CHAPTER 13

Rocky checked Bill McGinty through the mirror he'd been using to finish preparing for the big night out. The diminutive bronc buster looked good in uniform. He returned his attention to his own toilet, pleased with the fresh haircut from one of the Iowa volunteers.

He liked the fellows from Iowa. They were friendly enough and some rather ornery, as they'd run the guard more than a few times to town for some unauthorized entertainment. One fellow used banana peelings and pinned them to his shoulders, half-heartedly pretending to be an officer. The guard, a backward fellow from another unit, let him and his pards pass. It all amused Rocky Killebrew.

"Be ready in an hour, Rock."

"All right, Bill."

He sat on his cot and passed the time re-reading the letter from the two beauties he'd met that first night in Prescott. Every time he read those words, written in that lovely hand, he pictured them, sitting with him and Woodbury Kane in that posh hotel at the beginning of this adventure. He had to shove his nose into the envelope to catch the intoxicating odor, but it was still there, just not so plainly as when he'd first opened it.

This night he decided would be *the* night, as, with all the camp talk, Rocky was convinced he would have little chance of surviving Cuba.

It was mostly idle nonsense spun by the volunteers. Veterans and proper soldiers knew better than to dwell on statistics and theories on mortality rates. And, besides, most of the young men's frames of reference were fathers and uncles and grandfathers who'd fought in places like Fredericksburg or Gettysburg, Chickamauga or Shiloh, and predicated on the horrific numbers of dead and wounded back then. Young Killebrew thought, especially with his kind of luck, he stood less than half a chance of surviving.

He was nearly twenty and liked women. Loved women, at least the ones he'd known. But he was too damned bashful to do much about it. He loved his adopted mother and

Ellen and even had a romance, at the age of eleven, with Francesca, at least until Jonathan sprouted and became handsomer and manlier.

Yes, he loved women and thought that, with the prospects that he'd likely not see twenty-one, it was time for him to have carnal knowledge, and this was his primary objective this evening.

The whole thing, of course, gave him a terrific headache. Rocky harbored no illusions of bedding a pretty proper gal like the ones who'd written him or one like Francesca or, for that matter, any woman not in the trade, and, though it was all exciting, his heart beat unpleasantly in his throat and temples as he considered how he'd carry out the deed.

He never had any interest in whores, though he'd known a few who'd flirted with him when he'd visited the saloons in town and known more than a few fellows who'd slaked their passion via the services of the soiled doves. Those men thought it a convenient arrangement. But Rocky could not expunge the bad taste of it from his mouth. There was something cheap and phony about it, and of all he found reprehensible about life and the world in general, phoniness was the most repugnant.

Bill McGinty was no help, evolving into a sort of father figure when Rocky'd suggested they visit a whorehouse together, which was comical as, if anyone would run with whores, it would be the likes of a tough customer such as the bronc buster.

He remembered the conversation well enough, as Bill's face had contorted into an unpleasant grimace. "I would not lie with a whore even if *you* paid the tab, Rock." He turned his head from side to side. "Had a friend, a half Mex, caught somethin' from a whore once in Abilene, said it felt like he'd pissed a straight razor, and the stench, my God . . . what come outta him, Rock, it was frightful. You only ever have one Willy, Rock, and I intend to keep mine in working order. Believe they called it the gleet, the malady that Mex got for his trouble." He cringed. "You know the old sayin': one night with Venus, a lifetime with Mercury."

When that did not dissuade young Killebrew, the bronc buster tried another tack. "And besides, Rock, the colonel done forbade it. He says no lying with whores, you know that. You end up caught cavorting with the sportin' gals, well, by God, Rock, they might clap you in irons, might hang ya or put you up in front of a firin' squad, shoot ya dead, and then where would your beloved mules be? Might end up under the care of some blockhead who don't know how to treat 'em." He went on when Rocky sat, working away polishing a boot.

"Why don't you come along with me, Rock, gettin' some decent ice cream, not that bile they're peddlin' in camp. I heard they have the best ice cream in the state and a pretty gal servin' it up. Come on, Rock, buy some ice cream with me. Let's talk real nice to that pretty girl who serves it."

But, eventually, McGinty gave up, could see it in Rocky's preparation when the lad scarfed a couple of bottles of beer to bolster his courage, that nothing he could say would change his companion's mind. They'd walk into town together and part company, Bill McGinty for ice cream and Rocky Killebrew, more likely than not, for a dose of the French Pox.

It was much easier than he'd imagined, as the brothel stood nestled between two saloons in the part of town where one would expect such to be. A fat woman with halitosis and a Tampa cigar clenched between rotting teeth pulled him in by the neck. She squeezed him so hard that his vertebrae cracked.

"You are cute as a button, soldier."

A skinny man with about as poor dentition spoke up. "That's no soldier, Gert, that's a Rough Rider, one of Teethadore's boys, by God!" He slapped Rocky on the back. "Don't ride our gal too hard, young Rough Rider!" He laughed like an idiot, and Rocky wanted to punch him, but he did not. He was close to the ultimate prize, so close he could smell the sweat between the madam's breasts. Somehow it did not revolt him.

She held out a chubby hand. "That'll be two dollars for the ride and another three for a shot of courage." She handed him a glass of amber liquid, which he downed in one gulp. It tasted about as bad as the shoe polish concoction he'd obtained from the Australians back in Texas.

"Off with you." She pushed him toward the staircase, tucking the bills between her heaving bosom. "Second door on the right. Madeleine's her name; she takes care of all the first-timers."

He turned to face her, planning to lie and tell her he was *not* a first-timer, but it was for naught. She and the skinny man were greeting another customer. He turned back toward the stairs and became dizzy, as the rotgut was some powerful stuff.

He passed many men from other units,

realizing he was the only Rough Rider, and felt ashamed. He was one of the best, one of the men whom the colonel had hand-picked. One of the men the colonel had forbidden from such carrying-on, and now he was amongst the others, the common soldiers, the detritus who were commanded by hapless officers who did not care enough about their men to keep them from carrying on in such a way. He was with the common element, and he felt lower than he'd been since San Antonio when the Texan broke his nose.

He knocked on the door, which led into a closet, not much larger than the single bed it occupied, and Madeleine sat upon the greasy sheets, wearing nothing but a stained white-turned-to-brown chemise, Indian style. The odor of sex and sweat and excreta overwhelmed him.

She offered an inebriated smile. "Oh, a cute and clean one." She patted a spot on the bed beside her. "Have a seat, sweetie." She turned and downed a glass of the same stuff he'd been given by the madam and wiped herself with a soiled pillow, which she returned to the head of the bed, careful to turn it, dry and cleanish side up.

Little oval glasses with pink lenses perched on a red and swollen nose, and again all he could think about was Colonel Roosevelt staring at him through those pince-nez.

Otherwise, she was pale as parchment and as thin and shapeless as a boy, arms like sticks covered in blotchy skin. Her hair was not long and looked as if maybe it had been cut with a Bowie knife, uneven and dirty and yellow with streaks of silver. She, too, had few teeth, and Rocky sort of blurted, "Don't they sell toothbrushes in Tampa?"

She laughed and spit her answer in little fetid balls, slapping her knee. "That's funny, soldier." She patted the bed again. "Come on, have a sit down."

Rocky wanted to gag. "No, don't think I will."

She held out a hand. "That'll be five dollars."

"For what?"

"A ride, 'course; what ya think?"

"I paid the woman downstairs."

"Ah," she waved her hand, "that was to come *up* stairs, and for a drink. She give you a drink, din' she?"

"Yes."

"You're cute." She reached over to work his jacket off. Rocky pulled away.

"What's a' matter?"

"Nothing." He thought about what to say. He no longer was in a mood to learn anything of the mysteries of the fairer sex. He looked about as he pulled at his shirt collar, feeling as tight as a cinched noose. "Sure is close in here."

"That's 'cause it's a closent. So busy with you soldier boys, we had to turn it into a room." She shrugged, suppressing a belch. "No windas."

"What's that *stench*?" He watched her shift, evidently passing wind.

"The last fellow," she waved her hand like a fan, "he was not near so pretty and clean as you." She beckoned him closer. "Come on; we ain't gettin' a thing done lessen you come closer, sweetie."

She shifted again, and the odor wafted more strongly than before. He wanted to gag; he wanted to be somewhere else, anywhere but next to this pathetic creature.

"What's wrong, sweetheart?"

She smiled, exposing gaps in her dentition. He pitied her.

"What's your name?"

"What's yours?"

"Rocky."

"I'm Madeleine."

"No, your real name."

"What's yours?"

"I done told you, Rocky."

"Well, Madeleine's as real a name as

Rocky. Come on, Rocky, enough of the talkin'; I got a schedule to keep. What's your pleasure?"

Rocky had an epiphany. "How'd you like to put something on, have an ice cream with me?"

She harrumphed. "Hell no! Anyways, food makes me sick, soldier. Ain't got the time or interest in any *ice cream.* What are ya, a little kid or somethin'?"

"No, thought —"

She dropped a strap, exposing small nubs topped with pink nipples. The first he'd seen, and they were not as appealing as he'd imagined. She held her hands as if welcoming a toddler. "Come on, soldier, it'll be dandy." She winked and belched. "Promise."

He snatched a glance to the matted hair of her pudenda and wanted to vomit. He swallowed the nausea and pointed to her nether region. "You ain't got the . . . the . . ."

"Clap?" She grinned. "No, honey, cleaner than a fresh washed chitlin', but if'n you like, I can take care a' you the *other* way."

"No, no!" He pressed himself against the closet wall. The room began to spin, the closeness and stench and smoky wick of the lamp making him dizzy. "Let me outta here."

Hands were upon him, and the skinny man threw him out back, into the sandy, wet alley. The fresh air bringing him to his senses. "What the hell you doin'?"

"Move on, capon. Don't need your kind around here. We serve men!"

"Need my hat; where's my hat?" He attempted to push past the bouncer and was swatted on the nose for his trouble, dropping him on his backside.

From a second-story window, Madeleine threw his hat like a discus. "Here you go, soldier." She blew him a kiss. "Come on back once you've licked the Spaniards. Real name's Mary. Won't charge you a dime!"

He wandered to the decent part of town, discovered a fountain, and washed the blood from his nose and chin. He felt lower than he'd ever felt and thought about his home and father and Ellen and even Francesca. He was homesick and wanted to lie in his bunk with the men of the ranch and work the horses and never think about fighting Spaniards. Why was he there? What did he care about Spaniards? The whole ridiculous idea was Jonathan's. He didn't want to kill a man, Spaniard or not. He didn't want to die for his country. He wanted to live and maybe find a gal like Francesca and marry and just be. Just live. He didn't want to run his mules and horses into battle and see them cut to pieces.

On leaden legs he trudged to the ice cream parlor and wandered past it. He checked his watch, and it was late. McGinty was the last customer, and the beauty sat across the table from him, evidently entranced by the tales of his long and storied past. The tableau was overwhelming, the two seated in the warm glow of the electric light, the beauty, who couldn't have been more than seventeen, absently turning the gifts from McGinty, the mementos of a soldier, over in her hands — a Krag cartridge and a button from the bronc buster's uniform. If only he could know such love and adoration, be valued as a human being.

She was too young for McGinty, but that did not matter. There was nothing but friendship and perhaps a little hero worship between them. She sat like a starstruck schoolgirl in the presence of her favorite stage idol. And McGinty, with that look in his eye, as if he were beholding the paradigm of the fairest of the human species. They looked good together, she in her pretty, long dress, protected by a pristine, white apron, and McGinty looking damned fine in his sharp uniform, albeit absent a button.

Rocky moved on to the sound of music playing, yet another rendition of "A Hot Time in the Old Town Tonight." He was about sick of that song. One trooper kept whistling it. It so got on his nerves. He hated it.

He ended up at the hotel where the colonel's wife was staying. Where they'd received a little money from the paymaster who'd set up at the natatorium. Both Rocky and Jonathan had only received half of what was coming to them, and that had already been spent. No one could explain why. The colonel staked them, so at least they were not completely without means.

Throngs of people moved up and down the boulevard, and it felt better to be amongst normal, decent folks. He looked himself over, and his uniform was not so terrible. He wiped the seat of his trousers of the sand that clung to them from his fall in the alley. He rubbed the toe of his boots on the back of each pant leg. He rubbed his hat clean and felt a little better, as he had sobered.

The jolly voice brought him from his musings. "Young Killebrew?" Woodbury Kane called as he sat at a table on a veranda overlooking the hotel grounds. With him were William Tiffany, Ham Fish, a half dozen society ladies, Colonel Roosevelt and his wife, and Jonathan.

Rocky snapped to attention, speaking as he saluted. "Yes, sir!"

"Young Killebrew, you've been clobbered again!"

Roosevelt looked interested.

Rocky touched his nose, checking his fingers for blood. "No, nothing, sir. I . . . I tripped, fell right on my face, back at that ice cream parlor with Trooper McGinty. I'm all right, sir. Wasn't drunk or anything; tripped over a tree root in the dark."

"Good, come, sit down."

"Oh, no, sir, not my place."

"Nonsense." Kane looked to Roosevelt for approval. "We . . . need a guard, need a young trooper to guard these" — he pointed — "salt shakers."

Tiffany held them up. "Silver, I dare say."

Jonathan turned his attention to Rocky. "How's it going, brother?"

"Oh, all right."

Kane interrupted them. "Ladies, may I present young Killebrew, half man, half mule, half horse."

"That's three halves, darling." A stunning brunette with skin the color of fine china smiled at Rocky.

"Well, you know what I mean. Young Killebrew is handling the mules for our Tiffany guns."

"Oh, how exciting."

Roosevelt became animated. "Do you ladies know why the mule is a superior creature to the horse?" He did not wait for a response but rather stood, pushing his spectacles back into position as if he were about to address the legislature. "Hybrid vigor!"

"Do tell, Colonel."

"As you well know, the mule is an aberration. It is the result of cross breeding the donkey and the horse, and through the phenomenon of hybrid vigor, one obtains a creature with all the best traits of the contributing beasts, except they are far superior. Thus the mule, more intelligent and robust than the horse, more sure-footed and less obstinate than the donkey. Why, I say, with the proper scientific research, hybrid vigor could easily be applied to many —"

"Theodore," Edith interrupted, "I believe we should retire."

The colonel smiled. "Of course, of course." Roosevelt and his wife excused themselves. "Woody, ladies, gentlemen, we'll leave you to it." The colonel nodded to Jonathan. "Trooper Thomson, you may stay here, enjoy the evening. My servant Marshall can do any running if need be."

"Thank you, sir."

The men stood and saluted. Jonathan bowed to the colonel's wife. "Good evening, ma'am."

Kane nodded to Rocky, as a way of introducing the party. "These are some distant cousins, young Killebrew: Miss Simpson, Miss Davis, Miss Carlisle, Miss Stanton, Miss Gillespie, and Miss Crane. Ladies, I present to you one of our most talented Rough Riders." Kane looked serious. "And where is your sidekick McGinty?"

"Oh, still eating ice cream, sir."

"Good, good." He smiled. "Ladies, a tougher customer you will never meet than Bill McGinty, yet he has a sweet tooth to rival that of a child." He turned his gaze to Rocky. "Glad to hear it, young Killebrew."

And once again, the kind words of Woodbury Kane had rescued Rocky from his melancholy. He sat back, pulling himself into the shadows of the veranda's roof. Sat back and breathed the scent of the beautiful women, watched them laugh politely, watched them hold their cups daintily, watched them exude feminine charm. How could that poor creature back at the brothel look so completely different?

He sat and listened and gloried in the congress of decent human beings. By God, he was a Rough Rider! By God, he was one of Roosevelt's boys!

Jonathan was assisting the colonel's manservant, Marshall, in packing for the push to Cuba, when their leader burst into the room, rummaging about with an overwhelming sense of urgency.

He found the object of his desire, a leather fob in which was secured a tiny screwdriver. "There it is!" He began tightening the screws on a pair of sturdy spectacles, turning his attention to his runner.

"Trooper Thomson, how is your brother?" He screwed up his face. "He certainly looks nothing like you."

"No, sir, he's my stepbrother. He's fine, sir."

"From which side?"

"Beg your pardon, Colonel?"

"From which side, your mother or your father?"

"Oh, none, sir; he's adopted. The church folks found him as a babe, and my mother took him in."

"Oh, well, then, Trooper Thomson, he's

not your stepbrother. He's your brother. The definition of stepbrother is one who has been introduced into the family from another marriage, by either the husband or the wife. And then there are half brothers. That's when siblings share one parent. For example, in the case of my children, Baby Lee is half sister to her brothers Ted, Kermit, Archie, and Quentin, and her sister Ethel, born of a previous marriage." He appeared, momentarily, as if he might lose his composure. "May God rest her sweet and loving soul, but I am father to them all. A half brother would be one who shares one of the same parents. But an adopted brother, well, he's neither. He would be considered your brother, and that would be an end to it."

Jonathan spoke without thinking of the potential impropriety of the question, as the colonel was captivating. "How do you keep all that in your head, sir?"

Jonathan looked at Marshall, who wore a grin.

Roosevelt looked up from his glasses repair. "What?"

"*Everything,* Colonel. I never met a man knew so much about so much. If I did not know you were a man of such high morals, I'd think you made most of it up as you

215

went along, but I know you don't. How do you do it, Colonel? How do you know so damned much?"

"Language, Trooper." He nodded to his valet. "Give Marshall a quarter."

"Don't have a quarter, sir. Spent it all last night."

"Then you may owe it." He pondered the question. "Trooper Thomson, the answer to your question is clean living. A man has only three requirements: proper rest, proper nutriment, and proper exercise, both mental and physical." He turned to his valet again. "It keeps at bay the worst plague and cancer known to mankind."

"Yellow fever?"

"No!" He nodded to his valet again. "Tell him, Marshall."

The Negro spoke without looking up. "The seven deadly sins."

"Precisely! Which are: luxuria, gula, avaritia, acedia, ira, invidia, and superbia, at least according to the Italian poet and philosopher Dante Alighieri."

"I don't even know what those words mean, Colonel. Never heard such talk."

"Tell him in English, Marshall."

The old fellow spoke without stopping his work. Having heard the list recited in both languages so many times over the years, he

216

could repeat them without thinking. "Lust, gluttony, greed, sloth, wrath, envy, and pride."

"Capital!" Roosevelt returned his gaze to Jonathan. "Those are the seven deadly sins, Trooper Thomson. They are more deadly than the cartridges in our Colt revolvers, more deadly than any plague or pestilence known in the annals of history, as they not only kill the body, but as surely destroy the soul, the spirit, the very essence of mankind.

"Guard against them, Trooper Thomson, and you will go far. Avoid them, and you will have health and longevity and, more importantly, contentment. Why, with your eye on the avoidance of the deadly sins, you'll have time for rest, time for work, time for play, and time to nourish the brain and body. Isn't that right, Marshall?"

"Yes, Colonel. Absolutely right."

He inspected the work he'd done on his spectacles, flexing the temples. "There, fully functional." He put them on, shaking his head. "Capital."

As quickly as he'd burst in upon them, he rushed out.

Jonathan smiled at the valet. "He's like a whirlwind, ain't he?"

"Oh, you can say that again. One in a million is the colonel."

"All due respect, Marshall, but I'd say more like one of a kind. It must be right tiring trying to keep up."

"I'd have it no other way. He's an honor to serve. The best of men, that's the colonel."

CHAPTER 14

Sean Whelihan slept late, and Francesca did not disturb his slumber. She waited quietly and reread the letter from Jonathan and thought about the conversation she'd had with the old man the day after he'd had his fit.

The Dutch-uncle talk. That was what her father had called it. Now and again, from the time she was sixteen, he would demand she give the Dutch-uncle talk to any of the hands who'd misbehaved.

"Have a Dutch-uncle talk with them, Francesca."

It had infuriated her mother. "That's not for a young girl, Wallace, and you know it. A young girl should not know such discord and strife."

Her father would laugh. "We are not talking about *a young girl.*" Then he would kiss her, and she loved when he hugged and kissed her. "We're talking about *our* Francesca."

She remembered her first such talk, with a hand that was about as surly as Sean Whelihan and ten years older. He was competent with the stock but not so with the other men, especially Mexicans.

She'd turned sixteen, the same year she'd fully grown her splendid figure, her spectacular bosom, the year she'd blossomed from comely girl to beautiful woman.

The hands greeted her respectfully as she knocked at the open door and crossed the threshold into the bunkhouse. All but the surly man who sat on his bunk, occupying himself with a game of Patience.

She remembered that she trembled, not from fear or anxiety, but from the adrenaline rush of excitement. The kind of excitement she had known on her first elk hunt, the first time she'd taken an animal larger than herself. And that was how she felt as she addressed the old timer.

"Gus."

He responded, speaking to the cards. "Yes, missy?"

"I want to talk to you about something. Please, let's walk outside. And it's Miss Rogers, or Miss Francesca; you know that, Gus. Pop's rule, not mine."

He looked about at the men, busying themselves, trying not to appear as eavesdroppers to the unfolding drama.

"Anything you have to say, you say it here, missy."

"Fair enough." She nodded. "I suppose it's best everyone hears, anyway. You men, gather 'round." She turned her attention again to Gus. "We'll have no more ugly talk on the ranch, Gus."

He interrupted her. "What ya mean, ugly talk, missy?"

"You know well enough what I mean. No more calling these Mexican boys niggers or greasers or any other names." She shrugged. "No more ugly talk."

Again, he cut her off. "This ain't no finishing school, young missy." He laughed, looking about for some encouragement, but none of the men were having it. Most looked everywhere but in his direction. They had too much respect for Miss Francesca and her family.

She closed the distance between them. Caught herself, remembered what her father had taught her. Never fall victim to emotion. Never let them see they've gotten to you; never show your anger. She took a deep breath.

"Do not talk over me, Gus." She faced

him squarely. "Do not —"

"And don't *you* talk to your elders in such a way, young missy."

He stood, grabbing her before she had time to react. He twisted her by the wrist. "I ought to teach *you* a lesson. I ought to take you over my knee and give you a proper spankin'."

Before Gus could take his threat any further, Francesca jerked the thirty-two from her holster, pressing the muzzle to his forehead. She cocked the piece, pleased with how calm she felt.

"Let go of my wrist, Gus."

The old fellow paled. He could see it in her eyes; Francesca Rogers was not bluffing. He froze, not able to comply and not able to continue his attack.

"Gus, this Colt has less than a pound trigger pull. You don't let go of me this instant, I'll scatter your brains all over that bunk behind you."

He regained his senses, feeling the cold steel of the six-shooter's muzzle pressing into the skin covering the space between his eyes. He complied without further protest.

She turned on her heel, speaking to the men as she walked out. "Remember, gentlemen, no more ugly talk."

So, another successful Dutch-uncle talk

had resulted in a happy conclusion. She smiled when she saw he was awake.

"Good morning, Father!" She kissed him on the cheek. "Sleep well?"

He shrugged.

"Let's check to see if you've any strength back." She nodded as he tried to grip her hands. "Yes, I think maybe so, darling. I think you might be a-horse by winter time."

She fed him coffee through the tea spout, pleased that he liked it. "I brewed that batch. Been teaching Agata how to prepare a proper cup." She brushed the hair from his forehead. He gave her a crooked smile.

"Today, you'll tell them, Father."

After breakfast she washed his face and hands, gave him a proper shave, and dressed him, replete with vest and high collar and tie. She helped him into his upholstered chair.

"I'll bring them in, Father." She kissed him on the cheek as she hurried toward the parlor.

They sat around him in a tight arc. Francesca began. "Ellen, Louis, your father would like to tell you, you have his blessing to marry." She turned to Whelihan. "Isn't that right, Father?"

He nodded in the affirmative, reaching out with difficulty. He nodded again, forming the words the best he could. "You, together."

Ellen clasped his hands. "Oh, Father, thank you. Thank you."

He cried and quickly worked to gain control of his emotions. Francesca continued, sharing with the happy couple their future plans.

"When Jonathan comes home, we're to be married, and our ranches merged. Ellen, your father will have one of the largest operations in the territory, and Jonathan and I will run it." She nodded. "You and Louis will be equal partners if you wish, or, if you'd rather, we'll buy you out. You'll be free to pursue your own interests."

She retrieved a silver tray of filled cordial glasses, doling them out. "A toast, to the Circle W Bar Nine, the happiest and most productive ranch anyone in these parts will ever know."

Sean Whelihan nodded.

They stood by their boulder as Louis handed her the nightly cigarette. He took one himself, as the occasion seemed to call for it. With a full heart, he admired Ellen in the moonlight.

She seemed to read his mind. "I wonder what Francesca has done to cause such a radical change of heart?"

Louis stood behind her, wrapping his arms around her as he discarded his cigarette. He kissed her neck. "I don't know, Ellen, nor do I much care. But I am happy, whatever it was."

She turned to face him, running her fingers over his cheeks and down his neck. Taking the initiative this time, she kissed him on the mouth. "Now to deal with your mother."

"My mother will be fine." He pressed her head to his shoulder, breathing in her scent, running his fingers through the unencumbered locks. "I like the way you've changed your hair."

"Do you?" She pulled away, touching the ringlets Francesca had created. "A little like putting lip rouge on a pig."

"Do not say that about yourself."

She was taken aback by the forcefulness in his voice. Louis never said anything forcefully. She smiled. "I'm sorry."

"That's all right, Ellen, but, going forward, I do not want to hear any such talk. To me you are beautiful, and you are my woman, will be my wife, and only nice words will describe you from now on." He raised her head by the chin. "Do you understand, Ellen?"

"I do." She hugged him. "Oh, Louis, I

don't know. I don't know."

"You don't know what?"

"Have you ever been afraid to be happy? Have you ever felt that the feeling of happiness is nothing more than a cruel joke, a joke that someone or something was playing on you to watch you ride the high of it, only to wind up crestfallen?"

"No."

"No?"

"No, never." He kissed her again. "There is no evil god playing with us, Ellen."

"I know that."

"Then what you are saying is nonsense. What you are saying is an irrational play of the mind. It is not something that could happen without divine intervention, and you have already said, you do not believe there are such gods or demons or other mythical creatures to make it so."

"I know, I know, Louis. I . . . I don't know what it is, perhaps the war, perhaps Father having the fit, perhaps the stories I've heard about Francesca." She turned to Louis. "What do you suppose she said to him, Louis? What could she have possibly said to change his mind?"

"I don't know, Ellen, and to be truthful, I don't want to know." He pulled her by the arm. "Come, it's time you were home and to bed. Tomorrow we tell my mother."

CHAPTER 15

Juan José Julián Pérez stood at attention before Sister Bonaventure. As he'd done the night before, he bowed to Minerva and then to her companions, shaking each by the hand.

Clara smiled. So this was why Minerva had been walking on clouds all morning.

He was, to Minerva, even more handsome this evening. He was freshly shaved and had been to the barber, his hair not so unruly, but still retaining those handsome waves. He sported a different suit, newer, and a pristine celluloid collar and tie of bright red silk that complemented his complexion.

In a little while they were in the dining room of one of the finest restaurants for locals in all of Key West. He could not resist taking control, and ordered for Minerva. She let him, as somehow it was not off-putting. She liked his confidence. It felt nice to be taken care of for a change.

As they ate, he regaled her with stories of his home, told with unflinching enthusiasm everything he'd done, at least up to a certain point, to help liberate his Cuba.

She slipped a question in while he chewed his way through a tough piece of conch, fished from his soup.

"What was in that letter you wanted me to deliver?"

He grinned, exposing those pretty teeth. "Oh, you will laugh at me if I tell you, I think."

"No, I won't."

"It is a letter to my mother. And, well, some newspaper clippings and a few dollars to ease her way."

Minerva could not stop a smile. "Oh, that *is* rather funny. Not secret plans to blow up the capital. Just correspondence to your mother."

He looked young, boyish. Like a lad just home from his first term of school, proud to tell of his exploits. Perhaps he was not constructed of iron.

"Why not mail it, or deliver it yourself?" She looked east. "Cuba is not so far away."

"There is a price on my head there, Nurse Trumbull, and they are watching the mails. And the mails are not so reliable as they are here in the states."

"Why is there a price on your head?"

"For murder."

"Of who?" She felt the blood rise up her neck, into her cheeks. She was light-headed.

"Spaniards. It is not murder, Nurse Trumbull —"

"Minnie."

"I beg your pardon?"

"You may call me Minnie if you'd like."

"Minnie." He said it as if he were trying it on for size. "Minnie, it is not murder when you are fighting a war, when you kill the enemy, but that is what the Spaniards are calling it, and I may not return home until my people are liberated. That is what you Americans are to do for me."

"For *you*?" She smiled. "I have never known such passion in a man, Mr. Pérez."

"Please, it is Juan José to my friends."

"And I am a friend?"

"I hope so."

He looked a little vulnerable. A vulnerable rebel and assassin. Minerva was emboldened by her power over him. "I hope so, too."

An hour's dinner stretched into three. The place was comfortable, and they eventually moved, as the sun set, to a veranda overlooking the Atlantic. The cool breeze was invigorating.

"Why are you so angry, Juan José?"

"I'm not angry!" he snapped and as quickly realized his delivery did not match his words. He smiled. "Well, maybe I am angry, a little." He looked into Minerva's pretty brown eyes. "Is it wrong to be angry?"

"No, not as such. I have been angry from time to time, but is it right to be *always* angry?"

"What causes *you* to be angry?"

"Oh, I don't know. I guess . . . well . . ." She sat back, folding her arms, staring at a ship as it passed to the south. What a strange sensation, to be asked her feelings. Until now, no one had asked. Even her grandmother had not cared enough to ask. She enjoyed his philosophical interrogation. "I'm usually pretty happy, but, when I think on it, I guess what makes me angry is the idea that I have to travel far away to learn to be a nurse. To pursue my education."

"How so?"

"Well, there are only a few schools that will allow Negroes to study nursing, and all far away from my home in North Carolina. Well, except I guess for St. Augustine, but, well, that's not a proper school. At least not yet. They graduated only four students last year.

"There's a proper nursing school within

walking distance of my home, yet I may not study there. That makes me angry. What difference is there if I'm a Negro or as white as Nurse Maass? We still have the same brain. Still care for the sick, still serve God . . ."

He ejaculated, "Serve God?" He uttered a cynical laugh.

"Of course, serve God. Why is that funny?"

He waved her off, patted his suit pocket for a cigar, and then remembered the smoke did not agree with her. "It . . . it sounds funny to hear someone say it. At least among the company I keep."

"You mean you don't believe in God?"

He lost his smile.

"Let's say that I am more worried over the real than I am the ethereal, Nurse Minnie."

"It is Minnie, or Nurse Trumbull, but not Nurse Minnie; you make me sound like a Mammy from the plantation days."

"My apologies." He nodded. "Minnie."

"You are one of the modern thinkers. The ones who believe religion is for the old and stupid, aren't you?"

"No. I —" His face flushed. He waved the air dismissively. "I do not wish to criticize your beliefs. It is silly semantics, arguing over such trifles. My overall philosophy in life, dear Minnie, is to live and let live. If you have faith, I respect your right to it. If one does not, I respect his right as well."

She suspected that he was lying. "That's bleak."

"Why?"

"Because there's no . . ." She knitted her brow, not accustomed to philosophizing, thinking thoughts of the intangible, the metaphysical. "There's nothing to anchor us, nothing solid, nothing, how do I say . . ."

"Immutable?"

"I don't know what that means."

"Fixed, unchangeable, absolute."

"Yes, yes, that's it. That's what I mean. At least as a Christian, well, there are laws, good laws that stay forever, the Ten Commandments."

"Such as thou shalt not kill?"

"Exactly."

"Yet, dear Nurse Trumbull, here you sit, preparing to go off to war, to help your countrymen kill the Spanish despots." He gave her hand a squeeze. "To violate the immutable."

Clara reclined, pressing her head to her lover's shoulder. *Her* lover, her fiancé! She sat up, looking about to see they were far away, out of town, the twin dapple greys plodding along a road that paralleled the Atlantic. The sound of the surf mesmerizing, the moon electrifying. She thought that perhaps she could not be happier.

"Driver?"

The sleeping man sat, slumped and insensible, the reins loosely held in his hands. Mortimer awoke, pulling her back onto the cushions, as plush and comfortable as the bedchamber in a potentate's harem.

He kissed her. "I fell asleep."

"So did *he.*" She pointed and called out again. "Driver!"

"Shh." He pulled her more tightly into his arms. "Let him sleep."

"I don't know where we are. We could be anywhere. Far out of town."

"We are in Florida, on the island of Key West. That's all we need to know."

She snuggled against his chest. "What of the horses?"

"They're likely asleep as well. Sleep walking. They'll find their way. Come closer, love."

"I cannot move any closer, Mortimer. Any closer, I'd be inside you."

"Or perhaps the other way around."

"Shh! He might hear you!" She swatted him playfully. "You are wicked."

"Love me?"

"With all my heart."

He looked off into the sky. "There." He pointed. "At least we know where we are heading. That's the north star."

"Happy?"

"Yes and no."

"Why no?"

"Because I've only just found you, and I have to leave you. Tomorrow it is off to Tampa, and then God knows where." He rubbed his temples.

"Will you miss me?"

"That's a silly question."

"Say it."

"Say what?"

"That you will miss me."

"I'll miss you. I'll miss you as I miss you whenever we're apart. Oh, God, Clara, I miss you every moment we're apart."

"Even in bed, when you are sleeping in the officer's tent?"

"No, actually, not then. Then, I dream of you." He played with her fingers, pulling them to his lips, kissing each knuckle. "Then we are together and happy."

"Then we need to get this war over with. We need to make that dream a reality."

Chapter 16

Ellen awoke early from a slumber more restful than she'd enjoyed since her mother had become ill. She rose and fixed her hair as Francesca had shown her. She looked left and right and was pleased with the result. Perhaps she wasn't so homely after all.

She pulled the letter from her housecoat pocket and read it more carefully this time.

Dear Sister:

Well, we have made it to Tampa, Florida, and are chafing at the bit to board the transports to Cuba. Rocky is well. He has become friends with a rich New York gentleman by the name of Woodbury Kane, who might well be one of the wealthiest men in the world.

There are many such men, friends of Colonel Roosevelt. They're known as the Fifth Avenue Boys or the la-de-da boys, and some of the fellows thought they'd be soft and need nurse-maiding, but that has not turned out to be the case at all. Woodbury Kane is about the best horseman I've ever seen.

Enclosed is a copy of a newspaper article that tickled me and that I thought you might find amusing, as I remember how you liked to follow the sharpshooter Annie Oakley. She wrote a letter to President McKinley, offering to pull a squad of fifty lady sharpshooters together to fight the Spaniards. I won't repeat the details; you'll see it well enough, once you look at the story.

Things are going well enough here. Glad to be out of Texas, but then again, Florida offers enough challenges to go around. First, chiggers. They are a tiny insect with the power to cripple an army. They burrow into the skin and cause all manner of torture. One man nearly died because the skin around his belt line got so bad. He was wracked with fever for the better part of five days.

Colonel Roosevelt made an inspection and was pretty unhappy with a lot of the men. Seems they used this moss that hangs from the trees down here as bedding, and the chiggers live in it. The colonel said it was no wonder so many of the men got bitten, as they were fairly wallowing in chiggers the whole time they were asleep. It seems it's okay to use the stuff hanging in the trees, but once it hits the ground, the chiggers invade it. He said how chiggers were even a pest to the Roman army, thousands of years ago.

The colonel is funny that way, Ellen. I wish you could meet him. He is like a walking dictionary, I swear. I get to spend a lot of time around the colonel, since he assigned me as his runner. Pretty slick duty since I stand around mostly, listening in on what is happening at headquarters. He is dedicated to the cause and to his men. Everyone respects him, and he works hard to get around all the terrible delays and failures of the army.

Food has been a major failure. They say this is the first time that canned meat has been used, since the government is trying to modernize the army, which used to bring meat on the hoof and slaughter it as required. Now we have canned meat, and it is, mostly, not fit to feed to a dog.

On top of all that, many of the men are sick from the bad water and the sinks that were dug in the wrong places. The flies are amazing, and the word is still out on that, from the medical men, but, as far as I'm concerned, they carry disease. That's what the colonel says, and I'm inclined to believe him.

Colonel Roosevelt says there's not enough land for the army to remain in Tampa. He says there's all kind of higgledy-piggledy business going on. That's the words he used, higgledy-piggledy. Pretty funny coming from such an educated gentleman, but then again, you know right away his meaning when he says it. The colonel suffers the same as us. There's been rumors about other units, how the officers hoard good food and the best tents and bedding and uniforms while their men go without. Not with the Rough Riders, Ellen. Not by a long ways. The colonel's wife has come down and stayed in the best hotel, and, yes, the colonel visits her, but he always reports back every night to sleep in a tent with the men. That's Colonel Roosevelt. And the other officers, well, you know how father is about politicians and his time in the war, but it's not like that with ours. Buckey O'Neill is a first rate captain, Major Brodie is top rate, too, and there's so many more. We are in good hands, Ellen.

Equipment is good. We've been allowed to shoot our rifles a fair amount, and I guess it will do, though it kicks me too hard, as it has a pretty big cartridge. I prefer the .30-.30, like the Winchester Father gave you last Christmas. The action on the Krag is smooth, though; no one can say that it's not a well-built rifle, but I don't like it much because of the magazine. I'd as soon they issued us Winchesters. Almost every Rough Rider in our regiment knows about the Winchester, but they've gone with these Krags. It's kind of funny, because every now and again one will discharge out of the blue, and the man holding it will look as if he'd committed high treason. These boys know guns well enough, but they sure don't know these new-fangled Krags, and they touch off pretty easy if you don't remember to engage the safety catch. When that happens, a whole bunch of us cry out, 'Take it away from him, take it away from him!' and the offender looks all red in the face and feels a regular greenhorn, but it really is all in fun. Don't understand all that, how the government and the army decides on such, but what do I know? I'm only a private. Our six-shooters are regular Colts, like at home, but some are double action, which are all right, I guess. I like them well enough, though again, I'll take a .32 over the big .45 any day. Don't know how much gun you need to kill a Spaniard, but the government seems to think a pretty big one, certain enough.

Well, I better close. Please give the letter to Francesca that I've tucked in with this one. Take care, and tell everyone Rocky and I are all right.

Your brother, Jonathan

She dressed in one of her new outfits. Nothing fancy, but not like her old ugly dresses, either. That thought elicited a smile. When *did* she start dressing that way? Mother never encouraged it, for Mother was a rather stylish lady, at least as stylish as one could be living on the Arizona frontier.

She remembered: it was the winter after Mother's death; the year she'd had that growth spurt and no longer fit into any of her clothes and no one around to help her decide on a new wardrobe; the year Father was at his darkest. The worst winter of their lives.

She bought outfits from the local grocer's

wife, an old woman who'd been born old and into the Quaker faith and styled her creations accordingly. Even Jonathan could see them for what they were, declaring they were sewn from the same cloth and in the style of flour sacks.

Before her mother had become ill, they'd take long trips, the two of them, every spring down to Phoenix and indulge a little. Sean Whelihan never begrudged his wife the money. He was proud of how beautiful she looked in the new fashions, many of them straight from Chicago or New York.

Ellen laughed again as she buttoned the dress at the collar, remembering that Francesca likened her to a Quaker, at least as far as it concerned her hairstyle.

How did that all come to be? How did everything so completely unravel? She wanted to cry at the sadness that had befallen their home. All those wasted years of moping, negativity, ugliness; all those wasted years her father kept the place so sullen. It was like an infection of smallpox that ran through and wiped out an entire family.

When Mother was alive, it was a happy home. Mother could control Sean Whelihan; keep him from falling into the melancholy that had poisoned his mind. Keep him from dwelling on those terrible years during the war, the loss of his brother, the wasted life and stolen opportunity.

She thought of Francesca again, how Francesca would tell her, again and again: "No regrets, Ellen. No use in regrets."

What was done was done, and it was time to move forward, and with a deep breath, she pushed those sad feelings away, sat up a little straighter in the chair before her dressing table, and thought of Louis Zeyouma.

She considered her reflection, following the curves of her body. She did not look so mannish now. The new dresses were flattering, and, indeed, Ellen had a voluptuous figure, when allowed to be revealed with a correctly fitting frock.

She thought about intimacy with Louis, knew it could be pleasurable, thanks to Francesca's enlightenment, but also from the knowledge imparted by the books she'd read. That kiss of Louis's had triggered something. He was so gentle and loving. The thought of it caused her face to flush, the heat on her skin, a tingle traveling down her body, to the tips of her toes.

She stood abruptly, feeling a little silly for the titillating response, then as quickly sat back down.

Another of Francesca's influences. They'd

hired more staff to do what she'd done unnecessarily for the past several years. They had more than enough money, and, though Sean Whelihan was tight-fisted, he'd have never refused her if she suggested taking on more help. The labor was cheap enough.

No, if she were honest with herself, that was her idea, some kind of self-flagellation and, of course, a way to occupy her mind. Hours of toil kept her from loneliness, feelings of despondency, longing, and unhappiness. It kept her from dwelling on what the tragedy of her mother's death had both brought upon and simultaneously denied her.

But life would be different from now on. She stood, consulting the clock on the mantel, and decided to check on Francesca. Her future sister-in-law had taken up residency since her father's fit, despite Ellen's protests, as Francesca had her own ranch to run. But Francesca would have none of it. And the young woman was a comfort to her.

She passed Francesca's closed door, wandered out onto the veranda, and decided to sit for a while and wait for the sun to rise. She loved the hour before dawn as much as the period before bedtime. Most often they were hers to own exclusively, and she could catch a few moments reading or embracing the sights and sounds and odors of her spread. She had convinced herself that it could be enough, that it could sustain her for the many years of loneliness to come.

A sudden chill ran through her. Was it possible to be too happy? Would something happen to stop it? What? Father had given his blessing, which was strange, but there it was.

Would Louis's family be difficult? Why? His mother loved her. Everyone loved her. And, if they were married, was she too old for babies? Wasn't her mother nearly her age when she was born? Mother was thirty-six when she'd had Jonathan. No, she was not too old for babies, and her cycles were normal and healthy and regular.

How would her half-breed children be treated? She knew a few in her time. The good people she lived among would not mind it. The Hopi, though it would be an aberration to have a white in the mix, they were good, at least Louis's family; they'd never object.

And Father. He *was* a changed man. The fit had changed him. How? How could such a terrible tragedy so completely change a man? How much longer would he live? She swore the other day he'd had another in his sleep, sure there had been another attack, another deficit. He barely ate these days. How much longer could a man survive on the little bit they'd managed to feed him?

Francesca's chipper "good morning" brought her from her musings. She smiled and took the cup of coffee.

"Thank you."

"A penny for your thoughts."

Francesca lounged in her robe. Pulling a quilt from the back of a rocker, she scooted her chair next to Ellen's, giving her a peck on the temple as she threw the blanket over both of them. "Love mornings, don't you, Ellen?"

"I do, Francesca." She took a sip. "I was thinking of Father."

"Is he awake?"

"No. Anymore he sleeps until well past nine, God bless him. He'd say a man who sleeps so late is a hopeless idler and deserves to be shot."

"Tell me."

"I was thinking that he will not live long, that anyone who eats so little cannot live long, Francesca." She turned to face her. "And, frankly, that does not vex me. Does not sadden me so much."

"Good. I'm glad you feel that way."

She could never be angry with Francesca. The young woman knew a thing or two about losing family.

"Are you pleased with your father's blessing?"

"Y — yes, and, well, no."

"What does that mean?"

"Oh, I don't know. It seems — I can't explain it. Forced, in a way." She looked into Francesca's eyes. "I don't know if I'm looking for a way to find fault."

"Find a way out of happiness?"

Ellen smiled. "Am I that transparent?"

"Yes." Francesca sighed. "You martyrs are all the same, Ellen."

"Martyrs?"

"Yes. Please no offence, but you've been disappointed so many times in your life, you . . . your kind are compelled, I guess, perhaps, as a defense, to preemptively do your best to find the bad in something good, to prepare yourself for disappointment."

"That's cynical."

"Cynical or not, it's true. What did you want your father to do, cartwheels?"

"No."

"But you expected more enthusiasm."

"It . . . it all seemed" — she looked Francesca in the eye again — "frankly, coerced."

"What do you think, that I somehow forced him into it?"

"Why would you say that?"

Francesca took a deep breath. Ellen could be infuriating sometimes. "I want to be clear, Ellen. I want to be clear that I have only the best intentions for us all." She folded her arms, looking off at the horizon. "My relationship with your father has always been tenuous. I don't want you — don't want anything to come between us. Does that make sense?"

She'd never seen such vulnerability in her future sister-in-law. "Thank you."

"For what?"

"Without you, without your wisdom, Francesca, I'd be a basket of nerves. I'd be wringing my hands, admonishing myself for having such notions, for feeling any happiness."

"He's a tough old bird, Ellen. Don't worry so much about your father."

Ellen felt the blood infuse her cheeks. "He's more fragile than you'd think, Francesca. Remember that."

"Oh?"

"The war was hard on him."

"As it was on everyone who lived or died in it. But the war was more than thirty years ago."

"You know, he lost his brother."

Francesca spoke to the horizon. "That's

no excuse for bad behavior, Ellen. My father was in the war as well, but he moved on. Didn't torture his family with a lot of nonsense."

"*My* father was at Gettysburg."

"And mine was at Fredericksburg." Francesca turned severe. "I am not keeping score, Ellen, but your father lost his brother. Mine lost three uncles, a cousin, and his father. The rebels cut them down, then shot them as they lay wounded and helpless on the battleground. My father lay on the field for a night and a day, covered with the corpses and gore of his family. It was horrific, as it was for Sean Whelihan, but, again, I say, it's no excuse for his behavior."

She stood. Facing Ellen, placing a hand to her face. "I don't want to fight with you, Ellen, but I will tell you this. I will do *anything* required to ensure life as it should be for all of us."

"All of us?"

"Yes. You, Louis, Jonathan, me, even Rocky. When this ridiculous adventure is over, I'll marry your brother. I'll want a happy home in which to raise my family. No, that's not right; it's not what I *want*, it's what I *demand*, Ellen." She turned her head side to side. "And I will do whatever is required to achieve that end."

"Not, I hope, at the expense of my father."

"Your father." Francesca smiled. "Your father is, Ellen, not unlike a spirited mustang, allowed too long to run wild and out of control in the desert. Sometimes such beasts need to be broken."

"And sometimes they need to be loved." Ellen remembered the conversations she'd heard on the subject. Her father and Arvel Walsh, the mule breeder, considering the cruelty of breaking over taming with understanding and love.

"And sometimes they need breaking, Ellen." She pulled her future sister-in-law from the chair. It was time to change the subject. "How about a ride today?" She held up a hand. "And don't tell me you've this or that to do. Agata and the new girls have everything in order."

Ellen smiled sheepishly. It would take time to stop denying herself a little fun. "You are right." She saw the hint of pink on the horizon. "But we should go early; it will be hot today."

"Anything new from the boys?"

"None, Francesca."

"One lousy letter." She turned her head in disgust. "And nothing from Rocky."

"No, nothing from Rocky."

"I miss him."

Ellen smiled. "Rocky?"

"Of course! Well, both of them, but I miss and worry about Rocky. Worry about him more than I do Jonathan."

"I know. Poor Rocky."

Francesca blew steam from her cup. "Jonathan could fall face down in a pile of horse manure and come up smelling of lilacs."

Ellen smiled. "And Rocky could do the same and end up arrested for stealing fertilizer."

CHAPTER 17

They went about the business of packing
with a mood more somber than would be
found at a funeral. Sister Bonaventure tried
to be cheerful. "Well, ladies, at least we
know where we are heading. Jacksonville
will be busy."

And she was correct. Typhoid fever had
hit Tampa, and General Fitzhugh Lee's
Seventh Corps had established itself at
Camp Cuba Libre a little more than two
hundred miles away.

Thanks to the old confederate's expertise
as a soldier and organizer, it was the clean-
est, most efficient place for the afflicted to
recover. Trains were moving the sick over to
the east coast several times a day. Nurses
were desperately needed.

They'd take a transport up to Miami, then
a train to the camp. Sister Bonaventure tried
to comfort Clara.

"The captain is only a short train ride

away." She smiled as she regarded Minerva. There was less to encourage her. Juan José had left the night before, giving no detail on his plans or destination. Minerva had no idea of his whereabouts. At least she'd eventually agreed to carry the letter for her Cuban patriot.

An ominous knock at the door brought them from their various musings, and Sister Bonaventure greeted a portly man with a ruddy complexion, sweating in a worn winter suit. A northerner, no doubt.

"Good afternoon, ladies." He nodded resolutely at the neck. "I am Otto Smith from the United States Secret Service." He opened a wallet, revealing a card too briefly for anyone to examine. "I'm here to speak to a Miss Minerva Trumbull."

Minerva peeked around the sister's girth. "I'm Minerva Trumbull."

The man stiffened. "I see."

Sister Bonaventure replied, "How may we help you, Mr. Smith?"

"Miss Trumbull, what do you know of a man named Juan José Julián Pérez?"

Minerva raised her hands, palms up. "Very little. I've met him three times. He is a Cuban refugee living in Key West. That's about all I know." She considered her situation for a moment. "He . . . he gave me a letter, to deliver to his mother."

"Interesting." He looked the women over accusingly. Clara retreated into a corner of the room, busying herself, giving the impression that she had no interest or real relationship with her roommates or the current interrogation.

He turned severe. "This does not look good. A contract US Army nurse fraternizing with shadowy characters. Carrying letters, and *who-knows-what,* to Cuba." He impatiently snapped his fingers as one summoning a dog. "The letter, please."

Clara stopped her work, springing into action. She stood between them. "Just a moment." She regarded the agent suspiciously. "How does a German become a United States Secret Service agent?"

He looked upon her with disdain. "I beg your pardon? I am an American, the same as you, madam!"

"Since when?" She regarded her companions. "If that's not a Kölsch accent, I don't know what is."

He began to answer, caught himself, and tersely replied, "I am the one asking the questions here. It would be unwise for you to give me any opposition, young lady." He eyed her with contempt. "What is *your* name, by the way?" He pulled a small notebook from his pocket.

"Clara Maass."

"Oh, a German. Perhaps it is not appropriate for a German to be a US Army contract nurse, *Miss* Maass."

"Perhaps you can check my credentials and arrive at your own conclusions, *Mister* Smith, *if* that's your actual name. I was born and raised in these United States. I'm as American as President McKinley." She regarded Sister Bonaventure, who stood, jaw agape, still not accustomed to Clara's aggressive response to men whose behavior she deemed inappropriate. "And while we are on the subject of credentials, please, Mr. *Smith,* show us yours, more slowly this time."

"I need to show you *nothing,* young lady." He glared at the three of them. "This is an outrage!"

"Well, then at least a badge, some proof of your position. For all we know, you could be a Spanish spy!" She looked each of them in the eye by turns. "Everyone knows the Germans have a vested interest in the affairs of Spain." She snapped her fingers, mimicking the surly man's behavior. "Well, let's see them, let's see them this instant!"

"This is an outrage!"

"Yes, yes, we know, an outrage. You've

already intimated that."

"I'll have all of you clapped in irons! I'll have all of you in Fort Leavenworth breaking boulders, ladies. Do I make myself understood?"

Sister Bonaventure nodded for Clara to behave. She put on a show of diplomacy. "I'm certain none of that is necessary, officer. Minerva can certainly show you the letter. It is sealed, and I believe it should stay that way until we have everything sorted."

"Sorted?"

"Well, yes. No offence intended, Mr. Smith, but Nurse Maass has a point. We don't know you, and we haven't received any formal request for the letter."

Minerva handed it to Sister Bonaventure, who held it but did not offer it to the agent.

"May I at least examine it, in its current state, madam?" He nodded. "You have my word as a gentleman . . ."

Clara guffawed, eliciting a scowl from their interrogator. He returned his focus to the nun. "I'll not open it."

She allowed it, and he turned it over in his hands. He sniffed it and smiled as if he'd stumbled upon a brilliant discovery. "Ah, you see, ladies." He tapped it. "This is important. The odor emanating is distinctive."

Clara snatched it from his grasp. She examined it, holding it to her nose, and replied, "It smells of cigars and hair tonic."

"No, you are mistaken, my fine *Teutonic* nurse." He sneered. "Chemicals! You see, ladies, such letters contain chemicals so that the writing can be made invisible. When attacked with a reagent, they become apparent."

He was distracted, and Clara, taking advantage, blurted out, *"Kann ich der Stift leihen?"*

Smith absentmindedly reached into his coat pocket, retrieving a fountain pen. He held it in her direction as he read the address on the letter.

She pulled the pen from his grasp. "Not German, eh?" She approached a little too aggressively, and he quickly retreated. Clara pulled his coat open, revealing the name embroidered on the inside pocket. "Cologne, Germany. As I thought. I knew I recognized that accent." She pointed. "And the cut of that suit!" She turned to her companions. "This is no American agent. This man is a spy!"

They froze. A man was in their room, a spy, standing between them and the only means of escape. They held their breath, waiting, except, of course, for Clara. She would not cede the upper hand. "Out with you." She began pushing him toward the door. "Out, out, out!"

Slamming the door behind him, she locked it, sighing in relief.

Sister Bonaventure was the first to speak. "Clara, you are a force of your own, my dear."

"Oh, that was nothing." She hid her shaking hands, placing them in her deep skirt pockets. "I can tell a German fresh off the boat. They all stink of pickled cabbage."

She had a thought. "I suppose we should contact someone." She considered Minerva. "Or not."

Minerva dropped to her bed. She was certain she loved him. Why did she have to fall in love with a revolutionary? A man hunted by spies?

Bonaventure comforted her. "There, there, Minerva. No reason for tears."

"I don't know what to do!" She looked at them in desperation. "Please help me. I don't want to be sent to prison. I don't want to put Juan José in danger." She turned the envelope over and over in her hands. Throwing it on the pillow at the head of the bed, she replied, "I wish I'd never met him! I wish I'd never agreed to any of this."

Sister Bonaventure picked up the envelope. "Let's see what it's all about." She steamed it over the kettle on the hotplate. In short order they were examining each page.

Minerva sniffed. "It's all in Spanish. It makes no sense at all." She looked through the newspaper clippings, which were in Spanish as well.

The nun interjected. "I know Latin, and enough Spanish to order dinner. Let me have a try." She put on her reading spectacles and was soon smiling.

"It's a love letter from a homesick young man to his mother, Minerva." She turned her head slowly. "Nothing more." She held it to the light. "There's nothing to it as far as I can see. No intrigue, no secret messages, no invisible ink. Nothing more than a letter from a loving son telling his mother that he misses her and that he's all right." She looked at the articles. "And these, well, pardon me for saying so, but they are stories to make a mother proud. Articles about Juan José's exploits in the revolution."

Clara reached down, picking up dollar bills that had fallen from between the pages of the newspapers. "And, let's see, eighteen, nineteen, twenty American dollars. What a fortune!"

Minerva sniffed. "Really? That's what he

told me. He was telling the truth, then."

"Certainly, child." Sister Bonaventure folded everything back as it was; she stuffed the envelope and licked the flap, resealing it. "So, you see, there's no reason for you not to take it."

Clara paced, fists clenched. "I know one thing, ladies. There's a certain fat German who better pray to God he never again crosses *my* path."

CHAPTER 18

Camp Cuba Libre was well ordered, though woefully undermanned and under-supplied. The ladies were greeted enthusiastically by the overwhelmed medical staff.

An old sergeant had been assigned to assist them, though, other than procuring them a tent for sleeping and some meager provisions, he was otherwise useless.

"They said I was to be a nurse, a head of nurses on account of my stripes, ladies," said Sergeant Elijah Collings, "but I've done nothing but tended mules all my twenty-three years in the army. Know naught about nursing and don't want to know naught."

Sister Bonaventure hid her smile. At least he was honest.

"What physician is in charge?"

"What what?" He absentmindedly scratched his backside.

"Physician?"

Clara spoke up. "Doctor. Who is the doctor in charge?"

"Oh, Boovey. He's in yonder tent, upwind, but," he shrugged, "you ladies would be right wise to steer clear of that one. A regular damned fool he is, if any of the real medical folks is to be trusted." He cast a hand across the tents assigned to the nurses. "He don't come here for love or money. He pretty much stays in his quarters, some say he spends most his time drunk."

"Sergeant, we'll need three cauldrons: one for boiling bedclothes and bandages, one to mix disinfectant, and one to sterilize water." She looked at him. "The water is impotable, I presume?"

"Sister, yer goin' to have to use plain English with me." He scratched his backside again. "Not used to such big talk."

"I'm guessing the water is not good. Is that right, Sergeant?"

"Oh, no, the water's good. Gen'l Lee's set the wells and sinks right. Not bad water, no bad privies, ma'am. Hardly no flies even; it's all that clean here abouts."

"All right, well, we'll make do with two cauldrons then; can you find them for us?"

"Doubt it, ma'am. The army's sure fouled this one up. Never seen such bad supply." He pointed at the lumber yard. "Men's been using roof shingles for plates. Eat with their fingers *or* their bayonet knife."

He pointed north. "There's a bunch a' niggers, in yonder town; they can supply you lots a' provisions and food, mostly pork and catfish — you know, regular nigger food — but it fills the gullet."

"All right." Sister Bonaventure nodded. "In my part of the country, we refer to such people as Negroes, Sergeant." She regarded Minerva standing beside her. "Please fix that term in your mind."

"Oh, sure, ma'am, sure." He nodded in the way of an apology to Minerva.

"Ain't got any pick with Nig — I mean Negroes, ma'am, no offense intended. Fought alongside more than a few in my time, killin' Injuns. They's some fightin' sons of guns."

She sent the sergeant on his way to do what foraging he could. They had three long tents that would accommodate fifty men each. The floor was muddy sand, despite Lee's establishing them on high ground. There was too much foot traffic for it to be any other way. Many of the men had cots, but more were lying on the damp ground.

They had a proper little war council. "Ladies, your thoughts, please?"

Clara spoke first. "Mostly dysentery. We must keep them clean, and we've been assigned five orderlies per tent. As far as I've seen, about half of those men are willing to do the work. The others are scoffers and believe the task at hand beneath them. Some of the poor men have been lying in their waste for two or three days."

Minerva commented, "They aren't getting enough food or water, either."

"All right." Sister Bonaventure documented in her notebook. "Three tents, three proper nurses. Minnie, you have the first; I'll take the middle; Clara, the last." She looked behind them. "The lumber yard is a godsend, and I've never seen men yet who do not like to tinker with wood and hammer and nails. Let's find some of the more able fellows and have them build us proper floors and beds where we need them."

"How do we pay for all that, Sister?" inquired Minerva, forever the pragmatist.

"We don't, but we write requisitions." Bonaventure held up a stack of empty forms. "I found these on my way through the quartermaster's tent when we were checked in. They are as good as blank cheques."

Clara smiled. Evidently she was not the only one to buck the system from time to time.

"Let's determine which orderlies we can

trust. Assign each good orderly a bad orderly to keep the malingerers in check." She stood, regarding her watch. "Let's see if we can get these men properly cleaned and fed and hydrated."

Over the next eighteen hours they worked and cleaned, all the while training the men. There was eventually not the hint of odor anywhere.

Five soldiers had been busy with hammer and saw. Each tent was fitted with a proper, dry floor. Beds were hammered together for every invalid with no cot, and Sergeant Collings had three cauldrons working, two for disinfecting clothes and one for mixing the all-important carbolic acid solution used to sanitize everything.

Bed pans were properly cleaned after every use, and even the orderlies were a bit happier.

After twenty-two hours on their feet, the team of nurses settled down at sunset on their second day.

At lights out, Sister Bonaventure said her evening prayers, then took a deep breath and announced, with dignity, "Ladies, I must tell you. In all my years of nursing, I have never cleaned so much shit!"

They laughed until they cried and then fell into a deep, exhausted sleep.

Dr. Boovey wasted no time taking credit for the work, as his assignment was soon the model of medical care in all of Florida. Men recovered more quickly under the watchful eye of the Nun, the German, and the Immune, as they were affectionately known.

After the third day of the nurses' presence, Boovey deigned to make an appearance, unwisely choosing to review his charges with Nurse Maass.

She'd never been bested by even the most arrogant, German-trained physician, and the fool Boovey was to learn why.

He walked along, half-heartedly reviewing cases, nodding to men in their beds and cots.

"That man there, what's his problem?"

Clara did not need to consult a chart. She knew each man's diagnosis and the state of his condition.

"Typhoid fever."

"You mean to say, Typhoid fever, *Doctor.*"

"As you wish." Clara felt the blood infuse her cheeks. She controlled her fury. "Typhoid fever, *Doctor.*"

He scribbled some orders, handing them to her without looking up. She read them.

"Blue mass, acetanilide, and quinine?"

"Yes, that's correct."

"Why?"

"Because I said so. Nurse, what's your name?"

"Maass."

"Where did you receive your training?"

"At the German Hospital in Newark, New Jersey. I was the superintendent of nurses there before taking this assignment."

"Did they teach you to question a doctor's authority at the German Hospital in Newark, New Jersey, Miss Maass?"

"No, there was no need. We had competent physicians there. They did, however, teach us pharmacology and how to protect our patients. We also learned a long time ago that mercury is poison, and one does not give a patient with dysentery acetanilide, nor does one prescribe quinine to a patient who has no diagnosis of malaria. And, Doctor, it's *Nurse* Maass."

"And you are an expert on malaria? I did not know there was malaria in New Jersey, Miss Maass."

She wanted desperately to punch him; instead, she reached into the vast library of her mind and began reciting all that she'd committed to memory.

"Common symptoms of malaria include:

267

shaking chills that are moderate to severe, high fever, profuse sweating, headache, nausea, vomiting, diarrhea, and anemia.

"For dysentery, frequent near-liquid diarrhea flecked with blood, mucus, or pus. Other symptoms include sudden onset of high fever and chills, abdominal pain, cramps and bloating, flatulence, urgency to pass stool, feeling of incomplete emptying, loss of appetite, weight loss, headache, fatigue, vomiting, and dehydration.

"Typhoid fever: a feeling of weakness, often stomach pains, headache, or loss of appetite. In some cases, patients have a rash of flat, rose-colored spots.

"Cholera: watery diarrhea that can rapidly lead to dehydration often with a rapid onset of copious, smelly diarrhea that resembles rice water and may lead to signs of dehydration, such as vomiting, wrinkled skin, low blood pressure, dry mouth, and rapid heart rate.

"Yellow fever has three stages. Stage one, infection: Headache, muscle and joint aches, fever, flushing, loss of appetite, vomiting, and jaundice are common. Symptoms often disappear briefly after three to four days. Stage two, remission: Fever and other symptoms cease. Stage three, intoxication: Problems with many organs occur."

She looked at him. "And, for the record, *Doctor* Boovey, I would not treat a dog with mercury or, for that matter, arsenic, in case you get it into your mind to prescribe it, which frankly would not shock or surprise me."

"People are treated with metals all the time; look at silver, Miss Maass."

"No one poisons rats with silver, nor do they store wine in mercury-lined vessels. The metals are not remotely equivalent in the treatment of diseases."

Clara was pleased to remember Dr. Schroeder's lecture on pharmacology. He was adamant about it.

"And, as for the blue pills, we do not have a supply of patent medicine or any other hokum or gimmicks of the quacksalver available from the pharmacy. If you happen on a medicine show in town, perhaps you will find a supply from the local snake-oil salesman, but, Dr. Boovey, it will otherwise be quite impossible for me to carry that order out."

"Well, see what you can do, Miss Maass. And, one other thing, I believe a healthy dose of morphia tablets will ease the lads' suffering. See to it right away."

"To irritate an already irritated bowel?"

"Those are my orders."

She spoke through gritted teeth. "How many grains?" She had no intention of carrying any of it out but felt compelled to befuddle him further. Clara was convinced the fool did not know a grain from a dram.

"Oh," he shrugged, "the normal, based on their weight, Miss Maass." He waved her off. "I'm off to the commissary to procure, eh, supplies . . . items for the men."

"Dr. Boovey, before you leave, there's a man with a rather bad boil that requires lancing. Please, before you go, come this way."

"Oh, I've not brought my medical kit. I'll attend to him later. Which man? I'll note it."

"He really is in a lot of pain, Doctor. If you please, Sister Bonaventure has a sterile kit. It's in her tent. I'll fetch it."

"Oh, well, I'm sorry, miss. Have to dash."

He was away before she could fully comprehend his stupidity. Stupidity and arrogance. She saw double, the anger dizzying.

She wandered to the shade of a tree where they would take a few moments to rush through a meal before, as Sister Bonaventure would say, stepping back into the breach.

It all was, for Clara, overwhelming. She'd

270

never refused an order in her life. She thought about Mortimer. Missed him. Thought about home, her mother, her father, her siblings, and the wonderful folks at the hospital. She might spar and disagree with the physicians at home from time to time, but she'd never had to resort to refusing an order. She tried not to cry, but the tears came. She cried from fatigue and frustration and anger. She felt helpless. Balling up Boovey's orders in her fist, she considered throwing them into the fire.

A friendly voice broke in upon her. "Hello."

He was one of the newest physicians, an easterner like she, but from Boston, Harvard to be exact. Clara quickly dried her eyes. She was ashamed for letting the incompetent fool cause her to lose her temper.

"Is everything all right?"

Clara removed her glasses, pressing her lids as one would use a cork stopper. "Oh, yes." She waved her hand in front of her face, quickly drying her eyes. "The smoke, from the cauldron fires; some overwhelmed me a little."

She stood to attention. She'd heard about this one and respected him.

"You are Nurse Maass."

"I am."

He introduced himself. "Dan Regan." Not *Doctor* Regan, she thought. He extended his hand. "You and your companions are quite famous."

"We are?"

"Oh, yes. Dr. Boovey's team has the best record of any physician in, well, perhaps the entire army."

"You mean Dr. Booby!" She caught herself, holding a hand to her mouth. "Oh, I cannot believe I said that! It was most inappropriate!" She looked left and right.

He smiled. "It's all right, Nurse. We all have a pretty good idea who is running this outfit. We all know Dr. Boovey fairly well. May I offer you a cup of coffee?"

She immediately stiffened. Wished she was wearing Mortimer's ring. Regan had a sense for it. He diffused the uncomfortable moment.

"My wife says a cup of coffee is always a good way to recover from battle, and, Nurse Maass, that look on your face and those what I suspect are rare tears indicate to me that you've had one."

"You are married?"

"Oh, yes, to a wonderful nurse like yourself. It was everything I could do to keep Fabia from running off with me to war.

She's home in Boston."

He was kind, competent and not arrogant like so many in his trade. He looked with knitted brow at Boovey's orders while sipping from a tin mug.

"Was he joking, Nurse Maass?"

"Not that I could tell."

"Well, if you will indulge me." He folded the paper, placing it in his pocket. "I'd like to keep this. I believe General Stricker will be interested to see what kind of work our stellar Dr. Boovey has been carrying out."

Clara beamed. "Oh, Dr. Regan, you may have it with my compliments."

They spent two hours together. In that time, Regan had expertly lanced three boils. He had nothing but compliments for the women's care, nodding and agreeing with each of Clara's assessments.

The men were complimentary. Everyone who could sat up in bed to offer her a greeting. They called her Nurse, and Miss, and some, a few of the fresh ones, Clara, but she did not mind. One old-timer from out west grabbed Regan by the arm, giving it a tug, and said, "Ain't she a peach!"

Regan was disarming, delightful, as comfortable to engage as a kind older brother. She found herself prattling about Mortimer.

Regan smiled. "War suits you, Nurse Maass."

"How so?"

"You're glowing, and you've found your love. Isn't it ironic that, for some, it takes war to really start living?"

"Oh, no bullets have been flying, yet. I imagine the situation will become much worse than all this in time."

"I doubt it, at least for us. Dysentery will knock down more of our men than gunfire." He absentmindedly licked his thumb, using it to wipe a bit of dried blood from her forehead. Immediately sensing the impropriety, he went white.

"Do forgive me, Nurse Maass! You remind me so of my wife, it was sort of a reflex! I should never have touched you so familiarly."

Clara smiled. "You are forgiven." She turned toward him, lifting her face for inspection. "Is there anything else that shouldn't be?"

He recovered. "No, everything is in order."

"The other day, I wiped a streak of stool from Sister Bonaventure's chin. That was rather amusing."

"My wife generally takes a full bath at the end of each work day. Some of the items I've pulled from her hair," he smiled, "would inspire a layperson to gag."

Clara smiled. It was good to have a physician so intimately familiar with the plight of the nurse.

Regan continued. "It's a wonder we aren't all sick, I mean the medical personnel, isn't it?"

"I've heard a nun died, only last week, at a camp in Georgia."

"I did not know that."

"Typhoid fever."

He looked genuinely affected. He wanted a cigarette, reached for his pocket, then hesitated. Clara read his mind. "Please smoke. My fiancé smokes. I'm accustomed to it."

"Thank you."

They walked back to the tents, to Clara's tent, and he waited to be introduced to the rest of this wondrous triad.

Sister Bonaventure extended her hand; Minerva did a sort of little curtsey.

"Ladies, I've been explaining to Nurse Maass that you have the best record of all the camps in perhaps all the army."

Minerva beamed. Perhaps she was a competent nurse after all.

"I have a proposition for you."

Clara took the lead. "Dr. Regan will be replacing Dr. Boovey shortly. It'll be double duty, as he already has an assignment."

"Yes, and I'd like you ladies to superintend all my staff and patients. We'll combine forces, and you will apply your stellar practices to my current caseload." He held up a hand. "I'm afraid all I have to offer is more work and less sleep, but it's all God's work, isn't it?"

Clara could have kissed him. She could not wait to work with Dr. Regan.

It was approaching eleven when they broke for some sleep. Regan again extended his hand. It was evident to Clara, she'd indeed reminded him of his wife.

"Dr. Regan, I want to thank you for, well, treating us, Sister Bonaventure, me, Minerva — especially Minerva — as equals."

Regan smiled, pulling deeply on his cigarette. He laughed a little, blowing smoke over his head. "It was never my intention to treat you as equals, Nurse Maass."

She would not take the bait, instead smiling coyly. "Really?"

"No. We are not equals. Women and men are no more equals than dogs and cats."

"Is that so?"

"Yes." He turned, touching her shoulder. "And I am sorry to have misled you, for women are superior creatures. I am convinced of that."

CHAPTER 19

Sean Whelihan awoke with a start as Francesca sat too close. So close, he could see right into those jade eyes. He coughed to clear the secretions pooling at the back of his throat.

"Good morning."

He nodded.

"I've got to say, I'm not happy, Sean Whelihan."

He wanted to tell her to go to hell. The little bitch was pushing again. Hadn't he given his blessing? Hadn't he done what she'd wanted? He could manage only a nod.

"You know what I mean." She sat back, speaking in little more than a whisper. "Ellen's not convinced that you're sincere."

He regretted that. Of the many regrettable infractions he'd committed in his life, hurting Ellen was the most upsetting to him.

"Yes, now, that's what I expect to see." She leaned forward, placing a palm to his cheek. He, like a spirited puppy, pulled away.

"Oh, I'm not to touch you? That'll prove problematic, when I have to wash you. Clean you after you soil yourself."

He could not stem the tears.

"Sean Whelihan, I know you love animals. Know you treat them better than you do your own children. You'd never hang-tie or beat one of your horses, would you?"

He turned his head in disgust.

"Well, then, don't force me to do such to you." She sprang from her chair. Pressing her face against his, she grasped him about the throat. "Don't force me do anything you'd not do to a horse, Sean Whelihan. Just don't."

She kissed his forehead. "Do you know how to stop me?"

He shrugged.

"Do not treat your family worse than you would a horse."

The epiphany struck him like a lead slug to the brain. He nodded in the affirmative.

"Good. We understand each other. Now you understand me." She wet a wash cloth, using it to wipe his brow. "I'm not evil, Sean Whelihan. Really I'm not. But I will have things right, or kill you trying. I hope that's crystal clear. Remember, I break horses, and with methods that would cause the most hardened cowpuncher to cringe. Remember that, Sean Whelihan."

CHAPTER 20

Rocky watched as the navy's guns pummeled Daiquirí. It fully hit him that he was in a war. A real shooting war. He felt pity for those bombarded, even if they were the enemy.

He'd spent the morning below decks, checking the few horses and mules they'd been allowed, worried over how they were handling the noise of the shelling. He wondered how they'd act when they were outside, and worried more about the horses than the mules, as they were often more skittish to loud noises and unusual experiences.

Being with them reminded Rocky of the anger exhibited by Colonel Roosevelt, who was outraged that his cavalry had no significant herd. He quipped that it was as serious as if they'd forbidden them their rifles.

In a little while, the gangplanks were arranged as tenders came alongside. He watched man after man descend the narrow platform. Everyone was in good cheer. Captain O'Neill looked a bit like a pig on ice as he fumbled with his saber, which kept catching in the ropes. He cursed at what he called "the damned contraption," hanging, like a grappling hook, around his waist.

Eventually, Rocky was the only trooper on board with the navy men, who were by no means pleasant, as they were sick of the animals, as they would say, *"shitting up their ship,"* which was not a fair assessment, as Rocky and Bill McGinty had mucked out the stalls constantly. The horses and mules lived and ate and traveled better than the Rough Riders, thanks to them.

One surly coxswain called out as Rocky had a smoke and watched the fireworks. Throwing the butt into the ocean, he followed the man below decks. It was evidently time to move the animals to shore, and he was curious to see how that was to play out. Certainly the ramps used to move the men were too narrow and steep for the beasts to negotiate.

There were only thirty in all, some horses hand-picked by him and Jonathan for Colonel Roosevelt and a few key officers, and the balance mules. Sweetheart and Honey, the mare mules he'd picked for Woodbury

Kane's and Tiffany's machine guns, and a horse mule named Frank who'd carry the ammunition, stood close by.

The coxswain had opened a cargo door to bright sunlight, and the sound of explosions overhead streamed in, which did nothing to improve the mood of the nervous beasts.

The seaman glared at Rocky and nodded toward the opening and blue water below.

Puzzled, Rocky looked on. "What?"

"Get 'em goin', Trooper. They ain't doin' your Rough Riders any good standin' here, shittin' up my hold."

"Where's the ramp? Where're the barges?"

The seaman sneered. "Hell, son, this ain't the White Star line," and, with that, he cracked a horse, standing close to the edge, on its backside. The animal skittered, losing its fore footing; it tumbled into the sea.

Soon animals, like lemmings off a cliff, followed as the sailor laughed with puerile glee.

Rocky turned to him in disbelief. "You son of a bitch." He watched the animals bob and kick, attempting to gain their bearings. Some swam toward the open Caribbean Sea. "Jesus Christ!"

Rocky urged Sweetheart, his favorite bell mare, beckoning her to follow. Miraculously she did, and they fell for what seemed an eternity, he landing in the water beside her.

She whimpered and blew seawater from her nose while he mounted, holding onto the bridle in one hand, a fistful of mane in the other. He whispered into her ear, urging her away from the ship and the others, falling like giant meteorites, one after another all around him.

He watched Frank and Honey glide to shore. At least they'd make land without incident. Already a few of the horses had climbed onto the beach, shaking like dogs as several troopers converged upon them. They waved to Rocky, signaling all was well.

He turned his attention to the others. They'd made incredible progress and were more than a hundred yards beyond the ship, heading into deep water, into nothingness, into deep blue oblivion.

Rocky whispered again into his girl's ear. "Come on, Sweetheart, come on my girl, let's turn 'em, let's turn 'em, my baby. Get 'em to shore and safety."

Sweetheart kicked hard. She was, to Rocky's astonishment, a natural, as this was the first time she'd been in water deeper than a stream. They had done well until the first fin appeared.

Rocky heard the coxswain call out behind them. "Shark!"

And soon the water around him abounded with the dark fins. Sweetheart saw them as well and gave a little desperate whine, the instinct of imminent danger washing over mule and rider equally.

The sailors fired their Lee rifles, bullets whizzing all around them. A few found their marks, which did nothing but add to the frenzy. Blood leaked from the dead, permeating the water with the attractive liquid; scores more were drawn to them. He felt the first hit, and Sweetheart was momentarily pulled under. Three more struck at her hind legs and underbelly. Rocky went for his Colt, finding nothing in the unsecured flap holster; the impact had sent his six-shooter to the sea's bottom. Pulling his Bowie, he slashed at the doll-like eyes as the terrible creatures emerged to take bites of both of them.

He turned her, swimming her to shore, as the errant horses were nowhere in sight — either drowned or eaten, he did not know; to further pursue them pointless.

The coxswain shouted after him, no longer bearing the smug expression. He was pale as parchment. He fired again and again. "Swim for shore, Trooper. We'll cover you!"

But it was for naught. Sweetheart pulled herself onto land, and Rocky followed. To his horror, loops of gut, like freshly packed sausages, trailed behind her. He could see white bone and sinew where the monsters had savaged her.

She shook and stood uneasily, whimpering when Rocky held her head to his cheek.

"I'm sorry, Sweetheart. I'm so sorry."

He cried as blood pumped from the severed arteries of her legs. He knew she'd not survive. There was nothing anyone could do for her. He searched for a weapon as a soldier approached. It was the sergeant who'd lambasted him an age ago in Woodbury's tent.

"What's this all about, Trooper?"

Another man spoke up. "Sharks."

"Why's this man blubbering?" He looked Rocky over. "He's not wounded."

"He's the tender, the mule man. He and this mare where trying to corral the horses. Some of 'em swam to sea, Sergeant."

Rocky turned to him desperately. "Give me your weapon, Sergeant. Need to put her outta her misery. Please give me your six-shooter."

"You need to take hold of your senses, young Trooper. Stop that crying! This is the army. This is no place for men who blubber over beasts of burden."

Rocky pulled his Bowie. "Shut your goddamned mouth."

The sergeant retreated, hands up, palms forward. "Easy there, Trooper."

"Easy, nothin'. Give me your goddamned Colt, or I'll run you through with this knife. I swear to God and all these men, I'll run you through and then kill myself, you son of a bitch. Give me your Colt, goddamn you. Give me your Colt this goddamned minute!"

Sweetheart stumbled. She would not live long. She looked into Rocky's eyes as if to say, "I trusted you."

The sergeant could not let this insult and breech of conduct pass unaddressed.

"You need to calm yourself, Trooper. The beast'll die in due course." He looked her over. "She's bleeding out. No need to waste valuable cartridges on such nonsense." He looked for a corporal and found him. "Corporal Jones, take down this man's name. He'll be reported for insubordination." He turned his head from side to side. "I've never seen anything like it. Crying over a goddamned mule! Hell, one of your officers, Captain O'Neill, jumped overboard after a couple of niggers; couldn't save them, but no one shed any tears over that! I'll not have . . . ."

A pistol shot interrupted the sergeant's

diatribe as Colonel Roosevelt helped Sweetheart to the ground. He holstered his weapon and turned to Rocky, giving him a fatherly pat on the shoulder. "There now, Trooper Killebrew, I've put the poor creature out of its misery." He turned on the sergeant. "Who are you?"

"Tomlinson, sir." He saluted with little enthusiasm as the realization hit him that the colonel was not of the regular army.

Roosevelt adjusted his spectacles, pushing them back onto the bridge of his nose. "Why are you harassing my men?"

"Was assigned, sir, by General Williams, to help, sir."

"Help do what?"

"Add a level of military bearing to the, ah, your . . . begging your pardon, Colonel, your volunteers."

"Nonsense." Roosevelt called out. "Captain O'Neill?"

"Yes, sir." Buckey O'Neill, still soaking and not a little disappointed from his earlier adventure and failed attempt at rescuing the buffalo soldiers, stepped briskly toward the colonel. He frowned at the mutilated carcass at his boss's feet.

Roosevelt pointed at the sergeant. "Send this man back to the regular army. I'll not have such a rude and obnoxious fellow interfering with our men." He turned to the small gang of troopers who'd gathered around. "You men, find a litter or a board, or *something*. I want this mule buried with full military honors."

He patted Rocky on the shoulder as the lad sat, cradling Sweetheart's head, relaxed in death in the young man's lap. "You stay with her, Trooper. See they do a proper job of it." He addressed the crowd. "Mules are special creatures. You remember that, you men. You remember, the mule was prized by the pharaohs. President Lincoln himself worried as much over the welfare of army mules as for his men in blue. Honor the mule, gentlemen. Respect and honor the mule."

He pulled his six-shooter, replacing the spent shell casing with a fresh cartridge, re-holstering it once again. He nodded energetically. "Captain O'Neill, let's see what we can do about shaping this invasion force into some semblance of order."

The sergeant, furious, spoke up. "Hold on a minute, *sir*!"

Roosevelt turned, looking the man up and down. "Yes?"

"That trooper threatened a non-commissioned officer, sir. I'll not have it! I'll have justice or . . ."

Buckey O'Neill closed in. Towering inches from the man's face he glared down at him. "Or *what?*" He absentmindedly fiddled with the grip of his six-shooter.

Roosevelt interjected. "It would be wise, Sergeant, if you were to return to your unit and forget what happened here today. My Rough Riders are the finest fellows, but they are frontiersmen and are sometimes rather wild." He waved as if shooing a fly. "For your own safety, young fellow, return to your unit and leave us to our work." He turned once again to O'Neill. "Captain, follow me. I have a plan."

Jonathan was given a little time to check on his brother, who sat, exhausted and spent both physically and emotionally, next to the mound of sand covering his mule.

The other troopers had been good to him. Even the Texan who'd clobbered him when he'd remonstrated the fellow for calling Woodbury and the others the *la de da* boys had offered him condolences.

"I'm mighty sorry about Sweetheart, Rocky."

McGinty arrived with fresh coffee. He understood how affected Rocky would be by losing one of his charges.

He grinned at Jonathan. "Old Rock swam

a good many of 'em in." He patted Rocky on the shoulder. "Didn't you, Rock?"

"Saved Frank and Honey, and Little Texas."

McGinty twisted a cigarette for his partner. "That's one a' your geldings, ain't it, boys?"

Jonathan nodded. "A pony."

"How's it you named him Texas?"

Both lads looked at each other and shrugged. It was the old man's idea, and they could not understand why he'd named it such. Sean Whelihan hated everything and everyone associated with the lone star state.

McGinty looked at the tip of his cigarette. "Maybe 'cause Arizona would take too long to say."

Jonathan smiled. "Yeah, maybe. But then again, it isn't as long as *Rain-in-the-Face.* Who the hell thought that one up?"

Rocky looked up. "Did he come in? Last I saw, he was swimming, hell-bent-for-leather, out to the open ocean."

"No, Rocky." Jonathan looked at his hands. "He didn't, Brother. Sorry to say, he didn't make it."

McGinty turned to Rocky. "Rock, you look wore out, old son." He held a hand to his partner's forehead. "You feel all right?"

And, as if the question triggered the response, Rocky collapsed.

CHAPTER 21

Las Guásimas is what he heard Colonel Roosevelt call it. He found himself under the command of Hamilton Fish, who was a splendid sergeant. Rocky wondered why the la-de-da boy had not been offended by not receiving a commission as a proper officer. Fish should have been, at the least, a lieutenant.

There was no stock to attend, and both he and Bill McGinty were no more important than ordinary troopers with no troop, at least as far as the four-legged kind was concerned. They were common foot soldiers, which gave Bill plenty to talk about. Though he was fit, McGinty did not appreciate marching.

Rocky, ever vigilant, scanned the jungle for any glimpse of movement, for any enemy activity as they trudged along the most unforgiving piece of land in all of Cuba. Every so often, he'd spy Jonathan, running hither and yon as if he were competing with Louis in a Hopi tournament.

Rocky's headache was better at least. Someone suggested, with that dip in the ocean, that perhaps he'd caught the yellow jack. He'd be the first one to become infected, and it sounded like a terrible way to die. As one old soldier told him, it was days of horrible pain, then vomiting black blood, and then you died. Rocky did not want to die in such a way, and after a good night's sleep, convinced himself that he was just plain tired.

At least there were no horses or mules in the line of fire, which was as much a relief to Rocky as it was a point of contention for Colonel Roosevelt. It infuriated his boss, and Rocky'd not seen the colonel really riled, but when the army told them that they had no right to pack or riding animals the colonel lost his composure. And every time Rocky or Bill or any of the other fellows would find some, they'd be confiscated as well. It was as if the Rough Riders did not count.

The colonel turned three shades of red over all that, and one fellow was certain he heard the proper New York gentleman curse a time or two.

Sergeant Fish turned and looked at him

and then Bill McGinty. He cast his gaze forward to Thomas Isbell on point. The half-breed Cherokee, whom everyone feared and respected, was picking his way along a path that forced them all into single file. He knelt, holding up some barbed wire that had recently been cut.

They were close to the enemy, so close the tension was palpable, hanging in the stagnant heavy air like poisonous gas enveloping them, the heat nearly unbearable, and so humid that sweat leaked from every pore of Rocky's body. He was drenched all the time.

He fiddled with the safety on his rifle. It was a slick one, action smooth as butter, but not as good as his Winchester back home, as, he agreed with Jonathan, it kicked too damned much and was ponderous to reload. He could make his seventy-three sing when he wanted to. Jonathan said it was a waste of ammo to shoot so fast, but his brother could not deny it. Rocky was quick with a lever gun. Quick *and* accurate.

At least he shot the Krag well, and it had smokeless cartridges, unlike what those Negroes in the Tenth were issued. That was curious to him: the thought that he, that the Rough Riders, a bunch of volunteers, would have better equipment than the regular army. There was most certainly a pecking order, and Rocky was learning a little about it and perhaps why his adoptive father was so vexed by the bureaucratic nonsense of both the government and the military.

That all seemed a bit childish to Rocky. On one hand, the Rough Riders had the best gear; on the other, they were constantly referred to as the *red-haired stepchildren* of the enterprise. At every turn, at every opportunity, regular soldiers did their best to spite or belittle them or push them out. At every turn, their provisions were pilfered, their stock taken from them for more important business. No wonder the colonel was constantly pushing them forward. If it were not for Colonel Roosevelt, they'd have been relegated to the rear of the army. They'd have ended up a mere footnote in history, and, while Rocky was no glory-hound, he wanted all this suffering and misery and deprivation to count for *something.*

It seemed that the concept that all men were created equal was true only to a point when it came to such institutions, and Rocky was beginning to understand why Sean Whelihan was so bitter about them volunteering. Just treatment seemed haphazard and purposefully uneven.

He nearly stepped on Bill McGinty's heel

when they all froze. Isbell, as if lining up a shot on an elk, stood peering into the jungle. Snapping his rifle to his shoulder, he fired into a treetop. The first Spaniard Rocky had seen since arriving in Cuba thudded to the ground, not ten yards distant.

It seemed a hundred guns opened upon them, and bullets whizzed like angry bees all around. He watched McGinty run to Isbell as the Indian had taken a ball to the hip, spinning him about until the Cherokee faced his sergeant.

Fish turned to the men, beckoning them forward.

At that moment, many yards to the east, Jonathan Whelihan stood before the colonel, awaiting his command, when a diminutive German bullet zipped through him like a lightning bolt.

He spun as well, catching himself as he dropped to all fours. Roosevelt looked on, then up ahead for the sharpshooter who'd delivered the shot. Another round kicked dirt at the colonel's feet while he calmly helped his runner to cover.

"How bad's it, Colonel?" Jonathan was curious as it did not hurt as much as he'd imagined. Though he'd never been shot, he thought somehow it would feel different. The colonel examined him as one a child whose diaper needed a change.

"Struck in the gluteus maximus, Trooper Thomson." He squinted. "Interesting, four bullet wounds with only one shot."

"The what, sir?"

"Gluteus maximus." Roosevelt pushed his glasses to the bridge of his nose. "Lucky it was one of those metal encased Mauser projectiles. Why, if they were using the Dum Dum, Trooper Thomson, I dare say, you'd not have anything left upon which to sit."

"Is that so, sir?" Jonathan prepared himself for another history lesson, evidently on the finer points of military accoutrement.

"Oh, well, of course. The Dum Dum, invented by a British officer."

"You really need to speak English, Colonel."

"Dum Dum is actually a Bengali word, Thomson. It means —"

"No, Colonel, I mean Glutinus matimus or whatever you said."

"Gluteus maximus. Your ass, Trooper, your ass. You've been shot in your ass. Well, actually *through* your ass."

Jonathan suppressed a grin. Was vexed by the colonel's strange vernacular. Gluteus maximus. What a war! He nodded to Marshall, who fired into the trees. "You owe Marshall four quarters, sir."

"For what?"

"You said *ass* four times, and you weren't talking of donkeys. That's cursing in my book, sir."

"Duly noted, Trooper Thomson. Can you stand?"

"Think so, sir."

"Can you walk?"

"Oh, sure, I'll be fine, sir." He observed the blood oozing through his khaki trouser leg. "I'll be all right; bullet went through."

He attempted to put weight on his right leg, the side with the last exit wound, and immediately buckled. "Maybe not, sir."

"Report to the hospital, Trooper. Crawl if you must, but you are no use to me here. Get patched up, then stand picket there. These murderous Spaniards cannot be trusted to honor the sanctity of a relief station."

Roosevelt watched Marshall work his old Springfield. "Did you kill him?"

"Think so, sir."

"Capital! Take up Trooper Thomson's Krag and stop using that damned old trapdoor. You'll attract the attention of every Spaniard within a mile with that smoke."

"Yes, sir." He nodded to Jonathan, offering his relic as a crutch. "Don't like to give her up. She's done me good service for a lotta years, but the colonel's right."

Jonathan took it and smiled. "Sir, that'll be another quarter."

Roosevelt nodded. "Go away, Trooper Thomson. I've a battle to fight."

Rocky needed no encouragement from anyone. Seeing one of his pards hit infuriated him. He rushed abreast of Fish, looking ahead for targets. When he saw flashes among the thick vegetation ahead, he shouldered his Krag and fired at the flames produced by the enemy's Mausers.

He called to McGinty, who had the Cherokee on his feet. The Indian looked himself over and went about his business killing Spaniards. He refused to be removed from the line. Instead, he hobbled forward, his rifle at the ready, picking targets.

By day's end, Isbell had been shot in the neck, hip, and thumb. He'd not allow himself to be removed to the field hospital in Siboney until the next morning.

McGinty called out. "Come on, Rock, there's Spaniards in them trees up yonder. Let's light 'em up, old son!"

Rocky turned to the football player, as he would his old father for permission, at the moment one bullet's strike took down a fellow trooper and his beloved sergeant.

"Bill, Sergeant Fish is hit!" He dropped his rifle, grabbing the fallen young la-de-da boy in his arms. It was no use. Hamilton Fish was dead inside the span of a minute, a bullet through the heart.

Rocky turned toward the enemy, all fury, when another Mauser ball hit him above the brow of the right eye.

Chapter 22

Sean Whelihan awoke with a start, knowing in his bones that something terrible had happened. He tried to move but was weaker than when he'd retired.

He squirmed, attempting to move from the wet sheets, as he'd again lost control of his bladder. He heard the clock chime seven. It would be ten o'clock in Cuba. Were they fighting? Had his boy been hit? The thought of it sickened him.

He heard movement in the parlor. Someone was awake. Ellen? Francesca? He hoped one of the servants would come to tend to him. He felt so ashamed when either his girl or his future daughter-in-law cleaned his wrecked and soiled body.

He found he could roll. If he rolled with enough energy, could he eject himself from bed? Would the fall be enough to kill him? Fracture his skull? Break his neck? Did he honestly want to die?

The baby would come soon. How long? Francesca knew she was with child, but her belly had not yet started protruding. How many more months — six, seven? He'd like to live long enough to see his grandchild.

Would he come out dark as a nigger, as Francesca had said? That was silly. Preposterous. That little bitch invented that to vex him. Would it matter? Would he care? Had he really ever cared?

He thought about his Ellen lying with the Hopi. Was it so repulsive? Did he care so much? Not really, if he thought on it. How did Ellen arrive at such a conclusion? Why was he such a tyrant that what he thought would so profoundly affect her? The thought shamed him. Francesca was right. He was kinder to dumb animals than he was to his own flesh and blood.

The newest housekeeper, little Pilar, softly padded, barefoot, into the room. These poor Indians. Most had no shoes, would not wear them if they had. She smiled when she saw that he was awake. She was beautiful, long raven hair straight as sawgrass growing on the bank of a river.

She deftly removed his nightshirt, bathing him, always with dignity. In a little while he was lying in a pristine bed. She left him to rest a little longer.

He watched her leave and remembered that first year in Arizona. Wasn't it the Indians who helped him? The Navajos. The horse breeders. They did not need to help him, but they had. One had even died because of him.

Well, that was not actually true. He died, in Sean's company, but it was not Sean's fault.

That terrible day when he and his Indian friend Hosteen Redshirt had come home of a late morning after riding all night, to horses tied outside the place, what they thought at first were the gypsy-like Comancheros from the south, up to do some honest trade. But they were *not* Comancheros. They were a pair of devils from back East. White men who'd behaved worse than savages.

One shot Redshirt dead as he dismounted and then Sean Whelihan in the hip. He dropped as if pole-axed, stunned until his wife called out, bringing him to his senses.

"*Dó, m'fhear céile!* There are two, my husband!"

And he, like a wild bull, forgetting the searing pain imparted by the heavy rifle slug, dove headfirst through the front window of his homestead. Took another bullet in the shoulder before killing them both, one with his six-shooter, the other with his hands.

No, he had no pick on dark people. He thought about Francesca's lecture, her threats. A child of twenty, a *woman*, had broken him.

His father would not have been broken. His father would have fought her. Spit that mush right back at her, right in her face. He felt his dead body. He was too tired to fight like that. To what end? To prove he could not be broken? To prove that he was tougher than a young woman?

Francesca had always, at least secretly, amused him. Why secretly? Why could he not let them know what he'd thought, thought of her, of life, of how much he cared for them? Why could he have not counted his blessings before her threats of assassination?

He drifted, then awoke to his wife's lilting voice, happy and energetic and full of love. His dear Hortense. Was he dreaming of her again? He shook himself, awoke fully, and listened to the sound, the happy voice carried on the breeze over his head, through the open window from the veranda, where his Ellen and future son-in-law sat and conversed.

It was an engineering phenomenon, a

secret he shared with no one. The construction of the veranda, like a whispering gallery in a cathedral, allowed the voices to carry straight to his ear. He listened in on many late-night conversations that way: Rocky whining, Jonathan scheming, Ellen reading poetry to herself aloud, the gossip of the washer women about all the scandals and intrigues on the ranch.

It was Ellen, and he'd never heard her voice this way, never heard Ellen sound so much like his wife when she was alive, always happy and gay. There was no other way to describe it than elated. Ellen elated. His heart fluttered at the realization. He frankly could not remember the last time he'd heard Ellen so happy.

He craned his neck to eavesdrop. Louis's voice not so plain as he was always such a soft-talker, Sean Whelihan constantly had to ask him to speak up, repeat himself. But none of that mattered now; it was his girl's responses that he wanted to know, wanted so desperately to hear.

"Yes, she'd have his children, yes, once all this was over and Jonathan returned, she'd go with him to serve the church, serve the Indians as a missionary. Yes, she'd go wherever he went, do what he'd like, as long as they were together, carrying out God's work, helping the Indians."

He wiped the tears from his eyes as he listened to the happy planning of a loving couple's life. The excitement, the anticipation, not unlike his conversations with Hortense those many years ago when she'd convinced him to move west, to the wilds of Arizona, to escape the demons and crowds. Hortense knew what was good for him.

He fumbled for the bell, rang it awkwardly, beating it against the headboard more than ringing it, desperately, with all the energy he could muster. He had to tell Ellen what he'd heard, give his blessing, in earnest this time, from the heart, assure her that he'd do anything to ensure her dreams would become reality.

CHAPTER 23

Rocky's wound was cleaned and he did not look as ghastly as when he'd first arrived. The malaria was the most severe of his maladies, the delirium, the shivering so wracking his body, he had to be tied into bed.

Minerva took him on as her personal case, of course, as she was deemed immune.

She looked to Clara and the Sister for advice, as his fits where worse than any she'd encountered.

Dr. Church prescribed laudanum, and that seemed about the only thing to calm him, which was fortunate, as the battle of Las Guásimas had given them brisk business. They did not need the added stress of an out-of-control madman on their hands.

By early evening she found him sleeping and took the opportunity to replace the dressing, now saturated, as Rocky had leaked a lot of blood.

It was likely not the best strategy, as her ministrations awakened him, the fever once again eliciting the mania.

He shouted into Minerva's face. "Sergeant Fish is hit! Sergeant Fish is hit!" He shook her by the shoulders. "Come on, we got to help Sergeant Fish!"

"It's all right, Trooper Killebrew, it's all right. It's all over. You're safe."

This seemed to bring him from his trance, though it did not improve his attitude. He looked about with wild, unthinking eyes, turning on Minerva with a renewed savagery. He scowled, literally spitting the vitriol. "Don't you touch me, you filthy nigger!" He freed an arm and backhanded her; she tumbled over the man dying in the cot next to him.

He was up and running amok, blood once again pouring freely from his wound. Three troopers tried to contain him, too weak in their infirm state to be of any help. Sister Bonaventure took action. Manhandling him, she pulled Rocky into her arms, pinning his flailing limbs by his sides. She spoke, softly, inches from his face. "There, there, young Rocky, there, there, none of that."

He stopped momentarily, trying to focus, as quickly slipping into another rage. Struggling, hyperventilating, he attempted to free himself from her grasp. "Take your hands off me, you *bitch!*"

Sister Bonaventure would have none of it. She motioned to Clara for the hypodermic, but even a dose of morphia could not calm him. He continued to flail.

"Oh well." The nun shrugged, then punched him across the face.

This worked, and Rocky was soon resting in his cot. Sister Bonaventure patted him on his reddening cheek, whispering into his ear. "There, there, lad. Sleep it off. Everything will be better in the morning."

The men watched, jaws agape, as she helped Minerva with the rest of her charges.

By evening they'd had all the wounded accounted for, and there were many.

Dr. Church was most responsible for that, spending the day running back and forth, from front line to his makeshift field hospital, personally carrying wounded men on his back.

Jonathan limped in late, as he could not bring himself to retire until all his boys were fed and supplied with water. His backside was swollen around the bullet wounds, the pain beginning to make it impossible for him to walk.

He saw Clara, and his heart stopped.

She was beautiful, splattered with blood, tearing off a chunk of hardtack with the corner of her mouth. He sauntered up to her. She did not notice him, too distracted by her exhaustion.

"Hello."

She peered up through blood-stained glasses, evidently in no mood for a flirtation. He continued nonetheless, too smitten to read her attitude and apparent lack of inclination toward romantic frisson.

Pulling her glasses from her face, he cleaned them. She let him, too spent to slap him.

He held them up to the light. "There, much better." He smiled. She did not reciprocate, instead taking the spectacles from his proffered hand, as if none of it ever happened.

She blinked twice through the pristine lenses. "Why are you here?" she demanded.

"Three reasons." He grinned wider. "No, that's not right; let's see . . . six reasons, ma'am."

"Nurse."

"Beg your pardon, Nurse." He cocked his head in curiosity. "How's it lady nurses are hereabouts?"

"A mistake about which you need not

concern yourself. What six reasons?"

"Been shot in the rump." He turned, pointing to his backside. "Four wounds. Been told by Colonel Roosevelt that I'm to guard the camp while I get bandaged up, and I'm here to see my brother Rocky, Rocky Killebrew."

He counted on his fingers, offering a Cheshire cat smile. "Yep, that's six reasons, ma'am, I mean, Nurse."

"I'll take care of the wounds, Nurse Maass." Jonathan turned, gazing in awe at the massive, black-cloaked woman towering over them.

Sister Bonaventure led Jonathan by the arm. "Come with me, lad. We'd better have those holes attended to before they become mortified."

She delivered him to a cot in the corner, the only one to offer a modicum of privacy. "Let's take a look, Trooper . . . ?"

"Oh, I'm mighty rude." He pulled the hat from his head. "Trooper Whelihan, ma'am, I mean, ah, Nurse, I mean, nun . . ."

"Sister. You may address me as 'sister.'"

He looked over his shoulder as his savior attended to him.

"How's it look, Sister?"

"Not so terrible, lad. You are lucky." She considered the dried blood staining the seat of his trousers. "When did you receive these?"

"Oh, don't know." He shrugged. Knew full well but he did not want to appear a braggart. "I kind of got caught up, ma'am. Colonel told me report here, to guard the hospital, but the boys . . . well, ma'am, it was sure hot up on the line. Hot from gunfire, and hot from the danged heat around here. At first, I couldn't even walk. Then Dr. Church, he stopped, gave me a dose of morphine. After about an hour I was good." He smiled through gritted teeth, resisting the urge to cry out as she doused his wound with disinfectant. "That stuff smarts."

"It does, and I'm sorry, lad, but it will help the healing process. It will, hopefully keep the wound from becoming mortified."

"Mortified?"

"Infected. Gangrenous, my boy. Gangrenous."

He surveyed the tent as he stood to give the nun better access to the wound. He cast his gaze at the pretty nurse with the freshly cleaned glasses working on another invalid.

"You all seem to have everything in order here, ma'am." He pointed. "Who, may I ask, is the nurse with the golden hair and spectacles?"

"That's Nurse Maass, from New Jersey. She's engaged to be married to a handsome lawyer from New York, a volunteer, a captain." She considered Jonathan, who was evidently undaunted by her none-too-subtle remark. She continued. "They are madly in love with each other."

She smiled to herself. Young love. It was always, to Sister Bonaventure, thoroughly gratifying to behold, even when doomed to failure.

"How's my brother, ma'am? Rocky Killebrew. Took a glancing bullet to the head, at least that's what I heard. Old Rocky, he's a hard-headed son-of-a-gun!" He dropped his gaze to the tent floor. "Beg your pardon, ma'am. Should not say such words to a lady. Colonel Roosevelt would certainly charge me a quarter."

She ignored his apology. She'd heard worse in her time than son-of-a-gun. "Your brother is fine, Trooper. Fever will be the challenge for him. Malaria. But Nurse Trumbull is taking good care of him."

"Another beauty. You all sure have some handsome nurses, ma'am, present company included." He smiled bashfully.

"And you have a silver tongue, young Trooper. A silver, albeit forked tongue."

"Not a liar, ma'am, I mean Nurse, I mean

Sister. Not a liar."

He held a hand to his head. "Ma'am, don't know what's come over me. All of a sudden, I don't feel too well."

She controlled his fall to the cot, removed his boots and gun belt, then went about the business of caring for her many charges.

CHAPTER 24

Roosevelt eyed Jonathan with suspicion. "Why are you not back at the hospital, Trooper Thomson?"

"Oh, I'm all right, sir." He cast his gaze behind him, to his trousers, puffy from the heavy dressing applied by the nun.

Roosevelt spoke into a map he was reading. "We shall see." He remembered something. "You are the one who supplied me with Little Texas, aren't you, Trooper Thomson? You and your brother, what's his name . . . oh, right, Killebrew. How is your brother? I heard he took a round to the head."

"It only skimmed him, sir. He's all right with the wound, but now he's down with the malaria. But, yes, sir, we did provide Little Texas from my father's ranch. He's a fine beast, ain't he?"

"Isn't he." Roosevelt eyed him again. "Why is he named for Texas when he's from

Arizona?"

Jonathan suppressed a laugh. "Don't know, sir. Me and my brother and Bill McGinty were just talking about that. My father named him. I guess there's too many sylla— , sylla—"

"Syllables, Trooper." He gave Jonathan a sideways glance. "You need to bone up on your elocution, young man. You are a smart fellow, and there is no excuse for a smart and healthy American to speak like an ignoramus or a foreigner." He nodded. "You remember that, Trooper. When we return home, I want to hear that you are working on your education. Every man needs an education; it's not exclusively for lawyers and engineers and the like. It is for every man to take up the mantel of responsibility to be as educated as possible."

Jonathan grinned. The colonel sounded a little like his sister. Ellen was always after him to do more reading and study. "It's . . . well, there aren't many books, you know, in Arizona, sir." He thought of Ellen again, with her impressive library. He continued the lie, nonetheless. "School never had much, and, well, no libraries to speak of."

"Twaddle!" The colonel turned, looking a little annoyed. "That's no excuse at all, young man!" He wagged a finger at Jonathan. "Do not blame your environment, Trooper Thomson. Do not expect the government or society or even your friends or family to pull you up. That's why we have bootstraps, young Trooper. Bootstraps to elevate ourselves, on our own. Look at Captain O'Neill. He's a man who has spent most of his life in a rustic environment, yet he can speak intelligently on many subjects: philosophy, history, art, and politics." Roosevelt knitted his brow. "Even if he *is* a Georgist, he's still a bright and well-read man. No, Trooper Thomson, do not fall victim to such an excuse. It's up to you to improve your position in this world. Remember that, young man, and you will go far."

"Yes, sir. I guess it would be kind of silly to name a horse Arizona. Too many syllables, as you say."

"Well, perhaps." Roosevelt stood for a moment, cleaning his spectacles. "Trooper Thomson, how were you treated in the hospital?"

"Oh, well, sir. Those nurses are some wonderful ladies, sir."

"Ladies! Good Lord! Ladies, in combat! Preposterous!"

"Yes, sir. Kind of thought the same, but

they were there sure enough. Three of them."

Roosevelt turned, calling into his tent. "Marshall, fetch me Captain O'Neill, at the double!"

In short order Buckey O'Neill was saluting the colonel.

"Captain O'Neill, what do you know of women in the hospital?"

"Oh, yes, sir. There are many French nuns, and some American nuns as well, in Siboney."

"No, no, I mean to our rear, directly behind our lines, Captain. In our field hospital."

O'Neill cleared his throat, evidently found guilty of his own little subterfuge. "Well, sir, it appears that, yes, there are three nurses: a young woman from New Jersey, a nun from Baltimore, and an immune Negro from somewhere in the Carolinas."

"Why, Captain, is this so, and why have I not been apprised of it? Does Jim Church know this?"

"Ah, he does, Colonel. It seems the ladies were sent in error. They were first sent to Siboney and then somehow ended up with us Rough Riders."

"And did he not know I'd not have such a thing! It is out of the question to have females so close to the line. My God, man, it's bad enough to have American women in Cuba at all, at least until the savage Latins have been conquered. No telling what they are capable of." He glared at Marshall and Jonathan, as if they were conspirators. "What if the Spaniards flanked us? What if they'd been victims of sappers and infiltrators? Given the Latin mentality toward females, it is preposterous, Captain. Tell Church that these women are to be evacuated at once. And I don't mean to Siboney. I mean back to Florida!"

"Sir, with all due respect, Colonel, and in recognition of your military rank, Dr. Church said that he'd personally shoot any man or men or detail who so much as laid a finger on any of his nurses."

Roosevelt stood, brow knitted. His face flushed. "He said that? Church? My good man Jim Church said that?"

"He did, sir, and he's strapped on a Colt. He said that he'd commit high treason before he'd let his nurses be taken. I'm sorry, Colonel, I know it's not correct protocol, but Dr. Church has been without sleep since we landed. He spent all day carrying wounded back to his hospital, then operating on them. I don't see, sir, what we can do with him."

"No, no, you are correct. Church is a good man, and I don't believe he's bluffing." Roosevelt turned to Jonathan. "Trooper Thomson, you are no longer fit to be a runner. Return to the field hospital. Arm yourself, and protect those ladies. Understood, Trooper?"

Jonathan snapped to, offering an impressive salute. "Capital, sir!"

CHAPTER 25

Rocky felt better. The quinine was working, and a couple of days in a dry cot and some hot food had done wonders. Nurse Trumbull recommended a stroll to stretch his legs. He felt surprisingly well and at that moment realized he'd had no spirits for nearly a week.

Most of the past days were a blur, but he remembered his shameful behavior toward Minnie. Remembered it every time he encountered her, especially when he saw how hard she worked. It was as if another being, some otherworldly spirit, had possessed his mind. He felt mighty low to think about it while he wandered.

He could not believe it as he considered a pair of Cuban mules, standing in a field.

It had been that way ever since the rain and the incessant traffic on the primitive roads leading from the ships to the front. Mules would become mired. Even twisting their tails could not budge them, and the exasperated muleskinners would be forced to strip the poor creatures of their cargo and leave them to work themselves out of the muck.

The land was literally teaming with mules that had escaped the mud and now wandered freely, too wily to be captured. Of course, Rocky's luck was different in this respect. He knew how to woo them.

One animal was wounded superficially, around the region of the withers. The other was in good shape. They'd be good for packing, as Rocky was certain he could rig the wounded one so as to avoid any straps on the affected area.

A boy and girl plodded up to him. They could not have been more than six or seven. They looked him over, then smiled.

"Buenos dias." He nodded and wondered if they'd know anything of the mules.

"Go to hell, Yankee ass face. Good morning."

Rocky turned to face them, all incredulity. He looked at the little girl, who nodded and smiled. Neither could be filthier.

"Kiss ass, Yankee! Give us cigarette. Good morning."

Rocky admonished them in Spanish. "That's no way for little ones to talk. *Muy travieso,* very naughty."

They shrugged. The boy spoke up. "Give us cigarette, Yankee soldier man."

"I'll give you a horehound candy if you tell me about the mules. Who owns them?"

The boy turned his head side to side. "No candy. Cigarette! I'll tell you for the cigarette."

The mules would not budge, and, as Rocky did not know either one's name, he thought the whole enterprise might be lost. He twisted a smoke, handing it to the boy, who smelled the end, enjoying the odor of the Yankee tobacco.

The child nodded again. "*Y otro!* And another." He pointed to his companion.

Rocky complied, handing another to the girl. It was rather thoughtful of them. Little kids passing up candy for cigarettes to give to their pa.

"*A la luz de un cigarillo!* And the light."

Rocky handed them a box of matches. They were soon smoking like gamblers.

"My God!" He attempted to confiscate the smokes, but the children ran from him, laughing as if engaged in a game of dodge ball.

"Go to hell, Yankee shit ass! Good morning."

"Okay, okay." He held up a hand in surrender. "I won't take your cigarettes. Tell me the names, *niños*."

"Carl!" The boy threw his head back, laughing when the wounded mule turned in response to the lad's pronouncement. The animal certainly knew his name. Carl, not Carlos. That was right funny.

Rocky spoke to Carl, soothingly, in Spanish. The animal responded as all mules were wont to do for the wrangler.

He turned to the children. "And the other?"

"Carlita."

"Carl and Carlita." Rocky scratched his head. If the mules had not responded so quickly, he'd have been certain the children were joshing him.

He patted them. "Ain't you a nice pair of boys." He took hold of the hemp ropes hanging from each animal's halter. "Come on with me. Time you were mended. And you, too, Carlita. Colonel Roosevelt'll be happy to see the both of you, sure enough."

The children soon were beside him, walking along as if they were on a Sunday outing. "Yankee shit hand, we *muy hambriento,* very hungry."

"I bet you are." He looked them both over. He imagined how they'd be received in camp. "Come on with me. I'll find you some grub."

He turned to face them. "I'm Rocky. What's your names?"

They looked at each other and then at Rocky. The boy spoke first. "Carl."

"Is that so?" Rocky maintained a stone countenance. "And how about you, little girl?"

"I am Carlita."

"Well, bless my soul. Four Carls! That's easy enough to remember."

They whispered to each other and laughed again.

"Well, come on, Carl and Carlita. Let's get Carl and Carlita back for some veterinary. We got a war to fight."

The thought of the Carls hauling the machine guns pained him, as it reminded him of his dead sergeant. Hamilton Fish, the gentle giant, the man who taught him about the Tiffany Colts. The man who'd treated him so well. The man who loved animals as much as, or possibly more than, even he himself did, perhaps even more than Sean Whelihan.

He smiled a little at the memory of how impressed Fish had been when Rocky trained the mules to lie down on command. That would come in handy in battle, both to keep the animals out of the line of fire and for the men to pull the guns and mounts and ammo from their packs.

His daydream was interrupted by the children, swatting the mules' rumps with pieces of dried sugar cane.

Rocky turned a little tough. "No, no! You do not strike mules, little ones!"

They stopped, looking a bit forlorn.

"Gently, gently, little ones. That's what a mule likes. Gently, little ones."

He pulled his hat from his head, wiping his sweaty brow. The boy pointed at the gash freshly stitched up by Sister Bonaventure. "What happened you, Yankee shit?"

"I was shot in the head."

They crossed themselves, jaws hanging in disbelief. *"Muerto?"*

"No, I ain't dead. Skipped off. I got rocks in my gourd."

They laughed again.

"Come on, you Carls, let's pick up the pace a little. Pretty darned hungry myself."

CHAPTER 26

Minnie could not believe her eyes. The envelope read, Nurse Minerva Trumbull, USA, in pencil. She opened it immediately and began reading. It was brief, only one page on some cheap lined paper torn from a notebook, but it was a letter from Juan José and could not be better appreciated if it were penned on bleached parchment.

It was rather formal, which did not surprise her.

My Dear Miss Trumbull:

I hope this letter finds you in good spirits. Its purpose is to inform you that you need not worry about the communication I have entrusted to you. In fact, I strongly advise that you, as soon as is practicable, destroy it. I will be in Cuba by the time you will have read this letter and will deliver the message in person. When this is over, I hope to see you again and hope to speak of matters of a serious nature about our future together. Until then, I am your faithful servant,

Juan José Julián Pérez,
Captain, Cuban Liberation Army

P.S. You may be visited by a fat German swindler by the name of Otto Heinbecker. His method is to pass himself off as a government official. Do not be alarmed by him. He is a petty criminal of no consequence. He has no power to harm you. Ignore his threats.

Conversely, Clara's letter from Mortimer was significantly less formal. It read:

Dear Heart:

Well, another day survived without you, and it has not killed me yet. That is a good sign. The work schedule is brisk, and it helps. Seems the army is doing its best to ensure that life is as difficult as possible for us poor soldiers. No decent food, and, when there is, it's not in enough supply. No equipment, and all is confusion; no one seems to know much of anything. Day after day we are told that the transports will be arriving, but still, nothing.

I have a little confession, and this is not lawyerly of me to document in writing, but the conditions and ineptitude of the army necessitate that every good officer commit various acts of petty, and sometimes not-so-petty, larceny. I have a good old fud of a sergeant who retired and then came back into service in our unit. He is a magician when it comes to finding us food and supplies. I find I could not function without him. Oh, well, I'd rather risk jail than let my men suffer.

Tampa is pleasant enough, but the camps are overcrowded, too many men for too little acreage, and the sinks and wells — the bivouac areas — were not well planned out. I guess you know all this by now, my love, as so many men are shipped off to your camp for recovery. Typhoid fever will kill us all in the end, I believe.

I nearly forgot to mention that you are famous in Tampa. You and your nun and your immune nurse. The men who return tell about the pretty German girl with golden hair.

Dear heart, I have a little surprise for you and cannot contain it any longer.

Uncle and Aunt have given us a gift. A house. Well, more than a house; a manse in a little town near your hospital! Uncle says they want to retire to Portugal, and they no longer have a need for it. It's outside of Flemington. Perhaps you know the town? A home, love, large enough to fill with your family or our babies or both, as you like!

A lifetime together raising our family. Oh my God, my heart's breaking at the anticipation of it. It literally aches when I think about it, and there is but one cure. When will these damnable transports arrive? When will this war be over?

Well, enough. It is lights out, and I am so excited, as we are together in my dreams, always.

Love always, Mortimer.

CHAPTER 27

Marshall found his colonel standing over the brothers, sitting on upended buckets, working at pulling Spanish cartridges from their clips and loading them into the belts used to feed the Tiffany guns. The lads jumped to their feet, saluting smartly.

"What are you troopers up to these days?" He became distracted by the rifle Jonathan held at port arms. "Why do you have that Mauser, Trooper Thomson?"

"Oh, mine . . . remember, sir, at your order, I give to Marshall, when we were in the fight. I picked this off a dead fellow, knocked from a tree by Bill McGinty. And, sir, I like it better than what was issued to me." He addressed Marshall. "Your Springfield's in yonder tent. Knew you were fond of it; didn't want to wreck it."

Roosevelt adjusted his glasses; he waved a hand. "Give it to me."

Jonathan opened the bolt before presenting the rifle to his colonel. Roosevelt looked it over, held it to his shoulder, and sighted it on a distant treetop. He returned it to Jonathan.

"I will say this, men. The Germans produce a finer weapon than our own. Manufacture the finest weapons in the world. Why, were you aware that our own Kentucky longrifle was derived from the German Jaeger? The hunting rifle of Germany. The most competent rifle builders in America during the early years were German. The term Kentucky longrifle is a misnomer, men. Pennsylvania longrifle is the more appropriate term. The term Kentucky longrifle was coined after Jackson and his war, but Pennsylvania is the correct home of our forebears' smoke pole." He pushed his glasses against the bridge of his nose. "They do need to beef up the caliber a bit on these Mausers. Thirty should be the minimum, preferably forty-five, especially with the clad bullets." He looked to Rocky, who'd returned to his task. "Ah, you are preparing ammunition for the guns from Woody's sisters."

"Yes, sir." Rocky held up one of the canvas belts. "Only had four thousand rounds, sir, which ain't much when you have a shooting iron can spit out five hundred a minute.

Hamilton, ah, I mean, Sergeant Fish figured out pretty quick that the Spaniards' cartridges are the same."

Jonathan contributed. "Wish they didn't have them all hooked together with these little metal clips. Makes for a lot of extra work, and not all that easy to load the rifle, either, Colonel." He held one up for Roosevelt to see.

The colonel took it. "Trooper Thomson, this is a stripper clip." He motioned with his head. "Hand me one full of cartridges."

Jonathan complied.

"See here, Trooper Thomson." Roosevelt unloaded Jonathan's rifle, then opened the bolt. With his right hand, he placed the charged stripper clip over the magazine well and pressed the cartridges home, deftly discarding the object of Jonathan's derision onto the ground.

He closed the bolt smartly, seating a round in the chamber. He engaged the safety and returned it to the young man. "There, ready for action."

Jonathan stood, jaw gaping. "I'll be a son of a bitch! Makes sense now." He turned to his brother. "Knew there must be a trick to it. I was feeding them in one at a time."

"The Germans will never be bested in such mechanical wonders, gentlemen. Remember that. And remember, the German invents nothing that has no purpose. If they could be faulted at all, it would be for over-engineering. Heaven help us if we ever have to oppose them in war."

Jonathan called out as Marshall handed the colonel a report. Knew he had to speak quickly when it regarded his leader, as the man could take flight without warning. "Colonel, ready for duty again."

Roosevelt looked him over. "Really, Thomson? Your wound is fresh."

"Oh, I'm right fit for duty, sir."

"Run about for me."

"I beg your pardon, sir?"

"Run about; let's see how you run. I don't need a runner who cannot run, so show me."

Jonathan attempted to hide the effects of his wounds as he jogged. With each step, the pain was exquisite. He returned, sweat beading his brow. "See, sir, good as before I'd been wounded."

"You may not come onto the line, Trooper Thomson. You run like a constipated duck." He turned his head resolutely. "You stay here with your new Mauser, stand guard, Trooper. Keep a weathered eye." He looked into the trees. "I've heard the Cubans, the ones loyal to the Spaniards, are a ruthless lot. Shooting stretcher bearers, doctors, non-combatants. I would not put it past them to try a sortie on our little hospital, so, Trooper, keep a weathered eye." He turned to Marshall, then to the brothers. "And, Trooper Thomson?"

"Yes, sir?"

"Give Marshall a quarter."

Bill McGinty handed Rocky one of his horehound candies as he beamed at his fellow wrangler.

"Colonel Roosevelt said you must have got your name 'cause your head's hard as granite, Rock. That little Mauser slug skimmed off your gourd like when a kid skips a stone acrost a stream." He patted Rocky's shoulder. "It's sure good to see you back, old son. How's your brother?"

"Good to be back, Bill. Jonathan's good, still not up to much fighting. He's guarding the nurses."

"Where'd you find the slick Winchester, Rock?" McGinty admired the weapon slung over Rocky's shoulder.

"One of the officers. He's too banged up to fight. Loaned it to me, Bill. Can you believe it? And boy does this baby sing. Shoots these government cartridges to boot. Only problem is loading. Loads as slow as the damned Krags." He unslung it, handing it to McGinty.

"Why they have to ruin a good design, Rock? My old seventy-three, by God, you just shove the cartridges up the tube." He turned his head in disgust, handing it back.

"I know, Bill. Seems those pointy bullets . . . the ordnance sergeant told me, you put those pointy bullets in a tube magazine like that, and they can touch the round off in front when you fire. End up with a bomb in your holding hand."

"I'll be." McGinty scratched his head. "Never thought on that."

"Yeah, but I'll still take the Winchester any day. I can at least work the action without trouble. Still slick and fast."

He looked the defenses over. "You boys been busy, I see."

"They're called bomb proofs. Colonel told us how to build 'em. Funny, there was some high-tone regular army ass engineer struttin' around yesterday. Told the colonel they were amateurish." McGinty smiled. "Several of the boys were about to rough him up, then Captain O'Neill stepped in. Told that ass that maybe they weren't so text book, but seeing as all the regular army men and engineers were back hiding in the rear, that he was personally right proud of the work, and, well, the proof was that many had taken direct hits from the Spaniards' artillery, and we lost nary a man."

McGinty twisted cigarettes for them. "That shut the old boy up." He shook his head. "One thing a man ought not do is say anything bad about Colonel Roosevelt, least 'round his boys, anyways."

Rocky enjoyed the cigarette. "How's it you're always supplied with tobacco, Bill?"

"Oh, my, that's right, you ain't heard of the latest nonsense. Boys were startin' to smoke old dried-up palm fronds, Rock, and then we heard there was tobacco on the ship. They're chargin' us for it, by God, and not a man Jack one of us with two nickels to rub together. Lieutenant Kane staked us for it."

"He's something, ain't he, Bill?"

"He is."

"What's the plan?"

"Oh, we're going on the attack. All the men say it'll be soon. Waiting on orders, Rock."

They ate dinner and by early evening were visited by Colonel Roosevelt and Buckey O'Neill, checking the line.

The colonel nodded. "Finding enough to eat, lads?"

Rocky spoke, pleased to see the colonel

after so many days. "Oh, yes, sir. We put together a stew from that canned meat. Only one in ten's any good. The rest might as well be canned shit."

"That swear word will cost you a quarter, Trooper."

Rocky, without thinking, spoke out of turn, as he felt happy and thought a little sport with the colonel would raise the men up. "Shit, shit, shit, shit, make it five, Colonel."

He quickly lost his grin, as O'Neill did not find his joshing funny. The captain showed his temper. "Trooper Killebrew, you check your impertinence or there'll be more than fines."

"I'm sorry, sir."

"No matter." Roosevelt nodded to the captain, then considered Rocky. "You mind what the captain says, young man. Behave yourself."

"I will, sir. I'm sorry."

"All right, then." Roosevelt addressed Bill McGinty. "Bill, I want you and Trooper Killebrew to set up a Cossack post with two others." He pointed forward. "Out yonder hillock."

"Yes, sir." He thought a moment. "Okay to do it after dark, Colonel? We were . . . I mean, Rocky and me, we were about to hunt some tree dwellers with Goodwin and Proffitt. Near sundown seems the best time to pick 'em off."

"Very well." Roosevelt turned to O'Neill. "Captain, how bad are the guerillas further down on your flank?"

They moved off as they chatted, as was the colonel's custom. There was no keeping him for more than a minute or two in one spot.

Rocky touched Bill on the shoulder. "We hunting monkeys, Bill?"

"Monkeys?" McGinty grinned. "Where'd you come up with such a notion as that?"

"Well, the colonel was talking about gorillas. Only gorillas I ever heard of were big monkeys, you know in the zoo and the jungle."

"No, Rock. They ain't the same kind of guerrillas. Guerrilla is some kind a' military term. It means those Cubans still loyal to the Spaniards. They's the ones hanging in the trees, shootin' our lads. Bad devils for certain. Goodwin and Proffitt, they're our best guerilla hunters, by God." He stood, checking his rifle and cartridges. "Come on, Rock; it's pretty good sport."

In a little while they were among the two Arizonans, tough men, and, at first, at least to Rocky, a bit on the rude side, as neither man had much to say to either him or McGinty.

He soon learned otherwise, as both Proffitt and Goodwin never had much to say, good or bad. They weren't rude, just men of few words.

They went about their duty in a workman-like manner, scouting the places where the Cubans had fired upon their boys. On this day, the enemy had yet to draw blood.

One lanky Texan held up a hat they placed on a stick as a decoy. Proffitt examined it, instructing the trooper to show him the exact location of the hat when it had been fired upon. He bobbed his head left and right, eventually finding the trajectory of the bullet's flight.

He nodded to Goodwin, pointing. "In that tree yonder, two hundred yards."

"Understood."

A second later, the young man was off. In a little while, they'd hear the report of his Krag, and another tree dwelling guerilla would lose his life.

They travelled down the line in the same manner. Next would be Bill's turn, and the quiet man would point at another tree, this time a good three hundred yards distant. Bill grinned at Rocky. "See you a little later, Rock." He, too, went silently into the east, toward the ebbing light.

It was Rocky's turn, and it was plain for him indeed. One needed only to see where the shot had struck and interview the witnesses in order to determine the source of the firing.

His target was relatively close, one hundred fifty yards with good cover between the Rough Riders and the tree the assassin was certain to occupy. Goodwin nodded. He did not hesitate to offer advice, as this was no time to worry over a man's pride or his supposed knowledge or ignorance. He took Rocky by the elbow, pulling him close so that the lad could sight down his arm. "Follow the contour of that hill, Trooper Killebrew. It will take you three hundred yards out of the way, but you'll come up aside him. Don't try to take him until you can see him clearly, and in this light, that means within forty yards." He looked Rocky in the eye. "Do not let him see you, Trooper. He sees you, you are a dead man."

"Got it."

"And Trooper," he eyed Rocky with dead seriousness. "Make it a head shot."

"Yes, sir."

"Good luck."

Rocky picked his way along and soon realized he was far beyond the American line.

No-man's-land, that's what Colonel Roosevelt called it. It felt especially lonely when he considered it.

Mosquitos swarmed him, yet he dared not slap at them. He was sweating, wondering how Bill McGinty could call any of this good sport.

He snuck along, yard by yard, watching the ground cover, the way he'd learned to do hunting.

The Cuban's rifle cracked, and, in the dimming light, Rocky could easily observe his position. That Goodwin fellow was amazing.

Off to his right he heard a Rough Rider call for a stretcher bearer, as the Cuban's Remington had found its mark, and that is when a deadly calm fell upon Rocky Killebrew.

He was no longer fearful or excited. This was no time to be nervous or scared or even angry. It was time to be a hunter of men.

At sixty yards he could clearly see the white of the man's peon clothes. He stopped and squinted, wiping the sweat from his forehead. He watched the Cuban watch his boys off in the west, the guerilla working the action on his rifle as he chose his next target. Stretcher bearers were fair game to these fellows, and there'd be at least two in short order to offer him targets.

And now Rocky was certain the son of a bitch was lining up to take down another of his brothers.

But Rocky was too quick. Throwing his rifle to his shoulder, he put the front sight blade on the guerilla's cheekbone and fired.

It seemed a hundred or more Mausers opened at once, every one pointed at Rocky. Vegetation tore to pieces all around him. Dirt exploded at his feet.

He ran, zigzagging, until flopping down beside his Australians crouched in a trench, working diligently to feed the fire under the still from which they rendered their shoe polish drink. They nodded and offered him a good evening.

"What's all the shooting, mate?" they asked as if no more concerned than one on a Sunday outing.

"Sharpshooter," he answered breathlessly. "I killed one! Then a bunch started in after me."

"Good on ya, mate! We each took three this afternoon, along about tea time." The lanky one nodded to the tall one. "Let's see the ear then?"

Rocky looked confused. "The what?"

"The ear, mate. Don't tell me you didn't take his ear?"

344

"What do you mean?"

"Cut the ear off 'im; must be the left," he touched his own to clarify, "so's you don't try to take credit for two when you've only killed one." The lanky one smiled. "No ear, no kill: that's the motto."

"You're kidding with me."

"Didn't you hear, pardon the pun, that the Spaniards cut the ears off our blokes all the time? Make regular sport of it, don't you know? Turnabout's fair play, I reckon."

Rocky belched as his stomach turned, the thought of keeping a human trophy revolting him. "No, I didn't cut off any ears. I didn't know anything about it." He remembered that the Aussies enjoyed having a good joke on bumpkins such as him; knew it had to be the case now. "Let's see yours then."

"Our what?"

"Ears. You gents say you killed six between you today; let's see the ears."

"Oh, mate, they were too far off. Couldn't get to 'em."

The tall one changed the subject. "How 'bout a little grog to warm the cockles of yer heart?"

Rocky shook as the adrenaline took hold of him. The full realization of what he'd done had sunk into his battle-manic brain.

He had difficulty articulating his response. He held up his trembling hand and smiled. "No, thanks. Don't need it."

"Sure, mate? We don't charge any boys on the line. Matter of principle, that is."

"Nope, I'm good. You fellows be careful. Keep your heads down." He turned to walk away. And as quickly as the shakes had come, he regained his composure; felt that he could lick the entire Spanish Army singlehandedly. He wanted to tell his partner what he had done. He wanted to find Bill McGinty.

CHAPTER 28

Rocky was pleased to see the smile upon Sergeant Tiffany's face as he presented the mules and the belts of ammo he and Jonathan had loaded back at the field hospital.

"Where on earth did you find mules, Trooper Killebrew?"

"Just found 'em, Sergeant." He looked about. "Don't tell anybody. The damned regular army'll confiscate them if they find out. My brother Jonathan and me, we've been hidin' them in the jungle behind the hospital. Colonel said to keep 'em secret until we need them." He nodded to one. "That one with the healing wound is Carl, the other Carlita. They only speak Spanish, sir, I mean, Sergeant, I mean, understand. Mules don't speak anything, of course."

Tiffany looked them over, was impressed with Rocky's improvised racks.

Rocky explained. "I was able to cobble some strapping together. We ought to be able to load each with one gun and tripod. I think we'll have to hand carry the ammo, sir."

"This is capital, Trooper Killebrew." Tiffany turned to Woodbury Kane. "Our Colts are back in action."

Kane addressed Rocky. "I'll assign you back to William's machine gun crew, young Killebrew, as you know the mules' language." He sensed Rocky's concern. "Don't worry, young Killebrew, my troop will stay close by. The colonel wants our Colts under the direction of Lieutenant Parker, the master of the Gatling guns. He's a capital fellow; you'll enjoy serving under him."

Bill McGinty twisted a cigarette, presenting it to Rocky along with one of his horehound candies.

Rocky popped the candy into his mouth. "How many of these do you have, Bill?"

"Oh, a bunch. My ma said my sweet tooth would be the death of me, Rock." He shrugged. "Don't know, but I sure like sugary things, can't deny that. Could sooner give up tobacco than candies."

"Do you suppose we're going on the attack tomorrow?"

McGinty squinted off in the distance, raised his rifle, then changed his mind. He sat back down. "I think so, Rock." He blew smoke at the sky. "Worried?"

"Nah, not for myself." He looked back behind the line. "Worried more for the mules than anything else."

"My old uncle, he was in the war of rebellion, you know."

"Which side?"

"Oh, the north. Least I think it was the north." He grinned. "You know something, Rock? I don't know what side he fought on." He worked on his cigarette. "He said that horses and mules was the most heart breakin' to see knocked down, especially if you're a man who loves 'em. My God, my uncle loved horses the way you love mules, Rock."

"We hunting guerillas tonight, Bill?"

"No. Colonel says we all need to rest. We'll sleep out in one of them Cossack holes tonight. Keep a weathered eye by turns, but our main goal is a little shut-eye, Rock. Need to be fresh enough for running tomorrow. Running and charging."

"Wish we had our horses, Bill."

"You can say that again, Rock. Especially us bein' shortish in the legs. A-horse would be *the* way to fight."

But despite being "shortish-in-the-legs,"

both he and Rocky helped set the pace behind Woodbury Kane. Many men were hard-pressed to keep up as they marched all the day of June 30th along the road to Santiago.

That evening they dug in, then ran up and down the road, helping stragglers, carrying what little the men had left to carry, as many had abandoned packs and blankets and shelter-halves. Some even left extra ammunition, much to the men's consternation.

"How these boys expect to kill Spaniards without ammo, Rock?"

"Don't know, Bill." He turned his head in pity. "I think some of these boys would have been better left at home. Heat and walking's too much on 'em. They ain't fit."

By sunset they had a proper Cossack post set up, much to the delight of Kane, who rarely had to order either to do anything.

The lieutenant plopped down beside them, smiling, as usual, impeccably dressed and groomed. It was a constant wonder how he'd been able to pull that off. He worked as hard as any private soldier, perhaps more so, as he'd been known to pick up the loads of stragglers; yet he always looked as if he'd come from his morning toilet, freshly shaved and combed, uniform clean and boots polished.

"Young Killebrew, I have good news and bad news for you."

"Oh?"

"Yes. Which would you like first?"

"The bad, sir."

McGinty spoke up. "Of course."

"Well, the bad is that your procurement and training of the mules and your foraging for ammunition for the Tiffany guns has been for naught. William has been ordered to hold in reserve, to avoid any potential incidents of friendly fire."

A wave of relief washed over him. He was not disappointed, as Rocky had grown accustomed to doing work that ended up to no purpose. It seemed the army way. He'd certainly dug enough trenches and holes that ended up serving no significant utility. He smiled at the realization that the mules would be safe in the rear. "And the good news, sir?"

"The good news is that you'll be fighting with Trooper McGinty and me."

"Oh, capital, sir!" The thought of leaving the men when the attack was on vexed him terribly. "I'm glad, sir. Wanted to be with you when the bullets were flying."

"Well, young Killebrew . . ." He lit a cigarette and handed it to Rocky, then another for Bill. He lit a third for himself.

"Your wish has been granted."

They stayed awake mostly all night as they'd overheard Colonels Wood and Roosevelt conferring with the officers. Kane and O'Neill had received their orders. The attack was most certainly on for the next day and, by all estimates, would relegate Las Guásimas to little more than a minor skirmish.

Rocky let Bill drift a little at around three. He could not sleep, instead taking time to clean his six-shooter and, when finished with that, his Winchester and Bill's Krag.

He felt well, no longer scared or worried over the animals. He thought of Jonathan safe at the hospital, and that encouraged him, as, from the start of this adventure, he had the nagging feeling that one of them would not survive. He was resolved for it to be him. He was expendable. No woman, no real property, no responsibility, no father to cry over him. He thought of Ellen and became a little sad. Ellen would grieve over him but, then again, better him than Jonathan. Jonathan the golden boy, Jonathan the same flesh and blood. It would sadden her to know of his loss, but it would devastate her to know Jonathan's.

He watched McGinty sleep. The man could sleep anywhere, it seemed. He looked old when he slept, as he often did so with his mouth open, face relaxed. It was a good sleep for a man to have, and Rocky envied that. He hated to sleep. Most of his nights were interminable.

He thought of Sean Whelihan and the man's brother, how the wrong man probably died back on that field in the small Pennsylvania town. At least from what little he was told, Jonathan Whelihan the uncle was more like Jonathan Whelihan the brother. It would likely have been better all around had Sean bought it that day and his brother survived.

He watched the dawn come and prepared breakfast, some canned corned beef and hardtack mixed in a pot with a little lard. He'd squirreled away some coffee beans and crushed them with the handle of his Colt as Bill awoke, stretching and smiling as if he'd spent the night in a featherbed.

"Morning, Rock." He looked about, stirred the pot of gruel Rocky had started. "Sorry to sleep on you, old son."

"Nothing, Bill. Glad you could catch a little shut-eye. I don't sleep in the best conditions." He nodded. "Cleaned your Krag for ya. Loaded the magazine, and one's in the chamber, so take care. Would have done your six-shooter but didn't want to wake you tryin' to unholster it."

McGinty looked his rifle over. "That's fine, Rock. I'm thanking you."

By full light they could see the impressive army that had formed behind them, ready to take the high ground held by the Spaniards. Rocky felt invincible, sitting there at the spear's point. He felt as if he could take them all by himself. He was not remotely scared.

Off in the distance they could hear Lawton's guns open up. The battle of El Caney was on.

Much to their chagrin, their own artillery, not far behind them, opened as well. The men looked at each other, instantly knowing the other's thoughts.

"Start diggin', Rock. This Cossack hole ain't near deep enough. Those Spaniards will have that smoke zeroed, and we're too damned close for comfort."

Rocky pointed. "You can say that again, Bill, but look yonder. My God, who was the bone-head thought a observation balloon was a good idea?"

The balloon hoovered behind them, high enough for every Spaniard artilleryman within a mile to sight on. It might well have been a painted bullseye, and, as if their words had commanded the enemy, the

Spaniards' guns pounded the ground around them.

Colonel Roosevelt appeared amongst them, riding Little Texas, looking incongruous, too large and gangly riding the diminutive mount.

Rocky shouted, ignoring military decorum. He could think of no good that could come of his leader in such a vulnerable spot. "Colonel, please, dismount. Please, you're a regular target like that."

Roosevelt ignored him, instead surveying his prostrate men. At that moment, a shell exploded, wounding many around him. A chunk of steel fragment hit him on the wrist. It would be the only wound Roosevelt would receive in all the war, though his horse and the clothing on his back would be struck with both bullets and shrapnel.

The colonel, six-shooter in hand, waved in the direction of the enemy. "Hasten forward there, you lads. The Spaniards have us zeroed. Move forward, lads, move forward."

The ones who could did, some eventually taking shelter below the bank of the San Juan River. Disregarding their own safety, Bill and Rocky ran about, dodging explosions, pulling the wounded to safety, eventually also winding up crouched in the cool river water.

"Fill yer canteen, Rock."

He did and drank his fill, the muddy water as welcome as a cold beer. He gulped again, then topped the vessel off.

McGinty smiled. "They should have left those damned smoke poles back on the ship, Rock. They're more trouble than they're worth."

"Yeah, Bill. And what the hell with that damned balloon?"

"Don't know, old son, but seems our Rough Riders are the only ones ain't with shit between their ears, by God."

Roosevelt formed them up again. By columns of four, they followed the First Brigade to a sunken lane. The heat was intense, and few men had the forethought to take advantage of the river. Both troopers and soldiers all around them lay exhausted, a mix of volunteers and regulars. Ahead stood high grass and open jungle.

Despite putting distance between themselves and the artillery and the damned ridiculous balloon, the men were now the sole subject of the intense Spanish small-arms fire. The lads could do little but hunker down and receive it. Once or twice McGinty took a shot, but it was mostly for naught. They were too far away, and the enemy offered little in the way of targets as they were well-entrenched.

At that moment, Rocky observed Buckey O'Neill calmly smoking and walking upright, back and forth among his men, all lying in a ditch as close as they could to the ground. Killebrew turned, desperately searching for his boss. Certainly Woodbury would not be so reckless as to follow the Arizonan's lead.

"Jesus, Bill, look yonder at Captain O'Neill, by God, he's sure to get himself shot, sure as —" and, before he could finish, Buckey dropped.

"Oh, sweet Jesus, he's down, Bill." The tears came to his eyes as Rocky yanked the hat from his head, holding it to his heart, as one paying tribute to a funeral procession. "Buckey O'Neill's been killed, by God. Buckey O'Neill's dead!"

McGinty watched as the men pored over their fallen leader. Forever the optimist, he tried to encourage his partner. "Maybe he's only stunned, Rock. Maybe they glanced a round off his head, way they did you back at Guásimas."

"No, Bill. He's dead. He's dead. He fell like a dead man. Jesus Christ, they'll kill every good man we have."

He looked about him, taking in every terrible moment, McGinty trying, ineffectively, to force his friend to face forward, ignore the terrible carnage behind and abreast of them.

Off to his left Rocky watched the colonel, still a-horse, give one of his runners an order. The man saluted, then turned to leave and dropped much in the way O'Neill had when struck down. Another man came to the colonel's aid, and he, too, was shot. He thought of Jonathan, the golden boy would certainly have been one of these killed had he not been shot in the ass back at Guásimas.

"Bill, we got to move. Jesus Christ, we'll all lie here and be cut to pieces, friend."

"I know, Rock." McGinty pointed. "Look there: that's Colonel Dorst with our'n. He'll get us on the move, Rock. Sure of it. He'll move us out of this mess."

And he did. Roosevelt rallied the men, riding up and down, commanding his troop to move forward.

Small-arms fire raked them, mostly too high, and Rocky was surprised at his own ambivalence to the danger. It was mostly due to McGinty; the little bronc buster had no fear of anything, and the last thing Rocky would ever do would be to let his partner down.

In a little while they were plopped down among the men of the Ninth. Roosevelt and Kane were close to them. Thankfully the colonel had given up on riding Little Texas. Rocky and Bill took the opportunity to return fire.

"What you shootin' at, Rock?"

"Oh, off in the distance, there's a block-house. Putting a few rounds through the window, Bill. Can't stand all this lying about. Can't stand it."

"How you fixed for ammo?"

"Oh, good. One thing I never run out of, Bill, that's ammo." He looked himself over; he was carrying three belts.

They turned their attention to the colonel, presently lambasting a captain of the regular army, who sat, like a stone pillar. He'd not be moved without orders.

McGinty watched as Rocky drew marks on his canteen cover with a pencil he carried in a shirt pocket.

"What's that, Rock, your body count?"

Rocky grinned. "No, it's the number of swears the colonel's made. He has a filthier mouth than all us put together, Bill. I plan to present him with a bill when this is all over. We'll each be able to afford a fat steak from Delmonico's when Woodbury takes us on that trip he promised to New York."

"Look at General Sumner there, Rock. He's a-horse, like the colonel was. Guess we can take it if he can."

"Don't need some fool general to give *me* courage, Bill. Nor do you. Maybe that's needed with those regular army boys, but not with us Rough Riders."

At that moment one of their men, a tough Texan, jumped from his spot not ten feet from Rocky. He screamed like a schoolgirl, retreating from the battle line a good twenty feet.

At first, they thought he'd lost his nerve. Bill smiled in a way to reassure the terror-stricken frontiersman. "Easy, Hal. Easy, old son. Them Spaniards are missin' more than they're hittin'."

The Texan pointed to the ground he'd recently occupied. "Spi — der! Spi — der!"

A fat tarantula crouched in a crevice, looking as befuddled, if a spider indeed could look befuddled, as the panicked man.

They did their best not to laugh. The Texan cared naught about the Mauser bullets, but a spider, likely no bigger than what he'd known at home, had unnerved him.

Rocky called out. "Come on, Hal, lay back down; you'll end up shot, you dancin' around out in the open like that."

"Not until it's dead, not until it's dead!"

His voice quivered.

Rocky took aim, blasting the creature into oblivion. He nodded to Bill McGinty. "Hated to do that. Even a spider has a mom, I guess."

"I guess."

"But old Hal, he'd have ended up shot through the gourd we don't get him to lie back down."

And Rocky's actions had helped convince Hal to take cover. In short order, he was returning fire at the enemy. He'd fight as gallantly as Roosevelt throughout the campaign.

They rose in unison. It was time. First a low crouch, then a walk, a jog, and finally a full run. Kane appeared abreast of them, his Colt in hand. He motioned for them to follow, as Colonel Roosevelt was too far out front.

"By God, come on, Rock. We got to catch Lieutenant Kane and the colonel."

They rushed past the prostrate men of the regular army, now encouraged by the activity of the Rough Riders. They followed a mix of volunteers and regulars, blacks and whites and Indians. They charged, a motley crew of mixed races and creeds and classes, like the mongrels that they were, like Americans. They fought with one purpose. There

361

was no stopping them.

"My God, Rock, look at Henry Bardshar up there, runnin' like his ass was on fire."

They could see the enemy, and the first to be cut down were credited to Bardshar, a man as fearless and stealthy as a mountain lion. He'd become the self-assigned bodyguard to Roosevelt, shooting several Spaniards who would certainly have taken their leader down.

Men from the Tenth knocked down the barbed-wire fences; many more rushed forward as the Spaniards tore into them. Man after man fell, but neither Rocky nor McGinty gave them any notice.

They fought to a position behind a massive iron kettle, shooting Spaniards in the trenches and in the blockhouse.

Kane was standing beside them, directing men, cigarette in hand. Off to the right a Spanish officer and his manservant emerged, each wrapped in the flag of his country, as if they knew they would not live and were resolved to take as many Yankees with them as possible. The captain had pointed his revolver at Woodbury when Rocky pulled off two quick shots, into the head of each. They fell at his lieutenant's feet.

McGinty slapped his companion on the

shoulder. "Nice shootin', Rock."

"It's the Winchester, Bill. Sure you could do the same if you had one."

They did not have long to rest on their laurels at Kettle Hill, however, as Colonel Roosevelt pushed onward to the San Juan heights. Again they had to sprint to keep up with him. Fewer men dropped around them. It seemed they were gaining the upper hand.

Their attention was directed to the east where a hellish cacophony of firing sent a chill down Rocky's spine. Did the Spaniards have machine guns? All that would come to mind was the practice they'd had with the Tiffany guns. To be on the receiving end of such was almost too much to fathom.

Kane turned and shouted, allaying Rocky's fear. "It's Parker's Gatlings, boys. They'll make short work of the devils."

And he was correct. In a little while most of the enemy's fire had dwindled to a trickle. As they moved forward, taking full command of the high ground, they could see the full impact of the guns, as they had raked the enemy, hiding in their trenches.

Everywhere he looked, Rocky saw carnage. Gangs of men heaped upon each other, most with their heads destroyed. He sat and had a smoke and considered what had been done. What he had done with his Winchester and what he would have done had the Tiffany guns been allowed in the battle. Somehow he felt relieved. It was too much.

Bill McGinty broke his daydream. "Come on, Rock, them blockhouses are full of food. Good food. Let's wrangle some up for our boys before those fellows from the Tenth take all."

They found beef stew, boiled rice, boiled peas, all still warm, ready to be served to the hill's defenders. There were loaves of rice bread, preserves, and salt fish.

They eyed a tall trooper from the Tenth, working like lightning, filling rucksacks as fast as his hands would allow, but Rocky and Bill, being younger, were quicker yet.

Rocky held a can up to the light streaming through the window. "Bill, what's Foy Grass?"

McGinty looked the tin over. Shrugging he said, "Beats me, Rock. Some kind a' dago food, I guess."

A terse lieutenant pulled the can from Rocky's grasp. He read it aloud. "Foie Gras." He looked the young Rough Riders over. "Goose liver paté, men. No doubt some of your Fifth Avenue gentlemen will find it familiar."

They stood at attention, saluting smartly. "What is it, sir?"

"A sort of liver paste. You eat it on crackers or bread."

"Thank you, sir." Rocky stuck it in his pocket. He'd hold onto it for Woodbury.

They continued to race the men from the Tenth, numbering three along with the officer, when Bill nudged Rocky with his elbow, whispering as loud as he dared. "Hey, Rock, you know who that lieutenant is?"

"No."

"That's Nigger Jack Pershing."

Rocky's response was a look of disinterest.

"He's a famous officer of those Buffalo soldiers; went up to West Point and gave the cadets hell. They called him Nigger Jack 'cause of it being kind of an insult. One of the orderlies told me all about it."

Pershing turned, facing McGinty. "I prefer Black Jack, young man." He nodded to his Buffalo soldiers. "Come on, you men, back to the trenches. Leave these Rough Riders a few crumbs."

In the afternoon there was a brief counterattack. Rocky and Bill found themselves in the company of the Australians. Rocky did not wait for them to tease him, instead, taking the initiative.

"Where are all the ears, you men?"

The tall one grinned. "Oh, lost our ear-taking knives, mate." He raised an eyebrow. "How's the hunting?"

"Right enough."

"How many?"

Rocky would not answer. Killing was not something he took lightly, nor was it something, at least to his mind, about which one kept score. It was too serious an affair to turn into sport. "Oh, more than one, less than a hundred."

"Good on ya, mate."

As the afternoon progressed, he realized that, despite their devil-may-care attitude, the Australians were a fine pair of fellows. They worked hard reinforcing the trenches, did their duty with good cheer, and were deadly marksmen. Later, Rocky learned that the Australians were not unlike the American frontiersmen of the West, as they lived in a land not dissimilar, and many followed the life of the cowboy. They once again offered him and Bill some of their shoe-polish concoction, which both refused.

Throughout the next several days they'd play cat and mouse with the Spaniards, Rocky and Bill working constantly, one encouraging the other, not out of some sense of petty competition, but from the love only a soldier who's been in battle would know. They'd sooner die from exhaustion or a bullet than let their brother-in-arms down.

Woodbury Kane was especially impressed, as the lads seemed constantly everywhere at once, sometimes reinforcing trenches, other times bringing food and water to the men. They even formed part of the party of guerrilla hunters, numbering more than twenty, who'd venture into no-man's-land as twilight came of an evening.

That was particularly interesting to Rocky, as they'd deemed him an expert. He had four men under his command, giving them at least rudimentary instruction on killing the tree-dwellers. Only rudimentary, as these men knew how to take down game.

At one point, he and a fellow from New Mexico scored a hit on the same Cuban, and Rocky was at first confused, wondering if he'd had a double-charged round. He'd never seen such destruction on a head. Rocky, now as gentlemanly as Woodbury, gave the credit to the other.

Tiffany's guns were fixed on sandbags at the head of the outposts facing the Spaniards, the fortifications christened Fort Roosevelt as homage to their boss. The guns would not see any real action, and that was fine with Rocky. The mules were safely grazing near the field hospital, Jonathan in charge.

But, during the day, both Parker's Gatlings and the Tiffany Colts were used to defoliate the tops of many trees, hitting guerillas as far away as five hundred yards. Later Rocky observed the corpses, and that once again eased his mind that he'd not been involved in the operation of the hellish devices.

Well into July it became a routine. They'd had time to procure meager provisions, rest, wait, finish off guerillas, fortify defenses, hunt relatively clean water, and generally recover from battle.

Rumors were constant, but everyone was certain: the Spaniards were all but licked. Most theorized they'd be home by fall.

It was during this time that the enemy had begun purging Santiago of its civilians. A constant stream of half-starving women and children, the infirm, and the old began parading past them.

Roosevelt stood by, turning his head in disgust. "As I imagined, men. The Latin sensibility. They are as ruthless and inhumane as were the Roman Legions."

Bill and Rocky turned their attention to

the colonel, too overwhelmed to lecture.

Woodbury watched a singularly pathetic family pass by, a young woman with two children clamped to her back, walking unsteadily. She looked each of the men over as if entranced. She was young, perhaps once beautiful; now she looked like an old woman.

The colonel had forbidden the men from offering any assistance, out of fear they'd either contract disease or give up all their provisions. He knew his Rough Riders well enough. He constantly encouraged them, assuring them that the poor civilians would be cared for properly once they'd arrived in Siboney.

Woodbury could not restrain himself. Walking up on a woman pushing a wheelbarrow full of probably everything she owned, he shifted a table about to topple to the ground.

Roosevelt pointed. "You see, lads, this is why we are here. This is why our country must take on the role of protector, both inside and outside our borders.

"We will take care of these poor creatures; I promise you. We'll civilize this island, by God. We'll ensure it enjoys all the rights and privileges granted one of our states." He seemed lost in the idea of it. "I can see a

star added to our flag, a star representing
the state of Cuba."

CHAPTER 29

Clara slept for many hours and awoke to darkness. Movement caught her eye and the shadowy figure of Sister Bonaventure adjusted in her chair.

Her head ached and at first, she thought perhaps it had all been a terrible nightmare. It was too cruel a joke for it to be otherwise. The crumpled communication in her fist told her differently. It was no dream, no nightmare. She remembered the words. One sentence, or rather, one fraction of a sentence. *Captain Hollander Killed in Action Cuba.*

They hadn't even gotten the punctuation right. How could six words, only six words, thoroughly ruin a person's life? Destroy her happiness, her desire to endure.

The tears came again, not like any crying she'd ever known, not the crying from anger or exhaustion, or even on the rare occasions as she'd done as a child, before she'd grown up at age eight.

It was rather like faucets turned on. The tears poured from her eyes of their own volition. Beyond her power. Automatic tears. Salty tears invading her taste buds, invading and overwhelming her senses.

She put her palms to her eyes, discovering they were protected by the lenses of her glasses. She'd slept with them on.

Sister Bonaventure moved her chair next to the cot and scooped her up, pulling Clara onto her lap. She cradled her in her arms.

Clara could not help but speak of business matters. "It was kind of Major Johnston to send me this." She held the communication up.

"It was, child."

She cried into the nun's wimple as Sister Bonaventure rocked her.

"I wish we'd made love."

"I know you do, child."

"I wish I could have had his baby." She emitted a soft, low moan, "Something, *anything,* to fill this void, Sister. There must be *something* . . . my God, there must be *something* to carry me through this emptiness."

Sister Bonaventure held her more tightly. There was nothing to say.

"Dr. Regan, back at Camp Cuba Libre, said war suited me. He said that people like me begin to live when there's such a crisis as war. I say damn him for his blasphemy. Damn the war, and damn my ever knowing this love and damn it for this loss.

"What have I ever done to *Him*? Tell me, Sister, what have I ever done other than serve *Him*?"

"Nothing, child."

"I knew that war would be dangerous. I'm not afraid of death, of dying, I'm not necessarily surprised that Mortimer died; knew the risks, knew all that, but why, why did we have to be so in love? Why did He allow us to find this love? Why tease us and then rip it from our grasp? That's the cruelty of it."

She uttered a cynical laugh. "I've seen so many folks who married and could not stand the sight of each other. So few people find soul mates; so few ever know anything close to this love.

"Why, if God knew this would happen, why could I have not been given some little crumb, some tiny morsel to sustain me? One little thing to hold onto. Oh, God. We had so many close calls. So many times I was willing to give him the gift of intimacy. Now it's too late. He'll never . . . we'll never, know that."

She laughed again. "It was Mortimer who

cautioned that we should wait. It was Mortimer who said we would be married before consummating our love. It was Mortimer who fed my damned religious zeal! My worship of Him! He said it would be a sin in my eyes. Said, in the event of the unspeakable, he'd not send me home with a swollen belly, not ruin me, ruin my life, my career, my respectability, my reputation. My damned, damnable reputation. Oh, God, Sister, oh, God, I'd give up every vestige of respectability for the chance to have loved him. Damned my reputation! Damn it, damn it, damn it!"

"I know, child."

Bonaventure held her a long while, listened to her breathe, fall asleep, and hopefully rest her tortured mind.

She was placing Clara in her cot when Colonel Roosevelt appeared among them, turning his hat in his hands. Bonaventure nodded to a seat next to her.

He sat and watched Clara rest, her beautiful sleeping angel's face peaceful in sleep.

She awoke, sitting up abruptly.

He held up a hand, stopping her from springing from bed, coming to attention.

"There, my dear. Please stay put."

Sister Bonaventure took her leave. They were soon alone; both removed their glasses and began cleaning them.

Clara, forever German, looked up from her ministrations. She spoke in a wholly professional tone. "How may I help you, Colonel?"

"You may not, my dear." He replaced his glasses. "But I hope that I might help *you.*"

"Oh?"

She felt silly, inappropriate, vulnerable, sitting on her bed. She stood, covering herself with a robe, moving to Bonaventure's chair, so as to receive her guest properly.

Roosevelt took her hand. "I am here to offer some unsolicited advice, my dear. That is, if you will indulge me."

"All right." She looked at his battle-marred hands. Fought her nurse's compulsion to dress them.

"I once had a loss, which I can say with confidence was as profound as yours." He cleared his throat, the memory nearly too much to share. "I cannot give the details and maintain proper decorum," he took a deep breath, "suffice it to say, I am in complete empathy of what you are experiencing."

Clara peered through the lenses of his glasses, into eyes that betrayed the countenance of the ever-confident.

"Colonel, if what you are saying is true,

then I am heartbroken for you, as no one should ever have to endure such pain."

They comforted each other for a long moment, Clara transported into her lover's arms, and Roosevelt into his Alice's. Eventually, it was Roosevelt who broke the paralysis of melancholy.

"Now." He blew his nose into a pristine handkerchief, found one of Clara's by her bed and handed it to her. "Dry your eyes, young miss, and listen to what I have to tell you."

He waited. Clara, folding the handkerchief, looked up at him and smiled. "All right, Colonel, I am listening."

"I was a young man when I lost her, and I remember, as if it happened only yesterday, writing one line in my journal. *'The light has gone out of my life'*, and that was true, Nurse Maass. The light had truly gone out of my life." He took a drink from a glass by Clara's bed. Tears glistened in his eyes. It was clear, he did not mind sharing them with her.

"But I was young, my dear, nearly as young as you, and soon learned, I must carry on. People such as you and I, the special ones —"

"The special ones?"

"Well, of course!" The look of all-consuming confidence was back. He sat a little straighter in his chair. "Yes, the special ones, such as you and I. We must endure, Nurse Maass. We must carry on with our lives, flourish, and do whatever destiny demands of us."

"But I miss him *so!*"

"As you should." He patted her hand. "But, there is a time for that, and then there is a time for moving on. Give yourself time to grieve, my dear, but then, well, you must put it behind you. Put him into a special place into the farthest recesses of your mind." He held up a hand. "Not to forget him. Never to forget him. But to cherish him there, cherish your time with him, but then move forward. You have a long life ahead of you. A gift of intelligence and work ethic and moral compass. Why, that was precisely the reason for my visit today. To see you and Dr. Church and the other nurses who've taken such splendid care of my boys. I wanted to visit while there was a lull in battle. Come to pay my respects and to honor and thank you." He nodded. "And then I heard of your loss. I am sorry to have come upon you at such a tragic moment. I guess one could say, my timing was dreadfully off."

Clara smiled. "I would not say that, Colonel. It seems providential that you've come when you have." She grasped his hand. "Your words are a comfort to me. I thank you."

"I'm glad." He stood. "Nurse Maass, I leave you to it. You remember. You have much to accomplish before you leave this earth, much living to do, and inconsolable grieving is not conducive to it."

He turned to leave the tent, stopped, and touched her on the shoulder. "My dear Nurse Maass. My advice to you." He turned his head gravely. "Never speak his name, never speak of him. Never allow another to speak of him. Trust me when I tell you this. It is what has sustained me all these many years." He pointed to his brain. "Keep him here, to yourself; remember him, but do not dwell upon him. Forward, Nurse Maass, always and forever forward!

"Straighten up, get busy. Find another good man, marry him, have babies, pursue your passion, devote your life to service."

"Service?"

"Of course. Service. Service to God and country, my dear. To God and country."

"Perhaps country, Colonel Roosevelt, but not God. Not yet, at least. I am, at present, too angry at Him."

"Do not be. God is neither a genie nor a magician. We cannot blame Him for the injustices and cruelties put upon us. Don't do that, Nurse Maass." He reached over, kissing her forehead, and as quickly as he'd come into her life, he was away.

She stood, looking into the mirror hanging precariously from a wire, horrified at her terrible appearance, eyes red and puffy and a snotty nose to match. She worked at replacing several errant strands of hair when Roosevelt's manservant, Marshall, knocked on the tent pole.

"I'm sorry to disturb you, ma'am." He pointed. "Colonel left his hat; just fetching it."

"Certainly."

Marshall hesitated. "I am most profoundly sorry for your loss, ma'am."

"Who was the Colonel's?"

He responded in a hushed tone. "The sweetest angel you'd ever want to know, ma'am. His Alice."

"A daughter?"

"No, ma'am, the Colonel's first wife." He turned his head. "Those were some dark times, ma'am, darkest the Colonel's ever known."

"He won't speak of her?"

"Never. Won't say her name, and, boy howdy, you better watch it if'n you mention her! He loved her too much to say or even hear her name spoken by anyone. It's too much for him to bear, miss. Fact is, even his own daughter, named Alice, don't go by that name. She's called Baby Lee." He nodded, holding the hat as if to prove his point. "When he gets to pinin' for his late wife, he leaves items layin' 'round." He smiled.

"Well, best get this back to the Colonel. The man *hates* to be outta uniform. Thank you, ma'am, I'll be on my way." He nodded again. "You take care of yourself."

CHAPTER 30

"Where'd you find the scattergun, brother?" Rocky seemed genuinely interested. He hefted the dead birds, hanging from strings over his brother's shoulder. Jonathan admired them. "Colonel says they're Guinea hens. Told me the whole danged history of 'em, whether I wanted to hear it or not." He regarded the shotgun and recalled Rocky's question.

"Bill McGinty. Squirreled it away on the trip over; thought it might come in handy. That and a couple a' boxes of bird shot."

"What's put you in such a good mood?" He watched Jonathan hand the birds over to a Cuban the field hospital had talked into serving as cook for the staff and invalids. The man had taken to the buzzacot stove as if he'd grown up with it, turning the meager provisions into something not only sustainable, but easy on the palate.

The native turned his head sharply. Wagging a finger in Jonathan's face he said, "No hunting birds in the jungle. Bad Cubans in trees. In jungle! Hunt *you, señor.* Shoot you like birds. Then, no more!"

Jonathan ignored the cook's admonishments as he turned to face Rocky. "Oh, I'm pleased to kill some proper food for those nurses and . . . and the wounded." He smiled. "You heard that pretty woman, that blonde beauty, her beau bought it."

Rocky looked askance at his brother. "Yeah, I heard the poor man died. Heard she's broken up about it, too."

Jonathan smiled. "Tough luck, least for some."

Rocky waited for Jonathan to finish unloading the birds, take the shell belt from around his waist. He put an arm around his brother's shoulder, leading him away from camp.

"Come with me, brother. Want to take a walk."

When they were off the trail, Rocky turned and nodded to his brother. He looked left, then right. "Good. We're alone."

Jonathan smiled. "Guess we are. What's this all about?"

"Remove your hat, Jonathan."

"Why?"

"Just remove your hat."

He did, and once it was placed, carefully, atop an unopened palm frond, Rocky backhanded his brother so hard, the lad saw stars.

He fell on his wounded backside, then looked up at Rocky, towering over him.

"What the hell'd you do that for?" He felt the side of his face, checking it for blood; it stung so, he was certain it had been fileted open.

"Because of your ugly talk." He pointed. "Don't stand up, Jonathan, or I'll knock you down again. I have stuff to say to you. You sit there and shut up and listen."

"Like hell I will, you son of a bitch!"

He sprang to his feet, torpedoing Rocky in the abdomen. The two tumbled over and over, but Rocky was having none of it. All his life he'd been licked every time by Jonathan. Now things were different.

He rolled, freed himself of Jonathan's grasp, delivering a firm uppercut. The boy crumpled.

"Son of a bitch, Rocky! What the hell's wrong with you?"

"I done told you, don't stand up!"

"All right, all right. I won't stand up. Tell me what's got into you, goddamn it!"

"You! You!" He turned his head from side to side. "You act like some young colt, full of piss and vinegar. Pleased that some man's dead, 'cause you have stars in your eyes over that poor nurse. Goddamn you, Jonathan. It ain't right, and what of Francesca?"

Jonathan grinned, moving his jaw about with his hand. "Always the chivalrous knight, ain't you, Rocky? The drunken chivalrous knight! Stickin' your nose where it doesn't belong.

"Fact is, Francesca's not here. She's home, and I've been shot in the ass, and it might well have been my gourd, and we might not live another day, and, goddamn it, I'm planning to live life here on out to its fullest." He grinned. "Of all people, thought you'd understand that, Rock."

"Don't call me Rock!" It sounded ridiculous coming from Jonathan. Only Bill McGinty called him Rock.

"Yeah, yeah." He felt his jaw again. "Of all people, thought you'd know all about living for the here and now. Jesus, did that malaria finish pickling what's left of your alcohol-soaked brain?"

"No!" He wanted to punch him again. He wanted to shake some sense into him. *His* brother, the golden boy, talking like a senseless, selfish bastard.

"Everything's always been too easy for you, Jonathan. You act like some kinda royalty. Well, it isn't right. It's not right to treat Francesca in such a way. Not right to treat that nurse in such a way. You act like them fine ladies are whores you use and cast away. Goddamn it, I know you're better'n that."

Jonathan wandered to his hat as it swayed in the breeze, riding the palm like a wave crashing on the beach. He spoke into it while checking for pests. He spoke quietly, almost in a whisper. "I can't see her face, Rocky." He turned to his brother with a look of despondency. "I try so hard to see Francesca. Just can't. I . . . I don't know what's come over me. Don't know anything anymore. And, well, that day, when I came in to the hospital tent and saw that beauty standing there all worn out and tiny and gnawing on a piece of hard tack with her hands and face all covered in blood . . ." He turned his head slowly from side to side. "Something snapped, Rocky. I don't know how to explain it, but I swear to you, brother, if I could have, if she would have been willing, I would have torn her dress off and done her right there among the sick and dying men." He wiped his sweaty brow. "And the image of doing that keeps running over and over in my head, like those films we saw in Tampa brought down from that dude in New York. Remember? His machine jammed and the pictures kept flippin' of that acrobat juggling. Same ones, over and over. It is like that, over and over and over again. I don't know what's happening to me, Rocky. I have dark thoughts like that all the time. Dark and mean." He ran a trembling hand through his curly hair. "Don't know anymore."

"It's this goddamned place." Rocky looked around, remembered something. "What of that locket Francesca gave you? You said it had a picture of her. Look at it, Jonathan. Look at it and remember her!"

"Lost it."

Rocky paced up and down. All fury. "It's this goddamned place and the fighting and the malaria and the shitty food and no sleep, Jonathan. It's even the Colonel, God bless him, but he's . . . he's too goddamned much! Pushing us and pushing us. We'll all be dead or nuts by the end of it, I swear. You should have seen him, charging up that hill, like a goddamned madman he was. We . . . Jesus Christ, we followed him more to keep him from capture by the Spanish bastards than to kill 'em."

"I know! But, Rocky, I love it, too. Love it even if it's making me nuts."

Rocky smiled uneasily. Jonathan *was* acting nuts.

"Seems this war has filled your head with wisdom and mine, with shit."

They both had to laugh about that. Jonathan knew how to bring him down from a manic attack. He smoked quietly for a while, then Rocky broke the silence. "Jonathan, what *is* constipated?"

"What?"

"The colonel, he said you ran like a constipated duck. What the hell does that mean?"

"I think it means you can't shit, but tell you the truth, Rocky, don't know what a duck would run like if it couldn't shit."

"Well, I'm imagining not good." He twisted another smoke and lit it. "It's funny, him charging a quarter every time a man swears. I heard those Australian boys, the ones who sold me that terrible shit to drink, they've paid so many quarters, the colonel has almost enough to build a Rough Riders chapel. And, brother, you should have heard the colonel, when we attacked that hill." He remembered his canteen. "Look. See them marks? That's a mark for every swear word the colonel said, and I'll tell you, brother, he wasn't just sayin' 'damn' or 'hell' or 'shit.' He was cursing words I'm too bashful to say. I haven't had the nerve to present him with the count, but it's sure a good one."

Rocky turned serious. The thought of Jonathan alone with the nurse worried him. Not that he thought Jonathan would molest her, but he would not put it past his brother to work his silver tongue, torment her. She deserved better than that. She was a proper lady. She deserved to be left alone to grieve for her captain.

"Jonathan, please do me a favor. Leave that poor girl alone. Leave her be. It's not the right time, and, well, whatever's gotten into your head, you need to back away. You and me, we need to make it through this damned adventure and go home. After you see Francesca again, and settle with Father and Ellen and everyone, well, if you're still so preoccupied, you can worry about it then." He grabbed his brother by the suspenders, pulling him close, not a little threatening. "But until then, brother, you promise, you'll back away."

"My word of honor." He meant it, or at least looked as though he meant it. "You're right, and I'm acting stupid. My word of honor, brother, I'll treat her the way I treat that nun and that colored girl. No different from them. I promise."

But Rocky was too wise. He'd seen it, time and again, year after year. The golden boy with the golden tongue. Most of the time, Jonathan was about as genuine as a politician. Rocky grabbed his brother by the throat. Holding him in a death grip, he said, "Don't buffalo me, Jonathan! I swear to Christ, you hurt that poor woman, I, I swear I'll —"

Jonathan broke free. He grinned slyly. Certain Rocky was too weak to act on such bravado. "You'll do *nothing,* brother!"

Pulling his hat from his head, turning it over in his hands, he said. "Stay outta my way, Rocky. That nurse is a grown woman. An attractive woman. I'll guarantee it, it won't be the first time she's dealt with suitors the likes a' me." He winked. "Hell, she'll probably teach me a thing or two."

"Don't talk in such a way!"

Jonathan turned away. "You just remember, brother. She knows her mind, and I know mine."

CHAPTER 31

Minerva kept busy. The little urchins brought in by Rocky were a pleasant distraction. She'd stopped them cursing and had put them, with the aid of the cook, on the path to learning English. She thought it would come in handy, as the new occupiers of their land would no doubt require its use in all things official.

Clara's tragedy broke her heart. She watched her comrade move about, conducting her duties like an automaton.

Sister Bonaventure was most helpful. Minerva had never met so well-adjusted a human being. Too intelligent to be mindlessly happy all the time, but there was a contentment about her that Minerva had never known in another person. She wondered what they'd have done without her.

Rocky had returned to the front with the rest of the men fit enough for duty, and she missed him. The few moments she had to herself were spent re-reading Juan José's letter, and the one scribbled in pencil from Rocky, written with the aid of Woodbury Kane, which read,

Dear Nurse Trumbull,

This letter is meant to apologize for my rude behavior to you. I cannot bear to speak it in person. It was too mean a thing to say, and my actions too wicked to speak of out loud. The fact that I was sick is no excuse.

I am a rough and rude man, but I am a man and should know better than to speak so ugly to a lady who was only trying to help me. The fact that I laid hands on you and knocked you down is an offense for a court-martial and firing squad or the hang man's rope, and I am grateful to you that you have not demanded such justice. I would not blame you if you had me executed, and I am forever beholden to you for sparing my life.

I hope that you will find it in your heart to forgive me.

Rocky Killebrew, Private,
1st United States Volunteer Cavalry,
Arizona Contingent

The handsome brother interrupted her

thoughts. He stood, baring that ubiquitous Cheshire cat grin. The little girl held on, piggy-back.

"How you doing today, Nurse Trumbull?"

She looked up from her letter. "Fine, Trooper."

"What's got you so preoccupied?"

"Oh, nothing." She folded the letter, replacing it in her skirt pocket. It was her constant companion.

"Trooper —"

"Would rather you call me Jonathan."

"Jonathan, what do you know of the little hamlet between here and Siboney?"

Jonathan conferred with the girl, who turned her head. *"La Jaroba."* She spit rudely on the ground. "Bad land, bad land."

"What do you mean?"

Jonathan translated. The little one replied, this time in her English; it was that important to convey to the Yankee lady. "People sick all the times now. This time of year people dies all the times."

"Why do you ask?" Jonathan lowered the girl to the ground. She ran toward the cook, who'd been putting together something for the midday meal.

"I . . . no, nothing." Minerva looked off at the little one negotiating with the surly cook. "I . . . well, Juan José's mother lives there."

"Who?"

"Oh, of course. I am sorry. Juan José Julián Pérez." Her heart fluttered when she said his full name. "He's a captain in the revolutionary army. I . . . well . . . No, it's a foolish thought."

"What's a foolish thought?"

"He asked me to deliver a letter to her, back when we met in Key West, but then sent me another telling me not to bother. I wanted to maybe meet her, but, I know, it's a silly notion."

Jonathan turned to the girl, devouring a chunk of hardtack soaked in lard. He asked her, "How far to walk to *La Jaroba?*"

She held up a finger. *"Una hora."*

Jonathan turned to Minerva. "One hour by foot. We can use one of those mules Rocky found, hitch him up to an ambulance wagon. Can cut that by at least a half."

"You're not serious?"

"Sure, why not?" Jonathan smiled. "All the sick are doing good; they can miss you for a few hours. One of the boys is in tiptop shape; he'll stand guard in my stead. We'll take the little one as guide. Be back," he checked his watch, "if we leave in an hour, we'll be back by sundown."

"Why are you acting so queer?" Jonathan looked askance at the child, covered, like a diminutive ghost, in one of the bed sheets she'd stolen from their field hospital's supply.

She peeked up at him, disgusted, not happy to be volunteered for this duty, speaking in her native tongue. "You will find out."

At a dip in the road they did. Mosquitos swarmed, mostly attacking Minerva. Jonathan tapped the mule, urging it into a canter. He swatted mosquitos landing on his face and neck.

The girl told him to light a cigar.

"I don't smoke."

"Then light one of these." She handed him a pack of pre-twisted cigarettes and matches, stolen from one of the wounded men. "Smoke, Yankee, smoke."

Jonathan did and so did the girl. It seemed to help a little.

When they arrived at the hamlet, located on higher ground, the insects stopped molesting them. Both Rocky and Minerva looked terrible, welts raised all over both of them as if they'd been pelted by pea shooters.

The girl emerged from her protective shroud. She grinned. She smugly responded to Jonathan, "I told you, bad, bad. We should not be here, Yankee man."

Jonathan stopped at the town center, nothing more than an intersection of dilapidated hovels. There was a hitching post and trough of questionable water. He would not let the mule drink from it.

Two men approached. Dark men, African, not mulatto like Minerva's suitor. The girl asked them where to find the mother of Juan José, the captain of revolutionaries.

They bowed, as though Juan José was big medicine. They beckoned the troupe to follow, Jonathan bringing up the rear, his Mauser ready. He looked rather imposing in his Rough Rider outfit.

It somewhat confounded Minerva, as for some, frankly illogical, reason, she imagined a fine hacienda, to be greeted by an army of servants. The lady of the house, dressed in her finery, would lead her to an open terrace, where they'd dine on biscuits and English tea.

Of course, this was not Juan José's fault. He never remotely suggested such an upbringing. It was his carriage, his sophistication, his all-consuming self-confidence that suggested it. Merely suggested, but never declared it.

Instead, they were led into a darkened room that stank of old people, unwashed bodies, and bad breath, the sweet smell of decay and impending death.

Juan José's mother reclined on a narrow bed, blowing clouds of cigar smoke at the ceiling. She smiled toothlessly when she saw Minerva. Both women shared the same dark skin. Juan José's mother was the African in the equation. Minerva's heart fluttered.

Juan José's mother had no English, and Jonathan did the translating. He told how Minerva and her son had met in Florida. Minerva handed her the letter, which she could not read. Jonathan did so for her.

She extinguished the cigar and, with difficulty, moved to a chair. She pulled Minerva's hands into her lap. She pressed a palm to the nurse's cheek and whispered, *"Hermosa, muy Hermosa."*

"She says you're beautiful."

Minerva had to look away, cast her gaze to the old woman's legs, swollen and infected due to the ravages of poor health and flies and time. She grabbed her nurse's bag, pulling out some of its contents. She needed to do *something, anything* for Juan José's mother.

She was initially rebuffed until Jonathan

explained that Minerva was a proper army nurse. The old woman appeared pleased.

"Please tell her, Jonathan." She held up the rolls of gauze and ointment. "She must put on new dressing every night, change the bandages, and bathe with only water that has been boiled."

He did, and the woman smiled. It was unclear if she'd comply or even understood.

The old woman turned her attention to a scrapbook, stories about her boy. She showed them article after article, tapping each picture. *"Mi Juan José, mi hijo, mi hijo!"* She smiled and patted Minerva on the face again, turning to Jonathan. *"Te casas?"*

Jonathan smiled. "She wants to know if you will be married to her son."

Minerva smiled. The old woman was dead on her feet. There was no reason for Minerva to play her typical role of the self-effacing, the humble. She knew, if the woman were to live long enough, the match would please her. She'd not deprive her a little happiness. Instead she nodded resolutely. "Perhaps, *Señora*, perhaps. If God is willing."

The old woman pointed to a chest in the corner of the room, secreted behind a pile of old newspapers. She asked Jonathan to retrieve it. He did, placing it on the bed.

She motioned for him to open it. She removed what could only be described as rags, tossing them onto the floor. When the chest was empty, she removed a false bottom, revealing piles of American bills. To these she added the money from the envelope.

Jonathan looked up at Minerva. "My God, must be a thousand dollars."

The revolutionary's mother pointed to Minerva, speaking to Jonathan, and then pointed to the chest.

"She wants you to take it."

"Oh, no, no!" She turned her head. "Tell, her, please, 'For *you*, for *you, Señora,* for help; use it to buy medicine.' "

Jonathan translated. The old woman smiled. "I do not need medicine. I do not need money." She grinned. "I need a new body. I need to be thirty years younger."

A wave of exhaustion overtook her, and they helped her back to bed. She kissed Minerva on the cheek, pressing the letter to her breast with one hand. She squeezed Minerva's with the other. *"Que Dios te acompañe."*

Minerva stood, busied herself putting the chest back in order, returning it to its hiding place.

Jonathan whispered in his companion's

ear, "She said, 'May God go with you, Nurse Trumbull.' "

CHAPTER 32

Colonel Roosevelt's draconian method of grieving was no comfort whatsoever. How could she stop thinking of Mortimer? He was in all her thoughts and dreams and nightmares. He was with her constantly when he was alive, and the thought of taking the colonel's advice seemed counterintuitive. How could she grieve properly if she pushed him into the recesses of her mind?

But then again, perhaps it was not such terrible advice. She'd never in all her life met such a man as the colonel. As manly as they come, yet with the compassion and tenderness of Sister Bonaventure. He had evidently known the same love, passion, obsession, perfection in union she'd shared with Mortimer.

Around dark Minerva brought her a tray. "Some chicken from that boy shot in the backside. He hunts them. Cannot say they are much but skin and bones, but better than the canned meat they've been feeding us." She looked at Clara with her red nose and puffy eyes. She stroked her hair. "Don't guess you're much hungry anyway."

"I'm sorry for not working today, Minnie. I imagine you've been run ragged doing your job as well as mine." She rubbed her temples. "I can't seem to shake this headache. Dr. Church is convinced it's a migraine. Please forgive me, Minnie." She remembered seeing that Minerva had received a letter when hers had arrived. "What news have you received? Hopefully better than mine."

"Oh, yes, from Juan José, and, Clara, Colonel Roosevelt mentioned him. He was talking about the battle with the Cuba revolutionaries, over on the other side of the island. He mentioned Captain Pérez, my captain, Clara. He was with the Marines. Can you believe it? *My* captain!"

"I'm pleased for you, Minnie." She looked her partner over. "You look exhausted."

"No, I'm okay. The men are all good, hardly need nursing. Dr. Church has everyone tip-top. And the ones not so bad are helping, God bless 'em, the colonel's men, they're some loyal fellows. They're called Roosevelt's boys."

"Roosevelt's boys."

"Yes. He was mighty nice. He shook my hand, even with it all bloody on account I'd just changed that boy from Texas's head dressing. He told me that I was a credit to my Nubian race." She smiled.

Clara turned away, facing the tent wall. The tears came again, and she did not want Minerva to see them, afraid she'd try to keep her from working another day.

"I'm not hungry, Minnie. Why not take that and give it to one of Roosevelt's boys. I'm sure one could use it."

It was a few minutes after three when she dreamed so vividly of him. Dr. Church had offered her a sleeping draught; she had taken it, and it gave her queer dreams.

He looked well, not of a corpse but as alive as when she'd seen him leave from Key West. They were in the carriage and riding in the silver of the moonlight. A cool breeze of ocean air washed over them.

"Love me?" He was so handsome.

"With all my heart, Mortimer." She felt that rush of joy run through her. She loved him so.

"I love you, too." He shifted, pulling her into the crook of his arm. He kissed her temple.

"The colonel's right, you know."

She felt the joy drain, replaced with dread, replaced with a sense of despondency, as his comment reminded her that he was dead.

"What did you say, Mortimer?"

"I said the colonel's right." He held her in his arms. "Don't fight me on this, my dear little German Clara." He waited for her body to relax. "We had our time, a time that is not known in a thousand lifetimes. It was my happiest moment, Clara, and you've made me complete. I've left this earth full, but you must endure. You are too young to waste a life grieving. Move on, Clara. I'll be waiting for you."

"Where?"

She sat up, and the dream was fading. "Where, Mortimer, where?"

"On the other side." She could not see him; he was fading. "I love you, darling. See you on the other side, my love, but not too soon. Not for at least the full span of a lovely German nurse's lifetime. Good-bye, my love. God bless you. Good-bye."

CHAPTER 33

Clara's heart dropped to the pit of her stomach when she saw the brash Arizonan and his ubiquitous smile, swaggering outside her tent. At least his wound was healing, as evidenced by his ability to strut like a gamecock.

He tipped his hat, and she was encouraged by his expression, no longer that wild look of a rutting bull. He seemed kinder. Disarming. If this was an act, it was a good one.

He pulled his hat from his head, bowing, offering her a good day.

"Good day to you, Trooper Thomson."

"I'm actually Trooper Whelihan, Nurse Maass."

"But I heard the colonel address you as Thomson."

Jonathan flashed a toothy grin as he handed the Guinea fowl to the cook. "That's one of the colonel's little jokes. I'm a runner, ma'am. He says I run like a deer from Africa, a Thomson's gazelle. Colonel says, if I end up buying it, he'll ensure they use my proper name."

Clara looked the birds over, the shotgun in Jonathan's hands, his Mauser strapped to his back. She could not stop herself from liking him a little, especially after what he'd done for Minerva in her quest to meet her suitor's mother.

"I wanted to say, ma'am, I'm mighty sorry for your loss." He looked away. These days, any talk of death and killing overwhelmed him. He didn't know why.

"Thank you." Clara hesitated. "One moment, Trooper." She went to her tent, returning momentarily with a Red Cross brassard. She placed it above the elbow of his left arm. "Wear this, Trooper Thomson. We've been told the guerillas are shooting non-combatants, but who knows, maybe it will help when you are out collecting dinner for us. Maybe, God willing, they'll honor it. It certainly can't hurt."

She looked the plump Guinea fowl over and thought of Minerva. Dear Minerva, calling them scrawny to make her feel better about not having an appetite.

It all overwhelmed her. She pulled the glasses from her face, turned away, and

405

started cleaning them, hopeful that the young man would not see her crying.

Jonathan tried to lighten her mood. "Well, ma'am, I thank you. Fact is, I'm not really a non-combatant." He nodded to the shotgun in his hands, acknowledged the Mauser strapped over his shoulder. "I'm supposed to be guarding you ladies, but Trooper Wilson's taken over that duty, now that he's up and about. Guess those Guinea birds would not think me a non-combatant, either." He grinned, encouraged that she'd recovered a little, as evidenced by her thin smile.

"Glad to see a smile on that pretty face." He immediately regretted it. He was such an ass these days. What the hell was he thinking? "I . . . I mean, ma'am . . ." He felt a complete fool. "I'm not trying to be fresh." He felt his throat tighten, as it had the day Rocky choked him. "I'd like to be friends." He extended his hand. "May we do that, ma'am, be friends?" He pulled his hat from his head, speaking into it. "I don't know what comes over me these days. I mean, that day we first met, I was a regular scoundrel, pulling your glasses from your face, a regular brute and bounder, ma'am. Inexcusable."

"I think that would be possible." She shook his proffered hand. "I think we could be friends, and, yes, Trooper Thomson. I forgive you for your earlier indiscretion."

"Good. Well, I'd better be off; old Pablo has given me a quota. You all *do* go through these chickens. I need to kill another dozen before sundown." He grinned again. "And I hear there's deer about. White tails. Can you believe that, ma'am? White tails and wild pigs, too, in this terrible jungle. Would be nice to find the wounded fellows some hearty fresh meat instead of just fowl. We'll see, we'll see." He turned and walked away.

Clara called out. "Trooper Thomson."

He froze, turning his head hopefully. "Yes, ma'am?"

"*Do* be careful."

She bumped into Dr. Church as she entered the ward tent. He nodded, giving her a fatherly pat on the shoulder.

"How's the headache, nurse?"

"Gone, Dr. Church. I'm fine, really."

She thought a lot about Trooper Thomson as she worked, automatically, without giving much attention to the mundane tasks at hand. She'd worked automatically, almost trance-like, ever since she'd found out that he was dead. He was dead. Mortimer Hollander was dead.

How could Colonel Roosevelt have ever

arrived at such a ludicrous recommendation? Remove Mortimer from her mind? It was preposterous. The man must have had an iron will to have done it regarding the woman that meant as much to him as Mortimer had to Clara.

The wounded were always pleasant to her, always extraordinarily respectful, even more so than they were to Sister Bonaventure and Minerva, now that they knew her man was dead.

Why? They did not want to appear inappropriate, that's why. They did not want to appear lustful, hopeful. Hopeful of what? That they woo her? Never, never, never!

Dr. Church commented on that, before they'd found out Mortimer was dead. Church knew it, saw it. Women in combat were a liability, especially young and beautiful ones. He said it was best to have nuns for nurses, and old nuns at that. Ugly, old, and fat, preferably.

He was not mean about it, just pragmatic. Nuns and, of course, nurses and orderlies who were men did not distract soldiers. Did not allow their minds to wander to impossible situations. Did not remind them of their terrible situation. Did not remind them of home.

And Minerva, of course. Although she was

beautiful, she was a Negro, and these men were all white, except for the Indians, but they did not look upon Minerva in the way they regarded Clara. Even pure beauty could not span the gulf of institutionalized bigotry. It would likely take a long time for people to look on a woman like Minerva for what she was, a human being. Maybe such would *never* be the case.

Even back home in the German hospital, she was a celebrity. She had been a little flattered by it. Only a little; she'd never let vanity consume her. That was sinful. But she knew she was beautiful. She had been beautiful since she was a little girl.

Beautiful, beautiful! Damn her beauty; damn the fact that men wanted her. She did not want them, and she did not want them to want her. She wanted Mortimer, and he was dead.

Perhaps she'd have been spared all that, had she not been beautiful. Had she been plain, frumpy, or dumpy or downright ugly. Had she not cast her spell on Mortimer, he'd have never knocked on her door that first night on the ship. Lied to her, tricked her into dining with him and his uncle and aunt. Then she would have never known this loss.

The men were mortified at their unshaven

faces, disheveled hair, soiled bedsheets, the vomitus in the pails by the bed, the dirty bedpans. All the items she'd respectfully remove, clean, make right, always with that angel's countenance. Damn her beauty. Damn the feelings of hope, lust, anxiety, desire it evoked in herself and the damaged men.

Perhaps she should become a nun. Were there Lutheran nuns? Certainly there were the deaconesses. She knew a few. Were they the same as Catholic nuns? She'd never known any to marry. Did they live the same celibate lives? Did they consider themselves married to Jesus? She didn't know.

Oh, to be like Sister Bonaventure. To be free of this corporeal obsession. To be free of the longing and lusting in the men's eyes.

They never looked upon the sister in such a way. She was lucky; she was married to Jesus. Clara thought of the diamond-encrusted ring he'd given her, tucked away in her luggage. Thought of the plain pewter one the nun wore. She'd trade it in a moment if it would end this torture, this desire for him, this memory of the love they felt for each other. Why, oh why did she have to have ever felt that way toward any man? How could she ever feel the same for another? Betray him, moldering in his grave.

Betray him for another? Could she ever feel anything remotely as profound as what she'd felt for Mortimer? She doubted it — no, was certain of it. No man alive could ever compare.

A young lad smiled as she worked around him, unaware of her surroundings, unaware, really, of him, in the bed not three feet away.

"What's causing you such distraction, Nurse Maass?" He was a nice boy, young, likely the youngest she'd cared for, sixteen, *if that,* as he was known to be a fibber when it came to such detail. He'd not yet needed to shave; that was evident.

"Oh, nothing, Robert. I'm sorry. I'm a little tired." She inspected his dressing, sniffed it, and that elicited a chuckle.

"You nurses are some iron ladies, I'll say that!"

"Oh, the nose never lies, Robert."

"What's a bad wound smell like?"

"Oh, you would know it if you encountered it." She patted his shoulder. "And yours is not a bad one. You'll be home and back to work in no time."

He blushed. "I've never been to work, Nurse."

"Oh?" She remembered his youth. "Then school, perhaps?"

"Yes, ma'am." He blushed. "I'm not the

youngest, though, you know?"

"No?" She said it in a way that assured him his secret was safe.

"I heard that a boy of nine smuggled himself aboard our transport, had a cutdown .22 and three boxes of cartridges. Can you believe that, ma'am, nine years old, by God. What a story he'll have for his grandchildren."

Clara spoke without thinking. "*If* he survives." She looked into the boy's eyes, and her sadness weighed heavily on his heart. "*If* he survives, Robert."

"Oh, he never made it to Cuba. He was caught boarding in Florida. Sent back. Heard he'd become a mascot, along with the mountain lion and that eagle."

"That's reassuring."

She decided to change the dressing, pulled up an empty cartridge box, and began unwinding the bandage wrapped around his torso, revealing the gaping wound. She unpacked Minerva's dressing and smiled to herself at the memory of her fellow nurse's unwarranted self-doubt. Robert seemed to read her mind.

"That Negro nurse is a crackerjack."

"She is, Robert."

"I've never known a Negro before this."

"Where are you from?"

"Oh, Rhode Island, and there are Negroes up there, at least a few, just not . . . well, not in my circles, ma'am. All our servants are Irish." He smiled. "I've spent most of my time in New Hampshire, actually. At school." He stopped as if he'd remembered that he might not want to tell too much.

"College?" Clara knew that young lads were always pleased to be thought of as much older.

"Oh, no, ma'am. It's, ah, preparatory school, preparatory for college."

"I see." She busied herself. "Which school is that, Robert?"

"Oh, you'd likely not know it. Phillips Exeter Academy. It's kind of small."

"And you will be off to college next year?"

"Oh, well, no, ma'am, to let you in on a little secret," he looked about, whispering. "I've a ways yet till I attend college."

"How long, Robert?"

"Oh, five, ah, I guess five years, ma'am."

"So, you've either been rather a dunce, or you're not yet fifteen."

"Yes, ma'am, I mean, no, ma'am, I'm no dunce. Finished last term second in my class. Another fellow beat me by half a percent." He looked about for eavesdroppers, whispering again. "I'll be fifteen this October."

"And your mother and father. They can't know of this adventure."

"Oh, no, ma'am. They're in Europe. They're pretty busy. They think I'm off to a dude ranch in Colorado. I don't see them much. I didn't see them at all in ninety-seven. They're too busy traveling, I guess. I figured I'd be back for next term; no one would ever miss me."

She lingered about him for a while, as he was chatty and seemed to need the comfort of her presence. She liked the young fellow. Something innocent and pure about him. Likely too young yet to desire the opposite sex. At least if he did, he hid such desire well. He was gentlemanly. Gentlemanly. What an odd term for describing a child. He was a long way from becoming a man.

Jonathan felt good when she said that to him. Felt good and happy and alive. *'Trooper Thomson, do be careful.'* It tickled him to be known by the German beauty as Trooper Thomson. Maybe he'd change his name after all this was over. That would give his father a proper fit.

He no longer wanted to bed her. Despite her beauty, her allure, he no longer had carnal thoughts of her, and that made him rather proud.

Not that he was lecherous or weak or pre-occupied. He wasn't. He never considered women only objects, devices for the mere slaking of man's passion. Rocky's word came back to him. Shamed him. He'd no sooner treat the nurse or Francesca like a whore than he would rob a bank. He even treated whores with respect.

But some quality about the nurse had triggered something unnatural, and, as if a demon had been exorcised, he felt well to be shed of it.

He smiled at the memory of the drubbing Rocky had given him. Maybe his brother had knocked some sense into him after all. Maybe Rocky was right. Maybe it was this unholy place, the disease, the heat, the poor food, the trauma of war and killing and dying.

He checked his watch and the sky and clouds. He regarded the Red Cross brassard on his arm. It felt more like a target than a talisman against Cuban sharpshooter fire. Oh well, she put it there, and he'd sooner cut off his arm than remove it.

He followed a game trail, and the wind was right, in his face, but the heat was unbearable. Even the deer had more sense than to be up wandering this time of day.

He resolved to find a high spot and stand-hunt. A pleasant breeze rendered it bearable, and it was still good for hunting. He was downwind of several trails that converged on a clearing. There was plenty of sign about. It was likely he'd ambush some there, if they had a mind to wander by.

He pulled out the journal he kept, opening it to the letter to Ellen he was working on, read over the part he'd finished, and a cascade of emotion washed over him. All that he'd seen and done in a few days, enough experience packed in such a short span of time. He thought about that fateful day in Tampa, when it was learned, much to Colonel Roosevelt's dismay, that many of the troop would be left behind, along with most of their precious horses and mules.

It was a scandal, but the most moving experience for Jonathan was to witness the reactions of the rough fellows, the men a hundred times more worthy than he or Rocky, when they learned that they could not join the fight.

He thought back to the trip on the transport. Bill McGinty playing at a little cauldron, trying every trick he'd learned those many years on the frontier to transform disgusting things into something palatable. He'd done wonders with armadillo, rattler, even a Gila monster he shot as it stood on a little boulder, sunning itself one time. But no manner of culinary magic could transform that canned fresh beef into anything that did not resemble an old gut pile. Everyone agreed: the thick gel that encapsulated the tiny hunk of meat was all but impossible to overcome.

He thought of the flying fish. Flying fish, he told Ellen in his letter. She'd never believe it. But there they were, flying out from the wake of the ship, real fish, flying above the surface of the ocean. Fish with wings. Who'd have ever guessed such creatures inhabited the oceans of this world? The colonel even gave a little lecture on it. Told them the Latin name and that they were good eating.

Jonathan laughed at the memory when Rocky cocked his head, asking the colonel if they tasted like trout or prairie chicken. It was the first time he'd seen the colonel at a loss for words, as he initially thought Rocky was having some fun with him. Poor Rocky was not having fun, however. He did not know how to be ironic.

Soon he was drifting and asleep, propped up against a sturdy palm.

Francesca visited him, had come with a fresh canteen of water and was drizzling it over his head. He sat up and could see her face, and it was as he'd left it that day in Prescott. She was so clean, her raven hair freshly washed and brushed, with one of those fancy Spanish silver combs. She wore that dress he loved so much, the pretty sheer cotton one, the one that exposed her tan shoulders and collar bones and that dimple immediately below her throat.

Her belly was starting to grow, and that pleased him. She smiled when she understood his confusion. Yes, they could still make love when she was growing a baby inside her. It would not hurt either one of them.

So they did love in the Cuban jungle for a long time, and Jonathan awoke to the snap of a twig a few yards off. It was late, almost supper time, he'd dozed so long.

He leveled the front sight of the Mauser at the spot above the doe's foreleg, firing at less than twenty yards. She dropped, kicked a little, and was dead.

The bleating of the fawn brought him fully to his senses, as he was still groggy from his nap.

Father would be furious. Sean Whelihan did not like hunting, tolerated it grudgingly, but would never allow it in the spring and summer for this reason.

As far as the surly old confederate was

concerned, it was an outrage to leave babies orphaned and unable to fend for themselves. *Any* babies, whether they be deer, or foxes or coyotes or javelina.

But war was war, and meat was meat, and Jonathan worked the bolt and pressed the trigger a second time, as the baby was too young yet to live without its mother's milk. It was more a kindness than an acquisition for the stew pot, as the creature would render little useful sustenance.

It, too, lay dead, and another, the fawn's sibling, appeared, seemingly from nowhere, as if his deadly deed had caused it to sprout, like a mushroom, from out of the ground.

It was overwhelming, and, again, Jonathan took careful aim, dropping the diminutive creature, bewildered and frightened, where it stood, between its dead twin and mother.

He felt paralyzed; his legs would not hold him. Certain any minute he'd lose consciousness.

What would Father say? What would Father do if he ever found out? The thought of it mortified him.

He thought of Ellen and Louis and all the men on the ranch. He missed them. What had he done, why had he come here, why was he not home where he belonged?

He stood, resolved to finish what he'd

started, resolved to carry the freshly killed meat to the cook and the invalids. It was important for him to have the deaths serve some useful purpose.

He propped the Mauser against the palm, found his pocket knife, the one his sister had given him on his thirteenth birthday. He moved toward the nearest fawn, offering a clear view of the Red Cross brassard. The Cuban's bullet found its mark.

CHAPTER 34

It was nearly sundown as the nurses grabbed a few moments to take a meal together under the shade of the mango. It seemed the last of the battling was over and the wounded patched up as best they could do in the field hospital. The ones too badly injured were safely delivered to the hospital ship, *Relief,* lying off the coast. The ones not slated for evacuation were kept where they were, as Dr. Church declared he'd not send a man to Siboney, as it would likely be his death sentence, so disorganized and poorly run was the diseased place.

He joined them and looked to be about as sick as a man could be without outright dying. The fever was the next challenge, and, as if the gods had willed it, it waited long enough for the major hostilities to end. It then began afflicting the men with malaria, the Cuban fever, as it was known, and a few of the regular army with the yellow jack.

He patted Minerva on the shoulder as she cut the food on his plate. "It is a sad state of affairs when a surgeon is too sick to operate on a Guinea hen."

Sister Bonaventure poured him a brandy, a gift from her parishioners. When they'd learned, through one of Bonaventure's casual comments in a letter home, that they had nothing to give to the men, she'd received six bottles, a gallon each. She hid them well, and only Jonathan and another guard knew their location in a trunk under the nun's bed.

Church held the cup with a trembling hand. "Sister, you are a miracle worker."

When he'd consumed all that he thought he might keep down, he dropped the cup onto the camp table as if it weighed too much.

In a little while Clara stood as she finished her own meal. "It's off to bed with you, Doctor." She glanced at her companions. "Everything is under control."

He stood unsteadily, allowing Minnie to help him. She looked extra tiny as the imposing physician used her as a crutch.

Their quiet moment was soon interrupted by little Carlita, smoking a fancy, factory twisted cigarette. Clara smelled her before she saw her, quickly pulling the smoke from between the child's lips, throwing it to the ground. She stomped it as if it were a tarantula, wagging a finger in the child's face. "No smoking for little girls!"

"Lo siento, mucho." She offered an impish smile.

"En Inglés, Carlita, en Inglés," admonished Minerva, sitting nearby with Church, who was unable to travel the short distance between the makeshift dining spot and his tent.

"I sorry." She pointed in the direction of the jungle. "Jonathan, not back. Jonathan still in jungle, for chickens."

A chill ran through Clara. There could be no good reason for his tardiness. She looked each of her companions in the eye. Sister Bonaventure spoke.

"Tomorrow, we should find his brother. Trooper Killebrew should know."

Carlita smiled, pointing in the direction of Kettle Hill. "Carl already to find Rocky."

"What's happening?" Harry Thorpe, a physician who'd enlisted as a trooper, his skills soon discovered when he ended up amongst the wounded, walked up on the impromptu dinner party. He sat on an upended bucket next to Clara. He appeared alarmed by Church's pallor, as the doctor again rose, starting to limp off to bed.

Thorpe gestured, offering a hand, as Minerva herself had only recently recovered from a bout with fever.

She waved him off. "I have him, Dr. Thorpe. Sit and eat something."

Thorpe retook his seat, wincing at the healing bullet wound under his arm. He'd not argue with her. "Rest well, sir. We'll take care of everything."

Clara turned to Thorpe. "Trooper Thomson's missing." Clara corrected herself. "I mean Whelihan."

"Oh, the Arizona fellow. Good shot." He thanked Sister Bonaventure for the plate and immediately bit into a strip of breast. He picked a lead pellet from between his teeth. "I'm sorry to hear that."

Clara stood. The idea of yet another person dying whom she'd gotten to know and like made her extra melancholy. She wandered off without saying anything. Sister Bonaventure motioned for Thorpe to follow after her. He picked up the remaining piece of fowl, eating it as he walked.

They ended up in the hospital tent, as Clara needed to occupy her mind, and caring for the wounded was a comfort. Perhaps she could keep many of them from dying, about the only thing sustaining her.

He began automatically helping her. She

liked him. A New Yorker, he was competent, kind, self-effacing, not unlike Dan Regan, the doctor from Boston she'd met at Camp Cuba Libre, though Thorpe was significantly younger, likely not much older than Clara.

Despite the fact that he was far from recovered from his own wound, he worked with the diligence and efficiency of a fit man, and Church and the ladies found him indispensable. Their field hospital was superior to anything on the island, despite its remoteness and lack of ample food and medicine. No one could argue that, and an extra physician was welcome.

Jonathan awoke at dusk from what felt like one of those long midday sleeps that renders the body immobile. A fly had lighted on his nose, and it felt queer as he tried to raise his hand to swat it. Arm, hand, torso asleep. The deepest he'd ever experienced.

He breathed deeply and considered what had happened. He looked at his left foot, twisted into a most unorthodox position. That should hurt, but it didn't. Was again more fascinated than frustrated at the realization that he could not move it or feel discomfort.

He lay there for a long while, gazing

skyward. He could do little else. He worked from the top down, taking an inventory of what he could control. Brow was controllable, as were both eyebrows, lids; yes, he could blink both eyes. He flared his nostrils, moved his lips up and down, opened, closed, sideways. His tongue worked. He recited the alphabet until the letter *J,* then stopped. He tried to raise his head and could. He could look down his body, turn his head right and left. He could swallow and breathe all right.

Thankfully it was turning into a glorious night — rare, as, since they'd been there, it seemed to rain, as if on cue, every evening at around six o'clock.

The Cuban blocked his view, and that startled him.

He called out in Spanish as the man rifled through his pockets. This seemed to unnerve the guerrilla, who jumped a full foot at the realization that Jonathan was not dead.

They both smiled uneasily. The Cuban apologized.

"Oh, that's all right." Jonathan nodded. "Do me a favor, *señor,* fix my leg." He nodded further to his canteen. "And give me a drink."

The man complied, adjusting Jonathan's

body as would an undertaker preparing his customer for a viewing in the front parlor. He pulled Jonathan up so he was reclining against the palm, his head elevated to ensure the water would not choke him. The Cuban helped him to a few sips. It tasted better than anything he'd ever drunk.

"Muchas gracias."

"De nada."

It was the first Cuban Jonathan had seen. Really the first enemy he'd seen that was not three hundred yards away. He was a handsome man, dark, but not as dark as a Mexican or Indian. He wore peon clothes, not a proper uniform, looking more a beggar than soldier. His Remington was proper enough, though, and Jonathan felt a chill at the realization that it was what had been used to deliver the slug that had severed his spine.

"Did you shoot me?"

"Sí."

"Why the hell'd you do that? I was collecting meat." He looked at the brassard, now with a jagged forty-five hole through the center of the cross. "You sure as hell saw my armband. Used the son of a bitch for a bullseye."

The Cuban shrugged indifferently. He stood, taking an inventory of the dead animals lying about them. He smiled at Jonathan. "Good hunting."

He sat and twisted a cigarette and offered it to Jonathan.

"No, thanks. I'm a runner." He winced at the pain, like a lightning bolt, shooting up his back. "Least I was."

"Smoke, Yankee. It will not hurt your wind any longer."

Jonathan did, and the light head evoked by the harsh tobacco was nauseating. He fought the urge to vomit. He coughed and spat blood-tinged sputum onto his shirt-front. The Cuban helped him to another drink.

"I am sorry for killing you, Yankee."

"Name's Jonathan, and I'm not dead yet."

The Cuban looked gravely at the tip of his cigarette. "Why did you have to come here, Yankee?"

"To free, the . . . the Cuban people."

"Free us of what?"

"Tyranny, of course. The tyranny of the Spanish, and you . . . you blew up our ship. You blew up the *Maine.* Killed our sailors."

The Cuban stood, considering for a moment as he looked over the dead fawns. He checked the breech of his Remington, and Jonathan caught the meaning of his actions. He did not want to die but was surprised at his own feelings of ambivalence. He spoke, more in defiance than as a plea for his life.

"Haven't you done enough?"

The Cuban turned to walk away. Glancing over his shoulder, he spoke in a whisper. "I am sorry, gringo. *Que Dios te acompañe.*"

By late evening, Thorpe and Clara had found themselves back at the makeshift dinner table. He offered her a brandy, and she uncharacteristically accepted it. In a little while her teeth and toes were numb, her tongue feeling as if it had been sutured to the floor of her mouth.

"Dr. Thorpe, have you ever had an experience that caused you to question everything you've ever taken for granted?"

"Not really."

She held out her cup. He poured generously. Being a little inebriated appeared to agree with her. At least it had loosened her tongue, so the catharsis could begin.

"Oh, that's right."

"What?"

"I imagine you are one of those modern men. Ones who find religion silly and antiquated."

"No, I actually don't, Nurse Maass."

"Really?"

"So you doubt your faith, because your

429

fiancé died in battle?"

"I don't know."

"Well, I would not blame you if you did; it's only natural. But one thing is certain."

"Yes?"

"Surviving such a tragedy is much easier for the faithful."

She sat for a long while. She was tired, drowsy from the spirits and exhausted from the long day's work. She looked into the doctor's eyes and felt well. "Thank you, Dr. Thorpe."

"Nurse Maass, you are welcome."

He awoke at sun up, this time to Rocky, using the butt of his Winchester as a club, smashing the crabs surrounding them. Jonathan had not felt them working their way through the canvas material of his trousers in the night.

He smiled. "Hello, brother."

"Jesus, Jonathan. What the hell happened?"

"As you see." He remembered the guerrilla. "Rocky, there are sharpshooters about. Some fellow shot me yesterday. Have a care." He winced. "Pull me up a little, Brother."

The fire ants, as if on command, emerged from beneath Jonathan's body, as they'd been feasting on the parts denied the crabs. They engulfed them both, biting, stinging as Rocky jumped to his feet, beating and wiping in desperation at his brother's body, writhing with the red mass of insects.

"Jesus, Rocky, they're eating me alive." Offering a sly smile, he said, "Lucky I can't feel any of it."

"Jesus is right, Jonathan, *Je-sus*!" He reached down to pull his brother onto his shoulders as a bullet removed the top of his ear. Reflexively, he tumbled, landing atop his brother's wrecked body.

They regained their bearings, Jonathan struggling to see what damage had been done to his savior.

"Where are you hit?"

Rocky fingered the wound. "Just here." Blood flowed in a torrent over his hand and up his arm.

"That son of a bitch is still out there."

"No shit, Jonathan! No shit!"

"How bad is it?"

"Don't think all that. Just the tip of my ear."

"You are one lucky bastard, brother."

Rocky dragged him down the hillock he'd used to lie in wait for the white tails. Another slug from the Cuban's Remington kicked dirt into Rocky's eyes. He wiped them clean, then ran a bandage around his head to staunch the bleeding.

He pulled his canteen free of his belt and doused them both, wiping them clean with his handkerchief. At least the ants were mostly eradicated. Once or twice he felt the sting, like a red-hot poker, under his trooper shirt.

He'd learned well from his fellow Arizona troopers back on the front line. The hunters of men. He felt his ear through the bandage, remembering, in his mind's eye the attitude of his body when he'd been struck down. He looked up at the crease in the ground left by the sharpshooter's errant shot. He could pinpoint the son of a bitch.

"Jonathan, I'm going to kill that dago bastard; then I'll be back for you." He straightened his brother's body, hugging him about the neck. "Jesus, glad to find you alive."

"Glad you found me, too, brother." He felt queer as the brisk activity had loosened the clot plugging the wound near his spinal column. Dreamy, dizzy, as if he'd had too much wine on a Saturday outing with Francesca. He would not share with Rocky what he knew. There was no point to it.

Instead, he quietly, proudly watched his brother prepare, as he looked to be a wholly different man. A new man or, perhaps, just a man.

"All right, Jonathan. Cover me." He smiled at his own bad joke.

"Rocky?"

He stopped his forward motion, not a little exasperated. He turned impatiently. *"What?"*

"Wait a minute. That bastard's not going anywhere, and you have us well enough hid. Wait a minute. Stay a minute. I have something to tell you."

"It's not the time for a lot of talkin', Jonathan."

"Give me a moment, Rock." He smiled. *"Rock!* I like that name Bill McGinty gave you. You *are* a rock, by God. A *rock!*"

"Okay, that's fine, Brother. We got to get you back to the hospital. Let's talk about my new name then."

"No, it's not that." He nodded. "Hold my hand, Brother."

Rocky complied.

"You holding it?"

"I am, Jonathan. See?" He held it up. "Go on."

"I wanted to tell you I'm sorry for ever bringing you out here. Sorry as all hell, Rock. Sorry for all this. Forgive me."

"All right, you're forgiven." He began to pull away.

"Rock, one more thing. Tell Francesca I loved her. Tell her and Ellen and Father. Tell them all. And, if you don't mind, don't mention how I lost my head over that little blonde nurse."

Rocky pulled away. He did not like all this maudlin talk. "You tell 'em yourself once you're home, Brother." He thought a moment. "As far as I'm concerned, nothing whatever happened around Nurse Maass."

"One more thing, Rock. Take my belt. That Johnny Reb belt Father gave me. Put it on, Brother; maybe it'll protect you, way it protected our father."

Rocky rolled wide, crab walking forty yards to the south of the sharpshooter's perch. He'd killed close to a dozen tree-dwelling guerrillas. As Bill McGinty said, he was a regular pro at it.

Pushing the Winchester forward as he crawled, he moved to another hillock, to a rise that put him nearer to the height of the tree dweller, and to within a few yards of where he was positive the bastard lay in wait.

He stared at the spot, the way he'd learned, watched and waited, and eventually the Cuban gave his position away, reaching to scratch a mosquito bite on his temple.

Rocky threw the Winchester to his shoulder, the thought of demanding his surrender not remotely crossing his mind. He touched the trigger, and another dead Cuban tumbled to the jungle floor.

Clara could tell by the way Rocky walked that the young trooper's brother, carried on his shoulders, was dead. She helped him place the body on the ground, under the shade of the mango. She turned, preparing to comfort the young man; his thin smile was reassuring.

"He didn't feel a lot of pain, ma'am." He touched her shoulder. "He asked me to give you a message, Nurse. He asked that you please forgive his rude actions and talk."

She beckoned him to the upended buckets under the tree, took the seat beside him, and began redressing his wounded ear. They sat and said nothing for a long while, her touch electric, electrifying. Not provocative, but rather like a mother's to a child who'd skinned his knee.

She finished. "I know, Trooper Killebrew."

"Rocky, please."

"Rocky. I know he meant no harm."

"My brother was always happy-go-lucky. He treated life like a party, ma'am. Flirted with pretty ladies. Laughed and joked with everybody. Even in the end, this morning, when we were pinned down by the devil who'd killed him, Jonathan was making jokes. Father said it's how he'd slip into heaven. He'd get old Saint Peter distracted, you know, jokin' so much that he'd forget to see if Jonathan was on the list. He'd slip past and right on in."

"I'm certain he's on the list, Rocky. Your brother was a good fellow."

"I hope so." He looked about the little hospital. "How's Nurse Trumbull?"

"Oh, better." Clara smiled. "She had a day or two of feeling poorly, but she's much better today."

He stood, adjusting the rebel belt given to him by his brother. "Would you make certain they plant Jonathan in a good spot, Nurse Maass?" He touched her cheek. "One thing's for certain," he nodded, "if there was one person to lose his head over, you sure were the right one." He blushed and looked away. "Guess that's not military bearing, and I hope you ain't offended, but," he looked her in the eye, "I ain't sorry I said it."

"Thank you, Trooper — I mean, Rocky, and I'm not offended."

"Well, better be gettin' back on the line. These sharpshooters don't seem to know the Spaniards have given up." He adjusted his Winchester on his shoulder. "Please, Nurse Maass, tell Nurse Minerva I asked for her."

"I will, Rocky. I promise."

Rocky returned to the line, to Bill and the men, and felt better. Felt so well that a wave of elation washed over him, as Jonathan's death had left him numb. He was not sad, and he did not even feel all that much like crying. Just a horrible emptiness. A horrible hollow feeling, like someone had scooped out his insides. He trembled constantly. He'd never felt such a way before, but, upon seeing his brothers in battle, that terrible emptiness ceased.

He understood what Jonathan meant by loving it. God, he did love it, too, this perversion, this unnatural attraction, like a moth to a flame that was sure to incinerate it. How could men love this? How could any normal human being love this? But there it was. He loved it. He loved as much as he hated this miserable war.

The men had time to talk of battle. The fellow so petrified of spiders proudly showed the stem of his pipe, the only thing left after a sharpshooter center shot the briar bowl as he smoked. Rocky reached up and felt his ear. It was certainly almost as close a call.

Bill McGinty told anyone who'd listen about Rocky's quick shooting of the flag-ensconced Spaniards. How he'd saved Kane, and how the two adversaries were so close when Rock had cut them down, they actually splashed their leader's impeccably polished boots with gore as they fell.

Bill grinned. "Good thing lieutenant puts such a high shine on his boots, otherwise, he'd have had to throw 'em away."

Rocky was not back on the line long, however, before he was summoned, through Woodbury Kane, to report to Colonel Roosevelt. He stood at attention, waiting for the colonel to acknowledge him.

"Oh, Trooper Killebrew." He stood, extending his hand for the lad to take a seat beside him. "I am sorry for your loss, lad. Trooper Thomson, or should I say, Whelihan, was the best of men."

"Thank you, sir. You sayin' such sure means a lot. Would mean a lot to Jonathan."

He offered Rocky a brandy, which the lad refused. He had no use or interest in spirits anymore. Roosevelt poured the liquor back into its flask. He stood abruptly.

"Come with me, lad."

They walked back to the hospital together, Roosevelt beside him with an arm around his shoulder. The colonel didn't talk. He walked with Rocky, almost too quiet.

When they arrived, Dr. Church was there along with Clara and Sister Bonaventure, standing beside the freshly laid grave, as the less severely wounded had time to bury Jonathan alone, which was a comfort to Rocky. Mass graves seemed so impersonal, even when conducted with the dignity practiced by the Rough Riders after *Las Guásimas.*

Roosevelt nodded. "Dr. Church, Nurse Maass, Sister, thank you for responding to my man-servant's request to meet us here."

He turned to Marshall, who'd been waiting with a leather-bound book. He handed it to the colonel.

"I have a poem I'd like to share with you and Trooper Killebrew." Roosevelt adjusted his spectacles while leafing through to the page he'd marked.

"This is a poem I recently received from a friend in England. It reminded me of Trooper Thomson. By A. E. Housman, *To an Athlete Dying Young:*

The time you won your town the race,
We chaired you through the marketplace;
Man and boy stood cheering by,
As home we brought you shoulder-high.

To-day, the road all runners come,
Shoulder-high we bring you home,
And set you at your threshold down,
Townsman of a stiller town.

Smart lad, to slip betimes away
From fields where glory does not stay
And early though the laurel grows
It withers quicker than the rose.

Eyes the shady night has shut
Cannot see the record cut,
And silence sounds no worse than cheers
After earth has stopped the ears:

Now you will not swell the rout
Of lads that wore their honours out,
Runners whom renown outran
And the name died before the man.

So set, before its echoes fade,
The fleet foot on the sill of shade,
And hold to the low lintel up
The still-defended challenge-cup.

And round that early-laurelled head
Will flock to gaze the strengthless dead,
And find unwithered on its curls
The garland briefer than a girl's."

The colonel walked away alone. Jonathan had gotten to him.

Marshall watched his boss move on. Touching Rocky on the arm, he held out a rucksack. "These were your brother's belongings, Trooper Killebrew." He pulled a small cigar from his pocket, offering it to Rocky, who took it, and, together, they smoked over his brother's grave.

"I'm thanking you."

"Your brother made an impression on the colonel."

Rocky smiled. "My brother made an impression on a lotta people, sir."

"I know." Marshall took a long drag on his cigar. "I'll miss him."

They stood for a while until Marshall took his leave. Rocky wandered to the upended buckets under the mango. He opened the rucksack and began pulling out items: a notebook with some inconsequential scribblings; two framed photos, one of Ellen, another of his father; a small tintype of Rocky. That amused him. Why would Jonathan keep such a thing of him when they'd been together on this ridiculous odyssey? If he wanted to look at him, all he had to do was look at him.

He found a gold locket on a light chain, opening it to the provocative image of

Francesca, the one Jonathan had declared was lost. She was so beautiful. He closed it quickly, as if something forbidden to him. He had no right to look at it, as he was certain it was meant for Jonathan's eyes only. And besides, it might be spied by eavesdroppers, and he knew, he'd kill a man who'd dare snigger over it. He unbuttoned his chest pocket, placing it there, next to his tobacco pouch.

He walked back to his brother's grave. "Rest easy, Brother. God bless you. At least your worrying days are over. God bless you, you lucky son-of-a-gun."

CHAPTER 35

Francesca helped Ellen put him to bed. They kissed him in turn and gave him the sleeping draught the doctor had prescribed. The fit he'd suffered at the news was the worst yet, and neither held out much hope that he'd survive it.

He was insensible, and Francesca shrugged at the questioning look in Ellen's eyes.

"Time will tell." She motioned for Ellen to leave. She'd ensure he was comfortable. Francesca whispered in Sean's ear. "It's okay to go, Father." She kissed his cheek. "I'll take care of them. I promise, all will be well."

He was alone and began to drift and dream. It was a pleasant one, despite the news. Perhaps he knew all along that one would live and one would die. Somehow he was not angry about it. More of a sad resignation. Another Jonathan Whelihan cut down, stolen from him by a government accustomed to frittering away the lives of young men.

He awoke at midnight, to the striking of the long case clock his wife had purchased the second year they earned good money. Initially, he complained about it, said it would keep him up at night until she offered to silence it during bedtime hours. He didn't let her, as he'd quickly become acclimated to it. He'd often awaken, rarely slept more than a few hours at a time. He'd lie there and listen for the chime.

He counted until it struck twelve and watched a light rise slowly from the center of the fireplace, like in the Dickens story Ellen read at Christmas; up, up, up until it hovered next to his bed. He blinked, and the light became his wife, all aglow and as beautiful as the day they married. She even wore the same dress, as far as he could remember.

She kissed him, then turned to show him his brother, happy and young, as young as on that terrible day at Gettysburg. Next to him stood his boy in the good suit he wore the last day he saw him alive. He, too, smiled and kissed his father's cheek. Jonathan had something in his arms, and Sean Whelihan had to blink to see it plainly. A little bundle. His grandson, smiling up at him, the babe as beautiful as Francesca.

His wife and brother reached out, beckoning him to rise. Taking their proffered hands, he stood, felt well, as strong as if he'd never had the fit. Arm and arm they walked, his boy and grandson leading, toward the light, and, for the first time in his life, Sean Whelihan was content.

CHAPTER 36

Clara was wrong, as the yellow jack had a way of toying with its victims. Minerva had a reprieve, then quickly slipped back into the grip of the deadly disease.

Sister Bonaventure tended to her as Clara and Dr. Church and now Dr. Thorpe cared for the men, pouring in with regularity, not because of bullet or bomb wounds, but because of the inevitable fever, effects of starvation, and dysentery.

Minerva awoke to find the nun giving her a sponge bath. Minnie smiled. "I thought I had it beaten, Sister."

"I know, child. We thought so, too. I am sorry."

"Is Clara all right?"

"She is, child. Busy. She and Doctors Church and Thorpe are busy, but, you know, that's when Clara's happiest."

"Sister . . ." She tried to sit up but could not. She dropped her head to the pillow. "I think this might be the end of me. I don't think I'll survive this bout. *Everything* hurts. I've never hurt so bad in all my days."

"Oh, nonsense." She lied. The inevitable *vomito negro* was soon to follow. The signs were clear, and Sister Bonaventure was too well informed to put much stock in the theory that Negroes were immune to the yellow jack.

Clara arrived, and they continued to bathe her hour after interminable hour. Minnie was drifting, nearly too weak to speak. She grasped each nurse's hand, whispering, "Thank you for being my friend, Sister, Clara. It's been an honor to, to . . ."

"Nurse the sick together."

"Yes, Sister. To nurse the sick together. This has been the grandest time of my life."

"The honor is all ours." She kissed Minerva's forehead. Clara wept.

They sat with her, keeping vigil, waiting patiently for the pain and suffering to mercifully come to an end.

Rocky was waiting when Sister Bonaventure emerged, exhausted and filthy from the convulsive vomiting. He understood by her expression, the terrible disease had claimed another victim.

The emotion overwhelming him, he

turned away, wandering nowhere, finding himself at the upended buckets he'd sat upon with Nurse Maass the day he'd brought in Jonathan's body; it seemed a lifetime ago.

He'd spent the days since hunting men, killing many, exhausting himself, more emotionally than physically. He broke down when Sister Bonaventure sat next to him.

She removed his hat and unbuttoned his shirt collar. She wet his scarf, as Jonathan had done back in San Antonio, placing it across the nape of his neck. She held his hand as the catharsis continued.

"I'm sorry, ma'am. Right baby cryin' all the time."

"I don't think so."

"Tell me the truth, Sister. Did I cause Nurse Minerva's death? Is it my fault she's dead?"

"Oh, no, my lad, oh, my goodness, no! How on earth did you arrive at such a notion?"

"When I come in here, shot in the head, with the fever. Did I give her that fever? The fever, what killed her?"

"No, you did not, Trooper Killebrew."

"Rocky."

She patted his hand. Pulling a handkerchief from her sleeve, she handed it to him.

"Come, my boy, stop this crying and listen."

He blew his nose. Tried to stop his body from shaking. He could not seem to gain control of himself.

Sister Bonaventure disappeared momentarily, emerging from her tent with a glass and a bottle, pouring him two fingers of brandy. Rocky refused it.

"Go on, lad, drink it down; it'll calm your nerves."

"No, Sister, no. The drink has a hold on me. I don't want it."

"Come now. One won't hurt you. Strictly for medicinal purposes." She smiled. "Nurse's orders."

He eventually complied. Immediately the strong liquid worked its magic, as Rocky had had little to eat in many days.

She offered him a glass of water. "Drink this, lad. Drink it all."

When she was satisfied with the outcome, she continued.

"Minerva died of yellow fever."

"I thought that wasn't catching, you know, to colored folks, like Nurse Trumbull." He wiped his nose again, balling up the teary handkerchief in his fist. "I thought that's why the government brought folks like her out here to this hellish, Godforsaken place."

"Yes, lad, that was, but truth be known,

there's much we have yet to learn about yellow fever." She removed the scarf from his neck, rewetted and replaced it. She patted his shoulder.

"Rocky, do you know what Minerva said to me, before she became so ill, about you?"

"No, ma'am."

"She said that you were about the kindest trooper she'd met, and, lad, that's saying a lot. You Rough Riders are gallant men."

"I find that hard to believe, me bein' so mean and all. Hittin' her. Hitting a lady. Jesus, I hit a lady!"

"When you were fevered. And, frankly, because of that, it at least to my mind does not count."

"It does to me!"

"Listen to me, lad. Minerva said that letter you wrote comforted her. She said it was one of the kindest gestures she'd known from a patient, and all through her illness, even up until the end, she carried your letter and the letter she'd received from a nice Cuban she met in Key West. Your words were a comfort to her, Rocky."

"And you're sure I didn't give her that fever?"

"Yes, Rocky. You've contracted malaria and nothing more. Minerva most certainly died of yellow fever, two completely different maladies. Two completely different, unrelated diseases, my lad."

She stood, checking the watch pinned to her wimple. "She likely contracted it when she and your brother traveled to that village between here and Siboney. Jonathan likely had it as well."

"Do you suppose if that sharpshooter hadn't killed him, the yellow jack would have?" For some reason, the thought was a comfort to him. Perhaps dying from a bullet was a sort of blessing.

"Perhaps, Rocky, perhaps."

He stood, pulling the scarf from around his neck. He folded it properly, tying it in place.

"I'm all right, Sister. I'm beholden to you for talking to me. I feel a lot better. I'm sorry to see Nurse Minerva die, but at least it's a comfort to know she kept my letter. And I'm sure glad I didn't give what took her from us."

"I know, my boy." She patted him on the shoulder. "And I know for certain she appreciated your kindness. Sit a while. Eat something, rest a little before you return to the line."

One of the men interrupted. "Sister, it's ready."

"Oh, thank you." She pulled Rocky by the

arm. "Come with me, lad."

It was the idea of one of the men who'd been spine shot. He'd spent many years as a stonecutter, and some of the lads pilfered a property marker from a defunct plantation they'd passed on their march from Siboney.

He sat up straight in bed when the visitors arrived, turning, with the aid of one of his comrades, the improvised headstone. It read *Minerva Trumbull.*

The stonecutter smiled uneasily. "It's finished, Sister." He looked at Rocky and explained. "Some of the boys and me, we wanted to do something for Nurse Minnie."

Another man interjected. "We found some chisels and a hammer from an abandoned smithy's forge, found Walt the tools he needed."

The stonecutter pointed to his work. "She was a dear heart." He couldn't continue. One of the men finished for him.

"Walt says it's some of the nicest marble he's ever worked. A good piece, fitting for such a lady."

Rocky looked it over. The letters were beautifully rendered. "Sorry, Walt, but it needs a little more work, if'n you don't mind my sayin' so."

"Sure, Rock. What's it need, friend? You

want I should put an angel or something?"

Rocky wrote on a bit of his brother's notebook paper. He handed it over as Walt read it. "Put that under her name."

"By God, you're right." He smiled. He held it up for Sister Bonaventure to read. On it was simply written *Nurse*.

She patted Rocky on the shoulder. "Well stated, my lad. Minerva would be happy."

CHAPTER 37

It was heading into autumn by the time the government imbeciles had been sufficiently convinced that the men would not bring yellow fever home, and only after Colonel Roosevelt caused so much trouble was the vacillation ended.

The quarantine hospital in New York was pleasant and spirits high, even with the tragic loss of William Tiffany. Despite his family's employing the best physicians, the ravages of fever and privation were too much. William not-that-Tiffany died, literally of starvation and physical suffering, despite being one of the youngest and fittest in the outfit.

Like the loss of his brother and Hamilton Fish and Minerva Trumbull, the void left in Rocky's heart with the passing of Tiffany would sadden him for the rest of his days.

On a positive note, he was able to send word home that he was well. The army had already notified them of Jonathan's demise, but no news, of course, was communicated unless a man was killed or wounded, and Rocky's injuries were not enough to lay him up for any significant time.

Ellen had insisted that Rocky take his time coming home. Hastening him along would not alter the fact that Sean Whelihan was dead.

Woodbury Kane had plans for Rocky and Bill McGinty, but not before Rocky escorted his bronc busting companion on a ride from Camp Wyckoff to Oyster Bay, where the fellows delivered Little Texas to the colonel's home.

All along the route, souvenir seekers would accost them, cutting a bit of hair from the pony's tail. It vexed Rocky, though Bill took it in stride, waving his partner off every time he'd prepare to defend the animal's honor.

"It'll grow back, Rock. Don't fret over it. These folks want a little piece of the colonel. Can't fault 'em for that."

They were greeted by Mrs. Roosevelt and her staff, treated as the heroes they were, and even put up in the house proper, in Sagamore Hill's guest room.

That was all a bit overwhelming to Rocky. He was treated better than at his own home, where he'd been banished from the house, relegated to sleeping in the bunkhouse with the hired men.

On a crisp September day, the troopers found themselves standing in the tailor's room at Brooks Brothers, as Kane would not have them wandering about his haunts in New York sporting shabby, half worn-out, government-issued uniforms. A few hours later they emerged, looking much like the colonel and Woodbury that first day back in Prescott.

Bill McGinty stared in awe at the carriage waiting to take them to Kane's townhouse on Fifth Avenue. A footman held the door, and McGinty bowed, extending a hand for Rocky to enter first. Rocky grinned, feeling a regular fool for such high-tone treatment.

He turned the newly blocked hat over in his hands, never fully appreciating until now how beautiful the badge of the Rough Riders looked pinning the brim, on one side to the crown, in the manner of the warrior horseman. What was it that Dorst called them, the 11th US Horse? It was a high compliment.

"What do you suppose Woodbury's planning, Bill?"

"Don't know." McGinty pushed a pack of

factory-made cigarettes toward his partner. "Ain't these dandy, Rock? No more twistin'. What will they think of next, old son? Whiskey that pours itself?"

"Don't know, but it *is* mighty fine, Bill." Rocky looked about the cab of the carriage, smelling of freshly dyed crushed velvet and leather. "Never thought I'd be in anything like this till my final ride, you know, the one courtesy of the undertaker. My God, Bill, even the floor's covered in carpet. Hate to put my feet on it."

When they'd arrived at the townhouse they were greeted by Woodbury and his staff, to include a butler, housekeeper, three cooks, and four maids. They all stood at attention, with the precision of an honor guard, each bowing in turn as Woodbury introduced his Rough Riders.

The butler, an Englishman, lips pursed, nodded with military bearing. He'd spent some time fighting in the British army. Knew and appreciated men who'd seen battle and endured it.

"Gentlemen, welcome. I'm Hobbs. If there is anything you desire, please do not hesitate to inform me."

Bill McGinty proffered a hand. He shook each one energetically, even the dour housekeeper, not used to such informality. "Glad

457

to know you all. We're mighty beholden to each of you for your kind hospitality."

Over the next several weeks the men would be treated to comfort and opulence neither could ever, at least until now, fathom, as Woodbury spared no expense, from dining at Delmonico's, where they feasted on the best cuts of steak, caviar, and raw blue points, to a train ride south in a private car to Maryland horse country for dove shooting.

That was a failure, however, for Rocky when he'd learned about the curious mating habits of the dove. He'd dropped a fast flyer, and its mate landed nearby to see what had afflicted its companion. The loader pointed with a crooked finger, telling Rocky, "You know, they mate for life."

He banged away for the rest of the afternoon, enjoying the English doubles Woodbury had lent him without hitting another bird.

The gun handler could not be angry with him, even if their bag would be light. A GAR man himself, he knew what it was like to have a belly full of killing.

For that matter, none of Woodbury's friends or servants would make them feel foolish or out of place. On the fourth night of their visit, they were paired with two women, contemporaries of Woodbury, who took them in, quietly teaching each the various rules on dining and general etiquette.

One was Jeanette Danbury, or Jennie as she was known by her friends and admirers, a woman of forty who looked twenty-five. Tall and willowy, it was evident she spent countless hours maintaining an exquisite figure. She prided herself on the fact that she needed no corsets to maintain a splendid shape. It was all genuine. She was as fit as an Olympic athlete, yet as feminine as Cleopatra.

She smiled, nodding to her partner in all matters related to hunting men. Placing a diamond-bejeweled hand on Rocky's shoulder, she declared, "This one's *mine*, Lydia," who responded in kind, "Fine by me, because I'm keeping Billy."

McGinty blushed, smoothing his moustache and appearing slightly bewildered.

In a little while Rocky was alone with Jennie. She stood in the moonlight, as elegant as the ladies he and Kane had dined with that night in Prescott.

She maneuvered him to the balcony overlooking the busy street below, allowing him to light her cigarette as they took a seat on a long bench in front of Woodbury's rooftop garden.

Blowing smoke at the stars, she ran her fingers over the scar on Rocky's forehead, causing his heart to do flip-flops. She kissed his cheek, touching what was left of his ear. Rocky covered the hand stroking his healing wound.

He grinned. "Think it'll grow back?"

Jennie blew a smoky reply. "No, Rocky, I don't."

He grinned wider, pleased that he'd told a joke. "I know, ma'am. I'm thick, but I ain't *that* stupid." He felt the jagged edge. "Woodbury said maybe I ought to grow my hair longish."

"Thank you, Rocky."

"For what?"

"Fighting in the war, and helping Woody, bringing him back alive to me. To us. We all simply *adore* Woodbury. We heard you saved his life."

"Oh. That was nothing. It's Woodbury who kept us all safe, I can guarantee you that."

"Well. That's not how he tells it."

"Ain't surprised. Woodbury's a real gentleman. Never talks himself up. He's about the best man I've ever known."

"He *is*, Rocky."

"Are . . . are you two, you know . . . I mean . . . ?"

"Romantically involved?"

"Yes." Rocky looked as if his continued happiness hung in the balance. He was smitten with this woman, old enough to be his mother, yet he'd *never* cut in on Woodbury.

She turned, blowing smoke at the street below. "Woodbury Kane. What to say about Woody . . ." She smiled but was certainly not happy, her demeanor changing as a wave of sadness washed over her. "I have loved Woodbury Kane since I was nine years old." She sighed. "You've known him since the spring. I've known him for nearly a lifetime." She knocked an ash free of her cigarette. "But it will never be, Rocky." She nodded, staring off into the night sky.

"Yeah, I know all about *that* sort of thing." He smiled in a way that proved they were kindred spirits in suffering unrequited love.

She turned, her heart melting at the spell she was casting over him. She loved that look of adoration she evoked, every time.

She'd have to be careful with this one. She could see that her charms, her attentions, could easily be misread. The last thing she'd want was to break his heart, as, though Jennie was wholly dedicated to self-indulgence, a cruel and hurtful seductress she was not.

461

On a matter of principle, the liaisons had to be to the mutual benefit of both parties.

"I'm what is referred to, at least in my circles, as a debauchée, Rocky." She turned. "Tell me, what is your Christian name?"

"My what?"

"Your given name, your first name, Rocky."

"Oh, ma'am." He blushed, looking away, anywhere but into her eyes.

"Not 'ma'am;' I feel old when you call me that. Not 'ma'am;' 'Jennie,' please. Address me as 'Jennie.' "

"I'm sorry, Jennie. Of course. Well, my name, it's kind of a silly one. Would rather you stick with Rocky."

"Let me be the judge of that. Can't possibly be sillier than Woodbury."

He felt his ears redden. He didn't like that she'd have anything bad to say about his man. He recovered when it was evident there was no malice in her comment. She was teasing. Nothing more.

"It's Rockwell."

"Rockwell?" She sipped from her cocktail. "That's a lovely name. Rockwell Killebrew. Why, that's not silly at all. It has a noble ring. I rather like it."

"What's a debauchée, ma'am, I mean, Jennie? Is it some sort a' religion?"

"In a manner of speaking." She smiled at the irony. "Yes." She patted his cheek. "It comes from the French, Rockwell. It means — well, how do I articulate it? It describes a person who lives in the moment, and solely for sensual pleasure."

"Sensual pleasure?"

"Yes," she ran a hand up his thigh, all but intruding upon a place where no one had ever touched him. "Sensual pleasure is, well, literally, pleasure of the senses, the *baser* senses, to be precise." She cast her gaze downward. "The senses below the waist."

"I . . . I see. At least, I think I see."

She put her drink down, running her fingers over Rocky's scar again. She reached up, kissing him on the mouth. She pulled him close, grinding her pelvis against his knee, gyrating like a queen cat in heat as she used him to pleasure her body. She pulled away gently, rhythmically, as one engaged in a forbidden, ritualistic dance.

Taking a deep breath, she almost whispered, "*That* is a debauchée, my darling Rockwell." She grinned at the overwhelmed look as she pressed shut his gaping jaw, tracing her fingers up his cheek and again back to his scar. She'd most certainly have to be careful with this one.

"Do tell, Jennie." He ran a hand through

his hair. He was having difficulty breathing. "Do tell."

"Another drink, Rockwell?"

"Oh, no, Jennie." He glanced into his Manhattan, pleased to see it was nearly full. "I'm a, a . . . well, the drink has a bit of a hold on me. I kind of tone it down these days, on account, once I start gulpin', I turn into a regular fool. Don't want to make an ass of myself." He gazed into Jennie's blue eyes. "Especially not tonight."

"That's good, Rockwell. I'm glad you know it. Glad you're man enough to, as you say, *tone it down.* That's the sign of a *real man,* you know. One who knows his weaknesses and controls them." She dropped her shoe, revealing a pedicured foot, which she ran up the inside of his leg. Scandalously, she wore no stockings. "And it's imperative that you maintain all your faculties tonight."

She placed her foot into his hand, and he instinctively, seductively, began massaging it. "You sure have pretty feet, ma'am, I mean, Jennie."

"Thank you."

It was his turn to take the initiative. Much to her pleasant surprise, he pulled her into his lap. He kissed her, mimicking her passion. He was learning a lot, and quickly, from Jennie.

He massaged the nape of her neck, transferring the power from his grip, not unlike that of a lion's jaws, Jennie reacting to it most splendidly.

"Jennie," he whispered into her ear as he gave it a playful bite, "if this is what it means to be a debauchée, you can sign me up."

Her home, an impressive place on Central Park South, a quick stroll down Fifth, rivaled that of Woodbury's, if not in size, then in elegance. They held hands as they walked, the brisk air bracing, Jennie's grip firm and reassuring. Rocky was pleased he was sober. He was too excited for words. He wondered if Jennie could feel him tremble.

The townhouse was different than Woodbury's, however, in that there were no servants between the hours of midnight and noon. Jennie explained that this was so due to the fact that she could not afford prying eyes or the subsequent extra fodder it invariably produced for the scandal mongers and muckrakers who delighted in featuring her escapades in their newspapers. Not that she cared about her own ruined reputation, but it was imperative, in order to maintain her lifestyle, that the many men in her life continued to live theirs unsullied.

She took his hand, leading him up the marble staircase wrapping the foyer, to her bedroom. She opened the door, not a little dramatically. "Do you understand now what it means to be a debauchée, Rockwell? Are you absolutely certain?"

He felt overwhelmed. "I, I . . ." He cast his gaze about the room, to the impressive bed, neatly covered in satin sheets, tastefully decorated, though as provocative as a Parisian bordello. Everywhere he looked there were reminders of lovemaking, from oil paintings of nudes, both male and female, to marble statuary of beautiful women and men, arms and legs entangled in pre- and post-coital rapture.

She kissed him again. Gliding, as if on winged heels, to a corner of the room, she secreted herself behind a Chinese dressing screen, daring not to strip before him for fear of stopping his pounding heart.

She spoke in a kind of schoolmarm tone.

"Rockwell, a debauchée is a person who lives by a set of rules or standards that do not coincide with those of polite society, or, for that matter, the natural order of the universe."

He found his voice. "Jennie, you'll have to dumb down your talk, and I mean way down."

A sense of calm washed over him. He knew they would make love, and he knew that Jennie knew that he was woefully less experienced than she. He'd not have to woo her or seduce her or pleasure her or even impress her. He was like freshly thrown clay atop a potter's wheel. Pristine clay, the clay of youth, and Rocky *was.* He was the ideal man, at least to Jennie, and this is why he felt so good. He understood that he was exactly what she wanted. It was impossible for him to be a disappointment. He need only do as she wished, and a sense of joy ran through his heart at the prospect of his imminent deflowering.

"Folks like you and the colonel and Wood-bury say things that I've never heard of before. I'm thick that way, ma'am, I mean, Jennie. You got to be patient with me."

"You are *not* thick." She uttered a joyful laugh. "You are *pure.* Refreshing to people such as us. People who have had too much idle time on our hands. Too much time to learn vast amounts of worthless information. You are not thick, Rockwell. You are the ideal man, imbued with the knowledge of the practical, and nothing more. It's refreshing."

She emerged in a negligee of sheer silk, expertly fitted, leaving nothing to the imagination. She was barefoot, and that, of all the provocative images invading his senses, drove him to distraction.

She'd unpinned her hair, allowing the unencumbered locks to cascade, some falling over the fronts of her shoulders, revealing, according to her movements, pert, smallish, porcelain-white breasts topped with pouting nipples. The whore in Tampa came to mind, and Rocky again pitied her.

"Do you like it, Rockwell?"

"Oh, yes, ma'am, I mean, Jennie."

She took him by the hand, leading him to her bed. She sat nearly in his lap, her scent cascading over him, a mix of the musk of arousal and Eau de Verveine, the same perfume worn by the lovelies who'd written him, he was certain.

"Rockwell, I need to know before we carry on one step further if you will be able to keep from falling in love with me." She pressed a manicured finger to his lips, not yet allowing him to speak. "Because love is not my intention. Falling in love with you is not my intent, nor is it my intent for you to fall in love with me. To break your heart is the last thing I'd ever want to do.

"It is, however, to offer you the most sensual gift, the most profound pleasure a woman such as I can offer a man such as you. If you can do this, if you can accept such a gift, Rockwell, without the emotion of remorse or guilt or feeling beholden to me, then we'll proceed." She kept her finger to his lips, as she was not finished with her speech. "It is the most difficult commitment a woman such as I can expect from a lover, I know this." She smiled a little cynically, casting her gaze to her lap. "Oh, how I know this. It's why a man such as Woodbury and I will never be together. It is why women such as I will never be accepted into the Roosevelts' inner circle of polite society."

"It's hard, ain't it, Jennie?"

She looked up, into his eyes, as if his words brought her from some distant, melancholy place. "What's hard, Rockwell?"

"Being different."

The despondency, as quickly as it had come, evaporated from her expression. She shrugged, not prepared to share too much.

"Sometimes, I guess."

She cast her gaze over her body. "Do you find me attractive, Rockwell?"

"I do, Jennie." He swallowed, doing his best to control the trembling in his voice. "I find you to be about the most beautiful lady I've ever seen."

"Good." She kissed him. "And thank you. You are such a sweet man. Sweet and manly.

Those are the best men. But this is the danger, this and the aftermath of what we are about to receive — this congress, this interlude. Because I can assure you, Rockwell . . ." She hesitated, as if the thought had at that moment occurred to her. "May I ask you a frank question, and, if I do, will you promise me a frank answer?"

"I will, if frank means truthful."

She smiled at his innocence. "Yes, Rockwell, that's what it means."

"Then, yes, Jennie, I promise a frank answer."

"Have you ever been intimate with a woman?"

"No, Jennie. Never." He paused, thinking that it might be good to qualify. "If, if what I think being intimate means what it means." His gaze fell to her nether region.

"It does." She laughed. "Good. That helps." She kissed the knuckles of his battle-marred hands. "You are a beautiful man, Rockwell. Has anyone ever told you that?"

"No, Jennie, no, never."

"Well, you are." She held him, hugging him with a tenderness he'd never known. "You must be brave, Rockwell, as brave as you were facing the Spaniards' bullets and bombs."

"Why?" He could not fathom a need for

bravery now. He wanted her, and that did not seem to be something requiring bravery, though it caused his heart to pound with the intensity it had in battle.

"Because Rockwell. Because what we are about to receive, what we are about to do, violates every code of decency, every code, for that matter, of nature, understood by man."

"Do tell." He felt an idiot for such an ejaculation but could think of no more articulate a response.

"Yes, and this is the essence of the debauchée. The creed of the debauchée. Never, ever fall victim to the immutable. Never, ever fall victim to sentimentality. We will love, Rockwell," she sort of convulsed at the thought, her thighs, hips, pelvis, moving in a most provocative manner, her eyes rolling to the back of her head, shuddering, biting her lip. "Oh, *God,* how we will love."

He wanted her. Wanted to throw her onto the bed and ravage her. "I'm all right with that, Jennie. You can trust me." He held up his hand. "Soldier's honor."

"Good. But one more thing, Rockwell. You hold up that hand, pledge to me. Tomorrow, when we are together, in the calm light of day, and later still, when we are at the races or to dinner or to a party, do not look upon me as a possession. Do not think for one moment that I am yours. Promise me, Rockwell, because you will never, ever possess me."

He stood, holding up his hand as he'd done that crisp day in Prescott, certain he'd be as vexed, perplexed, heartbroken, and exhilarated as he'd been all through the campaign in Cuba. "I promise, dear Jennie. I promise."

"Splendid!" She began pulling at the buttons on his tunic. "Now, let's get down to business, my dear, darling Rockwell. Let's remove this uniform and have some fun."

CHAPTER 38

Rocky awoke at ten. Felt well. Fresh and invigorated and alive. Never in his life had he slept so late, realizing it had not been an incredible dream, as Jennie lie beside him, naked and unencumbered atop the satin sheets.

He turned to face her. Propping his head on an elbow, he ran his hand over the curves of her torso, tracing his fingers down her hip and thigh.

She awoke, smiling, giving him a long deep kiss. "What time is it?"

"A little past ten."

She turned away, pulling the pillow tightly against her cheek. "Too early, lover. Wake me at eleven." She was immediately asleep.

He watched her for a long while, thought of Francesca and then of Jonathan. He found a robe in her wardrobe, one of many for men, selected his size, and put it on. He found one of Jennie's gold-tipped cigarettes and had one as he wandered to the bathroom.

He sat, admiring his surroundings. Marble and glass and mirrors. Mounted on Corinthian pedestals sat stone carvings of ancient South American Indians, grossly exaggerated genitalia, in various, most unorthodox poses, the couples happily pleasuring themselves or each other. He wondered how, where she'd obtained them.

One featured a woman servicing a man in the way the whore in Tampa suggested. Isn't that what Jennie had taught him, that little, if anything, was disgusting or unnatural, between two willing adults?

He looked the sculpture over. Both participants seemed happy enough.

On one wall had been painted a fresco of Jennie in a flowing gown, perhaps from Bible times, emerging from a colossal clamshell. It was evidently rendered many years ago, and Rocky could see what effect the ravages of time had had on his lover. Though Jennie was beautiful now, she must have been stunning then. He was sad for her, as the loss of such beauty must be devastating to a woman who pursued such a life.

He looked to his left at a contraption, not a toilet and not a sink. He wondered at its purpose. There were so many items he was seeing for the first time. He fiddled with the taps and a fountain of water shot up, nearly hitting him in the eye.

He decided on a quick shower and remembered their midnight visit to it. He carried her, still joined, Jennie with arms and legs wrapped tightly about him as he shuffled more than walked.

Never would he have imagined one could pull off such a stunt. Never could he have imagined a woman would desire such a thing. It was both scandalous in its depravity and deliciously thrilling. The thought of it made him want her again.

He closed his eyes and remembered every detail as the water cascaded over him. His heart pounded, and his temples throbbed at the memory of it. He wondered at the hour. He wanted her again and could not wait until eleven o'clock. Another half hour. What could he do to pass the time? He dried himself, then wandered downstairs to the kitchen.

So this was what his brother had known of Francesca. This was what inspired men to marry. This was what his parents, the colonel, Sean Whelihan had known. He knew it would be fun, but not nearly so much fun as all that. Jennie was a phenomenon. She worked in lovemaking as an artist in clay or paint or marble.

He found things for breakfast, grapefruit and scones and biscuits and marmalade. Brewed coffee and presented all on a silver serving tray at a minute past eleven.

He kissed her on a nipple while stroking her nether region. None of that scared him anymore. None of that worried him, as Jennie had taught him what to do, how to elicit the response that would send her, time and again, over the moon.

She stretched and yawned. "Good morning, lover." Snuggling against his chest. "Still don't love me?"

He grinned at the irony of the question, answering with enthusiasm. "Not one little bit!" He was pleased in the knowledge that he was speaking the truth. He was certainly fond of her. Certainly found her fun and attractive, but, no, he did not, nor would he *ever,* love her. No strings, no expectations. Lovers loving. Friends sharing a profound intimacy.

"Excellent!"

He gazed out the window as she prepared her coffee. "Never would have imagined a big park, full of trees and grass, right in the middle of a city like this, Jennie." Rocky reached over to take in the scent of the arrangement by the window. "I wondered what smelled so nice," he smiled, "other than you."

"Jasmine." She sauntered up to him, pulling the robe from his body, letting it fall to the floor. She gave him a long deep kiss. "Some say the rose is the most provocative flower, others, the lily, and still others, the iris, but I've always found jasmine to be the scent that reminded me most of lovemaking."

She moved behind him, pressing her breasts against his back. She nibbled his earlobe, casting her gaze to the park.

"Up the street, in the zoo, there are lions, Rockwell. When the lionesses are in season the males roar night and day." She pressed her thighs against his body, rubbing her pubis against him. "It drives me wild to hear that, Rockwell." She smiled slyly as she pulled away, taking a long drink of last night's champagne. She offered him some, which he refused.

He considered her as she stood, posed really, as Jennie always posed.

She smiled and gloried in his admiration. Reached for him, arms extended as would a nanny for her charge, as Rocky was most certainly her charge, her apprentice, her protégé. He complied, of course, abandoning the breakfast.

She kissed and held him a long time, glorying in the union for a while. She pressed his cheek to her breast.

"Later, we'll have a ride through the park. Do you ride English, Rockwell?"

"Is that a kind of horse?"

She laughed. "No, it's a style, a matter of different saddle and tack. No matter; with a horseman such as you, you'll master it quickly enough." She assessed him. "I have a riding outfit that should fit you."

"Can't be any worse than those McClellans from the army. My God, they're the worst saddles I ever sat." He looked her over as she took his measure. He no longer felt embarrassed when she admired him. "That Woodbury, when he was playing polo the other day, my God, what a rider! He is a real Jim-dandy in the saddle."

She liked his admiration for their favorite man. "He is at that, Rockwell. He is, as you say, a real Jim-dandy."

She threw herself upon him, mounting his body as one would a spirited polo pony. "One more ride, then luncheon at Sheepshead Bay. I'm *dying* to show you my horses stabled there. How does that sound, lover?"

"Jennie?"

"Yes, lover?"

"Do you ever . . . I mean . . ." He had to speak quickly, as she was distracting. "Do you ever worry over getting in, you know, the family way?"

"Oh," she smiled down upon him. "No, Rockwell. That is not possible. I'm barren."

"Oh." He felt stupid for asking. Felt stupid as his dopey question seemed, at least momentarily, to sadden her.

She recovered, adjusting her body, finding him so deliciously responsive. It was why she loved young men so. They'd slake her passion long before wearing out. "Rockwell, please, no comments, no questions," she shuddered again, taking a deep breath, "at least for a while. Please love me, darling, love me as if the world was about to end."

"That sounds to me," he cast his gaze over every curve and provocative nuance, "my dear lady Jennie, like a wonderful idea."

CHAPTER 39

Chester Hogan sat in Clara's office at the German Hospital in Newark, fidgety and uneasy, as he did not like hospitals. They scared him, despite the fact that the one at Camp Wyckoff had spared his life as well as his leg.

He felt better when Clara glided into the room. Though she appeared gaunt and tired, she was as pristine and beautiful as the day he'd met her on the transport.

She extended her hand as Hogan jumped to attention. He bowed, mimicking his captain's behavior back on the ship.

"It's good to see you, Private," she glanced at the chevrons on his sleeve, "or should I say, *Corporal* Hogan."

"Oh, yes, ma'am." He nodded indifferently. "Wasn't anything. Nothing more than my turn to be made a corporal, I think."

They sat and said little for a while. Clara, as one pulling teeth, persuaded Hogan to tell about his life, that he was a train operator in New York and that his job had been waiting for him, and how he was settling in.

He produced a soiled letter from a jacket pocket. He tried to hand it over, hesitating, as if the act might kill him. He placed it in his lap instead, staring at it, daring not to look her in the eye.

"Ma'am, I'm having a hard time with this."

Clara moved closer, grasping his free hand. "I know, Corporal. It's been an overwhelming adventure for many of us."

"No, not that, not that. The captain, ma'am. The captain . . ." He searched her eyes, finding the common love they shared for Mortimer.

He mustered the courage to give her the letter. "This is from the captain. To you." He smiled bashfully. "That's pretty stupid. Of course it's to you." He nodded as Clara opened it. "It has some of his blood on it, and the boys said I ought not to give it to you, but I knew the blood would not put you off. The captain wrote that while he was dying in a trench."

"Were you with him?"

"Yes, ma'am. We were both wounded. We were on the attack when one of those Spanish bullets found me. Shot through the

481

thigh, and I spun around like a top. The captain saw me. He ran out to me as blood was shooting like a geyser from a hole in my leg. I yelled at him not to. Told him that I'd be all right, but he said I'd bleed to death, and the whole time the Spaniards must have turned a hundred guns right on our position."

He ran his hand through his hair again, cleared his throat. "But the captain made a tourniquet from my cartridge belt, and the geyser stopped pumping. It was then I saw that he'd been hit. Later we found out it was in the liver. I remember I said, 'Captain, you've been hit,' and he looked down at the growing stain on his jacket and smiled. He said it was not more than a scratch.

"He picked me up like I was nothing but a pound of flour, kind of carried me under one arm like a player with a ball on the football field, and then we were back in the trench again."

Clara closed her eyes and saw every detail. Saw that easy, confident smile, the twinkling in Mortimer's eyes as he likely lit a cigarette and considered his wound. Likely did nothing about it so long as he had his man, his private, his men to look after.

"Please, continue."

"Well, it was getting on night and the

captain was walking up and down the line, giving orders to the men to reinforce our defenses as we expected a counter-attack. None never did come. Later we heard there weren't all that many Spaniards left to oppose us, and that was all because of the captain. It was him who got us to fight like hellions, ma'am. Was the captain kept us calm, kept us from losin' our nerve. Some of the boys from the regular army, they said we fought like real soldiers. We sure laid into them that day.

"But he was calm, ma'am, like he was on a stroll with you on his arm on a Sunday afternoon, walked back and forth checking on his men. By this time all the other officers were dead. Even our sergeants were dead. It was pretty bad that day.

"By dark things were settled, and that's when the captain came back to check on me. A medical fellow looked at the hole in my leg and plugged it with some dressing. He said the hole in my artery probably sealed off. Nothing pained me, and the bleeding had stopped. They found me a crutch, and I used that. They wanted me to go to Siboney to be evacuated, but I wouldn't. I guess I was feeling no pain.

"But I sobered up real fast when I saw the state of the captain. By then his whole trouser leg was soaked with blood, and he looked as pale as white flour. I called for the medical boys, but they were nowhere around. The captain smiled and blew smoke from his cigarette. You know he liked his tobacco, ma'am. Always smoking was the captain." Hogan glanced up at Clara. "He said he'd have to give up the smokes once he returned home, as you didn't like it, and he said until then he'd do a lifetime of smoking." He smiled. "Captain was forever sayin', 'Miss Maass this' and 'Miss Maass that.' He sure did have you on his mind, in his heart, all the time."

The tears rolled down the corporal's rosy cheeks. "And then the captain pulled out his tablet and started writing." He nodded. "Wrote that to you, and when he was finished, he sort of deflated, like an observation balloon. Some of the boys and me found a rubber rain poncho and put it under him, keep him off that damned diseased Cuban ground. We gave him some morphine even though he protested on that. Said he needed a clear head, but we gave it to him anyway. He drifted off and that . . . that was it.

"Oh, ma'am, I'm sorry. I know what was planned for the two of you. My captain, your man, he should have lived, and I should have died. I'd trade with him if I could. I swear to you, I'd trade and be dead if it would bring him back."

She patted him on the back. "No one should have died, but someone did. Our man died, and it's no one's fault. Certainly, Corporal Hogan, not yours."

"I can't stop thinking about him."

"Nor should you ever stop thinking about him." She considered Colonel Roosevelt's advice. She'd never take it, never offer it. "Think about him every day, Corporal Hogan. Remember what a good man he was. Pray for him. Every day say a prayer for him, and let him guide your thoughts and actions."

She smiled, pulling his face up by the chin. "Look at me."

He complied.

"Remember this, Corporal. A good man died saving you. That obligates you from now on. That places a colossal burden on you, but a burden it is."

"A burden?"

"Yes. A burden to live every day as if it were your last; every hour, every minute, as if you were about to depart this earth. A burden to spend the rest of your days aspiring to be the best you can be. Be good. Be productive. Be the best train operator in

New York. The best son, husband, father you can be, but above all things, Corporal Hogan, be happy. If you can be happy, Mortimer's death will not have been in vain, and I can assure you, nothing would gratify him more than to know he had a part in your living a happy and fulfilled life."

Clara handed him a fresh handkerchief, stood, and pulled the curtains aside. Touching him on the shoulder, she said, "Isn't it a glorious day?" She smiled. "Come, dry those eyes and calm yourself." She held the letter to the light streaming through her window. She waited for him to acknowledge as he followed her gaze, taking in the autumn sun bathing her office in warm hues of yellow. "Hasn't our dear Lord blessed us with another beautiful day? Now, let's see what our man has to say."

Hogan sprang from his seat. "Oh, no, ma'am! That's for you. Personal for you!"

"Nonsense." She read it quickly to herself, confirming there was nothing embarrassing in Mortimer's prose.

"Dear Heart;
Please forgive the rough paper and rougher writing. Could only find a pencil, and this light is failing me. I regret to inform you that this is likely the end

of your man, as there are no pretty nurses about to take care of us wounded soldiers. This is my only regret, however, love, as these past months have been the happiest of my life. I honestly do not believe anyone could be happier than I am at present. I'm satisfied to know no more. Be good, darling. I'm certain this is not really the end, but rather a new beginning. I'll be waiting for you, and we'll walk the streets of glory, hand in hand, and it will be even more thrilling and fulfilling than our time in Florida. God bless you. I love you. Mortimer."

CHAPTER 40

Rocky sat in front of one of the baboon cages, smoking, waiting for Bill McGinty. He leafed through the book Jennie Danbury had given him. He thought he'd like a zoo, but he was sad for the animals. Not that they were cruelly treated, but there was something kind of lost about the creatures. They looked like jailed men. Jailed men serving life sentences.

McGinty brought him from his daydream, handing him a fancy gold-tipped cigarette given to the bronc buster by his lady companion, along with a peppermint wrapped in tissue paper he'd purchased in a sweet shop.

"How's everything, Rock?"

Rocky smiled, sharing without speaking, as each had received more education in the past few days than most men could hope to know in a lifetime.

McGinty pulled the book from Rocky's

hands. "*The Art of Reading and Speaking,* by Canon Fleming."

"Miss Danbury give it to me. Teaches elocution."

"What's that, politics?"

"No, Bill. How to speak proper. You know, 'ain't' ain't a word? You're supposed to say 'isn't.' Things like that."

"No kidding?"

"You think that's silly?"

"What?"

"Me, learning to talk right."

"No, Rock, I don't. Been thinkin' about all this. Me . . . well, I'm a cowpuncher from Oklahoma, and I'll never be anything else, but you, Rock" — he nodded — "I can see you as an educated man, and not some dude putting on airs. No, I see you as a real educated fellow. Hell, ain't no trick to it. Something you learn, like riding or roping, and you're smart, Rock. Smart and a hard worker. Bet you could have a proper education in no time."

Seemingly lost in thought, Rocky turned to his friend.

"Do you put much stock in folks, you know, predicting the future, Bill?"

"What ya mean?"

"Well, Jennie — I mean, Miss Danbury — she's all involved with these fortune tellers and the like. She had my cards and palm read. It was kinda creepy; you know what they say about you, and, you know, Sergeant Fish, before the battle — you know, Guási-mas — the boys heard him talking, saying he was sure to be killed, and well, there it is: he was killed. You suppose folks can see into the future?"

"No, Rock, I don't. Had a cousin once, she was all about that kind of stuff. Even talked me into visiting one of them palm readers running with a traveling show back home. Nothin' but tricks, Rock. That old gal, she had this thick accent; she was Romanian, I think. Couldn't hardly under-stand a word she said, and she read my cards and told me I'd be in the cattle busi-ness, told me I'd have all kinds of adven-tures. Hell, Rock, look at me. Don't take a detective to figure out I'm a bronc buster." He laughed. "My cousin was pretty vexed about it when I called nonsense on it. Then later on, I saw that fortune teller, out back of a tent, havin' a smoke and shootin' the breeze with a bunch of other carnival work-ers. That gal sounded like one of these New York boys. She was a faker. She weren't any more from Romania than you or me."

"But what of Hamilton Fish?"

"Don't know, Rock. I think you can talk

yourself into about anything. Hell, old son, we all had a fifty-fifty chance of buyin' it that day. Look at you, shot in the head; look at Tom Isbell — that old boy was leaking blood like you read about, hit three times; look at your brother, God rest his soul. No one can deny it was hot in that little battle. So, if you say you think you're goin' to buy it and end up buyin' it, well, does that make a fella a fortune teller? I don't think so."

"Do you ever sleep anymore, Bill?"

"Oh, sure. Always have slept well, Rock. Sleep like a dead man. That is, when Lydia's not pawin' at me."

The sadness enveloped Rocky. "I don't know, Bill. I sleep, maybe, three, four hours, then I get to thinkin' of the boys and Nurse Trumbull and my brother again. It's like I close my eyes, and they're all there. I hate to sleep. So damned tired all the time."

"I know, friend." He watched a baboon sit, hunched up as if he were bracing against a rainstorm.

Rocky stared off at nothing, speaking automatically. "I don't know, Bill. All the things I've been hearing, the newspapers, saying what we did down there was wrong. All the naysaying, all those good men dying, all the killing we did, it's kind of hard to take, kind of hard to figure out what it was all for."

"Way I see it, Rock, it's like an uncle I had. Helped a neighbor once, a mean old bitch she was. My uncle waded into the river during a flood, drowned while he was tryin' to save her milk cow, which he ended up doing. Well, everyone was saying this and that, how he died for a cow, how he died for a mean old woman's cow, how it was such a waste of a good man, to be traded for the life of livestock.

"Then the preacher spoke over him, and he said that my uncle didn't die for a cow, he said my uncle died helping a neighbor, being a good neighbor. See, Rock, that cow was that woman's life. If she'd a' lost it, she would have been in a bad way. About the only thing of value she owned.

"That's the way I see it with what we did down there in Cuba. Don't know how history'll treat us, but I know this much: some things were wrong down there, we seen 'em, sure enough, those little kids you found and all those old folks and refugees. All those filthy streets and bad wells. They say already Colonel Wood's got that under control. Already, Rock, in only a little while, he's making progress. Even less people are dying of the yellow jack. We did some good for 'em. I feel pretty good about bein' a

492

good neighbor. Whether the politicians move forward or backward is out of my hands. Know in my heart I have nothin' to be ashamed of. Know in my heart neither do you. We earned our pay, did some good, didn't do a thing my ma and pa would be ashamed of, and neither did you. I guess that's the best we can hope for, old son."

"I guess so."

"Rock, you're too good for your own good. That's *your* problem."

"What's that supposed to mean?"

"You care too much." McGinty took another long drag. He liked Lydia's Turkish tobacco, liked the way it hurt his lungs when he drew extra deeply. "I ain't sayin' that's a bad thing, old son, I'm sayin' it's the way you are. It's a tough, unforgiving way to live, but it's your curse, and blessing, all at the same time. What makes you such a good man." He looked at the glowing tip of his cigarette. "Man like you, you've got to be careful, Rock. Be careful of how much you care, or it'll eat you up inside. Do me a favor, friend. Go easy on yourself."

He reached over and gave Rocky a squeeze on the neck. "You're about the finest man I've ever known."

"Aw, Bill, you're having a joke on me."

"I ain't kiddin'. You're the finest man I

ever known, and that includes the colonels and Woodbury and Sergeant Fish and William Tiffany, Captains Capron and O'Neill, Major Brodie, Tom Isbell, Pawnee Bill Pollack, Henry Bardshar, and any of the other good men we've been lucky enough to know. I want to thank you for being my friend. Want to thank you for stickin' by me through it all."

"Same goes here, Bill." He worked on his cigarette. "It was quite a ride wasn't it?"

"Old son, you can say that again."

"What next?"

"Oh, I'm goin' home for a spell. See the folks, you know; my ma and pa are still kickin'. Want to see them all, but, well, Lydia asked me to come back here to New York. Work her horses on her farm. Funny, ain't it, Rock? They call 'em farms, not ranches here. Guess maybe I'll do that. Don't know. Probably not." He lit a new cigarette off his butt, handing it to Rocky, who always smoked them more quickly than did he. "Right now, like to sit a while with you, Rock. Let's us sit a while and watch these critters."

"Sounds like, what's that word Jennie always says? Oh yeah, *splendid.* Sounds like a splendid idea, Bill. A splendid idea."

McGinty watched another of the inmates

scratch its behind. "Nice to see some gorillas that ain't trying to kill us, ain't it, Rock?"

"Well, don't know if they count as gorillas, Bill. Baboons is what they call 'em. But
I guess that's close enough. All apes I guess."

McGinty looked his partner over. "For
two short-ish fellows, we sure give 'em hell,
didn't we, friend?"

"We did at that." He smiled. "What
amazes me, Bill, is how you got away without a scratch." Rocky absentmindedly felt
the scar on his forehead. His mutilated ear.

"Oh, you ain't seen my shins." McGinty
grinned. He should have, by all rights, been
killed ten times over. "But I know what
you're sayin', Rock. Can't believe, not one
hole, didn't even catch the Cuban fever or
the yellow jack, or even the shits for that
matter, by God."

Rocky laughed. "Remember, Bill, when
you were running that food up and down
the line. The Spaniards shot that can of
tomatoes you were haulin', and everyone
thought you were covered in blood?"

"Yeah, that was right funny, wasn't it,
Rock?"

"I guess one thing's certain."

"What's that?"

"You should never underestimate a man
on the short-ish side."

CHAPTER 41

Sister Bonaventure's colleagues survived the war, and soon the hospital and routine were back to normal. She'd lost twenty-five pounds, which she declared helped her move better on the wards.

Her bedroom felt strange. Even the bed was difficult to sleep in after so many months on a canvas cot; simply too comfortable. The books, book case; the small electric light with the pretty glass lampshade, given to her long ago by a grateful patient; the lithograph of Saint Bonaventure, after whom she'd taken her name; the print of the philosopher Democritus with his gay smile; the plain crucifix hanging over her bed: all felt remote, unfamiliar, as if she'd been away from them for decades rather than months. It felt, every now and again, as if she'd invaded a stranger's room.

She corresponded for a while with Clara, but lost contact when the feisty nurse from

New Jersey signed up again, this time for duty in the Philippines.

She spent many an hour, as she toiled on the wards, thinking about the friends she'd made in the war. Many of her prayers were dedicated to Minerva, and, though she had neither the energy nor the political acumen to force reform in her own hospital, she did what she could by helping the colored orderlies and housekeepers, both male and female, when any exhibited an interest in furthering their careers and education.

One young man had become a physician and attributed that success to Sister Bonaventure's encouragement and mentoring.

She thought a good deal about her father, who'd taught her many things; was such a man who could have easily taken a place alongside those Rough Riders. He taught her compassion and humility. He would have been proud to know of her exploits in the war, always was proud of everything she'd done, despite his misgivings about her decision to take vows. He felt it a waste of a clever mind. She could have been a scientist, could have had a significant impact on the world, but still she had no regrets, and when all was said, had he lived, she was confident he'd feel her life was not spent frivolously. Wasn't it he who introduced her to the laughing philosopher?

From time to time she'd receive holiday cards from some of the men whose lives she'd touched. Dr. Church proved prolific in his correspondence, and she could, at least monthly, count on a letter and an article from either the *Lancet* or the *Journal of the American Medical Association,* pointing out some item that might interest her. It was gratifying to be treated in such a way by a physician of the young surgeon's acumen. Church was, despite his brilliance, a humble man.

After a while, folks stopped talking of the war, stopped congratulating her or asking her about her adventures with the famous Rough Riders. To many, it was a footnote in history. But Sister Bonaventure would never stop thinking about and praying for those whose lives she touched in what had become known as, at least by those who'd not been in it, that splendid little war.

CHAPTER 42

Francesca Rogers concluded her lunch with a cup of tea as she lounged in a comfy chair, enjoying the view from the conservatory floor of the Palace Hotel. The Christmas decorations festooning the columns and rails put her in a holiday mood.

The nurse had advised that a regular dose of sunlight would be good for her, and, subsequently, it had become a daily ritual. She rubbed her belly and felt the baby move, which was altogether thrilling. She'd had a good pregnancy, little nausea in the beginning, but now it was nothing but joy to carry the life around in her body. Jonathan's life. At least there was some consolation in that. He'd, in a way, live on.

With the mild winter weather of San Francisco, it was the best place to spend one's confinement. She was thoroughly enjoying herself.

She learned from her father, from an early

age, to enjoy opulence, enjoy the fruits of her labor. She learned from her mother how to behave in such a setting, and the Palace was a place where one could obtain a belly full of it, even a pregnant one.

Not that Francesca was owned by the trappings of wealth. She knew her limitations and never overextended. Her motivation was also not to become something that she was not, and she was not remotely interested in rubbing elbows with the so-called elite of San Francisco society or any other, for that matter. She was keenly aware of the label placed upon her by the closed-minded, often dim-witted upper tier of the moneyed class. She was too dark, too Catholic, too free-spirited to fit in. She was a member of the working class, and she'd not have it any other way.

But, as was typical with Francesca, most of those lucky — or unlucky — enough to engage her, depending upon the individual encountered, learned quickly to accept, or at least quietly tolerate, her larger-than-life persona. She moved about with impunity anywhere she desired, remembering to accentuate her swollen belly, taking special delight in the scandal that resulted from her actions. She was a beautiful woman who happened to be pregnant, and what was more beautiful than a pregnant woman anyway? The world needed to move on from such Victorian stupidity, and Francesca decided to become a catalyst for the change in perspective so profoundly overdue.

She gloried in it. Derived a certain pleasure out of the glares and stares, the gaping mouths, the pointing fingers, the whispers. Shock, revulsion, disgust. It was about as much fun as tracking mountain lions through the Superstitions with a pack of good hounds.

If the fools really misbehaved, she'd give them a proper show. Whether in the grand court or the ladies' grill room or in one of the many parlors, she'd stand boldly, arching her back as she stretched, pushing out her belly as far as possible, rubbing it as one conjuring a genie from a lamp. She even caused one bitter crone to swoon, requiring the attention of the house doctor and a dose of smelling salts.

It was also why she'd become such a celebrity among the common clave. Guests, at least the ones of more humble stock, and hotel employees alike revered her as a working-man's muse and goddess. Many addressed her as the Widow Rogers until she'd correct them politely — or tersely, if the comment was meant in derision — announcing in a rather loud and offhand tone that she'd never married.

A hotel attaché, one of the many she'd wrapped around her finger upon arriving for her confinement, approached, bowed, presenting a card on a silver tray. It read *Trooper Rockwell Whelihan, 1st US Volunteer Cavalry, Arizona Contingent.*

She smiled at the attendant as she took in the scent of the card, smelling of Turkish tobacco and man. She was so enjoying the heightened olfactory powers her pregnancy had imparted.

She smiled. "Where is he?"

"Waiting in the bar."

"Of course he is." She stared off pensively, tapping her lips with the card, remembering everything about him. "Is he drunk?"

"Oh, no, madam. Sober as a judge. He's having tea, like yourself."

"You're certain it's him?"

"He's the one gave me the card. He's in uniform. Other than that, I cannot vouch for the authenticity of his person, madam."

"My name is Francesca, Harvey; you know better than to call me madam."

"Francesca."

"How does he look?"

"He's a rather handsome fellow, madam . . . ah, Francesca, if I may be so

502

bold. Battle scarred, but otherwise I'd say he was a man in top trim. Well-groomed and polite. He looks fit. A rather pleasant gentleman."

"Send him to my room," she handed him a tip, "but not yet." She worked to extricate herself from the chair. "Wait fifteen minutes."

She reclined on a divan, the winter sunlight playing on her hair and the stunning blue silk House of Worth gown she'd put on to receive him. She wore no shoes but stockinged feet, as they constantly felt cold now that she was so far along. Her belly protruded, and it pleased her when he did not avert his eyes.

It was as if he'd donned another man's eyes. They looked as a man's eyes *should* look, direct and with confidence, not downcast or wandering or ashamed the way she remembered them. Were they another man's eyes, or was it perhaps the way he directed them?

She extended her hands so that he could help her to her feet. She kissed him on the mouth. "Welcome home, Rocky, or should I say, *Rockwell.*"

"Oh, the card. Yes, that was a bit of fun. Had them printed in New York. Rocky's fine, Francesca."

"Where have you been? It's nearly Christmas."

"Oh, about. Went to Oklahoma with a friend; traveled around to some of the men's families, you know, the ones who died. I wanted to talk to their folks, maybe ease their minds, ease their suffering a little. Told them how they died; told them that they're safely planted. Things like that." He wanted a cigarette. "Rode the rails a bit, did some thinking." He looked up and smiled. "Even went to Chicago and Cincinnati for a little while."

She patted his shoulder. "I believe you've grown taller." She kissed him again. "Rocky Whelihan, not Killebrew?"

"Yes, well." He looked down at his hands, still embraced by hers. It felt good. Felt good to see her and to feel her touch, both on his hands and on his lips. It was much less intimidating than he thought it would be. In fact, it was not intimidating at all. It was rather thrilling.

"I never thought you could look more beautiful," he pulled her hand over her head, forcing her into a pirouette so as to take in a view from every side, "but, well, motherhood agrees with you, Francesca."

"Thank you." She smiled. "Some wine?

Or . . . or a whiskey, perhaps?"

"Oh, no. Tea or coffee would do if you have it."

"We're in the Palace Hotel, Rocky. We always have it."

He admired his surroundings. "Sure are some nice rooms, Francesca. Am I correct in calling it a suite?"

"Yes." She followed his eyes as they moved about the opulent parlor. "I know, quite rich. Matthews, Sharp and Archer have been good to me."

"Oh, the meat packers." He smiled. "You would either cry or vomit to see what they did to your beeves, Francesca. It's downright sinful."

"Well, the money was green enough."

He looked off in the direction of the window. "I guess."

"*And* the money from Jonathan."

"I remember. He bought that life insurance for you. He knew." He pointed at her belly. "He knew, Francesca."

"Well, God bless him for it. A hundred thousand dollars will last a long time."

"My God, it should." He reached into his breast pocket. "Oh, before I forget." He pulled out the locket, presenting it to her by the chain. "Jonathan's."

She took it, smiled, was certain Rocky had

had a look. "Thank you."

She watched him be for a while. It was as if she were confronting some manner of recast version of the boy she'd remembered: the same in body, but mind and spirit, quite different.

"Rocky, did you go off to war or to college?"

"I beg your pardon?"

"You don't sound yourself."

"Oh?"

"You sound . . . well . . . ah" — she raised an eyebrow — *"well!"*

"I met a lady."

"Oh?" Francesca felt her face flush. She wandered to the call bell to have the tea brought up.

"Yes, a fine lady, one of the rich New York folks. She gave me some books and kind of coached me."

"Some books?" She remembered how much Rocky hated to read. "And coaching?" She smiled coyly. "What kind of coaching?"

"You know, on how to speak properly. How to . . . I don't know . . . books, and advice on how to . . . I don't know." He smiled. "Do I sound a fool?"

"Not one bit." She wandered to the window and watched the street below. "You

506

sound different, look different," she turned, smiling pensively, "but, truthfully, in a wholly wonderful way." She turned to face him. "You're, well, *bigger,* Rocky."

"Not really. Maybe it's the shoes, and my hair, kind of growing it out, maybe to cover this mangled ear, but I'm no taller, and I'm actually skinnier than when I left. Lost ten pounds in Cuba, gained five back."

"Not that kind of bigger." She walked up on him, closing the distance, standing as close as her belly would allow. She touched the scar on his forehead, not unlike how Jennie often had done. She looked askance at his ear. "You certainly have been beaten up."

"Oh, I fared all right. Much better than some."

"Did he die well, Rocky?"

"If there's such a thing as dying well." He felt the tears, swallowed, and recovered.

"I'm sorry. That was a stupid thing to say. Of course there's no good way to die. At least not for the young. Please forgive me."

He moved to the window and spoke toward it. It, too, was not terribly unlike the view from Jennie's apartment. He missed his muse and mentor, more than he thought he would.

"No need to apologize, Francesca, but you

507

are right, there's no good way to die, and too many of my friends and, of course, Jonathan, died, and I don't feel like there's any glory in that. Can't find anything good in any of it. I miss them all." He stared at a distant bell tower, considered not saying it, but did. "Even all the men I killed saddens me." He turned, addressing her as if speaking to a priest at confession. "And there were many of them." He looked away, focusing his gaze at the floor between them. "It's empty and sad. My heart aches all the time." He turned to face her, feeling a little enmity toward her. Though he knew Francesca well enough, understood that she was not given to a lot of emotional expression, it vexed him to see her so cavalier. He spoke without really thinking. "Glad to see *you* taking it so well."

She held up a hand, her face flushing in anger. He hated when she looked that way, as she looked that way so rarely, and when she did, it meant things were about to go terribly wrong for the object of her displeasure. He thought about apologizing, when she replied.

"Do not presume that I have shed no tears, Rocky. Do not presume that I have found this easy. I haven't. I cried until I had nothing left to cry, but that was back in the summer; that was a while ago, and forgive me if I seem callous, but I'm not the type to waste my life grieving. It's why I would not marry Jonathan before this stupid adventure of his. This idiotic war. I refuse to be a widow, to grieve for the rest of my days."

Francesca was crying, and that scared all hell out of him. Francesca had never, in all the time he'd known her, uttered so much as a whimper. Even at her parents' funerals, she had been stoic.

"I know that sounds silly, Rocky. Know that makes no sense, but there it is. There it is."

He pulled her into his arms. He kissed her temple, brushing the tears from her cheeks. "Marry me, Francesca."

She swallowed, uncertain that her ears had not deceived her. "What did you say?"

"Marry me. At least for the sake of the babe. Marry me, and it won't be a bastard." He laughed at his ridiculous proposal. "I know I'm not Jonathan, know I don't have anything to offer, but I've always been fond of you and, I know, I'm not much, but I'll be good to you and the babe, our babe, if you'll have me. At least it'll have Jonathan's name."

She turned her head from side to side,

speaking with an ironic, clipped tongue. "You're not Jonathan!" She laughed. "You can say that again. You're definitely not Jonathan, Rocky. That's for certain!"

He smiled to hide the effect of the poisonous barb. Pulling himself together, he prepared to leave. Retreating toward the door, he turned one last time to face her. "I never expected any kind of big romance, Francesca. I thought, you know, now that Sean Whelihan is dead, and Ellen and Louis — they're planning to move away, become missionaries — I thought it would be a good business deal. We could merge the ranches." He held up a hand. "Nothing more. Didn't expect you to fall in love with the likes of me. I'm thick, but I'm not completely stupid."

She stopped him at the door. "You *are* thick, Rocky."

"Thanks." He smiled. "Should I lie down on the floor? You can stomp my heart out a lot easier that way."

"No, you *are* thick, because you do not *see.*" She pulled him into her arms. "You are one hundred times the man your brother ever was . . . would have ever been had he lived."

"Oh?"

"Yes, Rocky, but honestly, do you really

want to marry me?"

It felt cruel to say no, but now that he'd faced it, the idea did not agree with him the way he presumed it would. From the time he could remember, winning her affections was more an ideal than an obtainable reality.

"I want to do the right thing. Right by Jonathan, right by your babe, right by you, right by Ellen and Louis."

"And what about right by Rocky?"

He shrugged. Acting selfishly no longer interested him.

"Don't shrug, Rocky." She kissed him. "It is time to live *your* life, on *your* terms, and," she turned her head cynically, "you wouldn't be happy with me, Rocky. Don't frankly know if Jonathan could have been happy with me." She smiled. "The answer is no, Rocky." She held a finger skyward. "Not because you are not good enough. Not because you are beneath me or *anyone,* for that matter. You are not. Consider refusing your proposal my gift to you." She had to look away. "It might well be the kindest and most selfless act I've ever committed."

"Why would you say that?"

"Let's just say — and believe me when I tell you this — I'm more ruthless than you could ever imagine. I'd be poison to you.

Both of our lives would be miserable."

"What'll become of you?" He thought of Jennie, the deep loneliness the debauchée kept hidden behind the happy façade. "I can't bear the idea of you alone, Francesca. Seems so empty."

"Not all who are alone are lonely, Rocky." She smiled. She'd never been happier since her parents' death, all alone, at the Palace Hotel.

She pounded him on the shoulder. "You're as solid as the Rock of Gibraltar! You are such the man I always knew lived here." She patted his chest. "God bless you, Rocky, you've become a man among men." The tears came again. She could not stop them. "I swear, you remind me of my father."

"My God, what a compliment! If there was ever a man I'd feel honored to be compared to, it was him."

Rocky dried her tears with his handkerchief. "Will you be all right?"

"I will, Rocky." She smiled. "You remember the name they use behind my back?"

"Who?"

"The businessmen back home. The ones forced to deal with me. I'm *that little bitch*." She nodded. "And I am."

"Not to me, Francesca."

"That's because you are so pure. You are

pure and, because of it, don't see the folly in your fellow man, *or woman.*"

She let him kiss her again and felt her knees buckle.

"My God, Rocky, what did they teach you in that war?"

"Many things, Francesca, many things."

"You are as different as a body could be."

"Do you really suppose so?"

"Of course! You left us as a boy and returned a man. It's come out."

"What?"

"The maturity that my father and I knew was there, locked away, waiting to be born. And now it has. My God, it took a stupid, ridiculous war to penetrate that thick Ulster skull of yours, but it happened."

He could not contain himself. He kissed her with more passion than she'd ever known from her dead lover. Running his fingers through her hair, glorying in the effect his attentions were having, he whispered, "We'd better stop."

She playfully pulled at her dress, enough to give him a show. "Are you certain, Rocky? Because we aren't planning to spend the rest of our days together doesn't mean we can't comfort each other."

"I don't want to." He pulled her close. Hugging her tightly, he whispered in her ear. "Don't be offended. The last thing I'd ever want to do is offend or hurt you, but I don't want to."

Francesca looked up, incredulity reflected in her gaze. "You *can't* be serious."

She pouted, looking as would a spoiled princess who'd been denied her way. Pregnancy had heightened an already voracious appetite for sensual pleasure, and she'd been with no one since Jonathan. It was high time she'd gotten to know Rocky in a biblical way.

"Oh, yes, I can, *and* I am." He kissed her again. "Being together that way would ruin us, Francesca. And the last thing I'd ever want to do is ruin what we have; hopefully, what we'll have for all time."

"Oh, Rocky." She spoke breathlessly. "You certainly are *not* Jonathan." She pressed her cheek to his battered ear and whispered, "What, in heaven's name, did they teach you in that war?"

CHAPTER 43

On Christmas morning they stood over the plot in which was laid to rest, beside his beloved Hortense, the broken body of Sean Whelihan. Next to her had been placed a simple monument. An empty plot for Jonathan.

Louis stood by his wife and child-to-be, as they'd wasted no time; the newest addition to the Whelihan and Zeyouma clan would arrive sometime in June, by Ellen's best estimation.

She held onto Francesca as Rocky presided over the memorial service.

He looked upon his family and began. "I read a poem not long ago by the writer Ella Wheeler Wilcox, and I'd like to share it with you all, in remembrance of both of them. It's entitled *When the Regiment Came Back:*

All the uniforms were blue, all the swords
were bright and new,

When the regiment went
marching down the street,
All the men were hale and strong as they
proudly moved along,
Through the cheers that
drowned the music of their
feet.
Oh, the music of the feet keeping time to
drums that beat,
Oh, the splendor and the
glitter of the sight,
As with swords and rifles new and in
uniforms of blue,
The regiment went marching
to the fight.
When the regiment came back all the guns
and swords were black
And the uniforms had faded
out to gray,
And the faces of the men who marched
through that street again
Seemed like faces of the
dead who lose their way.
For the dead who lose their way cannot
look more wan and gray.
Oh, the sorrow and the pity
of the sight,
Oh, the weary lagging feet out of step with
drums that beat,

As the regiment comes
marching from the fight.

He turned, giving Francesca a gentle kiss on the cheek. He nodded and walked toward the ranch house. Francesca let him be. She knew he'd need to be alone for a while.

Ellen smiled as she dried her tears. "I wonder what happened to the old Rocky."

Louis led them both by the hand toward home. "Nothing, darling. He's still Rocky, only —"

Francesca finished his thought. "Bigger."

Ellen nodded. "Yes, bigger. That's exactly what he is. Bigger. God bless him."

EPILOGUE

Clara Maass continued her work as a contract nurse, spending a short time in the Philippines.

Undaunted by the heartache and privation of her duty as an army nurse, a year later she volunteered to return to Cuba, where she became a human test subject in Walter Reed's yellow fever experiments. One of nineteen participants, and the only woman, she allowed herself to be exposed several times to mosquitos suspected of being infected. She died of yellow fever August 24, 1901.

The public outcry at the news of her death ended yellow fever experimentation on humans. Her beloved German Hospital, relocated to Belleville, New Jersey, is now the Clara Maass Medical Center.

Except for a brief stint with the US Army in 1918 at the age of seventy-one, Sister Bonaventure spent her days serving the poor sick of Baltimore and as mentor and inspiration to another generation of caregivers. The *nice* nun died in her sleep a few days shy of her eighty-fourth birthday.

Ellen and Louis Zeyouma carried on as missionaries, working to help Indians navigate their way into and then through the twentieth century. They had two children, a boy, Jonathan, and a girl, Francesca.

Moving east, Rocky Whelihan worked for a while for Woodbury Kane, attending college at night. He became an engineer, specializing in bridge construction, finding solace in the creation of useful things. His rare fits of melancholy would be faced, not with drink, but with the love and support of his family and many friends.

He found a good woman who devoted herself to ensuring that he'd not tear himself apart, being, as Bill McGinty so aptly put it, too good for his own good.

Together, they taught their children to be independent, free-thinking individuals, constantly inspired to live up to the standard of their feisty Aunt Francesca.

Francesca Rogers furthered the cause of women's suffrage, doing all in her power to ensure that future generations would enjoy the independence she had the guts to take, sometimes by force, for her own.

Buying Ellen and Rocky out, she merged the ranches, maintaining her promise to Sean Whelihan, forming one of the wealthiest in the territory. She named her only son Rockwell Rogers, raising him alone on her ranch. She never married, nor would she claim that the little one was anyone but her son. No one, for fear of *that little bitch's* reprisal, dared to call him a bastard.

Woodbury Kane settled down to married life, but not with Jennie Danbury. He died of heart failure after a duck hunting trip in 1905. He was forty-six.

As her beauty faded, so did Jennie Danbury's popularity. She died in an apartment fire in 1927, where she lived in seclusion, ignored by her friends and many admirers, except for one, for every fifteenth of September, she'd receive a bouquet of jasmine, a tribute and reminder of the gratitude of an admirer and friend.

Bill McGinty traveled with Buffalo Bill's Wild West Show. He settled down with a good woman who gave him three boys. He formed what was considered the first cowboy band in his state and played on radio stations across Oklahoma. He was instrumental in forming both the Association of Rough Riders and the Bull Moose Party. He and the colonel remained lifelong friends.

Little Carlita, actually named Maria, became a nurse and spent the remainder of her days raising a family outside of Siboney. At every rainy season she'd ensure fresh mariposa decorated the marble gravestone of her friend and mentor, Nurse Minerva Trumbull.

And everyone knows what became of Colonel Roosevelt.

A NOTE TO THE READER

It was not the intent for *Roosevelt's Boys* to be a faithful chronicle of the Spanish American War, but rather a drama created to explore the human condition during this tragic time and to pay homage to the men and women, nurses and soldiers, who demonstrated what it means to make the ultimate sacrifice.

It was seventy-seven-year-old Clara Barton, not Clara Maass or the other nurses in our story, who actually saw action at the front lines during battle. Additionally, no historical record exists to either verify or refute that Clara Maass ever met Theodore Roosevelt, or engaged in the direct treatment of the Rough Riders.

Theodore Roosevelt did not visit the first Rough Riders in Prescott, Arizona. His initial encounter with his volunteers was in San Antonio, Texas.

It is the author's hope that the story is

received by the reader as an entertainment and will stimulate interest in and an appreciation for this adventure known by some as "the Splendid Little War," bringing to bear that no war is little, or splendid, regardless of duration or scale.

ABOUT THE AUTHOR

John Horst was born in Baltimore, Maryland, and studied philosophy at Loyola College. His interests include the history and anthropology of the Old West.

Roosevelt's Boys is his ninth novel. Other works include *The Mule Tamer Saga,* about the Walsh family in Arizona and Mexico, spanning two generations from the mid-nineteenth century to the early days of the Mexican Revolution, and the Allingham series, the story of a US Marshal in the wild lands of Arizona in the latter part of the nineteenth century.

He resides in Maryland with his wife and daughter.

The employees of Thorndike Press hope you have enjoyed this Large Print book. All our Thorndike, Wheeler, and Kennebec Large Print titles are designed for easy reading, and all our books are made to last. Other Thorndike Press Large Print books are available at your library, through selected bookstores, or directly from us.

For information about titles, please call:
   (800) 223-1244

or visit our Web site at:
   http://gale.cengage.com/thorndike

To share your comments, please write:
   Publisher
   Thorndike Press
   10 Water St., Suite 310
   Waterville, ME 04901